Woman's Own

Other books by Robyn Carr

Woman's Own

Robyn Carr

St. Martin's Press
New York

In loving memory of
Alice Entzminger,
"Grandmother E"

Design by Amelia R. Mayone

Library of Congress Cataloging-in-Publication Data

Carr, Robyn.
    Woman's own / Robyn Carr.
        p.   cm.
    ISBN 0-312-03837-2 : $19.95
    I. Title.
PS3553.A76334W6   1990
813'.54—dc20   89-48527
                                                            CIP

First Edition

10 9 8 7 6 5 4 3 2 1

A certain light was beginning
to dawn dimly within her—
the light which, showing the
way, forbids it.
But the beginning of things, of
a world especially, is
necessarily vague, tangled,
chaotic and exceedingly
disturbing. How few of us ever
emerge from such a beginning!
How many souls perish in its
tumult!

—Kate Chopin, *The Awakening*

Prologue

Philadelphia • April 13, 1859

There is no power so reckless as a woman's need to be loved. It is a hunger destined to be fed, a yearning that is oblivious to class, intelligence, discipline, and probity. Her urgency for a wholeness of the body and soul, to be made complete, to possess and be possessed, is an inevitable force. For some women it is an awakening of life. For others, their doom.

Mary Leshay, known simply as Old Mary, pondered the dilemma of this need routinely, for she was a midwife in a poor Philadelphia neighborhood. Her faith in God was unshakable, but she often wondered why so many of His children were created and then abandoned to desperate lives. Her patient might die, which was all too often the case, but the man who had answered a young woman's need with his own was not here to share in the meaning of life, nor to act as an escort to death's gate.

Old Mary mopped the fevered brow of the woman. Betsy, her granddaughter and helper, held the just born infant while the woman's first daughter, a blond tot of fifteen months, whimpered and clung close to Betsy's skirt.

"*Mama. Mama.*" The cry did not come from the small child, but from the mother's anguished mouth. Her second daughter had come forth with great difficulty; the baby was large and breech. Old Mary had been forced to turn the infant before it could be born, a procedure both torturous and dangerous. Now the bleeding would not stop and there was fever.

The woman Old Mary tended, Emily, had lived in this shanty for months, but little was known about her. The midwife was called by neighbors who saw Emily's child standing alone in the opened door of the shanty, her face tear-stained and her hair snarled. Emily usually kept the little one tidy and quiet and so those who passed her shanty daily knew something was wrong; they were afraid Emily was dead.

Old Mary mixed her herbs into water. "You're the mama here, child," she told her patient. "You think about getting well so you can take care of this new baby girl."

The midwife squeezed out a rag in cool water and placed it on Emily's forehead. Her eyes, glazed with fever, stared up at the old midwife. "My baby?"

"That baby's fine—strong and pretty. But you're a sick mama. Can you drink this?"

Old Mary lifted Emily's head and helped her. If the fever broke, Mary would go home and get broth and cider. Emily had stale water in supply but there was nothing in the little house to eat.

For several months Old Mary had seen this woman standing in the doorway of the ramshackle hut. Her little girl was either balanced on her hip or stood clinging to her skirt. She grew round with her second child. Once or twice Mary talked with her but the midwife's services were not requested. Mary had but to look around the room to see that the reason was poverty. Emily should not have waited for that reason; Old Mary had never turned her back on a woman in need.

Emily had very few possessions, none of them practical. A bowl and pitcher sat on the floor; a china chamber pot on the other side of the room. It was the first one Old Mary had ever seen in this neighborhood. Most people here had a bucket, if that. There was a small oval portrait in an ivory frame: a young girl. This girl? There was hardly any resemblance between this poor creature, her face bleached and drawn, and the robust blond beauty in the painting. A few dresses lay on the floor in the corner; a crate held two cups and two bowls. Emily's table. There was a miniature stool for the child, no chair for Emily. Did she kneel beside her daughter?

Old Mary called to her granddaughter. "Betsy, bring that baby here." Mary pulled back the thin quilt from her patient's breast. There was only an old, stained sheet between the woman and the rough straw tick on which she lay. "Emily, child, if you nurse this baby maybe the blood'll stop. It works sometimes with the herbs. It can hurt terrible, but we have to try. Can you try, child?"

Emily's eyes opened and she strained herself to concentrate on the midwife's instructions. "Emily," she whispered. "I am Emily. Please. Try. Please."

The midwife arranged the baby against Emily's breast, propping the infant with a rolled towel; Emily lacked the strength to hold her newborn against her. Then, as the baby suckled, Old Mary dug her wrinkled hands into the woman's flaccid abdomen, massaging deeply. She felt Emily's innards tighten underneath her skilled fingers in response to the babe's suckling. Emily moaned and cried as a bright river of blood flowed between her thighs. Then it slowed.

When the pain from the contractions stopped, Emily slept again. The bleeding had been so severe that if the fever didn't kill her, the blood loss might. Mary carried the newborn back to Betsy and began the arduous task of cleaning up. She should have guessed that poverty was the reason this woman did not hire her. Much of this suffering might have been avoided had Mary turned the baby much earlier to make the birth easier.

"She gonna live, Granny?" Betsy asked.

"Maybe. She's too sick to get well here, too sick to carry out of here. But these babies sure is pretty ones." She looked around the little shelter. Though poor and nearly bare, there were painstaking touches of home. Half a thick green velvet skirt covered the only window, wooden spools served as candle holders, rags used for washing had been cut from quality undergarments, a clothesline had been stretched between two walls at the corner. Right now, however, there was no food. Poor thing, Old Mary thought. How's she gonna feed these babies?

"She got any people?" Betsy asked. "I can't see 'bout these babies, Granny."

The little girl had crawled closer to her mother's pallet, curling up in a tight little knot on the edge of the quilt. She wore an old shirt, one that might have been found on a rag pile. On her feet she wore her mother's stockings, doubled over and tied with grass rope. Her knees were drawn against her stomach, probably in hunger. Emily had labored for two days and couldn't rise from her bed to see about her firstborn. The little one shuddered and whimpered from time to time.

"There ain't no one," Old Mary said.

"She's been callin' for her ma. And someone named Ned. Ned her man?"

"Women don't get this way alone, but there sure ain't no man here now."

The neighbors said that a man had moved this woman and her child into the little dwelling and left them. Shortly after he had left, they noticed her belly rounding out, but they didn't see him again. And from the way they lived, he didn't send money. The neighbors took pity on her now and then and gave her scraps of food and such, but they complained she couldn't do for herself at all. Someone gave her ground wheat and lard, but she only stared at it; she didn't even know how to make flat bread. No one understood how she had lived this long without starving to death.

But Old Mary understood. She had looked at the quilt that covered her patient. Emily had obviously sewn it for herself and her young. Her stitches were pretty, neat, and strong; she had cut scraps evenly, decoratively, though she had no batting to fill the quilt, which was thin as a sheet. But the child wore an old shirt. Emily had not cut down one of her dresses for her daughter because, although she knew how to sew and sew well, she did not know how to make useful things. Such was the case with many rich girls. Emily did not know how to do for herself, Mary decided, because she never had before.

"I can't see 'bout these babies while she's sick, Granny. I got my own babies to worry 'bout," Betsy reminded her grandmother.

"Just worry 'bout your own, then. I'll see 'bout 'em."

A sound came from the mat and Mary crouched down again. Emily looked like a china plate, her skin was so pale and thin. But her eyes blazed with a potency rare for a woman who had endured so much. "Please," she whispered. "Please, help me . . . my babies . . ."

"You're gonna be all right, child. You sleep if you can."

"My babies . . . my Patsy . . ."

"Old Mary'll see 'bout these babies, child. And you. We'll get you right."

Emily sighed and let her eyes close, exhausted sleep consuming her. Mary touched her forehead and found it had cooled. A slow smile grew wide and dark on her nearly toothless mouth. She had beaten the sickness again. The fever was waning. She pulled back the curious quilt and looked between Emily's thighs. There was only the old, dark stain; there was no new red glistening. They had gotten the bad blood out.

Mary had grown up in this neighborhood when it was far less crowded. Her husband had built the house she still lived in, but all around the waterfront little shanties like this one had taken over. Negroes fled from southern slavery to the northern cities and thousands of Irish and Germans clustered on American shores, light of money but heavy with dreams of freedom, opportunity, and success. Sometimes it seemed they never got farther than the docks, living in these little boxes—still, better homes for many of them than what they had left. The shanties were built against warehouses and against each other, far into the street. Some were made of wood, some were hardly more than crates discarded by shippers, tied or nailed together. They were never purchased or sold like real property, but traded, claimed, or just abandoned. One like Emily's, with a window of glass and a door that closed, was a quality shanty in a sea of waterfront hovels. There were no yards, of course, and it was not unusual for coaches or wagons carrying people and goods to the docks to scrape against these little houses and knock them down.

Old Mary had seen women in Emily's straits every day of her life. Alone by some misfortune, left to scrape together an existence for themselves and their young because some man's sin had been visited on them. They came from all manner of beginnings—poor since birth, immigrants from foreign lands, from good families, widowhood, illness, joblessness. Destitute women, trapped in poverty they couldn't escape, could be seen all over Philadelphia. Some could find drudgery work in richer homes or factories, and they left their children alone on the streets while they went in search of earnings. Some would take another man, sometimes for money straight out and sometimes with the hope that this one would stay and keep them fed. If they didn't take a man, a man might take them; many of the infants Old Mary delivered were the result of rapes, for these women were not only lacking in money and love—they had no protection.

Mary delivered their young whether or not they could pay; she had opened her door to them, had been called out to their shanties, to where they were. If called, she would go even to alleys to deliver women of their young.

Emily was older than most; had she lived this kind of low life through her youth, she would have some knack for survival and she probably would have birthed her second child at fifteen, not twenty. She offered to work in the neighborhood, but had no skills. Her skills or the lack hardly mattered here; there was no work. She tried to trade trinkets, so the neighbors wondered if she had stolen; people here did not have lace hankies, lockets, hair combs, petticoats, corsets, fans. Mary could guess why she had such frivolous things when she had no decent cooking pots. A man, Old Mary thought, took her away from a good family, filling her head with promises and her belly with his young before leaving her here. Such a story was not rare.

Emily wept and begged for help on behalf of her babies. When poor, broken women brought forth a child, all too often they cursed the offspring and, in despair and hopelessness, cried bitterly for death. Poor women learned early that the presence of children made life only harder, more impossible.

The light of dawn began to streak through the loose seams in the shanty walls. Everyone slept but Old Mary, and in the growing light she could see that the room was free of cobwebs, the dirt floor was packed solid and uncluttered. Emily had kept the place as clean as possible; other shanty dwellers battled vermin for they carelessly dropped food scraps and didn't dump their slops. Old Mary considered Emily's effort and pride.

It seemed she would live. Would her family take her back? What if she had food and a place for her children? If she were taken in, trained up, taught to bake bread, and put those neat little stitches to something that wanted mending, could she make her way? She had fight in her; it took fight of a powerful sort to survive childbed fever in circumstances like these.

Generosity was typical of Old Mary, but she had never before considered taking a woman in. She needed help now, because of her age and because her granddaughter had her own children to think about. Maybe if she could get Emily strong and teach her a few things, she might help with the midwifing and chores in exchange for keep.

Old Mary's hand had been grasped and squeezed by many a tortured woman, but Emily had reached out to her in a forceful way. Something almost radiant cut through Emily's pleading voice, through the gloss of fear and fever in her eyes. It was a quality rare in this part of the city, and perhaps it would die in Emily, too. But it could save her. It was the very thing to be blamed for creating this tragedy, yet the only thing that could give her the spirit and strength to free herself from this kind of life.

A willful spirit.

1

April 20, 1876

I don't think I can," Lilly said.

"Of *course* you can," Patricia insisted. "There's nothing to it. And men are very attracted by it; well, they're attracted to *frailty*."

Lilly frowned her doubt.

"All right, I'll show you again, so pay close attention. First, show that you're shocked—offended. *Out-*raged. Maybe bring your hand up to your mouth, like so, then begin to fade away, as if you're overcome. Turn your feet slightly, let your knees buckle, and . . ." Patricia, eighteen and slight of build, swayed downward in an authentic-looking faint. She melted to the floor where a collection of pillows, petticoats, shawls, and quilts softened her fall. Then she sat up smiling. "See?"

Lilly rolled her eyes. "It's so . . . *dishonest*, Patsy."

"Oh pish, men aren't interested in honesty, ninny.

Not at first anyway. I read about this in *Ladies' Own Magazine*—when men are looking for prospective brides they'll judge a woman's moral character by how she reacts to a slightly, well, provocative remark or gesture. They're supposed to protect and defend our moral character. Think about it, Lilly. You'll be tested. Why would a man want a woman who needn't rely on the strength of his protection? They count on us to be weak. Well, at least weaker than they are."

"This whole thing keeps sounding worse and worse," said Lilly. Seven years ago, when she was ten, Lilly had been the only child in the neighborhood brave enough to walk right up to the maggot-infested body of some unfortunate killed on the railroad tracks. Boys included.

Patricia stood up from the cushioning pile and smoothed her skirt. "Come on, try it. You said you would."

Lilly was almost a year and a half younger than Patricia, but larger of stature by three inches and fifteen pounds. Their mother had declared Lilly not quite graceful, and considering all the possible uses for grace, such as preening or pretending to faint so that some as yet unknown man might become attracted to her feigned weakness, it did not stir any excitement in Lilly.

"Try. Just in case you decide, as I know you will, that it's something you need to know. And try to look *womanly*."

Lilly took her place in front of the pile as Patricia had instructed, but she distrusted the reasoning. Their mother, Emily, whom they both considered the epitome of womanliness, would never faint. Though small like Patricia, Emily had the stamina of a general. And sometimes the air of command as well.

"Lillian! Patricia!"

Patricia made a face to show her annoyance, but she went to the bedroom door to answer their mother's call immediately. Emily stood below at the banister. "Yes, Mama. One minute more, please? We're pract— We're just cleaning up, Mama."

"Be quick then. Don't dally."

"Yes, ma'am," Patricia obediently promised. Then she turned back to Lilly. "Go on," she demanded. "Try it." There was an obstinate lift to Patricia's chin. Lilly was very well acquainted with her older sister's single-mindedness. "Do it."

Lilly concentrated hard for a moment. She thought this was probably foolishness, but she had to admit that Patricia had already mastered many feminine wiles by her seventeenth year. At eighteen she had a gallery of beaux. Lilly didn't have beaux, nor did she wish to, but Patricia kept insisting she would soon change her mind about that. These lessons, according to Patricia, were essential. Partly because Lilly feared her sister might be right and partly because Patricia would not give in before having her way, Lilly prepared to faint.

Lilly opened her eyes suddenly, as though she had just seen a naked man, drew up her hand to cover her startled, gaping mouth, and went backward. She forgot about turning her knees slightly, forgot about drifting slowly to the floor. She hit the protective pile in a stiff, poorly orchestrated thunk. Then there was the telltale sound of *ooofff.*

"For pity's sake," Patricia said in disgust, crossing her slender arms over her generous bosom.

"Well," Lilly said, sitting up dizzily, "it was my first try, you know."

"Hopefully, he'll catch you before you hit the ground or you'll kill yourself."

"Who?"

"Well, someone . . . surely." Patricia sighed. "You have to *fade.* You're not being thrown from a train, you know."

"I think I'd rather be thrown from a train, actually."

"You're being purposely uncooperative. Be an old spinster then."

"I'd prefer it to this if you want to know."

"Hah! That's what you say now, but just wait. If you think my husband and I are going to take care of some old spinster aunt—"

"You're the one who wants to be taken care of. You're the one who is pretending to be weak just so some—"

"Lillian Armstrong, you are the most bullheaded—"

"I'd rather be bullheaded than dis*honest.* And *weak!*"

"Sometimes you are such a *child!*"

"Lillian! Patricia!"

"Coming, Mama," they sang out in unison. Both girls grabbed armfuls from the cushioning pile, tossed the mess atop the unmade bed, and prayed their mother wouldn't inspect their room before they could tidy it. Then they bolted toward the stairs.

"Trade biscuits for dishes?" Patricia asked in a whisper.

"No." Lilly was firm. She knew what the trade meant. Biscuits

11

were set to rise before dinner. Dishes were washed after. Patricia must have evening plans. Again.

"Please? Roger is calling on me."

"I can't abide Roger. He smells."

"Does not," Patricia whispered furiously. "Please?"

"No."

Their mother was waiting. Both girls arrived at the bottom of the stairs together. Emily smoothed Patricia's collar while she assessed Lilly's appearance. She frowned. "Oh Lilly, how you do come apart. You might have to replait your braids. Who helps before dinner?"

"I do, Mama," Lilly said.

"Well, trade tonight. Or go back upstairs and fix these braids." Emily reached for her younger daughter, untying the ribbon at the end of one braid and retying it. Patricia glided away with a very superior air.

"That's what she wanted anyway," Lilly sulked. "Roger is calling on her tonight."

"Ah. That would explain her victorious posture. There, that's better." Emily put her hands on Lilly's shoulders. "Help Sophia anyway, Lilly. And set an extra place—we have another boarder coming."

"Another?"

"Yes. Goodness, you're wrinkled. What have you been doing?"

"Nothing. I mean, nonsense."

"Nonsense?"

"Promise not to get angry?" Lilly didn't wait for an answer because Emily never made such promises. "Patricia was teaching me how to pretend to faint."

"Whatever for?" Emily asked, wide-eyed.

"In order to make a man think that I need the strength of his protection for my moral character." She took a breath. "As Patricia tells it."

"I see," Emily said, her lips quivering with the temptation to laugh outright. "And? Did you learn?"

"Not so far. And even if I do, I doubt I'll ever use the skill. I don't have any interest in getting a man who's stupid enough to be taken in by something like that."

Emily patted her daughter's cheek. "It's just as well."

"It's written about in *Ladies' Own*, Mama. Did you ever faint so that a man would think you were weak and be attracted to you?"

12

"No." Emily laughed. "My weaknesses were much more obvious than that. I never had to pretend any of them."

"You? Weak? You're the strongest—"

"We aren't born with strength, Lilly. We develop it. And I was young once, too. As young as you." She smiled at Lilly's dubious expression. "Oh, honestly I was."

"It's hard to imagine," Lilly said, and then she began to color. "You being weak, that is."

"It takes a great deal of discipline to become strong. And faith," Emily said, but somewhat absently. She was thinking about Patricia. She would have to speak with her about this unwise practice of deceptive tricks to attract men, as if Patricia didn't have more than enough suitors already.

Emily had not feigned weakness at eighteen. She had been frightened, lonely, vulnerable, in desperate need of a man's love, and finally pregnant. The brief time with her husband had been intolerable, disastrous. The years of struggle to feed and clothe her children without their father's help had been harder still. She must convince Patricia. She might even tell how her own misconceptions about love and marriage had led her astray, but the very thought of such a confession made her stomach leap. Patricia was usually sensible; maybe a little advice would do.

"Does Patricia plan to entertain Roger here?" Emily asked.

"If she does I hope there's a good breeze."

"Don't be mean, Lilly. He works around horses."

"Mama, that's more than horses." Lilly wrinkled her nose.

"When you've finished your chores this evening, we should have a talk. You and I."

"About what, Mama?"

"About what you've been doing rather than going to Sylvia Stratton's School for Young Ladies. And what you've done with the money I gave you for tuition and horsecar fare."

Lilly's face paled and she felt her throat constrict. Caught. "Mama, I saved the money. I wouldn't—"

"After dinner will be soon enough, Lilly. That will give you plenty of time to think of all your excuses."

"But Mama, I was *bored!* It's terribly boring, Mama. And I haven't missed anything because instead of going there I go—"

"Stop, Lilly," Emily reproached, shaking her head. "I'm not going to discuss this with you now. Later."

13

During the fall term, from September until the Christmas holidays, Lilly had attended the young ladies' academy faithfully, completing all the required studies—reading, literary discussion group, book-keeping, sewing and design, deportment and etiquette—all things she could learn better from her mother. Sylvia Stratton's school was not designed for women with university ambitions, nor for rich girls whose families could afford sophisticated boarding schools or tutors, but rather as a place for the daughters of working people to fill the time between public school and marriage. The studies were intended to do nothing more than groom intelligent and sufficient wives. Lilly had tucked the tuition money her mother gave her into her satchel and did not enroll for the second term in January. But she left the house every day, going instead to the Women's Sanitary Gymnasium or the lending library. Lilly was not averse to studying, nor was she unmotivated. She studied independently, subjects of her own choice.

Lilly's grades had not been outstanding, because the trivial uselessness of the curriculum bored her. She was in a hurry. She wanted to read all the things that were considered unseemly or unsavory. She wanted to earn money, and she was not drawn to the few occupations considered appropriate for women. And, since pretending to faint held no appeal, she had decided she'd better have some resources other than marriage.

Patricia had always been pointed toward marriage; it was her unflinching target. Since the age of twelve or so she had been more interested in young men than any other thing. She had reached her eighteenth birthday last December and was determined to become engaged before she reached nineteen. She would be married the following spring and deliver her first child the spring after that. She collected essays on wifely occupation and protocol, domestics, manners, and even intimate practices. She had fabric samples snipped from great bolts of cloth and a collection of fashion plates from all the popular magazines. She had decided the menu for her wedding supper and the name of her first child, which would be a boy. But from the host of suitors who plagued the Armstrong front porch, Patricia had not yet selected a husband.

Lilly knew that Patricia was more like other young women in this pursuit than she was; most were preoccupied with becoming wives. But not Lilly. "Don't you have to be in love?" she had asked her sister.

"I will be," Patricia replied.

"But will you be in time?" she asked, referring to Patricia's rigid schedule.

"Don't be silly. Of course. I'm a little bit in love already. And I will marry when I'm completely in love."

"And what'll you do?"

"Well, silly, I'll get married."

"But what'll you *do*?"

"Oh, Lilly, you're such a ninny. I'll . . . I'll be like Mama."

"But Patsy, Mama isn't married."

"It's all the same thing. You're such a child sometimes."

Marriage was a state of grace for women. Lilly sometimes thought about the reasons for getting married. Wanting children, for example, for Lilly wanted children. She was very fond of babies especially, and often helped neighbor women by rocking babies or chasing the little tots who had just learned to walk. Patricia said she wanted to have a family but Lilly knew that Patricia was made nervous and cranky by crying babies, and chasing toddlers exasperated her.

And there was the physical aspect of marriage, the coupling. Patricia had shared an essay which not only explained that coupling was a thing *men* required, but also listed some methods a virtuous wife might employ to discourage her husband's conjugal demands, such as wearing a scratchy bedgown, complaining of fatigue and illness, even discussing household problems to divert his attention. It had all sounded to Lilly like more trouble and discomfort than simply letting him do as he pleased, which caused Patricia to gasp in disbelief. Patricia *dreaded* that part of marriage, whereas Lilly had never let it worry her.

Of course there was love, which was one of the greatest reasons Lilly was afraid she wouldn't marry. Not from the absence of love, but quite the opposite. There was a man, known to her only as Andrew, whom she had met at the library. He was forbidden, and Lilly knew it. He was far too old for her, maybe thirty, and very handsome. He was dark Irish and had a smile that cut through Lilly to her bones, leaving her with a vague unsteadiness. She knew he

15

was rich and well educated; his clothes were costly and new, his trousers did not bear a store-bought crease but were smooth and tailored from the finest, thinnest wool. She could tell from his diction, manners, and comportment that he was very sophisticated and refined, although there did seem to be a careless, almost reckless motion about him—even when he was silent and still.

Once there was some trouble with the librarian over reading she requested. She wished to read an essay about seances and spiritualism and was arguing for a old copy of *Woodhull and Claflin's Weekly* when Andrew had stepped in and instructed the recalcitrant librarian to give Lilly anything she asked for on his approval. The librarian looked disappointed, but he said, "Yes, sir." Even though Lilly wore a matronly bun rather than her braids so that she wouldn't be denied any reading because of her age, she learned there was plenty that was considered inappropriate for her gender.

She thanked him kindly, shyly, and was surprised to find him in the square later as she was leaving. She learned then that he was a patron of the library, but she did not learn his last name; indeed, she didn't ask. She didn't want to know; it could only bear testimony to his importance—and his distance from her class of people.

But he asked if she had found the essay interesting, and they discussed spiritualism for a long time. He knew about seances, though he said he wouldn't attend one. Once, he said, great stock was put in summoning spirits for a consultation; Cornelius Vanderbilt was known for seeking mystical insight. But lately seances had become trifling entertainment for bored rich people who didn't believe in the potential power. "How foolish to toy with something as provocative as spirits and magical entities," he had said, smiling slyly. "What if they get mad?"

Lilly wondered if he was bored as well as rich.

She saw him a second time and they had walked together in the square, almost *strolling* together as couples do, talking about Walt Whitman's *Leaves of Grass*. After that she began looking for him. He remarked that her determination to learn was delightful, her curiosity refreshing, her sense of adventure and daring fascinating— all this was complimentary enough, but affectionate? She wasn't sure. Maybe he considered her something like a younger sister—perhaps a pupil or protégé.

She had conjured up many vivid daydreams about him, but when he looked at her, she could not distinguish amusement from intrigue in his eyes. Inexperienced as she was, she couldn't tell the difference between admiration and desire. He had an uncanny knack for getting her to talk about things she had never guessed would flow so easily from her lips. She shared her ambitions, her frustrations, even the problem of an older sister with an unbearable quest for marriage. And she would die if he knew how attractive she found him.

Here was a man, Lilly was certain, who would not be won by a feigned swoon, nor be made malleable and contrite by a scratchy bedgown.

It seemed to Lilly that she, who would be pleased to find love, marriage, and children, would remain unhappily alone. And Patricia, who did not like children, could not abide the thought of coupling, and loved no one in particular, would marry in any case. There was much about life that Lilly found inequitable.   •

Lilly and Patricia had no models for marriage in their own family. Emily had been on her own since her husband, Ned Armstrong, left to fight in the Civil War two years after Lilly was born. In fact, Lilly's second birthday marked the day the Confederates had captured Fort Sumter; two days later President Lincoln had called for seventy-five thousand volunteers. Emily said that Ned Armstrong had been among the first to leave. Lilly could not remember him, of course. And Emily had not even entertained a gentleman caller since, although there had been a man or two who had expressed an interest in paying court. Emily was very self-sufficient and beautiful, and Lilly did not think that signs of weakness had attracted those occasional men.

Emily claimed to be very satisfied. She had work that was hard, but gratifying; her income was not grand, but decent. She was far from lonely, with a boardinghouse to keep. She had her family, her friends, her church, a neighborhood that thought highly of her, and she was content. Emily worked very hard, but it always appeared as though she simply followed a routine.

They had not always lived in this house. Lilly had very early memories of a small, crowded house near the waterfront where they lived with an elderly woman fondly recalled as Old Mary. When she died they moved into a three-room tenement, renting the second bedroom to two sisters who worked long days at the textile mill. Emily, clever enough to share her home for income, gave the women space and an evening meal for a fee. During those years the lamp had burned late in the bedroom Emily shared with her daughters

17

while she sewed for other women, saving every penny toward their betterment.

Year round Emily sewed for women who could afford her alterations and mending. Through those acquaintances she found buyers for preserves, jams, jellies, and baked goods. During the winter months, especially at Christmastime, she baked ferociously, and the coal fire served to warm the house while the baking provided income. As soon as Patsy and Lilly could help, they stood on stools around the worktable. In summer they pulled a wagon to market where Emily bargained expertly, as old Mary had taught her, for fruits and vegetables that were near spoiling; if the price was agreeable, Emily could stretch one dollar into ten with her culinary skills.

Lilly had fond memories of the days when her mother dressed them in their best and took them with her buying or selling. Emily always wore a very modest gray or brown muslin and her only pair of four-button gloves. And she was very precise about getting what she needed. She was soft-spoken but firm, her chin was high, and her shoulders square. More than once she had walked away from a purchase or sale if she did not feel satisfied.

In 1867 Emily received a settlement of some kind, probably from her father's death. With her savings, it was enough to buy this house in a better part of the city. It had three bedrooms then, but also a parlor, kitchen, dining room, pantry, and yard. Later, with the help of a mortgage, Emily added two bedrooms, which she instantly filled with boarders. She was clever enough to have a porch constructed, something she said was popular in southern climes; none of their neighbors had porches and the boarders liked hers very much in summer. Emily continued with her sewing and sale of foodstuffs, and even though times were less lean for them now, she was no less frugal.

Lilly admired her mother's industry and, faced with Patricia's flirting and fainting, she thought it was far more intelligent to work for one's own money than to try to trick a man into marriage. Emily had been married and had still been forced to make her own way.

"That's what I'll tell her," she said aloud.

"What'll you tell who?" Sophia asked.

Lilly hadn't realized she had spoken aloud. She looked over her shoulder almost guiltily at Patricia and Sophia. "Nothing," she said, turning back to the pot she had been told to stir.

Sophia sighed and went to Lilly, taking the spoon from her hand. "You're standing right here, but you're thinkin' somewheres yonder. These are potatoes, girl—don't keep mixin' unless you want mush." She turned away and lifted a tray from the worktable. "Here. You jes' take this cider out to the porch. Miz Fairchild been fannin' herself all afternoon. And Mr. Giddings be home from the newspaper now. And your mama jes' might go easier on you for it."

"You know?" Lilly asked in a whisper.

"Now how you gwine keep a secret in this house? Mind you don't make it no worse on yourself."

"Yes, ma'am," Lilly said, taking the tray with pitcher and glasses from Sophia.

Sophia wouldn't think she'd been foolish, Lilly thought. In fact, Sophia might approve. She had worked for the Armstrongs for seven years now, although she didn't live with them. Sophia said she wouldn't live with white folks again, no matter how highly she thought of them. She wouldn't live with her married daughters, either; there were three, and grandchildren. Once, a long time before the war, Sophia was owned by a white man. She had not only escaped bondage when she was just a girl, but she had married a free black man in Pennsylvania. He also died in a Union uniform. Then, in much the same straits as Emily, she had somehow managed to support herself and her daughters. The struggle must have been enormous for a Negro woman alone, but she had not only managed, her daughters were educated and, Sophia said, had made good marriages.

Lilly considered using Emily and Sophia and their widowhood as an argument for her independent study, except she could hardly explain reading philosophers and scientists as a way to earn money. Nor could she justify reading improper novels just because she was bored with comportment lessons. She liked newspapers that were considered dangerous, like the *Woodhull and Claflin* paper, which expounded on "free love" and communal living. There was literature on the suffrage movement and temperance that was difficult to come by, since the library stock was chosen by a man. She was delighted with *Oliver Twist,* but she wanted to read *Tom Jones* also. There were women who wrote essays about their belief that if Negro men could vote, women of all colors should be likewise entitled; Sylvia Stratton's school taught that a woman should accept and support the political preference of her father or husband, if not both. Well,

Lilly did not have a father, might never have a husband, and was certainly not without opinions of her own. She had decided she had better do some more extensive studying.

The reason Lilly had for doing what she had done would never satisfy her mother.

The boardinghouse was not neatly divided into tenants and owners. You could not share all your meals and rooms without also sharing everybody's burdens and triumphs.

Mrs. Fairchild had been with them the longest, since 1870. She was the most trouble. Emily said it was because she was unhappy, but Lilly thought that was just an excuse. Mrs. Fairchild's only son, Walter, had married a very domineering woman. Before their first year of marriage was over, he realized that his wife and mother could not live peacefully under the same roof. Mrs. Fairchild, whose husband had built the house she lived in, was put out to board. Although Walter visited her twice weekly, paid her board and expenses, and took her to church and dinner every Sunday, he lived with his wife and children in the house his father had built while Mrs. Fairchild lived in a rented room.

If this arrangement made Mrs. Fairchild unhappy, she showed it strangely. She was not only finicky, rarely finding anything to her liking, but she held up her son and daughter-in-law as examples to everyone. If the stew was too bland, Marlise used a spice that would make it right. And Marlise's biscuits were so smooth and creamy. Her grandchildren were so tidy and polite and her son's shoe-repair business was so successful he had taken on employees. "If it's such a good business, why doesn't he build a bigger house and bring you into his family again?" Lilly had once asked out of sheer annoyance. In her opinion Mrs. Fairchild ought to show more gratitude to the Armstrongs. But Lilly had been reprimanded and disciplined for being cheeky.

John Giddings had been in their house the second longest, since '71. He was nearly thirty, a newspaper writer, unmarried, and a perfect boarder. He always paid for his room and meals on time, even if he had not been in residence; he often traveled about in search of a story. John was punctual and polite. Emily would ordinarily consider it unpropitious to give room and board to an unmarried man; she could, on occasion, demonstrate such prickly virtue. But she had known John's parents before they died and John was very respectable. Lilly suspected that the fact that he was homely—lanky, bespectacled, rumpled, and timid—also put Emily at ease with the way the neighborhood would view this bachelor boarder.

Jamie and Annie MacIntosh, a young married couple who happily occupied the smallest room, had moved in two and a half years ago. They craved both privacy and economy, for they wished to lease a tenement of their own as soon as their first child arrived. But this arrival was tenuous; Annie was now pregnant for the third time, her first two pregnancies having ended in miscarriage. Those tragic losses had united the household in sadness, but this time it looked as though Annie would succeed. She was in her sixth month. Emily allowed Annie to help with light chores for a discount in their rent and they scrimped on the meals they ate with the others. Emily said they were happy crowded in that little room because they were young, in love, and couldn't get close enough. She had said so rather wistfully and Lilly wondered if her mother was ever lonely, despite her many protests to the contrary.

There was one more boarder, not in residence at the moment. Lilly hoped she wouldn't return. Miss Susan Pendergast was a middle-aged schoolteacher whose parents had died a few years ago. She had taken a room just after the MacIntosh couple, having found her parents' house difficult for an unmarried woman of limited income to maintain. Susan insisted on being addressed as Miss Pendergast by Patricia and Lilly. She had departed in a tiff two days ago. The issue was her annual summer visit with her brother's family in Newport. As she was discussing her summer plans, Emily asked Susan if she would kindly make her room, usually reserved for her, available. If Susan would store her more personal belongings, Emily could rent the room during the Centennial Exhibition, an event that was drawing thousands of visitors to Philadelphia.

Susan was outraged by this change; she had always left for the months of June and July, paying no rent and returning to her room in August. Emily had firmly and inflexibly explained that while such an arrangement was appropriate other summers when she could not attract short-term boarders, this summer, with so many visitors looking for rooms, Emily would be losing money by leaving the room empty while Susan was away. They finally reached a tense compromise: Emily would hold the room for Susan at half the usual price if Patricia and Lilly could use it.

Susan was angry but she knew that it would be difficult to find new boarding arrangements in August, especially during the Exhibition. So, she left early, moved in with another teacher for the remainder of April and all of May, paying her half-board to Emily for her empty room. Lilly suspected that Susan lived as a guest with her friend.

Susan might have thought herself clever in leaving early, but Emily would not be outfoxed. She moved Lilly's bed into the unfinished attic, though small and somewhat unpleasant, and planned to rent every corner of her house. While other owners of boardinghouses were considering putting up quarantine signs to keep the visitors out, Emily was dusting off the welcome mat.

Meanwhile, for the first time in their lives, Lilly and Patricia did not sleep with their mother. A room of their own was a great luxury and they used it greedily, staying up late at night to whisper and giggle, dividing their space judiciously and territorially. Neither considered that their mother had finally, after many years, achieved space of *her* own. They certainly did not wonder about how she felt with her newfound privacy.

This was the Armstrong household. Eight people, plus Sophia Washington, with one boarder away now but soon to be replaced with a visitor to the Centennial Exhibition and not quite a family, but more a community designed to keep its members safe and cared for.

As Lilly carried the tray onto the front porch, she saw that Mrs. Fairchild wore her usual grimace and John was smiling pleasantly. Emily looked up in surprise that faded into knowledge; very little escaped Emily. "What a thoughtful gesture, Lilly," Emily said, polite, but not fooled by this sudden considerateness.

Lilly served the first glass to Mrs. Fairchild, who sipped immediately, greedily. She passed the next glass to John; the boarders were always served first. "Too sweet," said Mrs. Fairchild. "Next time, Lilly, add more sugar."

"But if it's too sweet—" Lilly stopped herself. Mrs. Fairchild was getting old, her mother said, and they must be more patient than ever.

"Refreshing indeed. Thank you, Lilly," John said.

Lilly would have returned to the kitchen then, but she was caught by the sight of an unusual man walking toward their house. He carried a carpetbag and balanced a huge saddle on his shoulder. He was tall and wore a western hat and a ribbon under his shirt collar. His boots were brown, pointed, and dusty, as was his suit. He looked travel-worn and rumpled, almost as if he had ridden a horse all the way to Philadelphia from somewhere in the West. He moved gracefully down the stone-and-pansy-lined path to the porch. He carefully lowered the saddle, dropped the carpetbag, removed his hat, and stared directly at Mrs. Fairchild. "Mrs. Armstrong?"

"I am Mrs. Armstrong," Emily said, drawing his eyes away from the older woman. "You must be Mr. Padgett. The hotel asked if they could send you over."

"Yes, ma'am. I appreciate it, ma'am. Rooms are pretty scarce just now."

Emily stood to face him. He had a thick, untrimmed, unwaxed, sandy-colored mustache that lay like a limp cat's tail over his lip. Lilly would have found it comical if she weren't so fascinated. He must be a cowboy.

"Is it the Exhibition that brings you to Philadelphia, Mr. Padgett?" Emily asked.

"Yes, ma'am, from the territory of Wyoming as a matter of fact. But Philadelphia is familiar to me—I was born here . . . traveled west sometime later."

"If the hotel is already full, it must mean that visitors are arriving early. Were you informed that the grand opening has been postponed until May?"

"Yes, ma'am. Seems they ran out of money right at the last minute, but it looks like everything will be on schedule now."

"Well, Mr. Padgett, all I can offer you is my smallest room, an attic with a dormer window. As tall as you are, you might have trouble even standing to your full height. Did they tell you?"

His mustache moved slightly, hinting at rather than exposing his smile. "If there's a bed in it, ma'am, it'll do better than a bench in the train station."

"It is also very expensive—twelve dollars per week in advance." Lilly nearly choked. That was more than was paid for the largest room in her mother's house. "I serve both breakfast and supper. Seven in the morning and half past six in the evening. And I'm afraid I can't hold either meal for you if you're late."

The cowboy did not react to the high rent. Lilly began to

23

worry—when he saw the little room and short bed, he might refuse. How did Emily dare?

"Seems fair enough, ma'am."

"There is no water closet, Mr. Padgett. Although my house is not as fashionable as the hotel, I can offer you plenty of hot water, a basin, clean linens, good food. We have a tub in the pantry and can provide a closed door in the kitchen for your bath. I operate a very simple house. I hope you find it serves your needs."

"I'm sure it'll be just fine, ma'am."

If he could afford a hotel, Lilly thought, why would he accept these terms? He must be rich. And foolish.

Lilly noticed her mother's posture become rigid. "You won't be needing . . . a spittoon, I trust."

Mr. Padgett looked down at his boots for a moment. When he lifted his gaze to Emily again, his eyes twinkled exuberantly. His tanned face crinkled deeply at the corners of his slate blue eyes. "I reckon not, ma'am," he said with a laugh.

"I don't usually board men without their wives, Mr. Padgett, but I'm making this exception because the city is already overflowing with visitors to the Exhibition."

Mr. Padgett cleared his throat. "That's mighty generous of you, Mrs. Armstrong," he said, and Lilly was quite certain she heard a quiver of laughter in his words. Emily wasn't fooling him—not at twelve dollars a week with no water closet and a room he wouldn't be able to stand up in.

"The city will be full all summer," she went on. "I am a widow, Mr. Padgett, and I am raising two daughters. I'm sure you will consider these delicate circumstances and adhere to the strictest of protocol."

Lilly felt her cheeks grow warm. She wished her mother would not make such an issue over manners. Not everyone needed to be told. But Mr. Padgett did not blush or protest. Lilly saw that beneath his monstrous cat's tail of a mustache he had a handsome smile. And his eyes were firmly locked into Emily's.

"There is no Mrs. Padgett, ma'am, but I suppose I can behave to your liking. At least for a while."

"While you're in my house, Mr. Padgett. That's all I ask."

Behind the cowboy a ragged-looking character approached their house and Lilly frowned in embarrassment. The man shuffled, looked down, held his ruined hat in his hands, and patiently waited while

Emily was in conversation. Lilly could smell him from where she stood.

Mrs. Fairchild began to mutter disapprovingly and Emily looked around Mr. Padgett to the dirty little man.

"Yes?"

"Got any spare, ma'am?"

"You can wait by the back door, if you like, and if there's any spare after supper, I'll fix you a plate."

"Thankee, ma'am. 'Preciate the kindness, ma'am."

He shuffled off around the house, gaze low and manner ashamed. "Like feeding stray mongrels," Mrs. Fairchild grumbled. "Won't try to feed themselves after you start giving the handouts. Lazy filth."

Emily ignored her boarder's disparaging remarks; she was accustomed to Mrs. Fairchild's complaining and her less than generous nature. "Is that thing coming in the house, Mr. Padgett?" she asked, indicating the saddle.

"Well," he began with an apologetic chuckle, "it's a mighty valuable saddle, ma'am. I'd hate to lose it; it's broke in."

Lilly headed for the kitchen, but she listened raptly as her mother and the new boarder entered the house.

"There's a carriagehouse in the back; we don't have a horse or carriage. You're welcome to use it to store things you won't be using daily. You needn't worry that anyone in this neighborhood would steal it."

"Yes, ma'am."

"Would you like a tub this evening, Mr. Padgett?"

He chuckled. "It's been a long train ride, ma'am."

"I didn't mean to imply—"

"A tub would be welcome, Mrs. Armstrong. Thank you."

"I'll set water to boil after dinner and inform my daughters."

"Was that one of them there, ma'am? That one just gone off?"

"Lilly is my youngest, Mr. Padgett. I'll introduce you at dinner."

"Why, she's grown. You hardly seem old enough to have a grown child."

"Mr. Padgett, please be careful not to be too forward. I put great effort into keeping a respectable house. Being an unmarried man, your comments have to be—"

"I imagine looks can lie," he said, cutting her off.

Lilly smiled at the exchange and burst into the kitchen, exhilarated. There might finally be something of interest happening in the

25

boardinghouse. If he was really a cowboy from the Wild West then he might know about Indian wars, scalpings, mining for gold, trailblazing, and breaking wild horses. Maybe he'd fallen in love with an Indian maiden once. "He's a cowboy!" she exclaimed. "I swear!"

Lilly pumped water into the sink tub after scraping off all the dishes. She added hot water from the kettle. The spring breeze was heavy with the scent of apple blossoms and ruffled the kitchen curtain pleasantly, but Lilly was morose. She had been reprimanded at dinner, and over one silly question. What was the good of having a cowboy boarder if you couldn't learn? She had only wanted to know how Indians scalped people. Now there would be more to discuss than her absence from Sylvia Stratton's school. And her chance of convincing her mother that she had been wise in that choice was now reduced.

The smell of John Giddings' tobacco mingled with the fragrant scent of spring flowers; he was no more allowed to indulge his evening pipe in the house than the cowboy would be allowed to spit. John was talking to Mr. Padgett back by the carriagehouse, asking all the questions that Lilly wanted to ask. She couldn't hear them clearly, only the hum of male voices mingling with early evening sounds in the neighborhood, the splash of kitchen water being thrown on bushes, the jingling of the lamplighter's horse, the scraping of a fork against a plate on the back step, conversations in yards and in kitchens with open windows. Patricia's laughter punctuated the neighborhood sounds occasionally. She entertained both Roger and Arthur on the porch, having told each, by mistake, that the evening was his alone. Patricia made this mistake frequently and deliberately.

Lilly waited until she had done everything else before asking the man on the back step for his plate. She wished there was some way her mother could be convinced to stop feeding beggars. It was not Emily's compassion that disturbed Lilly, but people's comments on the inadvisability of having transients and indigents at the door on any regular basis. Emily, as frugal as she was in all other things, would not send them away if there was a little spare meal left over, although she wouldn't take food off the table for them. But who knew what illnesses they carried, Mrs. Fairchild argued. The neighbors said these jobless men stole, but the Armstrongs had never noticed anything missing.

"Have you had enough to eat today?" Lilly asked him. She could no more send away a hungry man than her mother could, but she wished, just the same, that Emily would refuse them. "There's a little more, I think, a biscuit and some coffee."

He looked up at her as she stood in the back doorway. His face was stubbled, dirty, and aged, yet there was a child's timidity in his eyes. Poverty must make even the aged feel like frightened children, she thought. The Armstrongs had once been very poor; Lilly was relieved not to remember that. He wore a Union soldier's coat, which tore at Lilly's heart. What if her own father had been reduced to this? "A little coffee'd be mighty welcome, miss. I got no money, but if there's any chores . . ."

"No," Lilly said, taking the empty plate. "There aren't any chores today." Could he have been indigent since the war? Eleven years? Surely he found the coat on a rag pile. The leftover coffee made half a cup, so she added hot water and cream, which they usually used very sparingly, to make it full. She put a dab of jam on the biscuit, knowing she could not possibly fill him up. Then she wished again that she could be spared this feeling of pity, and even guilt.

She heard the constable making his rounds, his nightstick on a fence, his cheerful "Good evening." "Stay right here now, and the constable won't bother you," she told the man.

"Thankee, miss."

"Wasn't that a kindness you jes' done," Sophia said. Sophia came into the kitchen, opened the pantry door, and began to drag out the tub. "I'll be fixin' Mr. Padgett his bath before I go. I think you wasted jes' about all the time you can, Miz Lilly. If you scrubs this kitchen any more, you're gonna see your first naked man."

Lilly made a face while Sophia laughed at her own joke. She dried her hands and reluctantly went to find her mother. She knew Emily would be mending in the parlor.

Emily Armstrong valued honesty, propriety, and industry above all. Lilly hoped to convince her mother she had been industrious even though she hadn't attended the school, but she had bungled honesty. That she had been less than proper, given the subjects she had been reading and her discussions with a forbidden man, she planned to keep to herself. It was not that Emily's punishment was likely to be

27

severe—in fact, it would probably be hardly anything at all—but her mother's discomposure would be unbearable. Lilly could feel destroyed just hearing "Oh, Lilly, I'm so disappointed in you . . ."

"Come in, Lilly. You've put me off long enough, don't you think?"

Lilly looked toward the open parlor window. Right outside, Patricia entertained her suitors.

"Don't worry about them, Lilly. They won't be paying any attention to our conversation. Come and sit by me," she said, putting her sewing aside and patting the settee.

Lilly perched on the edge of the settee and folded her hands in her lap. "Mama, I can explain."

"Let me speak first, Lilly. I apologize. I made a poor choice for you. Of course Sylvia Stratton's school is not right for you. You're too clever to make good use of all her subjects, and you're already a perfect young lady. But I was perplexed. I can't afford the university or a private tutor, and I couldn't imagine what you'd do without a schedule. I enrolled you because even if you didn't learn a great deal from the curriculum, I hoped you would make friends among the young ladies."

Lilly couldn't believe her ears. Her mouth was open, but she was speechless.

"You haven't gotten into any mischief with all that time to yourself, I hope."

"Oh no, ma'am," she said quickly, praying she wouldn't blush. She hated her tendency to blush. "I've been studying right along. I've been going to the lending library or the Women's Sanitary Gymnasium, or reading in the park."

"Oh, Lilly, not the Gymnasium. All the women there are so. . . . political."

"No, they're not, Mama. Not all of them. And I've read some of the most wonderful books: Dickens, Eliot, Sir Walter Scott, Emerson. I've even read parts of *Origin of Species,* although the librarian didn't want me to." She saw her mother frown, knowing there was great concern about Darwin's theory contradicting the Scriptures. "I've read *Leaves of Grass,* Mama." Her hands were no longer folded in her lap, but moving around in animated description.

"*Leaves of Grass,*" Emily repeated doubtfully. "Reverend Detwiler considered that unseemly for women."

"Oh, that old prude. Well, it's not—it's simply the most won-

28

derful thing in the world, and I wept and wept. One of the soldiers Walt Whitman visited might have been my own father. I simply had to read it. It was difficult, though, because I—"

Lilly abruptly stopped speaking as Patricia's voice, sharp and laced with anxiety, came through the parlor window. "Perhaps you had better leave, in that case." Lilly saw Emily's head instinctively turn toward the sound.

"Since this is between you and me, Patricia, why not ask them to leave. If you please."

That voice, Lilly knew, belonged to neither Roger nor Arthur.

"Can't you hear right, Montaine? She wants us to stay. It's you she wants to leave."

Emily rose and went quickly to the porch, Lilly close behind her. In front of their house a very rich covered carriage waited. Patricia had ridden in it a few times upon invitation from Dale Montaine, whose father was said to be among the richest men in Philadelphia. There was a fancy scrolled *M* on the door and a uniformed driver. Lilly remembered very clearly that their mother had not wanted Patricia to become enamored of a man who had so much, fearing he would not treat Patricia as respectfully as he might treat women of means equal to his own. Patricia had ignored her mother, and Lilly had not understood.

Patricia was sitting on the porch swing, with Dale facing her, and Roger and Arthur standing on either side of her. Dale seemed unconcerned with either of them; his head was bent as he spoke angrily to Patricia. "I don't understand the meaning of this; we spoke just the other day and you were looking forward to an evening with me, a ride."

Arthur responded for her, "She forgot your plans, then, so go on and leave the rest of us to enjoy the evening."

"Just shut your mouth, this has nothing to do with you!" Dale looked again at Patricia. "Why don't you just come along with me now and we'll discuss this misunderstanding. I'm sure you have an explanation for—"

Arthur made a move around the swing when Dale reached out for Patricia as if to pull her. Arthur's fingers closed around Dale's wrist and the contact seemed to incense Dale, who quickly snatched his arm away. He gave Arthur a shove that sent him tumbling over the porch rail and into a bush at the base of the house. Not only was Arthur no match for Dale in either size or strength, he was obviously unprepared for combat. Patricia gasped in surprise and Roger retreated a step. Dale's hand reached toward Patricia again.

"*Mister* Montaine!"

Dale whirled to face Emily Armstrong, a scowl on his undeniably handsome face. His features did not relax a bit, not even when facing the mother of the girl he was pursuing.

"I believe you have overstayed your welcome," Emily said, her voice steady and firm.

"As a matter of fact I've had no welcome at all, Mrs. Armstrong. Your daughter accepted an invitation from me and I have arrived to find her occupied with these fops and proudies; I believe this was intentional."

Lilly frowned. She had thought for some time that Patricia was probably headed for trouble with all her schemes, and now she had one angry young man on her hands.

Emily did not look at Patricia. She stared at Dale Montaine. "Whether you came by invitation or not, Mr. Montaine, you are no longer welcome. Patricia is done entertaining for the evening."

Patricia's face had paled considerably since her mother stepped onto the porch. She stood to go into the house, and as she passed Dale, he grasped her wrist. "Just a minute," he said. "I think maybe you ought to know, Mrs. Armstrong, that your daughter most enjoys leading her suitors around by the nose, making them all look like fools, full of insinuations and promises and plans, only to—"

"Get your hands off my daughter!" Emily snapped.

They stared at each other for a moment, Dale's face growing more red, his eyes narrowed and his brows drawn together. His voice became boyish and wheedling, but he had a mean look on his face. "Look, I'm willing to listen to an explana—"

"I said, *let go!*"

Reluctantly, Dale released Patricia's wrist and she skittered to stand behind her mother. But Dale did not budge.

Lilly was mesmerized by Dale's violent expression while at the same time the anger in her mother's voice fascinated her. She had never witnessed this kind of force; Emily was firm when she meant to be obeyed, but never snappish or loud. Standing behind her as she was, Lilly could discern a slight trembling in her mother's shoulders and she knew that it must be rigid, hot fury. Lilly had never witnessed such intense emotion in her mother.

Lilly felt a pair of hands on her shoulders and she was gently moved away from the door. Noel Padgett stepped between the women and onto the porch, where he faced Dale Montaine. They were the same height, but Noel was slightly more muscled. He was in an alarming state of underdress and must have come from the kitchen where he was preparing for his tub. He wore only his trousers, boots, and a ribbed undershirt opened at the throat. He surveyed the scene with his hands on his hips. Dale glared, Arthur pulled leaves out of his shirt, and Roger stood silent and shaken against the wall.

"Who are you?" Dale demanded.

"Just company, son. Now, were you asked to leave?"

"This is none of your concern. My business is with—" Dale made a move as if to pass Noel and approach Mrs. Armstrong and her daughter, but Noel took matters into his own hands. He lifted Dale by his very costly lapels and tossed him over the porch rail. It was so quickly done that Lilly hadn't even anticipated it. Arthur had to spring out of the way as Dale soon decorated the same shrub Arthur had just vacated. It took Dale a moment to roll over, get free of the crushed bush, and rise to his feet. The expression on his face passed the mark of anger and moved full steam into rage. His cheeks lost the color of temper, and his dark eyes sizzled with hatred. Noel Padgett calmly leaned both hands on the porch rail and met those menacing eyes with lazy poise. "That your horse and buggy, son?"

Dale turned and stomped away from the house. He arrived at the opened door of his carriage before turning back to the women to impart his final shot. "I'll be seeing you, Patricia. You can count on that!" Then his driver took him quickly away.

Noel stared after the departing conveyance until it was a mere cloud of dust before turning toward the gallery of women, Emily at their helm.

"Mr. Padgett, I'm sure you meant well, but you'll find that we're a family that abhors violence of any sort."

Lilly watched his eyes; his expression reflected the irony, and he grinned in amusement. But there was more in his smile, his eyes. Admiration. Approval.

Finally he gave his head a nod. "I'll try to bear that in mind, Mrs. Armstrong," he said. And he moved slowly past the women back into the house.

"You best tell them girls where they come from, Miz Emily," Sophia quietly advised. " 'Specially Miz Patsy—girls that age all the same, black or white, they think the world'll come to an end if they don't find them a husband."

Emily and Sophia stood in the foyer just inside the front door while John Giddings waited on the porch. All was quiet but for the soft creaking of the porch swing. John routinely took an evening stroll at the time Sophia walked home, never letting on that he played escort, no matter how inconvenient the hour of her departure.

Sophia was leaving far later than usual because of all the excitement. Lilly and Patricia had been sent to their room, and Mr. Padgett had finished his bath and climbed the back stairs to his attic room. The thing that made Emily most proud was the civility of her boardinghouse—quiet, decent, never any real trouble. The fracas had awakened Mrs. Fairchild, brought Annie and Jamie from their room; even neighbors leaned out of windows and doors to watch the Montaine carriage depart.

"I'll talk to Patricia. She might just listen to some advice now," Emily returned, expressing the hopeful thoughts she had had all afternoon.

"No, ma'am. We all got things we got to own, honey. You ain't gone and done nothing so terrible. Women been havin' trouble with men since Eve. You tell them girls where they come from. Sometimes all we got is our history."

"Did you, Sophia? Did you tell yours?" she asked. Old Mary knew what had befallen her, but Sophia had been the only woman Emily had ever confided in. And Sophia did not know everything.

"Yes'm, I had to tell my girls where I come from. You think it was easy tellin' my girls I was born a white man's property?"

"But that wasn't your fault!"

"We carry a lot o' burdens ain't ours, so how come we still ashamed? Ain't your fault neither. You was jes' a young girl like Miz Patsy. A young girl full of love and hope." Sophia squeezed Emily's hand. "You think about this, honey. You'll do right."

"Oh, I thought they'd be better off in innocence."

Sophia squeezed the hand harder. "Miz Em, you listen to me, Miz Patsy, she's a good girl, but she's foolish, not innocent. The things she does is deliberate. She does what she does *on purpose.* The only thing that girl is innocent 'bout is how much trouble she's gonna make."

Emily averted her eyes because she did not want to face that truth. She remembered how much her own ignorance combined with her absolute conviction had cost her. She sighed wearily. "It's been so good these past few years, no real troubles, no real dangers."

"Yes'm, you thought you was past all that. I think we don't never get past . . . we just get *on.*"

"They think me clever for thinking of a porch—they think I have intuition. Good Lord, I once called my private trap to the portico! Oh, Sophia!"

"Blamin' yourself won't do them no good, honey. Go see 'bout them girls—they're shakin' plenty by now."

Emily smiled softly. "I would be so alone without you," she

whispered. "I hope I haven't made a big mistake in letting Mr. Padgett have a room."

Sophia grinned, her large white teeth flashing against her beautiful brown skin. She was ten years older than Emily and had been through a great deal more. Her smile was beautiful, engaging, free. "Girl," she whispered conspiratorially, "you gone and forgot everything you ever knew 'bout men and women. Maybe we says we can get by jes' fine without a man, but I ain't never gwine to forget jes' how handy they is."

Emily hesitated after Sophia had gone. Dale Montaine had no idea whom he had treated so rudely. If he went home and told his father about his altercation with Mrs. Armstrong and her daughter, Wilson Montaine would have no idea who she was. In fact, if she visited Mr. Montaine to discuss his son's behavior, she would have to use her maiden name to be remembered. She would prefer to be forgotten, just as she would prefer to forget. One had proved quite possible; the other, tragically impossible.

She had stopped asking herself years ago whether she had created convenient lies for their sake, or to cover her own shame. How could the truth, that Ned Armstrong never loved her, never wanted their children, be useful to them? She had invented the knowledge they had of their father. The war had provided an expedient story.

She thought she saw him twice. Once a man, stepping out of a compact, smart, horse-drawn coupé ahead of a handsome woman, had met her startled eyes. Was there a frown and a flicker of recognition? Was it only confusion on the man's part because she stared, horrified and stricken? Another time, at Penn Square during a Fourth of July celebration when the girls were quite small, a man walked by. He didn't notice her but she had known it was Ned. By then her pain had turned to rage. That he had used her, led her astray and abandoned her, was insult enough; but he had left them all in deadly peril. That she could never forgive. She had barely forgiven herself her own gullibility.

When the Montaine carriage had gone and the crowd had dispersed from the porch she had faced her daughters, and it was like facing strangers. Things she had always known about them but had never quite taken seriously faced her down. Patricia's blue eyes blazed with annoyance because her flirtation had run amok. Her lips were tight, her face like carved, pink marble. She liked controlling young men, creating daydreams about whom she would have, when, and how life would be. When Patricia wanted something, no matter how foolish or reckless her desire, a team of bulls could not drag the notion away.

And Lilly. Her cheeks were bright with excitement. She craved adventure, intrigue. Courage and curiosity flamed on her cheeks and her lips trembled with a suppressed laugh or shout. Emily had not missed the way Lilly watched Noel Padgett; fascination, marvel, delight all glowed feverishly in her eyes.

In panic Emily had lashed out at them. In a voice more biting than she had ever before used, she ordered them to their room. For the first time in years she realized her lack of power and the limits of her protection. Her skill in mothering would be challenged, for if she could not influence her daughters now, she could not imagine the direction their lives might take.

She opened their door. They sat cross-legged on their tester bed, dressed in soft flannel gowns with bedcaps on their heads. Hair had been obediently brushed out, faces were rosy from scrubbing, and they waited, their eyes wide and fearful. They expected the worst of her wrath; she had not lost them yet. Ah, she thought, what beauties.

They were so different they hardly looked like sisters. Patricia was petite and fair—frail, one might think, unless acquainted with her stubbornness. Her golden hair cascaded down her back to her waist, the *tiny* waist she begged to corset. Her sapphire eyes were always bright with ideas. She was perpetually happy, filled with plans and schemes. She was small, eager, ripe with fantasies and the wiry strength and contrariness to pursue them. When she was tiny she played princess, draping towels around her shoulders and wearing bowls or pots for crowns. "What will you be after a princess?" Emily had asked her when she was perhaps five years old. Patricia had leveled her superior gaze on her ignorant mother. "A queen, Mama," she replied, perturbed at Emily's naiveté.

Patricia was aware of her beauty and had learned to use her flirtatious smile and audacious eyes to have her way when she was a mere tot. Patricia had no use for studies; the first time a boy had turned his besotted gaze on her, she accepted the power of her porcelain looks and used that power to her advantage.

So different from her older sister in many ways, Lilly was unaware of her own handsomeness. She was darker, taller, fuller. Her hair was brown with hints of red and blond. Her eyes were not quite blue, but a blue-green that changed with her attire and her mood. She despised her freckled skin; she didn't realize it was developing into a shimmering bronze. She would soon be a remarkably beautiful woman—more so if she did not become vain like her sister. And Lilly was less giddy, not given to whimsical ideas. She was serious about learning; she was solitary. Her studies, when not frivolous subjects like deportment, filled her with excitement. She liked having friends but it did not bother her one whit to be left out, to be less than the most popular. She'd brush off cruel and teasing little girls as silly, for Lilly was brave. Too brave sometimes. When a limit had been set, she went beyond it. She was drawn to the railroad yard and station, either watching trains pass or observing people who could afford travel. She stood outside the theater and listened to what people who had seen plays said about them. She did not complain that she could not afford a ticket but would not be denied the privilege of eavesdropping or reading the bills.

Emily smiled at them and shook her head. Had she thought to keep control? She, herself, had been impossible to control. Her parents before her had been headstrong, proud.

"You needn't look so frightened. As if I beat you."

They glanced at each other furtively, nervously. Emily had never lost her temper with them before.

Emily went to sit on the edge of their bed. Would they ever know this apprehension? she wondered. The fear of telling daughters about the less tender parts of life?

"I wonder if there ever was a daughter who listened to her mother's advice," Emily said. Patricia opened her mouth as if to speak but Emily sensed that a flood of excuses would be forthcoming. "I know you do as you're told most of the time, but do you really *listen*? I didn't listen to my mother, and there were cold and hungry days when I regretted that."

Their worried eyes told her that even now they were merely bracing themselves for a lecture to precede a punishment.

"You have many gentleman callers, Patricia. Some favorites among them, I think. But I have not yet met your future husband. Not Roger, or Arthur, or Arnold."

"Mother! Albert!"

"Of course," Emily said, her lips curving. Albert had been so singularly unimpressive that she had not remembered his name. "Albert," she repeated.

"When I was your age I had suitors also, though I can't imagine that I was as careless with their feelings as you seem to be. But now, if I fail to convince you of the danger of these flirtations, of the peril you approach if you—" Emily stopped herself. Patricia's face had lost color. "I know you're a good girl, Patsy. The fact is that if your intentions are not serious and honorable, you cannot expect the behavior of these young men to be decent. Perhaps young men like Roger and Arthur seem harmless enough, but it is cruel to lead them on, to pretend to take them seriously when you do not. I know you're only enjoying yourself. You met your match in young Mr. Montaine—he is not likely to patiently allow you to entertain yourself at his expense. And you are going to meet more young men of that temperament. There will be fewer overgrown boys like Roger and Arthur who are content to amuse you while you dally with their feelings."

Patricia's mouth was open and Lilly's ears nearly stood out straight. She thought this reprimand long overdue.

"This discussion is for you as well, Lilly. You see, it is not enough to tell you to behave responsibly where men are concerned. You must begin to realize that when you have made your choice, you must not only lie beside that man every night of his life, but even if he is absent, even if he *dies*, your life will be changed forever because of that choice. You cannot undo it."

She then began to tell a story they would never have guessed. Emily Bellmont Armstrong had grown up in a mansion richer than anything her daughters had ever seen. Her father, whom she had adored, had come from a respected family. Amanda Chase Bellmont, her mother, had come from a family not only prominent but fantastically rich. Emily admired her mother, but the warm rapport she and her father had shared was precious. Richard Bellmont was a gentle and loving man, a man of staunch principles, ethical courage, and profound public conscience.

Emily, raised as the only child of these two proud and dynamic people, had been surrounded by love and servants; she was indulged every minute and grew up very happily spoiled. Her dolls were created by French artisans, not made from sticks and rags as Lilly's and Patricia's had been. She had her own carriage and did not take the horsecar to a city school, but was kept busy by tutors. She had not learned to sweep a floor or bake bread, but by the time she was ten she could converse in French. This she told her daughters, who listened, enraptured.

"At sixteen I attended polo matches, lawn parties, afternoon teas, formal dances, and had a host of beaux. I confidently decided which one of them I would sit beside or honor with a dance. At seventeen my life changed dramatically when my father died very suddenly. He was a young man who had never been ill. My mother was an energetic, beautiful woman of only thirty-seven—pampered, aristocratic, very popular in her social circle. The shock of my father's death was quickly followed by visits from solicitors who came to see my mother to explain that the Bellmont finances were in trouble. Now I realize my mother had never suspected that my father's charity exceeded his purse and that his investments had been failing for some time. He was deep in debt when he died."

Emily, young and grief-stricken, had so ignored her mother's anguish that even when she strained her memory to recall signs of it, she could remember nothing. There must have been anger as well, since the fortune Richard Bellmont lost had come from Amanda's deceased family. A long while later Emily realized that the very thing for which she admired her father—his philanthropy, his social responsibility, his generosity—had probably measured significantly in the losses. But she had not thought of those things then. There is no creature, Emily had often thought since, more selfish than a seventeen-year-old girl.

"I thought my mother's absence of jewels had to do with mourning," she said. "I didn't know which kitchen maid had been let go or which gardener was sent away unpaid. My mother told me there was trouble with the will and debts, but I ignored her. We continued to live in the same house and socialize with the same families. But my mother was quietly dispersing property and possessions to pay debts, telling no one, trying to preserve some dignity for our family name. Then, when my father had been dead about a year, she allowed gentlemen to call on her. I was mortified. I hated her for it. I had no sympathy. It never occurred to me that marriage was her single resource. I also failed to see that she might marry a man she didn't love for my sake—my comfort and survival must have been paramount in her mind. I only know this now, finally, because I am a mother."

Filled with rage, consumed by loneliness, estranged from her mother, eighteen-year-old Emily was a perfect victim. She had plenty of suitors from good families, including several young men who would have supported her quite stylishly, beaux at least as dull as Roger and Arthur. It was an older, mysterious, and very handsome man who caught her eye and conquered her heart. Ned, more worldly, reckless, and exciting than all the others, said all the right things and was relentless in his seduction.

"My mother tried to convince me to be careful—she worried that I might fall in love too easily because of grief. She was unsure of your father's ability to keep me. She didn't know his family or his background. I thought she was interfering, and I fell helplessly in love with him."

Emily had never before known her mother to be so cruel, so heartless. She called Ned a fraud, a philanderer. The more her mother protested, the more desperately Emily loved Ned. Much of that had to do with Emily's despairing need for a man's love, still more had to do with Ned's skill at philandering. This she kept to herself.

"Despite my mother's warnings, I had never wanted for anything. It never occurred to me that your father's land business might not be successful. He, likewise, called for me at a very rich gate and must have assumed there was money in my family. Tossing all practical considerations aside, we married. Very soon I found myself alone, my husband gone, my mother lost to me, and two babies to feed. We do not always choose our futures—we only make choices toward them, that's all."

There was so much more, but she couldn't bring herself to tell the girls. Ned Armstrong had chafed at Amanda's reluctance to approve their marriage and he had laid siege. Emily was soon pregnant. He had been eager to confront Amanda then; he was quite confident.

Still, Amanda held the trump card. Emily had listened at the study door while her mother and lover conferred over their predicament. There was no money, Amanda had told Ned. Nothing. They would be lucky to get out of the house without debts. Fortunately there was a buyer, not a common thing during such hard times; people were hardly shopping for mansions. He was shrewd, however; he had knowledge of Richard Bellmont's financial debacle and knew how desperate Amanda would be. This buyer had made most of his own fortune by finding out who was most vulnerable and preying on them. Did Ned want Emily, she asked him, knowing there was no dowry, no property, no stipend?

Ned had been outraged. Even overhearing him declare his disbelief and denial, even hearing him slam the door as he angrily departed without her, Emily still wanted him. He had been like a sickness inside her; he had created a hunger in her that she could not satisfy.

She had begged her mother to employ the last bit of influence she still had to bring Ned Armstrong to the altar. Amanda Bellmont might have lost her money, but she had many powerful friends in Philadelphia and reluctantly used them for her daughter's sake; Ned was made to atone through marriage. "I hope this is truly what you want, Emily. There is nothing more I can do for you unless you will come away with me," Amanda had said.

Emily and Ned had lived in a two-room flat in the city. Patricia had been born with the assistance of a neighbor. Emily could barely serve her husband an evening meal, so ignorant was she of women's chores. Though she tried desperately to please him, to win his love, Ned did not return for days at a time, getting his meals elsewhere and ignoring the needs of his family. Emily traded her well-tailored and costly gowns for simpler dresses so her neighbors would not be standoffish because she did not even appear to be one of them. Amanda visited after Patricia was born. Emily's mother had disposed of all her material possessions; she had only her wardrobe, a fistful of invitations to visit friends in Europe, and a small sum of money. She begged Emily to bring the baby and leave Philadelphia. But Emily was far from giving up on Ned; it amazed her still how long she had embraced that lie, that delusion. She would not go. Amanda offered her half of what was left of Richard Bellmont's estate, a paltry sum compared to what it had once been, but Emily was indignant. Pride bit deeper than dragon's teeth, for Emily told her mother to keep it. Emily remained silent about these painful details.

"Even though I had very little, I was so righteous," she told her girls. "I still believed that love would mend our deeply rent pockets, making the whole world right. I knew my mother was going off to find another husband. Oh! I was so unforgiving. I told her to keep what was left for her retirement. I would rely on my husband."

Maybe they should know that their father beat her soundly for sending Amanda away with her money, a sum he said would have paid the rent for two years. Maybe they should know that Patricia was conceived on a lawn, and Lilly—ah! When she had crawled to Ned, begging him to forgive her for not accepting the money, his final gesture had been to give her Lilly. A week later he took her and

41

a few belongings to a one-room shanty in the city, near the waterfront. She had gone back to their flat two weeks later, but it was vacant. He was gone. He had disposed of her quite deliberately.

"There was war. There were many women alone, like me, without money or skills. It was hard for all of us. Do you remember Old Mary who gave us shelter? Or Nelly and Beth, the women from West Chester who came to Philadelphia to work in the factory? Or odd Mr. Conner who allowed me to bring the two of you along to his house while I cleaned it? There were kind and generous neighbors along the way without whom we might not have survived. I could not find my mother; there was nowhere to turn. If telling you this will turn your head to practical matters, I will be satisfied. Had I listened to my mother's advice, I might have suffered far less. There have been reasons why I've tried to teach you to find satisfaction in hard work—you might have to work hard to survive one day. I wanted you to have more than marriage as a means of survival. When I die, you have this boardinghouse. I've tried to teach you honesty, diligence, and decency—virtues that could save you when the money is gone. Without them no amount of money will ever help you."

"Mama, why didn't you go back to your old neighborhood when Papa was gone?" Patricia asked. "Wouldn't your friends have helped you?"

She *had* gone back, to the home of Lucille Sinclair, someone Emily had considered a friend. Her eyes misted as she remembered. She had not seen Lucille in over a year, but desperate and frightened, she went. She remembered her mother's comments about the odd cousin who seemed to be present in every household—the spinster or widow, down on her luck, too close a relation to toss out, not close enough to actually be one of them. Not much more than an extra eye for the children, an additional servant, better clad than the staff, perhaps, but ranked with the governess or housekeeper in a class just lower than the family who took her in. Emily, at that time, would gladly have taken such a post. Her clothing was clean but far less natty than what could be seen on the Sinclair maids. Her face was swollen from pregnancy and her hair, once so prettily coiffured, had lost its luster and shine and was tacked into a lopsided bun. She had insect bites on her hands and neck, and she dangled a child on her hip while another swelled in her middle. Lucille didn't bother with her for long. "Don't be ridiculous," Lucille had said. "Emily

42

Bellmont has gone with her mother to Europe." Lucille turned away in disgust.

"Pride, I suppose," Emily finally answered, brushing the tear away.

"Didn't your mother ever try to help you again?" Patricia asked. Emily smiled. Patricia always had a dozen plans to back up the first.

"Your grandmother. It was wrong of me to tell you we had no family, but my mother and I couldn't find each other for years. I always meant to tell you. Your grandmother is alive and well. She writes to me now and then, but our parting was bitter and angry and it was eight years before I had the courage to go back to the house of friends and ask if they had news of my mother. May you never know the agony of facing someone's pity! They offered to take me in or give me money! And by that time I was proud of the respectable life I had achieved. I learned where my mother was and wrote to her. She was living in England then and still does. Our lessons come so late, so painfully—even though you were the center of my life, I had not considered how my mother would worry about me."

Amanda had confessed in her first letter that she had hired Pinkerton men to find Emily, but they had failed. With the war they were so ineffective that Amanda had reluctantly dismissed them. Damn those Pinkertons, Emily had frequently thought.

"Mother had done as I expected; she remarried. I wrote that I was widowed and living happily with my daughters. She wrote that she was busy and content. It was not a settlement from the government that bought this house, but money from your grandmother, money that this time I accepted because I had finally learned how hungry one can be while feasting on pride."

Emily smiled a bit wistfully. Her opinion of her mother had gentled over the years. "She is now married for the third time. I wrote and asked her why she kept marrying. I had just learned that she had been widowed and remarried in the same letter! Even though I never proved myself any smarter than my mother, I never stopped being critical. She wrote back directly," Emily said, laughing. "She wrote, 'Be easier on me, Emily. I have no experience in being poor.'"

"Is she rich now?" Patricia asked.

"She is married to a wealthy man, but if he is anything like the last, his money will one day belong to the children of an earlier marriage." She shook her head, smiling, as she noticed their astonished stares; they would not understand the difference between having money and living among the rich. People who were born into wealth knew how to trade their dignity to remain among their class, even if they had far less than their peers.

"Why doesn't she visit us?" Lilly asked.

"She is proud, Lilly. I don't think she'll return to Philadelphia until she can come back here with her head high. The Bellmonts and the Chases before them were high families, Philadelphia belonged to them."

Amanda had once lectured Emily. "Don't speak loosely of society, dear. There are four societies. There is the first, the workers with muscle, the heart of society, for their muscle and toil makes the clock tick and makes it possible for some to rise to the top. And the second, the society of the parvenu, who will somehow achieve that amount of wealth necessary to buy entrée into luxury. His ambition becomes the arms and legs of society. And the third, the person who perceives himself an aristocrat, who was born to wealth and privilege, whose education was begun four generations before his birth—he is the blood of society. He neither works nor notices work and he resents the entrance of the parvenu into his clubs because he is afraid—he knows the parvenu wants what he has and doesn't know what that is." Emily observed then that they must be of the third society, but she was immediately corrected. "We are Bellmonts," Amanda said. "We work, but we need not speak of our work because we are secure in it. For the worker we have grave respect—his labor is worthy. For the parvenu we have suspicious respect—his ambition is not always honorable, yet it is ambition alone that will lead to progress. For the aristocrat we have guarded respect—we can appreciate his heritage yet be impervious to his hauteur. The fourth society, Emily, values work, pride, dignity, and success; it is the soul and conscience of society. And the soul is unafraid." Unafraid? asked Emily later. Then why did she leave Philadelphia, impervious as she claimed to be? "Because, my dear, I had nowhere to live in Philadelphia."

"She'll come home one day," Emily said, feeling a longing for her mother such as she had not felt in years. "When she's ready. When her losses do not hurt her so much."

The girls had questions, which she answered as honestly as she could. Why did Emily not write for the money for them all to travel to England? Because it was better for Patricia and Lilly to be influenced by the security of a humble but decent home and honest labor rather than by showy grandeur that could all disappear without warning. Did she regret her hasty marriage? The hardship it brought, indeed, but the result—her home, her daughters, her friends—never. Why had she never remarried? "There was no one," she shrugged, knowing it was not even half the reason.

"May I write to her, Mama?" Lilly asked.

"I think that would be lovely, Lilly."

"Mama, may we tell no one? Not even Agnes Marlene?" Patricia asked. "I mean, it is awfully stunning and it would simply shatter her!"

My dignity was so hard won, Emily thought. And Patsy would throw it to the gossips for the sake of prestige.

"It's Mama's life to tell or not tell, not yours. Don't you dare," Lilly warned.

"Telling won't do anything but cause people who respect me as I am to be either envious or suspicious of me," Emily answered. "It might give you a moment's pleasure and cause me a great deal of discomfort. Please, do not."

"Yes, ma'am."

Emily reminded herself that they were only girls, impressed for the moment at the mere thought of what their mother had once had, had once been. Girls have visions like no other creatures. Someday, she hoped, they might recall the story for the intended lesson.

"Patricia, as to my original purpose, you must begin to behave as a woman of taste and discipline. Those young men whom you do not seriously consider must be dismissed—you can no longer collect them. It is cruel and indecent of you. No more flirting, fainting, and tromping on their feelings. I'm afraid you're going to get a bad reputation if not some real trouble—you know what is said of girls of that stamp. It is better that you don't keep company at all than to have a lot of beaux at hand and not a one you could possibly marry. Retire your swatches and fashion plates for the time being. We are in no hurry to marry you. If you behave kindly and honestly, you will find a nice young man soon enough. And he will like it best if he has not come at the end of a very long line.

"And, you may not see young Mr. Montaine again. I will not have you in his company. It is a well-known truth that many an unfortunate poor girl has borne a bastard for a rich young man;

many a rich man has settled away a housemaid whom his son has tampered with. Since you do not come from the neighborhood into which he will marry, it is pointless to ride about in his coach."

"But, *Mother!*"

"Patricia, you must believe me. Your virtue is irreplaceable and the most important asset you can take to your marriage bed."

"But, Mama, I'm sure rich young men have married women without quite so much money because . . . because they are beautiful, or charming, or—"

"Not nearly so often as you wish to believe, Patricia."

In spite of herself, Lilly's cheeks became pink. She was thinking of Andrew. Her mother had verbalized her own dilemma. He seemed a perfect gentleman, but she was not of his class, and she knew she should dismiss him before he looked at her with real notice. When she stopped seeing him in the library, she knew she would never see him again. She already sensed that he was passionate. She swallowed.

Patricia did not heed the warning with the same earnestness. "But what am I to do with myself if I'm not to keep company with any beaux? I'll rot here!"

"You might rekindle some of your friendships with young ladies of your acquaintance whom you've cast aside for beaux. You might enjoy yourself, if you try, and in time there will be a good and mature young man. Meanwhile, I insist that you stop this trickery. It is not only mean-spirited, it is dangerous. More prudent behavior, Patricia."

Emily stood up from their bed. She leaned over and kissed each forehead, Patricia's second. "It is for your own good, my dear. Please believe me."

"Yes, ma'am," she said, but her heart wasn't in it.

It was a long while after Emily left their room before Patricia and Lilly turned down their lamp. Although they both discussed their mother's story, an eavesdropper might have thought they were talking about entirely different things. Each girl reacted differently to their mother's history. Neither realized she had arrived at a crossroad; it was at this juncture that they would separate and no longer understand each other.

Lilly recalled with pleasure their trips to market to buy or their jaunts to city brownstones to sell jams or breads. She liked to think about their mother's fierce but dignified bargaining. Patricia, on the other hand, had been bored and sulky during these excursions and had often wished to be left behind. Patricia had never liked any pastime that even vaguely resembled a chore.

Now Lilly was more impressed than ever. "Imagine," she whispered, "having nothing at all, not even food, and then someone shows you how to put up jellies and you begin to *sell* them! Do you know what that's called? It's called *enterprise*. Of all the poor women with children to feed, how many of them do you suppose have enterprise? Do you remember when Mama stitched dresses long into the night? I can remember when she was still awake, sewing, when we woke up in the morning."

Patricia was not thinking about that at all. For every comment Lilly made about industry or enterprise, Patricia wondered aloud what it might be like not to have to measure out the cream in a teaspoon, but pour as much as you please into the coffee. Or to buy whatever dresses you like, not make your own, limited to two good ones each year. Or to call your driver to bring 'round the landau, rather than asking your mother for horsecar fare. Imagine, Emily having been *that* rich. Patricia would die to be so rich!

"I'm going to be rich, that's what. Won't it be grand?"

"Just how?" Lilly asked. She was contemplating being rich as well, but she was wondering how many boardinghouses one must own, how many jars of jam must be put up, how many hems stitched.

"Mama is right. I have to stop just amusing myself and take the matter of marriage more seriously."

Lilly's brows drew together in a frown. She had not thought Patricia less than serious before.

"I've been giving far too much time to all the wrong young men. Roger has a cousin who is actually a lawyer. He's older than Roger, of course, but not yet married."

"Patricia, Mama told you to retire your swatches and—"

"Oh pish, you know what she meant. And she's right, too. I have to see myself as a marriageable woman, not a young girl collecting beaux. If I'm going to collect beaux, I may as well collect richer ones."

Lilly sat straight up in the bed. "Patsy, you know what Mama

47

said about rich young men like Dale Montaine. Don't you believe her? Do you think she was just *saying* that?"

"No, silly, I'm sure it is entirely true; that girls of lesser means are often taken advantage of by richer men. I certainly won't let something like that happen."

"But Patricia, if you keep playing mean tricks on young men, one might decide to get even."

"It's just that I think I ought to look a bit further, unless I want to measure out the cream and make do on only two good dresses a year for the rest of my life," she replied, unconcerned.

"Patricia, you're so dis*honest!*"

"No, I'm not. And so what? Men don't want honest women. All they really want . . ." And she listed all the same tricks and traps, tried and true, studied and perfected, only to be repeated on men of means. What was the difference, after all, between a rich husband and a poor one, but money?

As Lilly listened to her sister, she felt a knot grow and tighten in her stomach. She had previously found Patricia's quest for marriage tiresome and silly, but it was growing into a fearful obsession, a goal for which Patricia seemed willing to make dangerous sacrifices in her character. Patricia was becoming worse than dishonest, Lilly feared. She was becoming immoral.

"Patsy," Lilly said softly, "sometimes I wish I didn't even know you."

"Hah! You say that now, but wait till you're an old spinster, and I live in a big fancy house. Then you'll be glad enough to know me; you'll want to come to my parties and meet all my friends."

"I'd rather get a tooth pulled," Lilly said in disgust, slumping down into the bed and pulling the quilt up to her chin.

"That's what you say now."

Noel Padgett lay on his back, knees bent, on the bed that was far too short to accommodate his long frame. He could still hear a few sleepy murmurs from the room beneath his. Mrs. Armstrong would be embarrassed to know how thin these walls were; plaster didn't cover them all and there was no rug on the floor. Her voice had wafted upwards while she told her daughters her story. He sensed it was half a story.

There had been something nagging him all evening and now he understood exactly what it was. Here was a handsome woman who seemed to deliberately quiet her own good looks. She pulled her fair hair back into a conservative bun and wore dour gray dresses, buttoned high and topped with a white starched collar. Her attire and her behavior weren't out of place in this neighborhood of simple, hard-working folks. But he had sensed a provocative quality in her from the moment he looked at her, from the moment she spoke.

Noel had lived both rich and poor, both in the city and in the open western plains. He had been around all manner of people from country school masters to city women with lives so carefully drawn they could be framed. He knew bankers, politicians, cavalry officers and their wives and daughters; homesteaders, rangers, ranchers, miners, horse thieves, scouts, trappers, and Indians. He was forty years old and had never married because he had lived in worlds so different his tastes had become confused. He liked the soft, pretty city women whose hands bore no callouses; he liked their fresh clean smell and elegance. He had met a goodly number, both in Philadelphia where he was born and spent his youth, and out West when city women traveled with their husbands or fathers. He also admired women with the strength and courage to forge west, to homestead. But most of those women, if they made it, turned into tough old boots at a pretty young age. Only Indian women were both soft and tough, gentle and brave. And they had enough brothers who could wear the paint of war to start a whole uprising.

Emily Armstrong's own daughters did not understand why she had made it out of poverty when so many poor women could not. Plenty of people could put up jellies, sew hems. To turn such modest domestic skills into a living took gumption and sophistication, tenacity and intelligence, strength and determination, stature and decorum. It was always the confident man in a decent suit of clothes who seemed as though he didn't need the work who would get the job, not the poor jobless man in filthy clothes, hunched in a defeated posture. Emily approached people with that proud tilt to her chin, that painfully proper manner, her impeccable but not ostentatious diction.

Why had she not remarried? She had said there was no one, but

Noel had trouble believing that so handsome and clever a woman would be ignored. It must be more that she liked her independence, which made her all the more desirable. For the first time, he was not anxious to get out of the city.

There was iron under the velvet of her skin. Her voice, light and controlled, issued command. Her manners were not stiff, but natural and unstrained. She had a dignity that placed her high above those around her. And she was decent, good in her heart—good enough to share with hungry, jobless beggars even though there was no real bounty in her cupboards. Many women were polite without being good deep down. She was proud. If she ever got the notion he was taken with her, she would really get her bustle in a knot. She would have him down the road in short order. Despite her size, she was forceful. He would have to be careful.

He rolled over, tucking his long legs under the covers, bending them uncomfortably. Damned bed was built for a twelve-year-old. He was tired of thinking; it had been a long time since he had troubled himself over the character of a woman. He closed his eyes and wished for a whiskey. He was conscious of the easy warmth of desire. He hoped the feeling would stay easy with him.

John Giddings packed his pipe and struck a match against his shoe. It was nearly ten. Rare for him to be awake unless he was writing, and never, in his recollection, had he taken a second pipe in the evening. The Armstrong house was finally dark, but he would not be able to sleep yet. Perhaps it would be a restless night filled with disturbing dreams.

He was twenty-eight. His parents had been dead for five years. For five years these people had been his family. Yet they knew nothing of his other personas or his private ambitions.

He had watched her grow up and had dreamt of the day she would arrive at the door of womanhood and he would speak his mind. But as each month, each year passed, it became more and more obvious that he would never give voice to his visions. His pen could reveal his passions, but the words were difficult and bulky in his mouth.

It had all been so clear! Patricia would be the perfect woman to share the sense of adventure that lay dormant beneath his rumpled and timid appearance.

John had been reading voraciously and writing since he was a small boy. His eyes had gone bad from burning late night oil before he was twelve. John Giddings wrote a few stories and announcements for the *Philadelphia Inquirer;* his specialty was capturing the essence of the character of ordinary working people, their triumphs and their troubles. Under the name Thorn E. Briar, his identity secret, he wrote daring pieces that stirred political plots, upset rings of thieves, exposed graft. He had done several pieces for Horace Greeley about Boss Tweed. And now he was trying to merge the two writers—the gentle, observant pen of Giddings and the fearless, scorching pen of Briar—into a third.

He had written hundreds of pages already for a novel about the world in which he lived. He had re-created an aristocratic family, a sinister jobber of ruthless ambition, a crooked politician, fallen women and virtuous ones, orphans, thieves, and immigrants. It was his world, Philadelphia during the Centennial, filled with greed, heartless ambition, criminal bosses buying votes, while brimming with hopes, desires, possibilities. The city had its princes of industry, resented and feared by the fine old families, its immigrants with dreams of freedom and success, its simple, decent folks who believed in their work and their votes. Things were happening in America that had never happened before, that might never happen again; it was a time when a man like Wilson Montaine, an orphan who had pushed a knife-sharpening cart through Philadelphia at the age of seven, could become the richest man in the city. Known as the Philadelphia Landlord, he had stepped on many a fine old pocketbook to achieve his goals.

At the center of John Giddings' novel was the beautiful, naive, dreamy character of Chloe Tillets. She could not help the fact that her extraordinary beauty, inherent goodness, and charm caused men to want her, her family to resent her and use her, and women to hate her. She was victimized for all the reasons she should be cherished. She was a buxom, petite blond. She looked like Patricia, had the virtues of Emily, the intelligence of Lilly. She was in love with a man her family would selfishly deny her, a writer of modest income. A clever reader might find this character a composite of the women in the Armstrong household, but in John's mind this was Patricia . . . the guileless victim of her own remarkable pulchritude.

John had saved most of his money and hoped to own a press that would print fearlessly and would not be controlled by crooks or city fathers. He longed to share his life with a beautiful woman who believed in him. He had been so alone, living inside his stories. He knew that when people looked at him, they had no idea he was really a man of courage and passion. His clothes were clean but ill-fitting and rumpled, even after being pressed. His hair, already thinning, always appeared wispy and untrimmed, even after a haircut. He had never managed a mustache and he was small-boned and thin, although his ideas were muscled and hulking. No one ever imagined that his was a tempestuous nature, for he appeared timid and reserved. Yet the stories written by Thorn E. Briar seethed; they were intense, poignant, and relevant.

Passion of another sort caused him to toss against his mattress, imagining he made love to the woman he did not have the courage to embrace. To look at her beauty left him feeling drunk. He knew he was allowed a room in Mrs. Armstrong's house because he appeared harmless; he would be evicted if the depth of his longing was discovered. The young men who called on Patricia were all the sort he had always envied: they were handsome, amusing, and clever. Not intelligent, but what did a woman want with intelligence if she could be entertained?

John could put words on paper that would take her breath away. He would have her know him as he knew himself—those parts not yet revealed. But he feared Patricia would marry one of those idiots, one of the muscular proudies who came to call. In aiming for luxury, he feared, she might never know luxury at all, but would find herself wed, mounted, and ridden as some brainless dolt freed himself of his urge.

John wanted to love her, to make her body sing, to show her satisfaction that was complete, that was not his alone, but theirs, together, as one. He would make her the center of his world, feed her mind as he pampered her body, answer her emotional longings as well as her sexual cravings. If she invited him, he could say all the words that thus far he had only written, explore all the things that he had only imagined. And she would know the same joy that exhausted his nights when he thought of her. Her pleasure would be his pleasure, whether sought in quiet intellectual musings or in the most exotic of sexual passions. And he would not cease in his quest to completely satisfy her every desire until she begged him for rest.

But Patricia had not noticed him yet. Nor was she likely to, he reminded himself.

It was nearly midnight when Dale Montaine entered the foyer of his home. He had been to his club, had had drinks with the men, and then they'd gone to find some whores. Despite his effort to change his mood by drinking and watching the fellows sporting with the whores, he still seethed with anger. He poured himself a drink of gin in his father's study.

There was a tap at the study door and he hid the glass behind a pile of papers on the desk. The housekeeper stood there. "Is there anything you need, Mr. Montaine?"

"Nothing," he said, waving her away.

"Miss Dorthea Lancaster sent an invitation for tomorrow afternoon. I left it on your bureau."

"Thank you," he said, turning away, waiting to hear the door close so he could finish the drink. He poured another; when his father was not in the house, this study was his favorite place. The gin was in good supply and the room was broodingly dark, like his mood. He poured a third glass of gin. He relied heavily on the stuff; it blotted out much of his anger and worry.

He did not have many severe headaches when the gin was plentiful. As a youngster he had suffered wrenching headaches that had caused him to faint and vomit. There was once a housekeeper who would sit for hours and gently rub his temples and neck. She had been gone for years. He thought he remembered that she died. Another housekeeper had lashed his hands together when he was put to bed so he wouldn't be able to touch himself. She was gone, but not forgotten. A third housekeeper quit when she discovered him spying on her bath; he hated to see her go. He was relieved to be a man and no longer at the mercy of housekeepers.

Dale hated all women. It was one of only two passions he had in life. He hated the mother who had died when he was a baby, his first stepmother, whom his father had divorced ten years ago, his present stepmother, whom his father had married five years ago, various servants whom he had victimized or who had made him the victim. And Dorthea, to whom he would propose marriage within the year. He did not ponder his misogynous character, nor see this as an aberration, nor wonder if other men felt likewise. But this hatred showed itself in many ways. Sometimes it appeared in the blinding headaches and sleeplessness. Quite often a problem with a woman made him crave gin. In his treatment of women, he was perverse. He would not buy prostitutes, though he frequently went along with the boys when they were whoring. He despised the trade. He watched the other fellows at work, then did not pay. He sported young virgins, seducing them with vague promises until they nearly begged for it, then he would cast them off, not in a few days or weeks, but at the moment of his conquest. He wanted to claim not only a maidenhead, but the dignity of each one. And he had slept with Deanna, his present stepmother, but only a few times and only to degrade her. He seduced her, pleaded with her, crept to her, then called her a slut. Now, even though she was not a woman of high moral tone, she could barely look at him and had taken to tippling late into the night.

Dale planned to propose marriage to Dorthea Lancaster on her nineteenth birthday. Her family was prominent; they established and maintained the social standard for good form in Philadelphia. The Montaine name had never achieved any social distinction, despite their millions. It was a well known fact that Wilson was a parvenu, a jobber made good, and not a man of scholarship and heritage. This was Dale's second passion, to change the way *Montaine* was uttered in this city. He had been working hard at changing the image, though he worked against unbelievable odds. By getting himself an aristocratic wife, he would gain respect. He had finally compromised his goal; his father was sixty, and if the elite in society continued to tolerate Wilson so long as they accepted Dale, that would do. The old man could not live forever, and the Lancaster family would welcome him. He knew they liked the smell of his money; he considered it a worthwhile investment.

Wilson Montaine, an orphan proud to have made it out of an impoverished youth rather than ashamed of his lack of heritage, was an ostentatious bore in his son's eyes. He had no style or education, though he did have a knack for making money. He kept no records, belonged to no club, and had been married three times, once actually divorcing a woman. Divorce was completely unacceptable in polite society; Wilson would be banned forever. He was an atrocity, and he did not care. He was bright enough to make millions on property, but he refused to study the discriminating manners of his peers and attempt to cautiously enter their charmed circle. Instead, he spit in their eye. He was belligerent and careless and knew that people laughed at him.

Dale had found no advantage in being a rich parvenu's only son. He had been abused by the city boys who didn't have money, and when he was sent to Harvard, he had been snubbed by the rich boys who had as much as he. He had eaten plenty of dirt because he was the son of that clod, Montaine. He was alone, bereft of friends. But he meant to change all this, and so he went to their polo matches, their lawn parties, the Sunday evenings. He courted young women from prestigious families, thus finding Dorthea. Finally, after a very long struggle, he had overheard it said, "The old man may be a buffoon, but Dale's a decent enough fellow." He was their comrade now. Dale collected their secrets greedily, hoarding them for future use. He wanted only to be among them, held in high esteem, and when he was certain his position was secure, he would begin slowly, ruthlessly, to single them out for dismissal. Someday they would all feel as he had.

Patricia Armstrong had put him off and goaded him into a temper. His surprise had caught him off guard. He had *never* been treated so by a mere working-class girl; they usually groveled just for a ride in his carriage and wouldn't risk making him angry enough for him to withdraw his attention. This was precisely why he frequented neighborhoods like Patricia's. The girls were not desperately poor and dirty, nor were they shallow, haughty, and privileged like Dorthea. These were clean girls from strict homes, and they were pure—what else could they take to their husbands? And, they would do anything for a chance to be loved by a rich man. The worst that had ever befallen him was a payment of one hundred dollars to an angry father. He had hardly noticed the withdrawal from his purse.

But this one, Patricia Armstrong, confused him. She seemed impressed by his style and wealth, yet she risked losing him by playing coy. She thought highly of herself, apparently. And he knew she was just like the rest, another lying, using female.

When his better judgment warned him to forget Patricia Armstrong, he ignored it. He would find a way to teach her a lesson. Patricia was looking for a husband; she would learn the price of stalking such big game. Then he would see how highly she thought of herself. The notion of his vengeance caused him to smile. He had several more glasses of gin while he brooded on the girl and finally, full of liquor and plans, he fell asleep on the leather sofa in his father's study.

Above his head was a portrait that had once been a curiosity to Dale. A beautiful woman, her hair rich auburn, her eyes bright blue, her skin like creamed gold, had been the previous mistress of this mansion. Wilson Montaine said he had kept the painting to remind him of what happens to those who don't watch their money carefully, for when the woman was widowed, she found that her husband had mishandled all her money and everything was lost. Wilson Montaine had been able to purchase the house and most of its furnishings because she had been desperate to sell. But the staff nurtured a rumor that he had actually proposed marriage.

The intelligent eyes of Amanda Chase Bellmont stared straight ahead, as they had for twenty years, above the young man who had fallen into drunken slumber while contemplating the rape of her granddaughter.

illy, Lilly, wait till you *hear*," Patricia whispered in her conspirator's voice. "But you must swear you won't tell anyone. Especially Mama."

Lilly had been writing. She had been given a journal on her seventeenth birthday, less than a month ago, and she had thought it a useless gift. She wouldn't write about Andrew, and there was nothing else about her life she had found the least bit interesting. Was she meant to record John Giddings' most recent obituary? Perhaps Mrs. Fairchild's latest complaint?

Patricia had been writing in her own journal for two years. With all her various suitors, daydreams, romantic foibles and conquests, Patricia had provided Lilly with some blushing reading. Of course they had promised *never* to read each other's writings. Lilly had broken that promise quite soon after it was sworn. Lilly knew almost as much about Patricia's schemes and flirtations as Patricia did herself, but would never let on. Patricia might stop writing it down. Lilly read every word, some pages so often she feared she might wear them thin. Patricia had written of the daring liberties she had allowed Dale Montaine, and his passionate response. After Lilly had read that, she was warm for a whole day. That was a marvelous page.

Then Mr. Padgett arrived and threw Dale Montaine into the bush. Their mother had revealed a fascinating past and provided a notorious grandmother who lived in England and married rather indiscriminately, Patricia had launched a campaign to discover a rich man to marry, and Lilly's journal pages ached for new entries every day. Life had finally become interesting enough to write down, although Lilly was very careful—she assumed Patricia would peek.

"Do you promise?" Patricia asked.

"You know I never tell your secrets," Lilly returned, and in fact, she never had. "But Mama is going to discover exactly what you're doing, and you're going to get your ears trimmed."

"But I've taken her advice!" Patricia cried indignantly.

Lilly frowned, but said nothing. This was hardly Emily's advice, even if it was arguable that Patricia was becoming more serious in regard to marriage.

"Oh never mind, just promise," Patricia said.

"I did, didn't I?"

"Well," Patricia said in a hot little whisper, flouncing on the bedspread and nearly causing the ink bottle to tip. Lilly grabbed it, saved the quilt, and glared at her sister while she corked the bottle. Patricia didn't notice she had nearly caused an accident. Lilly had found Patricia's beaux, fabric swatches, and plans annoying, but her quest to marry well was unbearable. New schemes unfolded almost hourly.

"Remember," Patricia continued, "how I managed to meet Roger's cousin, the lawyer, and found that his younger sister who is nearly my age was in desperate need of a friend? She's just barely older, actually, and well, Mary Ellen Jasper has taken me under her wing. Truly! She is concerned with helping me to keep the right company. She is nearly betrothed to Thomas Markland of *the* Markland family. Surely you've heard of the Marklands? Well, Thomas has a very good friend by the name of Wilbert Kennesdow. Well,

Wilbert isn't much, really, a nice young man but, well, not terribly handsome, although he's quite tall. But his father is just *very* important, just *very*. Mr. Kennesdow is actually related to the mayor and was an alderman or some such. And Thomas thinks that Wilbert might be interested in keeping company with someone like *me!*"

Lilly moaned and rolled over on her back, her skirt up and her pantaloons flaring. She looked blankly at the ceiling. The names changed too rapidly for her to keep up . . . and worse, too quickly for Patricia to write them all down.

"Well," Patricia went on, completely nonplussed by Lilly's apparent lack of interest, "of course I complained to Mary Ellen, 'Oh dear me, how in the world could a man of such stature be interested in me when I come from such a humble home and have so little?' And Mary Ellen not only comforted me, saying that I came from quite a good family, if a little impoverished at the moment, but offered to help me with appearances. She has just piles of pretty dresses, some of them almost new and she doesn't even want them anymore. She has offered to share some of her *formal* attire, one dress in particular that could be worn to a ball or evening of opera! Oh, Lilly, can you believe it?"

Lilly's eyes narrowed. "You've told," she accused. "Don't even bother to deny it, I know you've told. You've been tossing out the Bellmont name!"

"I *haven't!* Not actually. Well . . ."

Lilly no longer reclined. "You *have!*" She was up on her hands and knees on the bed, her back arched like a cat's, her face pressed close to Patricia's. "How could you? You *promised*."

"I didn't promise. And I haven't actually said anything, I've only told Mary Ellen—who just happens to be my very best friend—a little bit about Mama. And so what? I won't ever say another word!"

"I would tell on you," Lilly said gravely. "I would tell on you for the very first time in my *life,* but I'm afraid it would hurt Mama terribly to know how you've betrayed her."

"Good gracious, Lilly! Mama's concern is with our friends and neighbors—Mary Ellen won't cause Mama any discomfort. Such a fuss. But never mind that. What do you think of me having a ball gown and keeping company with someone like Wilbert?"

"I hope Mama throws up your skirts and takes a switch to your fancy little ass!"

"*Lilly!* If Mama heard your language, guess who would get a switch! Now stop being nasty and tell me what you think of my news."

"What I've always thought of all of this," Lilly said, easing down on the bed again. "It all seems like a lot of foolishness to me. Are you going to marry him now?"

"Heavens! I've barely met him! I only mean to keep company with him—if he likes me, that is." She wrinkled her nose slightly. "He's not very handsome at all, and Mary Ellen says he's just terribly shy. But he is quite tall." She began to laugh happily, her teeth shining like drenched pearls. "And to think I once considered Roger, who wishes to drive the city horsecars! Mama was right—I must take this more seriously."

"Patsy, you are *not* doing what Mama suggested at all. Aren't you afraid people might get angry with the way you're simply using them to make more introductions?"

"But I'm not! I happen to like them. Especially Mary Ellen. I never thought I'd have such a dear friend."

"In just a week or two? You wanted to meet her brother!"

"We simply weren't well suited," she replied evenly, but her journal had told how the lawyer had ignored her since she'd been with Roger. The lawyer, apparently, had more integrity than Patricia. "But it wasn't a complete disappointment, you see, because Mary Ellen and I liked each other instantly."

"Patricia," Lilly began, her tone suspicious. She rolled onto her side to face her sister, propping her head on her hand. "Do you mean to say that you liked Mary Ellen Jasper *instantly?*"

Lilly had read about that, too. Patricia had found nineteen-year-old Mary Ellen spoilt, bossy, homely, and unsophisticated for a rich girl with servants. But she was also very lonely, and Patricia had simply behaved with humility and awe, and Mary Ellen swiftly saw Patricia as someone to advise, instruct, and promote. Mary Ellen had a faithful subject and Patricia had her entrée. Patricia had written that she hoped she came into the acquaintance of some people easier to abide than Mary Ellen—and *soon.*

"Very well," Patricia relented, "not instantly. I suppose she can't help it if she's spoiled and accustomed to having her own way. But now that we're better acquainted, I'm simply amazed by her generosity—it's awfully kind of her to bother with me. I'm certainly not like her other friends."

Lilly wondered if underneath Patricia's amazing ambition there was any decency at all.

"She does become a little irritable now and then," Patricia added indulgently. She went to stand before the small oak-framed mirror that Susan Pendergast had left behind. This had become Patricia's favorite place. "I suppose we all have our quirks, hmmm?"

"Do you think you're fooling Mama?"

"Lilly, Mama's so very strict and she doesn't approve of *any-*thing. I'm eighteen and a half, after all, and still not allowed to do anything stylish or choose my own friends or go as I please—not *any*thing. And there are some things I intend to do even if Mama doesn't approve. There's a party planned at the home of the mayor or someone, to celebrate the opening of the Centennial Exhibition. The Jaspers and Kennesdows are to be included. Dozens of rich and famous and influential people will be there. There'll be dancing and everything. I mean to go if Wilbert asks me and I daren't ask Mama. If she said I couldn't go, I would die. That would be just too unfair of her."

"You'll die if you *don't* ask her," Lilly pointed out.

"I'm going to ask Mama if we can invite Mary Ellen to tea so that Mama can meet her. Then Mama will be much more agreeable about our friendship."

"Patricia, we don't *have* tea!"

"Oh, silly, Mama will know what to do. These are all the sorts of things Mama understands. Imagine, if she had not told us all about her life before she married Papa, we'd never have known who we actually *are*. We're actually quite rich. We just haven't any money at the moment."

They called him Papa, this man neither of them could remember. It had only recently piqued Lilly's curiosity, the way their mother seemed guarded about him. She answered questions, but did not volunteer much. She had said he was quite handsome, but there was no photograph or painting. Agnes Marlene's father had also died in the war and her mother had kept his Union coat, complete with the sooty hole from the lead ball that had dealt him death. Emily had not one article of clothing, no letters, and she never provided intimate details about him.

Patricia swept up her shining locks to make a crown of curling gold on top of her head. She wanted to cut her hair into one of the modern styles, short ringlets framing the face, set off by a headband,

61

but their mother wouldn't allow it. Emily said the style was suggestive.

"Mama told us about her family so you'd learn an important lesson. She wouldn't have you repeat her mistakes."

Patricia stopped preening to meet Lilly's eyes in the mirror's reflection. There was a look of serene and detached power on her face. The chill in her cool blue eyes sent a shiver through Lilly. "And I shan't," Patricia replied. Then she broke the gaze and went on twisting and turning before the mirror.

"She asked you not to tell," Lilly softly reminded her.

Patricia ignored Lilly. She let her hair drop and unbuttoned the top buttons of her blouse, pulling it down so that the lace edging her camisole showed. Patricia wanted a corset, but Emily wouldn't allow her to be bound so young. She had just lately achieved a coveted bustle. She examined her cleavage. Then she swept up her hair again.

"Mary Ellen's favorite dress, which she has offered to let me wear, is lavender. It's scandalously low cut so that one must wear a sheer tulle about the shoulders. There are layers and layers of puffs and flowers and lace, and a tight corset and larger bustle are required. Do you think lavender a good color for me? I'm so fair as it is and—"

"Have you considered blood red?" Lilly asked sarcastically.

Patricia let her hair fall and turned slowly toward Lilly, her hands on her hips. "Is there any particular reason you're being so hateful?"

"At least you've stopped demanding that I practice fainting," she replied.

"Because you're perfectly hopeless. Be an old spinster then."

"I'm sure I will be, and it's just as well since I'm not willing to go through all that you are to get married."

"Just when I thought my own sister would be thrilled for me—just when there are so many exciting things happening, you're being perfectly hateful."

"Mary Ellen needs your company more than I do. You could move in with her and have full choice of her second-hand gowns."

"You're jealous," Patricia said, slowly advancing on Lilly. "Oh, my dear Lilly, you're jealous of all the time I'm spending with Mary Ellen!"

Lilly shook her head and rolled her eyes. There were times it was impossible to believe how desirable Patricia found herself.

"You're looking for trouble, Patricia. You don't even *know* these people."

"But Lilly, they're all the very *best* people. And don't you ever worry that I'll forget you. Why, I couldn't. You're my sister and will be my best friend forever!" Patricia leaned over and kissed Lilly's forehead. "Don't worry, Lilly, I'll always love you best. I'll even help you one day." She smiled sweetly. "I have to ask Mama if we can have Mary Ellen to tea," she remembered brightly, and out the door she fluttered.

Lilly had a momentary wish that Patricia would forget to fasten up her blouse buttons before facing their mother. It was not a vengeful wish, just a rational desire for their mother to discover Patricia and take action. No one knew Patricia the way Lilly did. Patricia had always been bright, happy, loving, and filled with fantastic plans. She could also be single-minded and selfish when there was something she passionately wanted. Lately her virtues were disappearing. She was more deceptive than ever and daily put her plans and wants above any consideration for others. Patricia was no longer charming, unless she could get something by it.

Lilly had a niggling feeling that Patricia was in danger, that her schemes had outgrown her ability to carry them off. According to the journal, Patricia had discovered men to be the most predictable creatures alive. They were outlandishly physical, partial to frantic kissing sessions. For a caress or nuzzle they'd trade *anything*. Fascinated with bosoms, they became panting, breathless beasts for a touch. Patricia found their wet mouths and roving hands disgusting, but she had developed a talent for pretending to be as desirous of all this fondling as they. She had allowed Dale Montaine a bold caress, but *not* under her camisole, which had driven him into a temper that she took as a warning to be careful of him. But he, of all her beaux, had been the most desperate.

Lilly was worried, but not inclined to confide in her mother. Patricia had always been a schemer when it came to these courting games. She had always been deceptive with the young men, if not a downright liar. But she had never before lied to their mother. Still, looking for a rich husband was certainly more logical than looking for just any husband. Somehow, teasing and flirting with the likes of Roger and Arthur did not seem as dangerous as all these little tricks being played on "all the very best people," whoever they were.

63

Lilly faced her journal again. She had written a very long letter to her grandmother, brimming with news and filled with questions. She longed for a reply and could barely stand the wait. In her journal and in her letter to her grandmother she had speculated over how long it would take, how many hems stitched and jams put up before a second boardinghouse could be mortgaged. A boardinghouse for women who were not yet married, perhaps. Or women who had no interest in marriage. Young women, not old widows like Mrs. Fairchild who complained incessantly and were only fading away amidst strangers because their families could not tolerate them.

If women with skills shared bedrooms and chores, such a house could virtually run itself. Another might be started for young couples who did not yet have children. She had read about the Swedenborgian cooperative community where a group of women with children lived together and shared responsibilities, each contributing her best skill to the good of the group. Lilly thought this was a sensible idea and not unlike their own boardinghouse, especially since Annie MacIntosh had begun to help with household chores. There was only one element missing, a thing that Lilly would not consider sacrificing: profit.

The worktable in the kitchen was covered with cinnamon buns. The aroma filled the house and wafted down the street. Mrs. Armstrong was baking, a pleasurable event for her neighbors and tenants. The crisp redolence of cinnamon had become frequent since Emily had gotten a lot of it in a good barter. Her sleeves were rolled up to her elbows, and Sophia had a streak of flour along her brown chin. Annie's growing middle was pressed against the table as she kneaded dough and hummed an Irish tune. "We'll keep that last batch, Annie—my orders are filled. I can't subject John to the aroma all Saturday and not give him some with his dinner."

"Mama," Patricia said, entering the kitchen tentatively. She didn't want to be called upon to help. "Mama, I'd like to ask you something."

"Ah, I was just going to find you and Lilly. You can deliver these buns for me and collect for them. They should be warm when you go. Mrs. Wilder will be trading butter and eggs, so go to her last."

"Mama, I've just come from Mary Ellen's house."

"I don't usually bake on Sundays, but with all those eggs I might do some cakes. Patsy, you can ask the people who take buns if they'd like an apple bottom cake—that will make good use of all our apple preserves. And with the price on cinnamon . . ."

"Mama, I'd like to ask you something."

"Yes, Patsy, what is it?"

"You've heard me mention Mary Ellen Jasper, Mama? Roger's cousin? We've become such good friends; I've been to her house every day this week."

Emily smiled approvingly. She was pleased that Patricia was spending more time with young ladies.

"She's been so nice and generous with me, Mama. Could we invite her to tea? She might meet you then."

"Tea?" Emily looked up from the mixing bowl.

"Well, Mrs. Jasper serves tea every afternoon, and I just thought we could too. I mean, you know all about that sort of thing, don't you?"

Sophia made a sound that was not quite a word but carried a distinct tone of disapproval.

"What sort of thing, Patricia?" Emily asked, an edge of suspicion in her voice.

"It might make Mary Ellen feel more at home."

"The idea is not to make her feel at home, Patricia, but to make her feel like a guest. This is *our* home. Would you like to invite her to dinner?"

"No, ma'am, I'd rather not. I mean, there are so many for dinner every evening, and I'd like you to know Mary Ellen without having Mrs. Fairchild . . . well, you understand."

Emily looked into her daughter's eyes for a long moment, her features tense. "Would you have me put on airs?"

"Oh, Mama," Patricia whined, "I'd never *had* tea in the afternoon before. It's fun. And elegant. We *drink* tea sometimes. Why can't we *have* tea?"

Emily's expression relaxed. Patricia was only a girl, she reminded herself. "I suppose we could. Next week?"

"Sooner, Mama? Mary Ellen has had me to her house so many times."

Emily thought for a moment, thought of all her work and all the people who expected her good services. "Tuesday?"

"Tuesday! That would be perfect, Mama."

"And will you be inviting Mrs. Jasper to come with her daughter?"

"I hadn't thought so."

"Well, it might be nice for her to get out of the house and meet the family of her daughter's newest friend."

"Yes, ma'am, I could invite her, but she doesn't need to get out of the house; she has her clubs almost every day."

Patricia had been watching the table, six hands working on the buns. Mrs. Jasper's housekeeper frequently bought items and services for the Jasper household from women just like Emily. They came to the door with baskets on their arms. She had a sudden, desperate hope that her mother wouldn't try to sell Mrs. Jasper something.

Emily's hands stilled. "Her clubs?" Only women whose husbands were well to do could afford to occupy themselves with clubs. Emily had recently joined her first organization other than the church. Temperance. Even one monthly meeting had proved a difficult schedule.

"Will you have everything for Tuesday, Mama? Four o'clock?"

"Four? But Patricia, we serve dinner at half past six. That's a little late in the day for working people."

"But Mary Ellen isn't a working person, Mama. She's just my friend. With Lilly and Sophia seeing about dinner, we could—"

"I'd be pleased to help with the meal on Tuesday, Mrs. Armstrong, if it will help Patsy with her party," Annie said. Patricia smiled at Annie, but it was a guarded smile. All this business of chores and duties seemed so ordinary. One day, she silently promised herself, she was going to demand that her kitchen girls get it all done on time.

"Very well, then, if Annie can help in the kitchen. But Patricia, I can't spare more than an hour for this." She locked on her daughter's eyes for a moment. "Don't be pretending we're something we're not."

"No, ma'am," Patricia said, but she was smiling very happily, not the least concerned with her mother's wishes.

Emily's eyes were drawn away from Patricia then. Noel Padgett stepped into the kitchen, lifting his nostrils into the air as he appreciated the aroma of warm bread and cinnamon. Patricia backed away. She was hoping to disappear before her mother remembered about delivering the rolls—later she would pretend to have forgotten. As she slipped out of the kitchen, she noticed that her mother's smile for Mr. Padgett was a sort she had never seen before. It was lively and girlish and did not look quite right on Emily's lips.

"Mmm-mmm, I was hoping all those good smells were coming from this house."

Sophia laughed at him. "That ain't no way to ask, Mistah Padgett. Not if you want to taste as I 'spect you do."

"Well, I'd be obliged," he said, grinning broadly.

"Sit right down here, Mr. Padgett, and let me see if there's any coffee to go with that roll. Have you had any dinner yet today?" Emily asked him.

She wiped her hands on her apron and pushed back a strand of hair that had escaped her bun. She opened the hutch cupboard and looked over the cups, selecting the largest and best mug. Sophia lifted one eyebrow and let her teeth show in a hint of a smile.

"I'm a little dusty from the road," Noel apologized as he claimed the stool near the worktable.

"Don't worry, Mr. Padgett, you could hardly avoid that. Would you like some jam?"

"Just the roll would be welcome, ma'am. Mrs. Armstrong, I haven't been to services in a mighty long time and I wondered if you and your daughters attend church on Sundays?"

She looked into his eyes as she handed him the coffee. She knew he didn't like it weighted down with cream. He had just come from a shave and a haircut; there were little snips of hair on his shoulders that she felt an urge to brush away. In fact, she wished to run her fingertips slowly through the shiny red-gold hair over his ears. His mustache had been trimmed and waxed. How atrocious that mustache had seemed when she first saw it. In her mind it was becoming more noble.

"We attend the Presbyterian church, Mr. Padgett. Services begin at nine o'clock in the morning."

"Is it near? Will I need to hire a coach?"

Emily found she had to hold her hands together at her waist so she wouldn't reach out and brush that hair away. "We walk, Mr. Padgett, and you're welcome to join us if you like. We start out at half past eight."

"That sounds just fine, Mrs. Armstrong. I believe that's exactly what I'd like to do."

"I didn't know you were a Christian man, Mr. Padgett."

He smiled just slightly as he gave his head a tilt that was not exactly an affirmative nod. "My mother was Presbyterian, and my father, well, I suppose he wasn't much of anything, especially since my mother died. I was pretty young then, but I guess her lessons must have been powerful ones because I still want services now and then."

"Your mother must have had a firm hand with you. Is there a suit you'd like me to press for you?"

"Yes, ma'am, since you ask. I'd be pleased to pay—"

"Nonsense. It's the least I can do. It does my heart good to hear a man asking for church services. Have you just come from the barber, Mr. Padgett?"

"Yes, ma'am, I have. Did he do a poor job?"

"No, no, he did a very handsome job, but he neglected to brush off your coat. Come out on the back step and let me. Otherwise those little snips of hair will drop all over my house."

"We wouldn't want that, Mrs. Armstrong," he said, setting down his cup and roll and preceding her to the back door.

Emily stood just inside the house, door open, brushing off his shoulders, while Noel stood on the ground below her so she could reach. He made a remark or two, she laughed lightly, and Sophia leaned closer to Annie. "That man's a whole lot smarter than he looks," she whispered.

Annie's eyes came up from her dough. Her mouth stood open in surprise. "You don't think—?"

"I try not to think too loud, girl," Sophia said in a tone of warning.

Annie's mouth relaxed into a gentle smile, and she looked back into her dough. Emily Armstrong was so beloved to her that nothing would please her so much as to have Emily happy and in love. Annie thought nothing so vital as being in love.

"There," Emily was saying as she came back into the kitchen, Noel right behind her, "that's much better now. You know, Mr. Padgett, I can manage a snip or two that isn't very fancy, but it serves to trim away a few shaggy ends when there's need."

"Mrs. Armstrong, that surely is generous of you. I believe I could make use of that skill now and then."

"I can't possibly help with something like shaving, of course."

He took his place on the stool and Emily handed him his cup

and roll. Her fingers lingered for a second against his—a second long and warm and sensual. He met her gaze, and she met his. He had wonderful eyes, not in their color so much as in their depth. Willing, serene, kind eyes, so gentle that she almost felt embraced by them. " 'Course not, ma'am," he said at long last.

Emily had to shake herself free from his gaze. She felt a little light-headed. "Where is Patsy?" she said, turning about. "Now she was just here—where has that girl gone?" And she whirled away in search of her daughter—and composure.

Lilly leaned against a tree in Rittenhouse Square with a closed book in her lap. She stared straight ahead, her brow wrinkled with ideas that disappointed her. For once she had collected reading material from the librarian that he had no compunctions about letting her have. In fact, he had raised his eyebrows above his spectacles and smiled at her as he wrote out her withdrawal card, pleased to be loaning her something that could improve her. She held in her lap a recent Boston edition of Mrs. Hale's handbook titled *Happy Homes and Good Society All the Year Round*. Lilly was very *un*happy with the reading. It seemed all wrong, and not only for herself, but especially for Patricia.

Mrs. Hale had covered the appropriate manners and dress for tea. There was the proper glove for the theater, the lawn party, Sunday church, and the formal dinner. The manners at a banquet versus those at a small dinner. And she pointed out the *faux pas*— "A gentleman does not blow his nose with his fingers," which had caused Lilly to hoot with laughter rather than shudder in revulsion. The tone of Mrs. Hale's book suggested a preference for revulsion from her readers. Lilly also read: "A gentleman should restrain himself from all manner of showing affection."

I am not capable of this kind of life—the pure dullness, the loneliness, the bland domesticity of it. No hilarity, no affection, and no nonsense? What about it is worth living it?

She did not see Andrew approach her. The smooth brown wool of his uncreased trouser leg and the shiny, slender booted foot came into her vision. Her pulse quickened before she even looked up at him. She met the bright Dublin green of his eyes, saw the anthracite black of his hair, his generous, careless smile. He was tall and broad-shouldered, of powerful form. She tried to pretend confidence—or at least friendly nonchalance.

"Lilly," he greeted her. There were so many glaring reasons they were opposites—his maturity and her youth, his wealth and her austerity, his worldliness and her naiveté—yet he always seemed as pleased to see her as she was to see him. She loved to hear her name on his lips, said with strength and approbation. He crouched down to see the book in her lap, and his smile widened. "So, you've finally selected something Mr. Wendell approves of. This is quite a change for you, Lilly."

How does he think of me? she wondered. As a girl? As naughty sometimes? Would he be shocked to learn I'm only seventeen? Does he find me remarkable because he has no obligation to me? Would he *marry* a woman of independent tastes?

"I'm afraid I don't find it the least pleasing," she said, feeling the predictable, despicable flush warm her face. But Andrew brought these alarming sensations, and part of the allure was that she knew she was being too daring, ungovernable, treading on forbidden ground. Just looking into his eyes filled her with a panic of desire.

"I wondered how your studies had been progressing, and now I see that since we last spoke you've been led astray. What brought this on?" he asked, lifting the light-weight volume from her lap and reading the title on the deep blue cover. "I suppose it's a special gentleman."

"Hardly that. Curiosity."

"Ah. But you're more inclined to *Woodhull and Claflin's* scribbling on spiritualism. Or Fielding. Other women read *Godey's* and tear out the fashion plates, Lilly. Not you."

She was unsure whether he was disappointed or relieved that she had finally become like other women. What other women? she wanted to ask. "I rather doubt I'm going to get ahead by reading this," she said morosely.

"Have you given up your ambitions then?" he asked. He straightened to his full height and held out a hand to help her up. "Tell me."

Something tugged at her conscience—she should not be with him. There were her mother's warnings about the dangers poor girls faced in the company of rich men. His close presence never failed to titillate her, and she knew she was not allowed to be titillated. But she put her hand in his, and they walked.

"What's driven you to study domestics, Lilly?"

"I have no interest in a domestic life, though my sister keeps insisting I will change my mind. I hoped to understand what makes women *desire* this role."

"And?"

"It is unbearably dull. The entire plan for women must be to remain as stolid as possible, as restricted as fish in a bowl."

"Now, can domestics really be so dull as that? What about holding the family together through all sorts of hard times? What about raising a great inventor or the next president of the United States?"

She gave a little huff of rueful laughter. "Have you ever bothered to look at some of the books or essays written about raising children? A good mother ties the children to the porch post, worries their hides with manners every minute, and teaches them to be still and silent. Having children sounds like a wonderful notion, unless you look at how it is to be *properly* done. Why, look at me, as an example. Look at the books I would be denied had you not stepped in and spoken on my behalf. And I am not a dowager yet, but I am not a child."

"No," he said, his voice silky, "hardly a child."

"Why shouldn't children be told about cooperative communities, seances, and how apes might have actually preceded men? I told my mother I had a look at *Origin of Species,* and I thought she might faint! Mrs. Hale says that intellectual discussions are for gentlemen, never during mealtime, and best confined to his study or his club." She kicked a pebble off the path. "I often suspect that rule protects most men from being discovered to be idiots by their wives."

Andrew's mouth opened and his eyes widened briefly before he let his head fall back in a large and deeply sincere howl of laughter. "My God," he finally said, "but you're priceless!"

"But am I right?"

"Yes, Lilly, you are indeed!"

"Then it's a shame, don't you think?" she asked very sincerely, her voice a little sad.

"Yes, Lilly, yes. But some women actually lead very happy lives in the pursuit of good manners and family."

"I don't know of one."

"Of course you do."

"I don't. Not my mother; she is widowed and works very hard to keep us—her work is her love and a great challenge for her. Not our neighbors; they may be in pursuit of good manners and family happiness, but the screaming from their houses would indicate it's not going well. Nor the reverend's wife; her face is so pinched into a grimace she looks as though she'd just eaten a bad pickle. If that's domestic happiness, why should I want it? I am going to be a miserable hostess. And wife."

"I doubt that. You're very entertaining."

"I'm not meant for it, that's all. I don't mind domestic work—Mama taught us early how to cook, clean, sew. But Mama earns her own money and decides how it will be spent. I dread the idea that someone might tell me what to talk about, what to read, how to spend my time and money. What if there is no challenge for me, Andrew? What if I'm expected to remain still and quiet and dull?"

"Surely not, Lilly. What man in his right mind would not want you for yourself?"

"Every one, I promise you!"

"Lilly, no—"

"Mrs. Hale says men are to restrain themselves from all manner of affectionate behavior. How in the world is a woman like me to choose a man when all I want is one who—" She stopped herself. An affectionate man? A *passionate* man . . . like Andrew? Somehow his simplest comment could bring the most personal responses from her.

"Perhaps you should rely on Mrs. Hale's expertise in table manners and trust your heart for the rest."

"*My* heart?" she laughed. "My heart just isn't in it at all," she confided honestly. "My sister has proclaimed me hopeless and destined to be an old spinster!"

"Are there no young gentlemen at all?"

"Not a one! They're all so boring!"

"But one *will* come along to change your mind."

"But don't you see? That's what I'm waiting for! Not a man, but something, maybe an essay, that will show me the virtue in living a quiet and mannerly life."

"You won't find that in a book, Lilly," he said, laughing. "You're looking in all the wrong places." When he looked down at her, she noticed his cheeks were lightly flushed, as if he'd been sailing, and she wondered about his life, what he did for work, for fun. But she was afraid to know very much about him; knowledge of his life could only widen the gap between their worlds.

His eyes became intense, serious as he looked into hers. "You really don't know, do you, Lilly?" he asked, his voice soft.

"No, I—"

"Let's hire a coupé, Lilly," he suggested. "Come for a turn around the square with me."

"Would that be proper?" she asked, though acceptance was on her lips.

"Now Lilly, you're bored with propriety, and you'll be completely safe with me. Come along, we'll find a lot of them setting up in front of the theater."

"But why?"

"We'll have a frank discussion about domestics and what drives women to it."

"Well . . ."

"There's my adventuress! Lilly, I find it difficult to believe you're not being chased by every young man in Philadelphia. Some bad fellow *will* come along and turn your head away from the scientists and philosophers. And I'll come looking for you in the park, and you will have given me up."

No, she wanted to say. No, never. There could never be a man to replace him. Never. He led her across the square where a number of brown coupés were lined up. She felt an odd shiver run through her at the thought of being alone with him in a closed carriage, but instead of finding the feeling fearful, it was delicious.

When he helped her into the coupé, she felt a moment's hesitation, but stronger still was her craving for intrigue. It was a very strange mixture of apprehension and pure delight. She tried to remind herself that despite their many conversations, he was still a stranger, but one whose knowledge, worldliness, and mysterious allure she wished to grasp. A voice within her warned, that voice sounding remarkably like her mother's, but Lilly was *not* afraid.

He sat beside her in the coach, twisting on the seat to face her. He pulled her hand into both of his. "Now, you have curiosity about what compels women to sacrifice their independence for a life of domestics. Correct?"

"Yes, but," she began, noticing that her voice had become smaller, "I think I know what compels some of them. I don't know what makes them *welcome* it."

Andrew laughed, shaking his head. "Exactly, Lilly. I flatter myself that you consider me a good friend, and a good friend would let you in on the secret. A secret that's not very well kept, as a matter of fact."

She'd never had a friend like this! Was he so bored that she had the power to entertain him with her choice of readings? Was he so unfulfilled that her interest flattered him? Friendship? If it were not such a ridiculous notion, she could admit that she wanted far more than friendship from him. But that was absurd.

"Interested?" he asked.

She nodded, but slowly. She was so lost in his handsome features that she didn't realize she bit her bottom lip.

"Lilly, do you find me attractive enough so far as men go?"

Her cheeks darkened to the shade of good wine. She had never known so handsome a man! Her voice was lost for a moment, but when it did emerge, it had changed to a squeak. "I . . . I . . . yes, I suppose so. But—"

"I want to kiss you, Lilly. Now, a kiss is more than just the meeting of lips. It must be done with the heart and mind. A kiss from me isn't likely to do anything for you if you don't like me, trust me, and find me somewhat appealing."

"But . . . why would you want to?"

"No matter what Mrs. Hale says, if you don't feel something special when you're kissed, you will be perfectly miserable as a wife. I promise."

"You're sure?"

"Absolutely, Lilly. Have you ever seen a picture of Mrs. Hale? How dare the woman speak of affection! Why do you think she's so square-faced and miserable looking? She's never been shown any affection, and she's a jealous old biddy."

Lilly laughed in spite of herself, but nervously.

"Just think of it as part of your study, Lilly. And if it is meaningless to you, I stand corrected!"

All she knew of kissing was what she had read in her sister's journal! She swallowed hard, praying Patricia was wrong. Her heart raced ahead of the clip-clopping of the horses that pulled them.

"There's always the driver, should you become worried."

"Yes," she whispered. "The driver."

"Close your eyes, Lilly." Before doing so, she searched his face for a moment to judge whether there was evil or even carelessness there. She felt instead a brazen desire for his lips, and it grew within her. How do women function, she wondered, when filled with this giddiness, this unsteadiness? How had Patricia neglected telling this part of it? She slowly let her eyes close and heard his voice. "There's my lass. Now, don't open your eyes until I tell you to.

"It is all in what is *felt,* Lilly. Here is my hand," he said, and she felt his warm palm against her cheek, his fingertips touched her hair at her temple. "And don't speak, Lilly, just allow yourself to become accustomed to this first touch which is barely a touch at all, it is so gentle."

Soft and sweet and delicate. His thumb moved along her jaw, and she was aware of a callus on his palm, a rough place along his thumbnail, but in all his hand was velvety smooth and well cared for. She leaned against his palm in mindless trust.

His other hand touched her other cheek; the soft caress lulled her. His hands were caring, tender. First touch, she thought distractedly. So pure. So subtle.

"My breath," he said, his mouth very close to hers but not touching. "Feel my breath touch your skin." His lips lingered over hers, and the sensation was so new and startling that she almost withdrew, then she realized that his breath, like his fingertips, caressed.

"The touch of my hands, the warmth of breath against your mouth and skin, and the sound of my voice must have appeal. But more important than the sound are the words, chosen for you and you alone. And the way the words are said; they must be precious words, and true. Do you know, my Lilly, how beautiful you are? How wondrous? Delicate but strong. Tender of heart, yet courageous of spirit." His voice had dropped to a whisper, a husky and seductive male scratching that could barely be heard above the sound of clopping horses and wheels turning against the stones in the cobbled drive, yet a voice that roared louder than a waterfall inside her brain because it was laced with secrecy and sincerity. "I think I have never known a woman lovelier, more enticing than you, Lilly."

A young girl's first words of seduction and she felt a sultry kind of smoldering begin inside her as she listened, wishing these words said of her to be true.

"My face against yours," he said, and she felt the coarseness of his clean-shaven cheek against hers. His words were like soft sand against her ear, his breath tangy and pleasant.

"Don't think about what you feel, Lilly. Just let yourself feel whatever is natural, and if anything in my voice or my touch makes you feel peculiar or afraid, pull away from me. My only desire is to bring you pleasure so delicious that you will glow from the memory of it."

Lighter than air was the swirl of longing she felt embrace her, enclosing her in a dream softer than a cloud yet more violent than a thunderhead. She wished for the passion to build and culminate while she hoped, at the very same moment, that this tranquil, rocking ecstasy would never cease.

"Lilly, lovely Lilly. Feel my lips. Here," he said, moving his cheek just enough so that his lips brushed lightly against her temple. "And again," he said, his lips falling to her cheekbone. "And here," he murmured, dropping his lips to the corner of her mouth so lightly that his mustache left a lingering tickle there. She felt a shiver of excitement and hungered for more, for a deeper taste.

"I'm going to embrace you, Lilly, so that I can draw you nearer. I want you to feel comfort, trust . . . and desire," he said, pressing his mouth to one corner of hers, then the other.

Lilly nearly swooned. She did not think about what she was doing as her hands gently slid up against his arms and she tentatively squeezed. The desire, growing and growing, seemed deeply rooted in her groin. She became aware of her body in ways that were new —an aching in her nipples, a pulling in her secret place where a man puts his seed. For a moment she had an understanding of coupling; this must be what a woman feels when she longs to pull a man inside her own body. The emotion that accompanied these physical sensations was strong enough to make her shout—or cry.

"Feel my lips here," he said, moving them gently across her mouth. "You need not keep your lips tightly closed—lips pliant and trusting and willing need not be braced against assault. There is so much more to a kiss than lips, Lilly. A kiss is best done with the heart."

And then he gently pulled at her lips with his. She felt his teeth delicately nip, peculiar yet oddly natural. She had never considered this, but of course it was right. And then his tongue gently outlined her lips, probing the place where they were joined. She let him open

76

her lips. And she gently caressed his arms. She was so weak with desire that she could feel her pulse beat in her temples.

She was won, she was his. His coaxing, his tantalizing invitation, so skilled and experienced, was victorious. She was filled with sensual stirring that had no physical meaning for her, even though it was all physical. She thought love, love, love. She welcomed him, all of him. He nibbled, pulled, tasted.

"Now, Lilly, I'm going to kiss you very gently. Just allow . . ." And she felt the soft press of his lips, a gentle movement of his mouth over hers. His tongue touched her lips. "And again, very softly."

Her head tipped back as she met his kiss; she welcomed the added pressure. His lips, on hers in moist command, whispered, "You may hold me, Lilly, for I am going to hold you. And if your heart tells you it is right, you shall have your kiss."

Right. Nothing in her life had ever been more right. Nothing in memory had been more luxurious, more thrilling, more consuming. Her arms went around him to pull him closer, to hold him against her heart, to invite him into her soul. And she welcomed his mouth, open now, soft and warm and powerful, taking control of every feeling she had ever had. Her chest, pressed hard against his, hungered to be touched harder still, and she didn't know whether she clutched at him or he clutched her. Her tongue joined his willingly in play. Beneath her fingers she felt his shoulders, hard and wide, and within the depth of her mouth she could taste him, a taste new and bold, the tangy yet sweet nectar of man that caused a wondrous aching to wrap itself around her and squeeze, strangely blissful pain that filled her up inside, drew her tight in her very center. She embraced him fiercely, so close that not a gasp could separate them. Her mouth demanded much of his—pulling, pushing, tasting, molding, searching, delivering her away from curiosity and straightaway into knowledge. *Never leave me. Never let me go. Never.*

This was not the kind of kiss a boy stole behind the house. It was a man's kiss, filling, tempting, and perturbing her body to want more. For a long, long time they were embraced, their mouths moving together in a lovely tug of war.

Then she felt his embrace slacken, the power waning, with the same finesse he had used to conquer her lips, he slowly began to retreat, withdraw, placing a light tongue here, there, a little nibble, a slight tugging, until she was free and could no longer feel his breath or his hands. She had never felt so alone.

"Open your eyes, Lilly," he gently entreated.

She felt as though she were just waking up. He produced a handkerchief, which he used to dab at her lips, wiping away the moisture from his kiss. She was breathless, speechless, fulfilled in one way and shattered in another. Does one become more insensible with practice? she wondered.

"Lilly?" he whispered. "What did you think, Lilly?"

In a moment she became aware of the coupé again, the sounds of the horses and wheels, the rocking and squeaking. He was not nearly so disgruntled as she, but he frowned slightly. Had she somehow disappointed him? "Shall . . . shall we be trying it again?"

His eyes grew dark, perhaps sad. "I think not, my lovely Lilly. It would be wrong for me to be tempted beyond your lips. It is one of my greatest disappointments that you are not for me. But if you will have me for a friend, I would be honored."

Her lips formed an 'O' that she did not utter. Of course she knew that, even if she had allowed herself to believe, however briefly, that a miracle might change their destinies. The book had slipped from her lap to the floor of the small coach, but she hadn't noticed. She was torn. She wanted to thank him, for nothing to match the experience had ever before been hers. Still, she wanted to shout, *what have you done to me?* She knew she could never find those feelings again, not with another man, not now.

"This was to be a discussion of women . . . and domestics."

"And it was, my darling Lilly. There are three reasons why women give themselves fully to a domestic life. There is the sheer love of building a home, a family. Perhaps they are few, as you say, but I think there are some women who love a domestic life. If they seem unhappy to you, perhaps it is because it is so difficult. And there is the woman who has no choice, really. Perhaps her parents have her wed, or perhaps she is too unimaginative to capture any other kind of life. But you are neither of those and if you enter a life of domestics it will be for love and desire. You will deeply love some man and soon you will see that one of you must bear the children while the other brings home the money to feed the family. For you, Lilly, if you are brave and stubborn, you will have a clear choice, and you will be happy in it because you will have *love*. And love makes so much possible."

He reached for her chin and lifted it slightly, looking down into her eyes. "Don't marry a man before you know him and trust him.

Don't accept his promises until you kiss him. And demand much of that kiss." He smiled. "Until then, worry the scientists and philosophers with all your grand questions, and no matter what the writers of etiquette say, tell your children all that you've learned and encourage them to be as free as you are."

A tremulous smile appeared on her lips. He reached for the bell to signal the driver to stop. "I suppose you could have taken terrible advantage of me," she said softly. The feeling was still new with her—that feeling of welcoming him into her.

"I wouldn't hurt you, Lilly, because I care about you. But your curiosity is infectious. Your questions lead me to questions of my own. Now, I'm leaving you back at the square, and I'll use this coach to get back to my own. Run along, Lilly. I'll see you again."

She wanted to extract a promise about that, but she only nodded. Andrew helped her out of the coupé and left her standing by the road. He waved to her as he left, and she lifted her hand, watching sadly as the coach rattled away around the curve of the square. Lilly suddenly felt like crying—as though she had lost something. Now she was even more convinced she would never marry. She wanted a man who could draw that sense of passion from her, a passion for all the things in life. She must be encouraged to question and seek answers; the man she wanted must delight in her intelligence yet find her beautiful and desirable. And it was not enough that he be able to give her all of that, he had to take from her the way Andrew did, finding her curiosity stimulated him and caused him to ask his own questions.

She wanted Andrew.

"I will be alone forever," she said, her voice distant and very quiet.

It was then that she realized the book was gone, and she knew it was in the coach. She couldn't have run after it even if that was her desire. Her legs would barely hold her up. She resigned herself that she would tell the librarian the book was lost and pay for it. She glumly considered the cost for what she considered worthless drivel.

She didn't see the coupé travel back to the library. Andrew Devon left the conveyance with the book in hand and returned it in Lilly's name. Then he returned to the coach and the hired driver took him half a mile to where his own covered carriage waited. It was a rich trap, identical to the one Dale Montaine owned and had taken to the Armstrong residence two weeks before. The scrolled *M* was on the door; five people had their own rich, monogrammed Montaine gigs, all members of the Montaine household.

"To your office or home, sir?" the driver asked.

"Home, thank you. My wife is expecting me."

I am nearly thirty-eight years old, Emily thought. I have grown daughters who could make me a grandmother before I am ready. I must send Mr. Padgett away. I must.

She lay in her bed, in her darkened room, unable to stop thinking about the way he made her feel. "Would it be too forward to use only our first names when it is just the two of us?" he had asked her. "Emily?"

That question had come after ten evenings of sharing the porch, the cool spring nights, conversation. He whittled on the porch steps, promising not to leave his shavings for her to clean up. John had been taking his pipe, Mrs. Fairchild had retired, and the evening breeze was cool. It gave her an uplifting feeling, such a feeling of renewal. She told him it was her duty to clean up after her boarders; he paid his board on time. But he left no shavings. And he agreed, there was nothing like a spring breeze in the evening to make a man feel like a boy again.

She felt like a girl. There had been other springs, but none that caused such a restlessness in her spirit. At least not in many, many years.

Night after night he whittled and told stories. She could have gone to the parlor to use the lamp to mend, but somehow the mending seemed so much less agreeable than listening to Noel. When John walked Sophia home and all the others had found their own diversions, it was only Emily and Noel . . . and their voices quieted instinctively. Alone. Nothing untoward was even uttered, yet her heart beat more frantically when it was just the two of them. Because if he stood from the step and walked over to the swing where she sat, if he bent down and touched his lips to hers, she would embrace him. He did not. Not yet.

I don't want these feelings, she kept thinking. Under the down quilt her hand moved across the coarse linen of her nightdress to stretch across her flat, firm stomach and she was reminded of her body. Her flesh nearly quivered with the desire to be touched by a man. I don't want to feel this way. I can't! I can't bear those kind of feelings again!

First it was something as simple as a good scrubbing to wear away his travel dust. He shaved and bought new clothing. She could not imagine what industry allowed him to have costly suits tailored so quickly. His tastes were experienced and smart; his choice of fabrics and style was learned and yet uniquely individual. He kept a western influence; he would not give up the hat or boots.

He was not shy of stories of his past: his mother's death when he was small, his father's quest for gold, his education in the East, his experiences in the West. He had a love of space and rich dirt and mountains that he brought alive in his slow, unhurried drawl. Emily was amazed by all that he had done and seen—and by the way she looked forward to the evenings.

She was drawn to a certain sadness in him, the grief of a small boy whose mother had died and father had left him with relatives who never missed an opportunity to let him know he was a burden. That was the reason he did not stay with his family when he visited Philadelphia; he disliked them. His cousins, he said, had always considered him an outsider, always been annoyed by his presence, although his father sent enough money for his keeping to allow the family to live in style. His father had been lucky during the gold rush—how lucky he had not divulged. Emily wondered briefly how rich he was, but decided he would not be content in a boarding house, in an undersized bed and room, if he had a great deal of money.

He said he had wanted for playmates when he was small, which accounted for his attraction to the West—out there a man could be alone as much or as little as he liked. And he appreciated good city manners, he told her, but proper manners that covered up bad behavior rankled him. Out West, he said, people spit on the street, but they did for each other. Emily thought hard on that.

Even with that hint of sadness from a hard youth, he was not a bitter man. She felt compassion for that small boy, orphaned and left with people who considered him a nuisance, but respect for the man who lived his life simply and honestly. These were virtues Emily aspired to.

Then she began to think him handsome. He was so well muscled from his years of riding, ranching, mining. He made that kind of life sound so ordinary; he answered Lilly's many questions almost shyly, making very little of himself. He'd fought in the Civil War, but in a secret detachment of frontiersmen in Colorado. His hand, so large, was gentle on her elbow when he escorted her into the house at evening's end.

She had no idea how he spent his days, but he returned almost every afternoon in time for dinner. Twice he had had to miss the evening meal and he had told her beforehand. She guessed he visited his family, reacquainted himself with old friends. He didn't bring home tales of the day's activities. He had stayed away until late one night, returning in a hired coach. A woman? she had asked herself.

The neighbors will notice, she reminded herself. I sit on the porch swing until nearly ten, when a proper matron has long since turned out her lamp. But Noel whittles and talks, and I sit, fascinated, hungering for the evenings, for the sound of his gentle voice . . . a voice, given a chance, that would be so loving, so dear. I drink in the stories of the life he says no woman has yet shared.

She told him about herself when he asked. The replies she had given to innocent questions had begun to sound like excuses even to her. Why had she never remarried? There were two daughters to raise; that alone took all the energy she had. Had she never been in want of companionship? In a house filled with boarders and children and work? she had laughingly countered. Oh, she said, she had often prayed to be lonely.

I am so lonely, she thought now. So hungry. So weary.

It had been years since she had thought about Ned's skilled seduction with any emotions other than guilt, shame, or fury. Now she remembered all too well how she had fallen his victim; his touch was fiery, his male scent intoxicating, and the words he had plied her with were so convincing, so tender. She had been only a girl, and, not knowing the dangers, she had let Ned show her the secrets of her own body; the carnal thrill of his possession and the blinding joy of that intimate completion had once bound her to him.

Then there was shame. The cost had been high because he had only used her. Desire, once a driving force in her, turned to repugnance. Even the casual touch of a widower's hand on her elbow could make her shiver with apprehension and anger. No woman, knowing her mind and body, would willingly allow a man to blind her with the momentary gratification of intimate pleasure. She had not considered her loneliness, nor thought of the physical wanting that had once, so long ago, so briefly, felt natural and right to her. No one since Ned had awakened any feeling in her. It had been painless to send those few bachelors and widowers away.

Then Noel Padgett. Her hand moved under the quilt to touch the firmness of her own breast. Emotion had been reborn in her. Everything that passed through her mind brought a bodily response. She had begun to doubt her own sanity, for she watched him hungrily, listened raptly to his every word. Then he said the precious words that thrilled and terrified her. "I've grown very fond of you, Emily. You're a remarkable woman in so many ways, and our evenings are more special than any I've ever had."

It had taken her a long, dangling moment to reply, "Thank you . . . Mr. Padgett." She wanted another chance, a chance to say she felt the same way . . . or at least to use his given name. But she couldn't. She had felt fear.

I am a woman of nearly eight and thirty, she told herself again. These feelings belong to young girls, new brides. Why has no one told me about this rebirth? Why did no one mention this dilemma? I thought it was over for me by now. Does a woman of virtue wish to be touched by a man? Does a woman of dignity allow herself to be reduced to this longing?

But as she listened to the night sounds through her opened window she was filled with a tender pull she could recognize from her youth. It frightened her, yet her body welcomed the sensations, the spiraling yearning, and the power of her great discipline was useless. She wanted a thing she had denied herself for many, many years. Pleasure.

The tea for Mary Ellen had been sufficiently ghastly to convince Patricia to proceed with her plans in secrecy. No one understood her, not even Lilly. Emily, had she tried, could have impressed Mary Ellen, but she made no effort; she would not purchase new tea linens or borrow a better service, and she insisted on including Lilly, though Lilly was bored by such pastimes. Then Emily conversed on the drab subjects of temperance, recipes, and even household economics.

Still, Mary Ellen had delivered as promised and Wilbert Kennesdow had agreed to escort Patricia to the fancy reception and ball at the home of Senator Williamson. On the tenth of May, dawn would break to the chiming of all the bells in Philadelphia, and President Grant would open the Centennial Exhibition. The senator, a patron of the event, was hosting an extraordinary party for honored visitors and guests and the president would be there. The city was already brimming with the rich and famous; with inventors, artists, and craftsmen who would be displaying their creations; with politicians from all over the country and dignitaries from foreign nations. There was simply no better environment in which to meet and intrigue a rich husband.

Until now Patricia had only misled her mother without actually lying. But this was an *occasion,* and she was not willing to test Emily's strict, prudish behavior against such an opportunity. Emily might prohibit her from attending the party, using the excuse that Patricia did not know these people. Or perhaps Emily would be honest and admit she did not like Mary Ellen.

"Your friend could use some lessons in grace," Emily had commented.

"Whatever do you mean, *grace?*" Patricia had returned peevishly. She had counted on her mother employing her knowledge of the delicate tastes of the well-to-do to make the tea elegant. Instead, Emily flaunted her ordinary, working-class existence.

"What I mean, dear," her mother had replied, "is that money cannot disguise bad manners. Your friend was very obvious—she thinks herself high above us."

Well, Patricia had thought, she *is.* Patricia was so disappointed in her mother. Didn't Emily see the possibilities? If Patricia could "marry up," above her class, then the whole family could rise above this mundane environment and enjoy prosperity. Doing so only meant attracting a man of means through influential friends. They could live fashionably again, as Emily had in her youth, for Patricia would share her good fortune. But Emily actually resisted this opportunity. She told Patricia very sternly, "Don't be fooled by money, Patricia. My mother, who was once extraordinarily rich, taught me early that money is no guarantee of quality."

Mary Ellen's comments after the tea had been likewise disparaging. "My goodness, your family *has* been humbled. How sad. I asked my mother if she remembered the Bellmonts and she said she did. They were simply the most prestigious family in all Pennsylvania. She would never believe—"

"You didn't *tell* her?" Patricia asked.

"Of course not, I only asked about the Bellmonts. I can see why your mother is silent. How perfectly humiliating for her!"

Patricia had been tempted to defend her mother, but only briefly.

Truthfully, she preferred Mary Ellen's pretentiousness to her mother's strict doctrine of a simple life and hard work.

Since she couldn't risk telling her mother that Wilbert Kennesdow had invited her to the reception and ball, she had asked permission to spend the night at the home of her new best friend. There they would dress their hair, don their frocks, and be called for by Wilbert and Thomas. Patricia would wear Mary Ellen's scandalously low-cut lavender satin. Mary Ellen had promised they would dance and drink champagne.

She carried a bag holding a few overnight articles and horsecar fare. She left the modest clapboard house and picked her way down the dirt road, stepping carefully around garbage and muddy patches from kitchen drains. The sour, telltale odor of outdoor conveniences rose in the heat of the afternoon. Soon she would be leaving for good; no more muddy shoes or smelling garbage piles. She looked back at the house, Emily's pride and joy.

Patricia had been ten years old when they had moved in. It had seemed like a mansion. She had been overpowered by its size and many rooms. Then she visited with Mary Ellen and her home became smaller, poor, shabby, and embarrassing. Even the chintz curtains she had prized looked dowdy to her now compared to the immense, luxurious satin brocade draperies in the Jasper home. She, Lilly, Sophia, and even Mrs. Fairchild had sewn the braided rag rug in the parlor; the Jaspers had woolen, manufactured carpet in every room, soft, deep, and artistically patterned.

How could her mother keep herself from longing for riches and prominence? Had the years since she had been wealthy damaged her memory? How could she argue that simple and uncomplicated things could mean a great deal? It was beyond Patricia's ken; one had but to look down the trashy, muddy street at the neighborhood to see it was nothing.

She turned away from the house. She walked away from her neighborhood and knew she would not miss it, not for a day. Tonight was just the first of many, many wonderful nights.

Noel Padgett ran a finger around the collar of his silk shirt. He recalled the look on Emily's face as she looked at his formal attire.

"My goodness, Mr. Padgett, what a magnificent costume," she had exclaimed. And he had replied, "A might too fancy for my tastes. I'm happier just sitting on the porch step."

That comment had caused her to smile in a way so warm he felt as though his heart melted within him. She could be here, he thought, looking around the senator's ballroom. If he could have invited her without causing offense, he would have done so. But he knew she had no fancy dress. He could buy her dozens, but she would decline even a lace hanky. Not only was she proud and proper, theirs was not a formal courtship.

Noel played his hand close to his chest in this precarious business of pursuing Emily. She was a complex woman, obviously suspicious of money, maybe even frightened by it, as she showed through her disdain. The things she claimed to admire, simple and uncomplicated things like a man looking for Sunday services or honest labor for honest pay or an evening on the porch were free of any risk.

When he had taken the address from the hotel, it had been his plan to spend a night, perhaps two, until more spacious and convenient lodgings could be found. Emily's neighborhood was a long ride from Fairmount Park, the Centennial Exhibition site, and from the business and government district of Philadelphia. Besides, he would have slept on a street corner rather than spend a single night in his aunt's house. Then he saw Emily. And before closing his eyes on that first night, he knew he had met the woman he wanted.

He planned a slow advance. If she learned that he boarded in her house because of his desire, her morals might be outraged. She could evict him. Meanwhile, he was trying to think of a way to convince her to take a stroll with him or pack a picnic lunch for two. He'd suffer through Sundays of services if he could sit beside Emily. He wasn't sure how long he could indulge this idea of temperance, and his impatience for a drink made him chuckle aloud. No woman had ever persuaded him to forego a late night card game or a glass of whiskey.

"You're about the only man I know can look so damned amused all by yourself."

He turned toward the familiar voice and accepted a glass of champagne from an old friend.

"Thank you, General."

"Think you'd call me Daniel at least. I got scars all over my backside from where you unloaded me of shot. I still don't sit a horse good." He sipped from the glass and made a face. "It just doesn't go down right, does it?"

Noel took a drink. "Keep your eye on the senator. He must have a private stock somewhere."

"I reckon he'll open it up later. If he leaves the party and ducks into a parlor or library, I'm on his trail."

"And I'm on yours," Noel laughed. He gestured to the ballroom at large with the hand that held the glass. "Nice little place the senator's got."

"Twenty-five acres all told. Sixteen bedrooms; fanciest damned thing you ever saw. I'm staying in one that looks like a damned bordello. Have you met Senator Tilden yet?"

"Nope. Do I need to?"

"Yessir, before we find the senator's private stock. Tilden's pure temperance. He's got more goddamn virtues than I got shot scars. You're gonna have to shake a lot of these hands."

"Sure is a mess of silk out there," Noel said.

"Yep, but I don't see it. If my eyesight is worth a damn, Mrs. Wilkensen gets her liver up." Daniel Wilkensen lifted one bushy gray eyebrow as he surveyed the room filled with whirling, beautiful women, a sparkling rainbow of frocks, furs, gems, laces. "There a Mrs. Padgett to make your life miserable yet?"

"Not yet."

"Well, you always did like buckskin on a woman."

What would he think, Noel wondered, if he knew that I was turning myself inside out over a woman in plain gray muslin with a white starched collar? Emily dressed like a preacher's wife or a country schoolteacher. No matter how sincere the attempt, she could not make herself ordinary; she was beautiful, her skin creamy and smooth, her hair lustrous and thick even though she pinned it back, tamed it down. Were she to wear evening toilette or a ballgown she would be more beautiful than any woman in this room.

Daniel Wilkensen's low monologue interrupted his thoughts of Emily. He had met the general fifteen years ago in Colorado. Daniel had been a colonel back then, commander of a special detachment of frontiersmen. He was shot in the rump by a bunch of advancing Free-Soilers who confused the un-uniformed pack of soldiers for the enemy. Nothing can humble a man like retreat, except maybe getting shot in the sitting joint. Noel had been an infantryman. It had taken Noel just about as much whiskey to get up the nerve to pick that shot out of a colonel's butt as it had taken the colonel to endure the pain.

"How's your pa?" Daniel asked.

"Dead now, Daniel. He died last year."

"Great loss," the general said after a somber moment. "Was he sick long?"

Noel remembered his father's tenacity. "He'd been slowing down, had a bad cough for a few months, but an expedition came through, and he wouldn't be left behind. He'd been up the Oregon Trail enough, you'd think. But no amount of coaxing or bullying would get through to him. He died on the trail." Noel looked down for a moment. "Almost like he planned it," he added sentimentally. And then, more brightly, "He was sixty-eight; a long life for a man who lived like he lived. Hope I see sixty-eight."

"Ahem," the general cleared his throat, "I'll see it first. You ought to dance, Noel. Now that the old man's gone and there ain't no one to badger you, get a woman."

"Maybe," he said, seeing nothing on the ballroom floor that intrigued him nearly so much as another evening on Emily's porch.

Daniel leaned closer to provide commentary while Noel mentally compared each woman who swirled by to his idea of perfection. "That's George Corliss—his machine engine will start the Exhibition by lighting all the lights. I ain't never seen the like . . . Walt Whitman—that man still don't own a decent suit of clothes . . . See Julia? There's a lesson. Even getting her husband elected president can't make a woman pretty."

Spending the next few months with a bunch of eastern politicians and businessmen was the last thing that interested Noel, but the territory of Wyoming had sent him as a representative to the Centennial. They needed a great deal from the United States government: cavalry support to quell the Indians, guns, money, land grants, homesteaders. They needed major connecting railroad lines for their towns, for towns to become cities. All Noel could think about tonight was how far Wyoming was from Philadelphia. How long before Emily would use his first name without whispering?

There would be many gatherings like this in the course of the fair. The more he could get out of one, the fewer he would have to attend. He was just about to excuse himself from Daniel and start shaking hands when a flurry of lavender silk and satin distracted him.

He squinted in the direction of the young woman. His mouth dropped open. She danced gaily, tossing her blond curls with coquettish intent, smiling suggestively into the handsome face of her young partner. She was one of the most beautiful in the room and he could not help but notice the eyes that followed her. She swayed gracefully, beaming with rehearsed, flirtatious guile. She was an artist, and this room was her canvas.

She had somehow fooled her mother. Emily could not have provided such a dress, would not have helped fashion a coiffure so modern, and must be ignorant of her daughter's whereabouts. The handshaking would be delayed for Noel, for he felt compelled to keep an eye on her.

"Maybe I will dance," he told Daniel.

"Patricia," Mary Ellen whispered furiously. "What do you think you're *doing?*"

"I'm dancing. Isn't that what I'm supposed to be doing?"

"By now I'm certain Wilbert regrets bringing you. You're ignoring him completely!"

"I am not! He's ignoring me! He hasn't come near me all evening. He was very precise in telling me that he did not like to dance and that I should enjoy myself while he talks to his father's friends."

"He hasn't come near you because you're dancing with all the other men! How do you expect to impress his family when you're acting like this?"

Patricia wrinkled her nose. She hadn't been particularly impressed with the Kennesdow family: they were all as awkward and withdrawn as Wilbert, and no one seemed to know them. All the important introductions of the early evening were the first for them, too. "Wilbert doesn't want to dance, Mary Ellen. He *told* me to enjoy myself, which is more than you've done."

"Enjoy yourself? You're making a spectacle of yourself! Don't you see how people are looking at you?"

Patricia glanced around and saw two men watching her from a short distance away. She met their eyes shyly, one at a time, and received a smile from each in return. "For goodness' sake, Mary Ellen, don't you even know when a woman is being admired?"

"Where'd you stuff the tulle?" she asked hotly.

Patricia's cheeks became rosy. She had removed the sheer tulle wrap that served to keep the low-cut gown which dipped off her shoulders more decent for a young woman her age. She had left it in the powder room with her borrowed cloak. Bosoms had great power; she wasn't very tall, and the men she danced with would be looking down at her all evening. She wanted to be asked where they might call to see her again. And she had been.

"Why don't you want me to have fun?" she asked Mary Ellen.

"Fun? Is that what you call it? It looks more like P. T. Barnum's Greatest Show on Earth."

"Oh, Mary Ellen, don't be mean. I've never in my life been to a party like this . . . and I may never have such an opportunity again!"

"There's a clever girl, you may not indeed. I tried to warn you, but since you won't listen . . . if Wilbert never calls on you again, it won't be anyone's fault but your own."

"Very well, I'm warned. And I can't help it if he won't dance and is just too awfully shy to even stand beside me."

"Not that you will be standing still long enough for him to approach you," Mary Ellen returned, the sarcasm in her voice bitter as bile. She lifted her nose and glided away.

Patricia pursed her lips in annoyance and glared at her friend's departing back. Then she looked uncertainly in Wilbert's direction and found his eyes were on her. She flashed him her most dazzling smile, lifting a hand as if to wave, but he started to grow pink immediately, a wash of color flowing up his neck, through his fuzzy new beard, scorching the pimples on his cheeks. Although Wilbert was twenty-four years old, a graduate of Harvard, and involved in the working world of business, he had all the physical attributes of a seventeen-year-old boy. Except for his height: he was well over six feet and lanky, towering above her with rounded shoulders and a head hung as if in perpetual embarrassment. He was polite enough, but he had said hardly ten words. He remained in conversation with his father and a dowdy looking old man with a horrid gray mustache—a poet of some kind, Patricia had been told.

Mary Ellen had enjoyed the task of making Patricia beautiful right up until the moment she had accomplished the feat. The dress, lavender satin covered with an overskirt of white Chambéry gauze, was layered in a series of puffs that led back to a demitrain skirt, each puff caught up with garlands of silk flowers. It flounced and moved and seemed to breathe with her while she danced. And of course the tulle strip had been added about the shoulders because the straps were little more than a thread of small flowers that dropped off. Far too brazen, Mrs. Jasper had said, for a young virgin. The tulle strip covered the white lace ruche at her breast, the prettiest part of the dress. It also obstructed the view of her bosom, upon which Patricia depended.

More daring still was what she had encouraged Mary Ellen to help her do to her hair. Copying a fashion plate in *Harper's Bazaar,* they had clipped the hair around Patricia's face and curled tiny ringlets with a hot iron. Patricia knew Emily considered this latest fashion hoydenish, but all the women in this room wore similar and even more provocative styles. Her mother would be furious, but she decided to face that predictable wrath. It was time her mother let her make a few of her own decisions—at least about her appearance.

When they had arrived at the ball, it had been easy to see that the gown Patricia wore was nothing in comparison to the others. Women were arrayed in all manner of expensive and flamboyant frocks: dresses were sewn with jewels, stones, feathers, pearls, and even costly furs although it was spring. The coiffures were far more extravagant than Patricia's; women wore peacock feathers, gems, and even sprinklings of gold dust in their hair. But it didn't matter that there were newer and more expensive dresses; no one could outshine Patricia in natural beauty. In fact, it brought a smile to her lips to see the number of painfully homely women who were expensively bedecked. More money than the Armstrong household spent in a year had been wasted in efforts to cover fat, fill in thin-boned figures, or draw the masculine eye away from a long sharp nose or dull, vacant eyes. Patricia, in her slightly out-of-date dress, was not left wanting for dance partners.

Mary Ellen was more than piqued. The moment Patricia stood before the mirror in Mary Ellen's gown, looking far more fetching than Mary Ellen could with the help of a hundred dressmakers, Mary Ellen had become surly and envious. Whereas she had earlier promised dancing and champagne, now, after the third dance and the second glass, she had begun to grumble and scold. Patricia felt the knot in her stomach tighten, but it did not show on her face. She was accustomed to envy in others. Mary Ellen would probably rescind the invitation for the over-night stay unless Patricia dashed to the powder room to retrieve the tulle wrap and proceeded to stand with her back against the wall, lonely and perfectly miserable.

But she would not. She had saved enough to ride the horsecar, although a number of pleasant young men seemed generous enough to hire a coach for her. And Wilbert, although timid and gawky, was probably decent enough to see her home even if he had a terrible time with her. She had overheard a young lady in the dressing room comment that at the senator's last ball they had all danced until dawn, and that had filled Patricia with hope; she would happily sit by the roadside in the early morning and await the first horsecar of the day. She did not consider dangers; there were no dangers tonight. It might as well be the only night of her life.

She danced again and again. She had a third glass of champagne and a fourth. She gave her house number and street three times, ignoring the frowns of confusion from rich young men who were unfamiliar with her neighborhood. It was midnight and from what she saw, the party was just beginning. She was very tired, but she wouldn't stop dancing for all the world.

"I could hardly believe it was you," someone said.

She turned toward the familiar voice with a ready smile on her lips which faded when she looked into the brown eyes of Dale Montaine. She formed a little pout, her lower lip thrust out, and opened her borrowed fan. "I saw you earlier," she said. "Of course, you were . . . occupied."

"I escorted someone else, is that what you mean? Well, I was hardly encouraged to invite you."

"Would you have?" she asked, turning her liquid blue eyes up, tilting her chin invitingly.

"Why not? But then, since our falling out—"

"Yes, that. I suppose one of us should apologize."

"Ah. I suppose."

"Oh Dale, you purposely misbehave! Especially around me. Who is that girl you're with?" Patricia happened to think she was one of the poor wretches on whom a fortune had been wasted.

"The woman I brought tonight is a close friend of the family and it was suggested that I escort her. Her name is Dorthea Lancaster."

"A friend?"

94

"Are you jealous?" he asked, smiling roguishly. "I hope the fact that I've brought her won't keep us from patching things up."

"Has she gone home now?"

"No," he laughed. "No, dear, she's gone to fix her hair and get her wrap. I'll have to see her home. Naturally."

"And so we won't even dance . . ."

"I'm sorry, Patricia, not tonight. But I'll be more than pleased if you'd invite me to come 'round for you again . . . so long as there is no confusion about who's calling on you on that particular evening. That isn't asking very—"

"Oh . . . um," she faltered, embarrassed. "There could be . . . well, a problem with that. My mother . . ."

"Has she told you otherwise?" he asked, his dark brows drawing together.

Patricia looked away thinking of what her mother had said. She couldn't tell Dale *that*. "Perhaps if you came 'round to tell her of your regret about—"

"Better still, why don't we plan to meet? Then we don't have to go through all that bother."

"Meet? How in the world do you expect me to do that? My mother doesn't let me run skitter-tail all over town."

"We have soirées and dinners nearly every day. Would you like to come to my home, meet my family and their guests?" He leaned his head to the side, not really pointing. "See that man over there? That's my father talking with President Grant. They're very old friends. Any night of your choosing there is bound to be something happening at the house."

"My mother wouldn't allow it," she said sullenly.

"Say you're going somewhere else, then, and send a note for me. I can send the coach for you. Anywhere."

"I wouldn't have the first idea how to go about arranging something like that."

"You're joking? Haven't you ever gone off without Mama? Pack your good dress and hide it around the corner and set off for a lecture like a good little Christian girl. Give me a little warning of the day and time, and I'll come for you."

She laughed with amusement that was wholly contrived. She didn't notice the way Dale's smile turned into a smirk, the way his eyes boiled with dark contempt. She had taken her fill of champagne;

95

she felt, erroneously, in control of the situation. And she did not see that beyond Dale, Wilbert cast a last, baleful glance in her direction just as a cloaked and bonneted Mary Ellen pulled him away. Patricia had no idea she'd been left behind.

"Choose a day and time in advance, when your family makes plans and you can beg off. Think about it," he urged her. "If there's no party at the house, I can take you to the theater. Edwin Booth is playing *Richelieu*. Or, maybe we'll borrow Father's yacht."

Patricia's eyes had grown wider, apace with his suggestions. She was possessed by an aching urgency for all those things, not once, not twice, but every day. A trip to Saratoga or Newport for the summer. Yachting. The polo matches. The horse races. Gowns, not wasted on her, for she could do them justice. Her eyes dropped to the diamond stickpin he wore in his lapel.

Dale's smile was lazy and shrewd as he watched her reaction. This was the type of woman he understood perfectly. Not only had his father married two such creatures, he had made a sport of similar ingenues for the past few years. He could tease her with fancy dinners or a ride on his father's yacht. He would soon part that reluctant virgin's flesh. The worst that could possibly befall him was to be forced to drop a little money into the widow Armstrong's palm to atone for her daughter's poor judgment. This was just another up-start; it would be no more than she deserved.

The mere thought put a strain on his trousers. He felt the familiar ache of impatience begin to swell.

"How'd you manage an invitation to this?" he asked.

"Oh . . . a friend of mine, Mary Ellen Jasper, introduced me to my escort, Wilbert Kennesdow." As she said this, she glanced around a bit, but she didn't see anyone she knew. It didn't worry her much. There were still many floating dancers.

"Wilbert?" he laughed, now more aware than ever how much Patricia would sacrifice for a single opportunity to be among the fashionable rich. He suddenly found Patricia's desperate attempt hi-larious. "Good God, you must have nearly caused the old boy to faint! He wouldn't know what to do with a beauty like you!"

She flushed slightly at what she believed was a compliment. "As it happens, he doesn't know what to do with me. He hasn't spoken a word to me all evening."

"But you weren't lonely, were you, darling?" he asked, and she cocked her head, unsure whether there was a mocking quality in his voice. "You *did* have a good time?"

"Oh yes, certainly."

"Will you send 'round a note for me?"

"Well, I'd like to," she said, her eyes not on his face, but on the stickpin. "But . . . well, here's something I can do. I can attend a lecture with my sister next Thursday afternoon. We'll be passing by the theater, and Lilly always stops to read the bills. Meet me there at half past one, and I'll tell you if I can plan a day for you soon? Hmmm?"

"Wonderful."

She dropped her gaze, feeling uncertain for the first time that evening. "I . . . you know . . . I don't have a deep wardrobe, Dale. I . . ."

"We'll do something that will make good use of your dress. There is no one more beautiful than you in that lavender."

She raised her eyes, reassured, feeling confidence surge through her once again. Her mother and sister were so wrong about these people, these very rich members of elite society. She had never met such an indulgent and generous lot. No one had yet spurned her for her lack. All had offered to share with her. Her mother, who had been one of them, should know this.

"I have to find Dorthea—can't have her looking for me." He leaned closer to Patricia, and his voice was husky. "Don't let me down, darling. I want to see you again. I want to take you someplace . . . special. Very special." He brushed his lips against her cheek. She shivered at the sensation, withdrawing slightly. She disliked his breath.

She watched him stride across the ballroom toward a small gathering of young people waiting in the foyer. He had a handsome enough face, and he was large. She had witnessed his quick strength, but his physique was somehow bulky. He was more bearlike than lithe. He swayed as he walked, unsteady and lurching. His carriage must be aristocratic, she decided.

She watched Dale take the cloak of the homely young woman and solicitously drape it over her shoulders. The ugly girl glanced back at him, an affectionate glance. Then she touched the hand that lingered on her shoulder. Friends, Patricia thought. Humph. If I can't get him away from *her,* I am nothing!

A shudder ran through her. It didn't occur to her to think about the reasons she disliked Dale Montaine. He was not nearly so solicitous of her as he was of this *friend*. And, largely due to the fact that she had not eaten, had consumed a great deal of champagne for a girl who had never before sipped alcohol, and was awake later than ever before, she made an excuse for the reason that Dale did not whisper to Dorthea Lancaster to sneak away to meet him. Dorthea's mother was not angry with him, after all.

When feelings of distaste and suspicion threatened to rise in her as she watched him, she forced herself to think about yachts and diamond stickpins. No man had succeeded in causing her to feel any desire; it hardly mattered that Dale had not. She doubted she would ever feel anything other than the shuddering revulsion that consumed her when a man touched her. From all that she'd read and heard, her feelings were completely normal. Women disliked this need in men. But she *still* intended to marry—and marry well. There simply wasn't anything else she could do with her life.

Dale gave her one last lingering look over his shoulder as he was leaving. He smiled briefly, suggestively, lifting his dark brows. She responded with her most fetching smile, raising her chin slightly in what might be a secret little laugh, a pact. Then she sighed heavily, rather exhausted by all of it. She hoped all the coyness, the acting, the pretending to be gay every moment and intrigued when she was bored would soon culminate in a successful marriage. She doubted she had the stamina to go on like this for long.

After Dale had gone, she began to search more sincerely for the people who had brought her. She was invited to dance, and she obliged though her feet were blistered. The satin-covered slippers lined with white faille that Mary Ellen had provided were too small, but she was without options; she could hardly wear her brown leather kids, and she would *not* be seen limping about.

She danced twice more, though she was less happy about dancing now. She scanned the room, seeing that there were most definitely fewer people; the walls, papered in a French design, were glaringly easy to see. It was not long past midnight—what of the dancing till dawn?

"Excuse me, but I simply must find my escort. I don't see him."

"Well, darling, a little late to think of that, isn't it?"

She stared at her grinning partner. He smiled as though he had some secret on her and she felt her cheeks flood with embarrassment.

The Jaspers and the Kennesdows were not in the room. Her heart began to race in the panic of defeat and she hurried in the direction of the powder room where she found the uniformed maid drowsing in the chair.

"Excuse me," she said, gently jostling the girl's arm. "I'm looking for my friend, Mary Ellen Jasper. Have you seen her?"

"I don't know ma'am. There's been so many."

"Well," Patricia faltered, "she's about so high," she said, using her hand, "wearing a faded rose satin, roses in her hair and along the bodice, and a white fan painted with roses. Oh, and spectacles." And mean as a rabid cat, she wanted to add.

"Oh! Oh, ma'am, is this you?" she asked, reaching into the pocket of her white starched apron and pulling out a note card. Patricia looked at it closely. It bore her name in perfect, large script.

She nodded and took the card, reading the other side. Her face slowly grew crimson. "Keep the dress. You'll need it. I'll have your clothes sent to you. MEJ."

"Well! Of all the—"

"Everything all right, ma'am?" the little maid asked. Clearly the girl could not read, or she would know.

"Fine," Patricia said, lifting her chin and trying to look as though she faced only a minor inconvenience. Or, that she had a plan, which she did not. "Will you find my cloak for me, please? The black velvet with otter trim." If she's bothered to leave me the wrap, she thought venomously. When the cloak was delivered to her, she felt a slight victory—for a moment.

Even within the folds of the costly wrap, no solution came to mind. She wandered down to the foyer, looking into the ballroom. Only a few people were milling about. The members of the orchestra were putting away instruments; the dancing was over. No one she knew was in the room, not one of the nice young men who had danced with her and asked where she lived.

A thick knot of young people stood in the foyer. They seemed to stare at her as a group. She sensed their amusement and superiority, and her throat begin to ache at the thought that she would have to pass through them to leave. Earlier it had seemed worth the risk to wait near the roadside until dawn or to walk the great distance from the senator's house to the park where she could find the first early morning horsecar. She had really believed that some gentlemanly fellow would offer her transportation. Now, when it was so late and dark, and the dozen or so gay young people in the foyer were just waiting to make fun of her as if they knew she'd been abandoned, she felt both foolish and angry. Had they been watching her all evening?

She made her way toward the door, and someone leaned aside and said to his companion, "It'll be our turn to make love next, if she's been left without a gig."

Her cheeks burned, and she bolted toward the door where a servant seemed to bar her departure. "Your escort, madam?"

"He's . . . he's waiting for me in the coach," she stammered.

"Yes, madam," he said, opening the huge double doors. She stepped outside. There was a full moon in a clear sky, better to light her way. She nearly choked on her tears of humiliation. Left behind, her escort and friend gone! How could Mary Ellen do such a mean thing? She would never forgive her!

The drive was lined with five or six coaches, each one monogrammed and therefore not for hire—not that she had the money. The tears filled her eyes, but she walked past the coaches with her chin high. When she had passed the gigs, she stepped off the stone drive and onto the lawn, pulling off the shoes and lifting her bulky skirts. She gulped on a sob. Damn them. Damn them all! Had she thought them generous and indulging? Mightn't Wilbert have fixed her a ride home if nothing else? Didn't he worry what might happen to her, abandoned and left to traverse a dark, country road alone? He could have afforded the cost of a hired carriage even if he didn't wish to share the ride.

She heard laughter behind her as the group she had passed went to their coaches. She refused to turn, knowing they were making sport of her. Were they all so high and mighty that they could laugh at the bad manners of one of their number? Did they think this was *her* fault? She held in her tears.

She walked toward the iron gate that was fixed open for the departure of the rich, horse-drawn traps. Despite her efforts to be stronger than the pain, she limped slightly. A coach rattled by, followed by a second and a third. The horses churned up dirt that she feared might ruin her cloak and gown, the least she had earned from this mortifying night. Damned rich fools, she thought vindictively. I'll show them someday—I'll show them all. Someday the bloody lot of them will be walking home barefoot from my house. Somehow. The tears filled her eyes so that she couldn't see the face of the young man who leaned out the window of his passing coach, waving and shouting, "Have a decent stroll, darling!"

A servant was following her at some distance. It didn't occur to her that he was going to lock the gate; she knew only that she couldn't bear to face even a servant in this disgrace. With a strangled sob, she rushed through the gates and began down the road toward the city. The knotted and gnarled branches of trees formed a dark canopy over the dirt road, blocking the light of the moon, and she cried aloud, her feet throbbing and her heart breaking. This was to be her beginning, her chance to do better with her life! What had gone wrong? What secret little things should she have been told about people with money? Would they have treated one of their own— one like Dorthea Lancaster—with such cruel dismissal? How had they been so certain she was not just like them? How had they *known* she was a nobody?

She was in such misery that she couldn't see very well, and she didn't hear a sound above the noise of departing coaches, their dust only thickening an already dark passage. She was startled when she heard a male voice. She nearly jumped right out of her precious lavender satin.

"It's a mighty long walk," Noel Padgett said. "Like a ride?"

*E*mily didn't sleep, and the reason was very difficult for her to accept. Noel had been wearing a formal suit when he departed in a hired coach, and her curiosity, indeed her *concern* had been provoked. She would hear him return; her opened window above the porch faced the street. Would the scent of perfume waft upwards? Why would he dress so for the evening if there was not a woman? Not for men.

By the chimes she had heard from her highly prized Swiss clock on the pie safe downstairs it was after one, but she waited. To judge his mood, to listen to whether he whistled as he came into her house, to know the exact time, for she cared more than she liked. She hoped she had not contrived his interest, that he would come home tired and bored. And soon.

These worries were both painful and delicious. The

exquisite suffering of wanting a man, barely a memory to her after so many years, made her every sense sharper and more alert, every feeling more intense. She was aware of the risk, the danger of feeling so—but she had never felt more alive! Like being born, the slow, dramatic unfolding of emotion grew wide and full, like the opening of a rose. Noel was not like Ned. Emily Armstrong no longer had anything for which she could be used.

She heard horse hooves and squeaking wheels, hinges and straining bolts that rattled and creaked as horses pulled a gig through ruts on their pot-holed, uncobbled street. If she peeked out the window, she could watch the coach pass under their only gas light, but instead she lay still, anxious, waiting for the sound of his boots on the steps, then on the porch, then on the stair, then— But there were voices! Emily's heart began to pound. She heard Noel's voice and a woman's, both hushed and secretive, the words cloaked by the sound of the hired trap's departure. Surely he wouldn't! He could not imagine she would allow him to bring a woman into her boardinghouse. Yet the soft scream of the screened door as it was being opened was loud. *How dare he!* was her desperate, furious thought. She flounced out of bed instantly, rummaging for the tinder box to light a night candle. She had to search for a wrapper to cover a bedgown that was every bit as concealing as her muslin daywear.

She flew down the hall to light the wall lamp to illuminate the front staircase. In her panicked thoughts she had imagined herself chasing Noel and some evening mistress out of the house, but she was frozen in shock as she looked down toward the front door. Patricia stood at the foot of the stairs, but Emily barely recognized her.

For a moment Emily couldn't move. Patricia stared back, not embarrassed or afraid or ashamed. Her eyes were red as though she'd been crying, but filled with defiance. Emily noticed the daring ringlets that framed her new coiffure. The clothing she wore was strange: a rich, fur-trimmed wrap, buttoned gloves, satin slippers, and peeking out through the folds of the cloak was a shiny gown. Her first frantic conclusion was that Patricia had lied and sneaked away for an evening with Noel!

Noel looked up the staircase at Emily. He had loosened his tie and removed the top two studs so that his shirt was finally comfortable. He observed Emily's mute surprise and confusion, though it was hard for him to remember their problem when he was distracted by the sight of her loosened hair. Long, dark burnished gold hung in a thick mane down her back, just as he had always imagined it would. He had no experience in dealing with problems between mothers and their daughters, but forced himself to seize some instinct. "Mrs. Armstrong," he whispered. "Please. Come downstairs."

Her bare feet were slow on the steps. When she reached the bottom, her gaze drifted between them, her lips parted in question. "Let the girl go to bed," he said. "She's all right, just disappointed."

"Patricia?" she asked.

Patricia lifted her chin. Emily was actually relieved to see her eyes well with tears, replacing defiance. "I was afraid you wouldn't let me go, Mama. Mary Ellen invited me to the party . . . a fancy party at a mansion and then Mary Ellen just *left* me and . . ."

"What have you *done? Oh, Patsy!*"

She felt Noel's fingers gently pinch her elbow. When she looked at him, she was astonished to see pity. "Mrs. Armstrong, I expect you'd like a few answers. We can talk a spell in the kitchen. Let's don't wake up the whole house over this."

Emily reached out to touch Patricia's arm as if to reassure herself that her daughter was here, home, but Patricia actually pulled back. Emily could taste something metallic in her mouth and knew that what she tasted was fear. A distinct image of herself, an image of a girl nineteen years old, sneaking into her mother's house after Ned had seduced her and spoiled her was as clear as if it had happened yesterday. What had her daughter done? And why? Am I too late? Emily asked herself. How can I make her see she must listen to me, believe me? She *must!*

"Mrs. Armstrong. Emily."

"Yes. Yes, we mustn't wake up the boarders. Patsy, go quietly to bed. We'll talk in the morning," she whispered. She wanted to say, "I love you, Patsy." But she didn't.

Patricia rustled noisily up the stairs in her full, borrowed petticoats; Lilly would be awakened and startled but Emily couldn't worry about that now. When Patricia closed her bedroom door, Emily turned to Noel. "Do you know what's happened to my daughter?"

Noel had a heavy kind of weight in his gut and wondered if this was a fatherly feeling. But wouldn't a father have pulled Patricia out of there, or maybe put a strong arm on a few young men? At the very least a father would want to throw up that young coquette's skirts and paddle her rump. He had been trying to decide all evening how he was going to do the right thing—tell Emily the truth about her daughter's behavior—and yet remain in her good graces. "Maybe we could put that teapot to boil?" he asked.

"Oh . . . Mr. Padgett," she began, her hands pulling at the sides of her robe as if considering her state of dress, the hour, what people might think. A naked foot popped out, and she jumped quickly to conceal it. Noel was surprised she didn't gasp and blush. He found her notions of propriety suddenly ridiculous.

"Aw, spit," he muttered, taking her elbow and steering her toward the kitchen. "You know something, Emily, there's nobody can't appreciate all your prim little manners more than me, but you have a young 'un in trouble, and I'm the one brought her home for you." He found a match by the stove and lit a lamp. He then crouched down and found some kindling in the wood box and lit it. When the coal took light off the kindling, he stood and faced her. "There's manners and there's manners. Just now I think we'd all be a sight better off if you'd make yourself a cup of tea and let me tell you what I know about this here party." She stared at him for a long, quiet moment. He lifted his eyebrows. "Find the teapot, Emily," he slowly instructed, and she lurched into the task as though she couldn't have done it by rote and needed someone to direct her. Once in motion, however, she moved with dispatch.

Noel took a step backwards to stay out of her way. She whirled around her kitchen, finding a kettle, ladling water from a bucket, reaching for the china pot high up on a shelf and opening a tea jar. Noel appreciated the sight of her moving around the kitchen in her sleeping clothes, hair unbound, feet bare.

"Emily, you fix that tea. I'll be right back," he said, and went quietly up the back stairs to his attic room, some twenty-five steps, the last twelve nearly straight up, but as soundlessly as a mountain lion. He dropped his tie and coat on the bed and pulled a bottle from his carpetbag; it was time to get a lot of things opened up. Twenty-five steps down brought him back into the warm little kitchen where he found cups and saucers had been placed on the worktable, plus a dish of butter and three fresh buns. He liked the way Emily could gain control by moving around her kitchen. She was the kind of woman who, if she had work, some mission, would be all right. It was only when she didn't know what to do that she could appear

106

helpless. Noel pulled the cork from the whiskey bottle, poured a small draught in each teacup, and placed the bottle on the table.

When Emily turned from the stove she was holding the handle of the steaming kettle with a towel. She stopped short when she saw the whiskey bottle. Her pause was a studied one, but she had recovered her composure by working in her kitchen. She poured the hot water from the kettle into the teapot. "You'll have to get rid of that bottle, Mr. Padgett. You know the rules of this house—spirits are not allowed. And should any of my boarders come into the kitchen and see—"

"Let's just this once drop all these fancy ideas. First off, this isn't spirits—it's whiskey, and I need a shot. You might decide you need one too when you hear about your young woman. Second thing is, ain't no one coming down here tonight. Little Annie and Jamie are all cozy, Mrs. Fairchild sleeps like the dead, you won't see those young girls, and if John Giddings pulls on his drawers to come down the stairs, he'll join us in a drink. He's the only one might, and he thinks so highly of you that you could be sitting here naked with a fistful of playing cards and a cigar in your mouth and he wouldn't say a word to condemn you."

"Mister Padgett!" she whispered almost pleadingly, shocked.

" 'Spose that's about ready?" he said, pointing toward the teapot. "Pour yourself a little over the whiskey and add some sugar. It'll warm you up and calm you down."

"I'm perfectly calm," she replied in a tight voice.

"That might not last long." He waited. He gave a nod toward the teapot, and finally, sighing, Emily poured tea into her cup, but when she moved the spout toward his, he stopped her.

She didn't approve of liquor, but she liked independence. She found his tenacity admirable. It was only whiskey. Noel was not a drunkard. Also, she was grateful that he had brought Patricia home and would not repay him by judging him.

But rather than saying what she felt, she said, "I assure you, Mr. Padgett, I won't be needing this brew for the courage to face whatever my daughter has—"

"Never meant to imply you did, Mrs. Armstrong. Emily." He smiled and lifted his teacup, taking his whiskey neat in one swallow. He held his breath luxuriously, eyes closed, then smiled again. "Just keep it handy, ma'am. Think of it as a tonic."

107

"What happened to my daughter?"

"Well, Emily, I reckon you already figured out she lied to you. She found herself some fancy friends who would take her to a fancy party. And, like she told you, they left her there."

"The Jasper family? Why would they do such a thing? I thought Mary Ellen Jasper was Patricia's good friend." She shook her head in disappointment. "Thank the heavens you were there. She saw you and asked you for a ride?"

"Nope. It wasn't quite that way. I saw her, saw how she had a new partner every dance, and decided I'd better keep an eye on her. Never could tell which young man was her escort. Get her to show you that dress she wore. Now, I'm a man to admire a woman with a nice, plentiful figure . . . unless . . . unless maybe it was my daughter. Seemed like Patricia lost track of the people she went to the party with because she was too busy."

Emily felt her insides tighten; her neck was suddenly stiff and aching. She clasped her hands together to keep them from shaking, and she kept her eyes locked into Noel's, waiting, although she wasn't sure she could bear to hear any more.

"I couldn't really see the point in stepping in to stop her, but on the other hand I knew she didn't have any experience with fancy parties, and I didn't want to leave her in trouble. Beautiful girl, Emily. I reckon she was the prettiest one there. Oh, for a while there I think she was maybe the happiest girl in the whole world, too, because she was sure the one with the most dance partners. The men couldn't keep their eyes off her. Got a few green stares from women, too."

Emily didn't need his delicate explanation. She glanced away, feeling as foolish as if she herself had made a scene. She had seen the new hairstyle and was afraid to have Patricia model the dress. A vision of her daughter came easily: a cheap, garish creature, flirting outrageously, ignoring protocol, dismissing her escort, collecting partners indiscriminately. "How . . . how did you happen to be there, Mr. . . .Noel?"

"Oh. That. The territory of Wyoming, where I have a considerable piece of land and a goodly herd, they thought to make me a representative to the Centennial.

"Truth be known, Emily, I'm here to politic. The territory needs a lot of money; they need railroads, cavalry, land grants, the like. Part of my job during the Exhibition is to shake a lot of hands, get politicians interested in the territory, and maybe bring some business and some money home. I'll have to go to a fancy party or two, meet the people whose influence will help Wyoming."

"You must have a great deal of money," she observed.

He cleared his throat. "Doesn't make me any different, really, if I have some money."

"It does make it a little strange that you're content to stay in a boardinghouse like this one. I'm sure you could afford—"

"The truth is I like it better here than in the hotel. I'm not much for big doings, and I like the company. Turned out to be a good thing, all around, though, that I happened to be at the senator's fancy party."

Noel uncorked his bottle and poured himself another draught. He didn't look at her. "Turned out to be good that Patricia got left behind." The teacup, petite and fragile, looked clumsy in his large, thick hand. "I don't know how I'd have done her any good if she'd gotten in a coach. And that young fella I tossed in the bush was there, talked to her a long while. I weighted the goods against the bads if I had to toss him in another bush."

For me, Emily thought. He'd have done it for me. But what would have happened to Patricia?

"I guess it's no surprise she thinks she's a lot smarter than the rest of us. I remember thinking I was a whole lot smarter than my pa. And he let me think so, too, because telling me different wouldn't have worked. Nope, he let me find out for myself just how smart I was. Wasn't long before it was mighty clear. Maybe Miss Patricia had a lesson tonight."

Emily's hand rose to rest on the table, gingerly reaching for her teacup. She remembered, too. Amanda had tried so desperately to make her listen, but she wouldn't. Her fingers shook slightly as she lifted it to her lips. She took a tiny swallow, letting the burning whiskey warm her all the way down. Then she took another, grateful now for the tonic.

"You must think I'm a terrible mother," she said, her voice hoarse from the drink, which covered any fearful tremors. "Not even knowing where my own daughter was."

"How do you reckon you'd know? She meant for you not to know."

"But it's my *obligation* to know! I should have seen—"

"So you've seen. Now it's your place to be sure she can't fool you again."

109

Emily fought the urge to cry. She was so afraid, so confused. Despite the struggle to feed them, she wished the girls were babies again. What could she do to keep Patricia from getting herself in all manner of terrible trouble? She believed somehow this was her fault; somehow she had failed.

Noel's hand tipped the bottle toward her teacup, and she waved it away. "No . . . no, I despise that terrible brew."

"Go on," he said, brushing her hand aside. "Takes the sting out of nights like this." And she let him pour another small amount, noticing in spite of herself that she did feel slightly less panicked, but a great deal more emotional.

"I suppose," she began while Noel added tea and sugar to her cup, "that many young girls behave rather . . . ah, spontaneously when they become interested in marriage."

"If that was the reason for Miss Patricia's getting herself to that fancy party and getting herself left behind, you wouldn't have any problem at all, ma'am. The problem is a whole lot bigger than marriage."

"Whatever do you mean?"

"I mean, if there was someone she wanted to marry just now, you could sashay around the problem by letting her have him. The problem is that Miss Patricia wants a fancier life than what you have here. And that's a real shame."

Emily let her eyes drop. "I just don't want her to be hurt," Emily said very softly. Without raising her gaze, she lifted the teacup again. She sipped. "Thank you," she said. "For bringing her home and for . . . for the tonic."

"Pleasure, ma'am. And don't worry too much about that young woman getting herself in trouble."

"Do you think I'll be able to talk some sense into her?" she asked, not finding it at all odd, given the tonic and her unsteady nerves, to be asking advice of an unmarried cowboy.

Noel smiled. "Nope. Time for talking's past. Just bolt the door for a spell."

"Yes," she said in resignation. She stood then, feeling a little light-headed, but better. "I'll talk to her in the morning. Good night."

Noel stood. He reached out for her hand. "Emily," he said quietly. "I think the time has come to talk about us. You and me." She let him detain her, blaming the liquor. "There's a reason I'd rather not go to some hotel now. And I think you know what it is."

110

"Mr. Padgett, I think—"

"No, Emily, this time I don't want you to get around it by refusing to say my name. Look here, I want you to listen to me. It's you, Emily. I want to be here with you. I won't pay you any disrespect. I won't hurt your good reputation, but I want you to know—"

"Mr. Padgett, it's after midnight, and I'm wearing my bed-clothes!"

Noel pulled on her hand to draw her closer, and then, slipping his arms around her waist, he embraced her. He waited for a moment, his mouth above hers, giving her a chance to protest his kiss, and when she didn't, he gently lowered his mouth. He regretted that he'd never done a great deal of kissing because he would have liked for this to be the most powerful kiss she'd ever had in her life, and he was unpracticed. He tried not to hurry and just gently coaxed her lips, tasting a bit of her mouth. She didn't invite a deeper kiss. And she didn't embrace him, not quite. She was little, but strong, firm, and she felt good in his arms, against him. The feeling was still easy in him; holding her was right. Her hands lay on his forearms, and he wished she would cling to him, pull him nearer. He kissed her a bit harder and felt her fingertips move into a clench. He wanted to feel more of her, feel some of the signs of a woman liking it, but with all those bedclothes and such there was only her small but solid body and her barely squeezing fingers. Still, she didn't pull away. That wasn't much on which to form a conclusion, but Emily wasn't shy. She wouldn't let him kiss her if she didn't want to.

He continued to hold her, but he took his mouth from hers. "Will you hold me?" he asked her. "Will you kiss me?"

Her eyes didn't open. "I . . . I can't."

"Can't, Emily? Or won't?"

"It's been . . . it's been too long, too—" She was unable to say anything more, unable to open her eyes. She let her head drop against his chest, eyes downcast. And so Noel wondered, too long, too *painful?* Too *lonely? Frightening?*

"Do you miss him? Mr. Armstrong?"

She lifted her head and her eyes opened. "Oh! No! It's not that, it's hard to explain, but I . . . oh, please, don't ask me, don't!"

He didn't try to kiss her again, but he couldn't quite let her go. The feeling was a little less easy in him. That was the only thing he needed to know, that she wasn't pining after someone long dead. In a lot of ways, he decided, Emily was more like an untried virgin than young Miss Patricia. Emily knew about love, about men and women, but she'd learned how to live her life without thinking about that, without yearning or daring or wondering or trying. How else could she have managed, and with a feeling of contentment? It had to be that she'd never considered finding someone new to replace her dead husband. Maybe she had never acknowledged desire.

"That's fine by me," he said softly against her cheek. "You'll tell me all about it when you're ready. But I won't have lies between us. I'll call you 'ma'am' and 'Mrs. Armstrong' around the others and I won't embarrass you—I want you to be happy. But it's you I care about, Emily, and I want it to be right between us. And I think you better know something else. I never cared for a woman like this before."

He let go of her very reluctantly. He took the corked bottle, smiled at her, and turned toward the back stairs.

"Good night," she said.

He turned, not exactly hopeful, but feeling a great many years younger than he was.

"Noel," she softly added, her lips curving.

"Good night. Emily."

The horsecar was nearly full so Lilly and Patricia had to sit on benches opposite each other, their knees nearly touching across the narrow, hay-strewn aisle. Patricia had lifted the hem of her skirt slightly, showing her leather buttoned ankles. Lilly, too, kept her hem off the hay. Although spitting was not allowed, there were telltale brown tobacco spots there, not to mention plenty of mud.

Beside Lilly slumped a twelve- or thirteen-year-old boy, holding newspapers and a lunch tin. She guessed from his posture that he'd already finished a full day's work. On her other side was a slim, mustachioed man who chewed noisily on an unlit cigar and supplied the acrid odor of a chimney sweep. Patricia was wedged tightly between a large, bosomy woman whose wide-brimmed and feathered hat occasionally dipped right over Patricia's left eyebrow and a young woman wearing a maid's cap and a long, heavily starched white apron.

Had the horsecar been less crowded, Lilly would have taken a seat beside her sister and would have been unable to look at her face. Had Lilly really wanted a more exciting life? Since Patricia's evening out in Mary Ellen's second-hand frills, the entire household had become strange. Emily had declared that the gown and accessories would be returned, but she had made no attempt to take care of it. Rather than doing as she'd been told, Patricia had concealed the clothes in the bottom of their armoire. She didn't lie or pretend to have returned them; she simply hid them and said nothing. And neither did Emily!

Lilly had heard the story from Patricia's own lips: Mary Ellen had become jealous of Patricia's prettiness and immediate popularity and sneaked away from the ball, abandoning Patricia. Rather than being contrite and sorry, Patricia seemed rather proud of the fact that had she not been left behind Emily might never have known.

Emily did not scold or lecture. She did not ask Patricia any questions, and Patricia did not supply any explanations. Looking piqued and headachey, Emily had entered their bedroom early on the next morning and was very brief. "Obviously you think yourself a great deal more experienced than I," she said icily. "Since you will not listen to me and you will not let me help you, I am not inclined to try very hard. Consider yourself confined. You will not go out of the house unaccompanied. You will not have visitors. Nor will you attend any functions without my permission."

Today Patricia rode into the city with Lilly to attend a lecture presented by the Presbyterian Women's Lyceum Series on Chinese Missions. Lilly was interested in China and all foreign countries, but she definitely did not care about missionary work. One, unfortunately, went along with the other. But Patricia? Lilly had underestimated her sister's need for fresh air.

Patricia gazed across the aisle, over Lilly's shoulder, at the passing houses and businesses. Her eyes were cool, her expression remote. Lilly had tried to get her to tell all; surely there was a great deal more. How Mr. Padgett had come to be at the fancy party, for one thing. But Patricia had never asked, didn't care, and since she was now confined to the house, Lilly had not been able to read the wonderful pages of her journal where she believed a great drama lived. She had worried that Patricia suffered from melancholia, so distant was her gaze, so detached was her behavior, but, in the days since, Lilly had decided that Patricia displayed derision. Resentment. Haughtiness!

"Aren't you afraid Mama will never forgive you?" Lilly had asked.

"I imagine she won't, and who cares? I knew Mama would not have allowed me, and so I went without permission." Patricia had shrugged, dismissive, as though she had little connection to this irate mother. "Mama is angry, I won't be allowed out, and what does it all matter? It's over, anyway."

"But was it wonderful? Elegant?"

"Do you mean until suddenly, left without a proper escort home, I was forced to begin walking? As you might imagine, a very lovely night ended badly."

"But *why?* Oh, Patsy, why were you left? Did you do something daring? Did you say something mean? Did you dance with a lot of men? Did you tell where we live so that they could call?"

Patricia's expression never changed from that perturbed, but sullen look she had been wearing since returning from her fancy ball. She was barely civil and, for the first time ever, had no grand ideas, plans, or melodramatic descriptions. But in answer to Lilly's questions, a spark of anger had lit Patricia's eyes. Looking away, she had answered, "I did not say or do anything to warrant Mary Ellen's shabby treatment of me. I'd rather not talk about it."

"Well, it's the first time in history you haven't been able to talk about something, Patsy Armstrong. Just what are you plotting now? Come along and tell, then. Don't I keep all your secrets, even when I shouldn't?"

"How am I to plot when I'm not allowed any farther than the porch swing? It would be a waste of time, wouldn't it?"

Lilly paid close attention. No gentlemen who met her at the fancy ball had come to the house, Mary Ellen did not attempt to reconcile, and Emily and Mr. Padgett whispered quite often. Patricia wore an air of superiority, censure, but for whom and what, Lilly was unsure. It seemed as though Patricia had dismissed them all—the fancy people at the party, the friend who had loaned her clothes, the mother who disciplined her, the sister who was nearly dying of curiosity. She was not warm or grateful toward Mr. Padgett, who had rescued her. She had not apologized. Indeed, she did not show remorse or express any regrets, as though *she* were above reproach. The fact was, Lilly believed, Patricia had gone completely hardboiled.

The horsecar slowed as they came to Rittenhouse Square. Lilly wanted to get off here, walk across the square and pass the theater. She glanced around for Andrew, but couldn't imagine what she'd say to him with Patricia present. She was frankly surprised that Patricia did not protest. There was something quite peculiar about Patricia's docility.

"I can't imagine why you'd be interested in this lecture," Lilly said as they walked.

"Well, it's not as though I had plans of my own," Patricia said.

"You have no plans of any kind," Lilly said. "And it's the first time ever." Lilly looked at Patricia, but Patricia stared straight ahead. She looked older somehow. Her neck was long and lovely above her high-collared, starched blouse. Emily left the whole matter of the forbidden haircut alone, and Patricia pulled her hair into a clutch of curls on the back of her head and wore her ringlets around her face. But it was not the hairstyle that changed her, it was her lifted chin, her cold eyes, and her obstinate posture. "I wish I knew what you wanted, Patsy," Lilly said. "I'd get it for you so you could be happy again."

"I'm perfectly happy," Patricia replied, her voice chilly.

"You're about as happy as a corpse. And I don't understand it at all."

Patricia had the simplest of desires, the simplest of goals, and no one understood. While she wept from a broken heart in Mr. Padgett's coach, he lectured her that she'd mistaken all those fancy strangers for decent people. In her heart she ached to have something to be proud of, something to flaunt, something that would impress people, and Mr. Padgett had only misinterpreted this, suggesting that she was foolish to forsake a perfectly nice lot in life. He did not understand that she was only trying to better herself. She was *striving*. In the only way she knew.

She hoped Lilly would sympathize, understand she had only intended to meet people, to make friends, perhaps find a new beau —a man of greater possibility. Even Lilly ridiculed her, calling her deceitful and selfish, asking straight out what she'd done or said to warrant mistreatment.

None of the fashionable young men who had danced with her

bothered to call on her—another failure. And their mother! Emily acted as though Patricia were a fallen woman, someone shameful. She didn't say so, but it was all in what Emily had *not* said.

Patricia wouldn't talk to them, not even to Sophia. But *they* were talking about *her*. Even John Giddings somehow knew. John almost never spoke to her, but he shyly asked her if there was any way he could help her! As if she were at the fulcrum of a great scandal!

As she walked across Rittenhouse Square with her sister, she imagined this outing a mere formality, another disappointment to be shouldered. She supposed that Dale Montaine would not appear, just as her escort had failed her at the party and her dance partners had forgotten her address. Patricia didn't know exactly where and how she had miscalculated in her plan. She didn't feel she wanted very much from life. Unlike her mother and sister, she just wanted to have a life that was as little trouble as possible. She wanted only to have fun and couldn't imagine a woman wanting to have a lot of work. Perhaps if she were naturally quite smart, like Lilly, she would want to become the smartest woman in the world. Or, if she were naturally energetic and proper, she might want a boardinghouse full of people to take care of like her mother's. In Patricia's mind Lilly and Emily proved themselves daily, through studies or chores or good deeds. People often commented on Lilly's intelligence or Emily's fortitude and charity, but the only compliments Patricia received concerned her good looks and charm. Among so many homely and boring women, she found it odd that a nice, well-to-do gentleman hadn't discovered that what Patricia had to offer was worth a great deal.

She finally came to the only possible conclusion: Mary Ellen had let her down. Perhaps she had been just a little bit too flirtatious, a trifle too daring. She had learned a few things. Given her enforced seclusion, she had plenty of time to think things over and decide on a better way to proceed. She was relieved in a way. She was tired of being alluring, of being pawed and slobbered on by potential husbands. She needed a little rest. She was almost glad that the fancy party had not proved to be the beginning of a wonderful and elegant life. Apparently, an elegant life was more exhausting than it appeared to be.

It's just as well, then, she thought glumly.

Lilly read the theater bills over and over while Patricia waited, faintly envious. It would be nice to have some interest she could pursue alone, some fascinating study that did not involve acting out

parts and worrying constantly about whether there would be someone at hand to admire her. It would be nice, she thought, not to be
lonely.

"I wondered if you'd come. I'm glad you did."

She had so convinced herself that he had forgotten, his voice
actually startled her. "Dale!"

"My coach is just around the corner. Come for a ride?"

Patricia glanced at her sister.

"She won't tell anyone, will she? She's your sister, after all."

It occurred to Patricia that Dale had proven himself, in a sense.
His presence confirmed his genuine attraction to her. She decided to
challenge him further, to find out just how much he was willing to
endure to have her.

"You might as well know," she said, "that I'm in terrible trouble
over that awful party. I didn't tell my mother I was going, and my
friends abandoned me there, left me without an escort or a ride home,
and now my punishment is that I'm confined. If I failed to attend
the lecture with my sister today, she would not only tell Mama, my
punishment would stretch out for the rest of my life."

"Why didn't you tell your mother about the senator's party?
Wouldn't she have been delighted that you'd been invited?"

"Of course she should have been, but Mama isn't like that at
all. She isn't impressed by fancy parties, and she is just *very* strict.
When she makes up her mind about something, she is impossible!"

He smiled, though his lips hardly moved and his teeth did not
show. He put his hands in his pockets and rocked back on his heels.
A lock of his dark hair fell forward on his forehead and his brown
eyes were leveled into hers. "And, she's made up her mind about me,
has she?"

"As a matter of fact—"

"Then we'll have to be very careful to show her I'm not such a
bad fellow. Anyone would let his temper show when the girl he wants
is taken by another."

"I haven't been taken by anyone. Not yet."

"Perhaps you'd rather a beau who doesn't care how many other
men you're interested in. Hmmm?"

"You were jealous?" she asked coyly.

"Come now, you know perfectly well you're the most beautiful
woman in Philly. Don't pretend you don't know it."

"I don't know any such thing," she said, lowering her eyes and

117

her chin. Underneath her downcast and demure posture, her lips curved upward. This was how she intended it. Didn't men want beautiful and charming women?

His finger lifted her chin. His dark eyes were strong, intense. "I want you. And you know it. And I think you want me as well."

"What do you want me *for*, Dale?"

He dropped his hand from her chin. His concentration caused him to frown slightly. "I want you to be on my arm at the balls, at the parties. I want you to ride with me to the horse races and cricket matches in an open carriage so that everyone in Philadelphia knows that the most beautiful woman in the city is mine. And if you don't have any intention of being the woman with me, tell me now. I don't want to waste my time."

For a moment Patricia thought about her actual dislike for him. But there was no other, and she wanted those things he described. "Of course I want it to be me, Dale. But I can't defy my mother without making it much more difficult than it already is. She is angry, you see."

"Well, we can't have that. When do you suppose the cage will be opened and my little bird will fly again?"

Lilly turned from the bills and saw Patricia talking to Dale. Lilly glared at them, then turned back.

"It won't be soon," Patricia said. "On the other hand, if I'm very well behaved, Mama can't really hold me prisoner forever."

"It will seem like forever," he said. "I've looked forward to this day all through the week."

"I think you're only trying to flatter me, Dale. Didn't you have anything more exciting than this to do with your time?"

"I have plenty to do, but I would like to do it with you."

All along I was right, she thought. It was too simple an idea to be wrong—men, especially rich, passionate, and popular men like Dale wouldn't waste their time on ugly, boring women. Why should he treat a woman from a rich family with any more deference than he would show me? Doesn't he already have piles of money? Why should he want a more prestigious bride? Everyone in Philadelphia knew about the Montaines! Dale wants beauty and charm. He *has* everything else already. "I'll be allowed out. Soon."

"When?"

"Be patient, Dale," she whispered. "I simply must show Mama that I can be a good girl."

"Do good girls go to lectures?" He smiled, and she smiled with him. "Next week?" he asked.

Patricia thought there was no better way to intrigue him, to force him to prove his stamina and desire, than to have him consume an entire day to gain only a few moments in civil conversation. Of course there was also the fact that under these circumstances she needn't endure his clumsy caresses.

Patricia didn't hear the lecture. It didn't matter. She wouldn't be asked about it. No one asked her questions of an intellectual nature. She thought of the future in the way she had before the ball. It was a good thing that she hadn't let her head be turned away from Dale, for he was going to be the one. He wanted her. To have her he would have to marry her. In her married state she would be elevated to a position so high above Mrs. Jasper that the overfed, arrogant gorilla and her monkey of a daughter would grovel for a kind word.

"Did you *know* he was going to be there?" Lilly asked when they were waiting for the horsecar to go home. Her tone was accusatory and her manner piqued.

Patricia looked into her younger sister's eyes. "Did you see me do *anything* wrong?" she asked in an angry, whispering voice. "*Anything?* Did I behave badly? Flirt more than you like? Faint, swoon, tromp on his feelings?"

Lilly was struck silent by the cutting edge in Patricia's voice.

"If I did nothing wrong, must we make an issue of it?"

"Patsy, Mama doesn't think you should see Dale."

"Then if you choose, you may tell her. I'm sure she'll come up with some horrid punishment so that I'll never see him again. But *why* would you betray me when I haven't done anything bad? Don't you love me anymore, Lilly? Can't you let me be happy? Ever?"

"I don't want you to be hurt," Lilly said quietly.

"No, that's not it. You and Mama *judge* me! You don't understand that I'm not happy doing my chores or reading a book about apes!"

"No, Patsy, no—"

"Did you see anything harmful in my conversation with him? Did you see him do anything I should be protected from?" Lilly shook her head, but she didn't feel right. "Lilly, you and Mama are made happy by the same things; by work and study and strict behavior. If I do anything different, it seems wrong. It is not wrong!

119

Dale is a handsome and rich young man, and it makes me *happy* that he pays attention to me!"

"Patsy, Mama wants you to tell the truth. You're lying again! Keeping these secrets!"

"He happened past and saw me, and he was delighted to see me again! Lord knows he would be tossed over the porch rail if he came like a gentleman to my home! If you spoil everything by telling, I will never forgive you! Never!"

f anyone had suggested to me two months ago that I might be courted by the same shaggy cowboy who toted a saddle up my front walk, I would have declared that person mad," Emily said.

"Courted?" Noel replied, his mustache tilting.

Emily laughed, a bright sound full of sparkle. "I hope that's the worst anyone would say. Are you not at all worried that someone will discover what we've done?"

Noel, who had been reclining on the blanket, sat upright, reached into the picnic basket, and took out an apple. His sleeves were rolled up, the top two buttons of his shirt unbuttoned, and he would have taken off his boots, but he did not dare. Even though Emily could now respond to his kiss, he suspected she might still be outraged by the sight of his naked toes. In due time, he told himself. "Nope," he answered her.

"And if someone asks us what went on in Penn Square today, and we say, 'Why, not a thing of interest,' when there happened to be an orchestra giving an afternoon concert and the word has gotten back—"

He laughed at her. He chewed a mouthful of apple and swallowed. "Would you feel better if we drove past the square and asked some of the people there if there was any event worth mentioning?"

She shook her head. Her lips, bright pink from kissing, curved into a smile. "How did you find this place?"

"I looked."

"For a private place. If I didn't know better, Noel, I would think you were ashamed to be seen in public with me."

He reached toward her, giving an affectionate squeeze to the knee nestled under her long skirt. "But you do know better."

She had been skittish at first. Just getting her to consent to a picnic had taken some time. Noel believed she had discussed it with Sophia; the black woman smiled at him in a knowing way, both amused and approving. Emily worried about the boarders, the neighbors, her daughters. "What will they *think?*" she had asked him. "Why, they might accuse us of keeping company," he had said with a smile. "How terrible!" They had exclaimed this in unison, finally laughing together.

Actually, for a woman to keep company with a boarder in her house was not of the worst improprieties. In fact, this happened among working-class people with regularity. It was not unheard of for a boarder to make his intentions toward a landlord's daughter known. There were circumstances that made it decent: a number of household residents keeping watch, thin walls between the rooms to discourage any sneaking around, and of course an established reputation. Emily Armstrong's morals had never been questioned by any member of her church or neighborhood in the nine years she had lived in her house.

Emily had finally accepted. Perhaps Sophia had convinced her.

When they finally rode away from the boardinghouse in an open buggy, he told her that he had a place other than a public park in mind. A private place, far off the country road. Appearances, she had said. Reputation, she had whispered. Her eyes were bright and almost alarmed. Also, perhaps, intrigued. "If you're afraid to be alone with me, Emily, you just have to say so," he had told her. "I sure don't want you to have a bad time. But if you reckon you're safe, I'd far rather be with *you* than a whole crowd."

He had ridden around the countryside with a mission, searching for a nice place where they could be alone, where he could take her into his arms, kiss her and hold her, and no one would see. He'd been giving her hand a secret squeeze, stealing a peck on the cheek, brushing up against her quick and then jumping out of the way before a boarder or daughter caught them. She wanted a private place, too, but couldn't say so. And she'd nearly twisted her neck into a knot surveying the area he'd finally chosen for their picnic. Now, finally, she was not only calmed down, but happy.

It was a beautiful place, up on a little hill in tall grasses, open for quite a distance around. There was a shallow brook running below them; had he been alone, he might have dropped a line. The horse that had drawn their buggy grazed nearby. They walked, ate a delicious cold lunch, held hands. And did a great deal of passionate kissing. He finished his apple and tossed the core into the stream. Then he reclined again, putting his head in her lap.

She touched the red-gold hair by his ear. His scalp was beginning to show through the more sparse hair on top. She touched his mustache. "I'm thinking I might shave it," he said.

"Oh, you couldn't!"

"It leaves too much proof on your skin." His finger came up to her lip, and she gently kissed the tip. "What will we do next, Emily?" he asked.

"Oh," she sighed, sounding either sad or tired. "I don't know. I've barely accepted the here and now."

"It can be any way you say."

Her memory was tugged and it brought a woeful sigh. "More than anything else, Noel, you've been the dearest friend. I hadn't thought I needed a friend this much."

"You have a lot of friends. So many friends a man can hardly—"

"Not friends, really. Boarders, neighbors, family. Except Sophia, who is truly a friend." She tweaked his mustache. "Lacking in some things," she teased.

"Would you tell a good friend?" he asked. "Tell me, Emily, what worries you? What holds you back?"

"I think you've guessed. Haven't you?"

"Nope. You been alone sixteen years and you don't seem the kind of woman should be alone."

"I hope you won't think poorly of me, Noel. I haven't confided to anyone before. I've told Sophia a little, but Sophia is the kind of woman who understands a great deal without needing to be told. And my daughters . . . well, I find the truth too cruel for them. So cruel that there are times I wish I didn't remember so well. My marriage did not last long at all. Exactly two years after Lilly was born, President Lincoln called for Union soldiers—and I was not sorry that my husband left me. I have not seen my husband, nor his body, since." She let her eyes meet his. She felt stronger by telling him this much. And she didn't think for one moment that he would think poorly of her; it had become a habit of hers to apologize for unseemly behavior ahead of time. "I have never missed him."

They were surrounded by quiet while their eyes embraced. "I was afraid you missed him," Noel finally said. His voice was quiet as a whispering breeze, filled with relief.

"I was not so young that I should have been so foolish," she said. "My father had died, and my mother and I, in our grief and fear of being alone, could not agree on anything. I believed I loved the man I married. Worse, I believed he loved me. We were together very briefly, a harsh time. My daughters don't remember him. He was a terrible, angry man, a liar of the worst stamp. He had given no clue that he would abuse me. He had courted me gently, but he was not a gentle man. I should have acknowledged his lies, but young love," she said, "is too ignorant for words."

Noel's complexion darkened in anger. His lips were tight. He wanted to know what her husband had done to her. He wanted to ask, but didn't dare. First, he had to let her tell her piece at her own speed. Second, he didn't know how he might react if she told the worst. He watched her eyes.

"I don't want Patricia and Lilly to know how mean and uncaring their father was, but at times I'm nearly persuaded to tell Patricia, shock her into hearing me, frighten her into taking fewer risks. I defied my mother and Patricia defies me. I married impetuously, full of ridiculous notions of how many ills love would cure, and the truth came hard. I'm afraid it could happen to my daughter, yet I don't know how to prevent it."

"Are you ever afraid that's how it would be with me?" he asked

124

her. "Do you ever think I'm well-mannered now, and later you'll find out the truth about me?"

"No," she said honestly. "The past two months have been like growing up all over again. I had been afraid of these feelings. And . . . I had been afraid I was long *past* feeling them." She massaged his temples with her fingertips. "What about you, Noel? Why haven't you married? Is there a broken heart in your past?"

"Well, I don't know," he said. "Once." He laughed. "Not like yours. I found me a woman on my second trip out to Colorado to visit with my pa. My pa wasn't a talker—he pretty much snorted and grunted his answers and never sat me down to talk. By the time he died, we had a whole language of just sounds. When I was young and was with him for a while between schools—a real stickler, he was, determined I'd get schooling—he kept himself busy with the land, traps, horses, the ranch. He was tough and silent. There was a trading post down river, and I'd go there sometimes. The biggest event of my week was when my pa would let me take the wagon or boat to the post. And I fell in love with this woman who lived near there. Seemed she was always there when I passed by and always smiled at me. I thought she loved me, too. Now I was seventeen, mind. I don't know her age. And, never wondered if she was married, or how she earned her keep, or why she was always free to be sitting out front, smiling and waving and talking through the door rather than working. So, I told my pa that I wanted to see this lady, court her, take her a present, and maybe have her fix me a supper. And my pa looked at me real peculiar, a frown like, and then he said, 'Well, then, I reckon you're ready.' That was the extent of his lessons about men and women. Can you guess the rest?" he asked.

"No," she said, innocent, curious.

"Do you think you can stand to hear it?"

"Why? Is it shocking?"

"Well," he chuckled, his cheeks darkening in spite of himself. "It's pretty well accepted out West, especially around trading posts and forts. There's a lot of men, tired, hard-working, long-traveled men. Not a lot of women—just a few wives and daughters. And a few like that one I thought I loved."

"Oh!"

"Turned out she just wasn't the marrying kind."

"Oh! You must have been outraged! Poor boy, to stumble into the path of a woman without virtues!"

"Now there you go," he laughed. "She was a good woman, more or less. She wasn't proper, I don't mean that. But she wasn't a liar or thief. She was fair and pretty and kind to everyone. The other women wouldn't talk to her. I reckon they were afraid their husbands went to her house."

"But you didn't *respect* her!"

"I never disliked a person with a tender heart. She lived an honest way. Now, if she was pretending to be the preacher's wife when she was really something else, then I wouldn't respect her. But she didn't pretend to be anything she wasn't."

"But you didn't—?"

"Now, Mrs. Armstrong, you don't expect a gentleman would talk about a lady." He smiled broadly at her crimson blush. "Shame on you. You're hankering to know."

"You're teasing me! You and your tall tales of the West!"

"What's going to happen with us next, Emily?" he asked again, causing her smile to fade into that serious, contemplative expression.

"I don't know. I'm afraid to think about that yet."

"There isn't any reason for you to be afraid. Of anything."

"So easily said. I'm not a young girl, Noel. I have a house to keep, daughters to raise, responsibilities. I can't ignore all that, I can't start over, I can't just pretend that at this age I can—"

"I love you, Emily. Aside from that one time, when I was just a boy, I haven't loved a woman. You don't have to make up your mind about me, but you don't have to be afraid. I'm a forty-year-old man, Emily. Can't neither one of us start over. All we can do is go on."

She looked away, and he sat up. He put an arm around her waist. "All this talking," he said. "That's what I missed growing up. I think that's what I like second best about us." She glanced at him, smiling sheepishly. "You're a good talker, Emily. Good listener, too. Do you reckon that since we're as old as we are, we'll do more talking than anything else?" He waited for her answer, but it didn't come. She was covered with evidence; her eyes were fever bright, her lips were chafed from kissing, and there was excitement, temptation in her smile. "You stop talking, though, when it comes to your worries. You just can't ask me, can you? But you know the biggest reason you had yourself a bad husband is because you didn't talk things over much first."

126

When she didn't reply, he took her by the shoulders and gently lowered her down on the blanket. She lay on her back, looking up at him; Emily had a way of looking at him so head-on that he felt the same as when her arms held him close. He kissed her lips, softly, not wanting to chafe her skin any more than he had. Then he stretched out his long legs to lie down too, on his side, his chest against her chest.

"I'll marry you," he said. She looked away instantly. "Or not, whatever you say. But we're going to be together, you and me, pretty soon."

"I'm thirty-seven years old, Noel. In some ways that's old—in other ways it's not old enough."

"I know a few things, Emily. I know how to keep from giving you a baby."

She gave a little huff of rueful laughter.

"But I'm telling the truth," he said, as if he knew she'd been told that lie before.

"There is no way to prevent that."

"There is. More than one way. If you're worrying that you're too old to have any more children—"

"You don't want a child of your own? A son?"

He shrugged. "A little late for all that, I think. But now I've found you, I'm not letting you get away."

"You're hurrying me. You're—"

"No, Emily, there ain't no hurry. On the other hand, let's not waste a lot of time. We've both been alone long enough."

He kissed her again, and again his lips were gentle on hers. His fingers, a little clumsy on the tiny buttons, opened her blouse at the throat. He kissed the hollow of her neck and felt her pulse. He lowered his mouth to the lace top of her camisole and nibbled at it. Her skin became flushed, fragrant, salty, warm. Against his cheek, through the blouse and camisole, he felt her nipple become hard, and he raised himself up, looking into her eyes while he gently worked open three more buttons.

He remembered twenty-three years back. He'd washed, put on his good shirt and jacket, and taken a fistful of wildflowers to the shack by the trading post. Her name was Rosemary, and she came to the door in a shift so transparent he could see the two dark spots on her full breasts and the shadow of dark hair where her legs were joined. Two men sat at her table sharing a bottle. He'd been so angry he dropped the flowers and ran back to his pa, but he hadn't told anything.

He asked around then and found out how much, found out who she'd do it for. Then he went by in the daytime and asked her if she'd do it for him. And she said she would, but she looked pretty doubtful, like maybe she didn't really want to. But he squared off his thin shoulders—he'd been six feet tall for a long time but hadn't filled out much—and said he wanted to be sure he was the only one that night. Double then, she said, still looking like the idea didn't sit well with her.

He didn't bother with the flowers or his best shirt. He did take a bath in the river, though. And he would never forget how scared he had been—not that it had changed his mind about what he'd wanted. And he vaguely remembered anger, like a boy left out of the game.

She asked him why he came to her. He told her that if she was bedding with all the other men she didn't love, she shouldn't mind doing it with him. She did love some of them, she said. The ones that were lovable. Most weren't, she added. But a few of the men who crossed her porch and went inside were like angels; they knew what to do, how to make a woman happy, and she hated to take their money. She wouldn't, in fact, if she didn't need it. He told her he wouldn't likely be one of them, since he didn't know much about it. Well then, she had said, come here and let me show you how to be one of the angels—where to put your fingers, your lips—because you would be an easy one to love. And she had refused to take his money. She had gentled him into manhood, and the fear, the anger, the disillusionment—all the things that had driven him—fell away.

Noel cupped Emily's breast in his large hand. He used his thumb to slowly lower her camisole. Even though each was with someone new, in part they loved from memory. It was not other people they thought about now, but how their bodies were meant to respond at a time like this. This was not the frenetic, excitable whimsy of the young; it was not the giddy yet explosive need of curious children. They shared a tender passion that was effortless, natural, yet new. First love was clumsy, wildly expedient. This was mature love—love that knew how to reach out and touch in an almost familiar way, taking simple, solid, uncomplicated pleasure from each other. It was good that they were older. There would be less nonsense, and loving was serious business. It was easier to accept the joy of a lover's touch and feel grateful.

His tongue teased her erect nipple, and he felt himself grow hard. He wished he wouldn't yet, but it was too late. He figured he was going to suffer some. He sucked at her gently and grew stiffer when she moaned. He was going to actually hurt, but he'd have to be willing to hurt some for her. His hand ran down over her slender skirt and he began to slowly gather it up while his mouth played leisurely against that prominent little knob. Underneath he found a bounty of underclothes; enough to have done a dry goods store a good day's business. But her pantalets were short and loose around her thighs. His fingers entered; he spread his hand across her abdomen. He was slow; he wanted her to know from his unhurried caress that he regarded this as a luxury. His fingers, though thick and callused, moved delicately over the hair and down.

He pushed himself against her thigh so she would know that what had happened to her had also happened to him. There was no resistance in Emily, and he knew this meant trust. Her body yearned. As did his. The feeling was not easy with him anymore. He took her mouth with his while his fingers moved deeper. Deep, into her, where she was lush.

"Not yet," she whispered after the kiss. "Not yet."

He had really known that. Still when the time came it was so hard to accept. Her body was ready, but her heart and mind were reluctant. Grown-up lovers, he reminded himself, didn't only know how to respond genuinely, they also knew how to savor each touch and taste ... and how to wait. He wouldn't make the mistake of forcing her to repeat herself even once. He didn't have to win. Even if he could have her despite protests, what would he have? Not enough. He would hear her invite him sometime, and that would make it right. He pulled his hand away from her flesh and smoothed down her skirt. He lay his head on her shoulder and began to attempt to redo those tiny buttons.

"I'm sorry," she whispered.

"Never be sorry with me," he returned. "Let's just lay here quiet and still for a minute."

"I shouldn't have let you—"

"You should have. Shhhh." He resigned himself that he could not, under the circumstances, handle those little buttons. He pulled the blouse closed and left it like that. And it was quite a while before he trusted his breathing enough to rise up, look in her eyes, and say, "Don't ever be sorry with me. I'm a patient man, Emily. And I promise I won't hurt you, hurry you too much, or be angry with you. It's high time you stopped blaming yourself for the things other people say and do. That was him, not me."

He wouldn't be able to forget, though, how quickly she was ready for him. She was so contradictory, which only made her more desirable. She was proper, generous, and always caring about doing the right thing. A good woman. And then there was that heat in her blood, as natural in Emily, who had remained chaste, as in Rosemary. Who would think, to look at Emily, to listen to her, that she had such passion? She was afire with it. He promised himself he would not let her down, not ever.

Their ride home in the afternoon in the open carriage was sweet in silence, their hands touching now and then. It was curious the way he'd remembered Rosemary. When he'd seen her again a few years later, she'd gotten a lot more than a few years older. He remembered her prettier, softer, younger. But she was still kind and good in her heart. Tender. Soon Noel realized that the feeling of love made people appear more perfect than they really were.

Noel had not been with many women. There had been only a few. He didn't know whether he was good with them, whether the things he'd been taught were useful. He wasn't a confident lover, only sincere. He'd learned that grown people can cry like small, hurt children on the inside and pretend they didn't. So he was careful, meaningful in what he did. Especially in the act of loving. He wanted to be pleasing, and usually women acted pleased if he judged right. For the first time in all those years he had a feeling like he'd had with Rosemary—that feeling that he wanted to crawl inside a woman and be part of her. He loved Emily. Like her, he had feared he was past that.

"Thank you," she said quietly when they were on her street. "It was a lovely, lovely day."

"Was it?" he asked her. "Did it make you happy?"

"Oh yes, Noel. Yes."

"And not afraid?"

She touched his hand. "Not afraid. Just give me a little time to get accustomed to this. It's been so long since I've trusted good feelings."

His mustache lifted, and his teeth showed in a grin. But behind his grin he had a thought. *She hasn't said she loves me.*

Lilly was aware of a new conspiracy in the boardinghouse, and for once it didn't involve Patricia. Because of Lilly's age and the limited experience she had with romantic love, she was slow to realize what was happening. To begin with, hushed conversations continued long past Patricia's troubles. Emily, with uncalled-for gravity, had talked to Lilly.

"I have been invited to make a picnic lunch and go for a buggy ride with Mr. Padgett, Lilly. Next Saturday."

Lilly had stared at her mother, not at all sure what was expected of her. She finally shrugged.

"And would you approve?" Emily had asked, her brows furrowing as though she braced herself for a response.

"Well, yes, I suppose, I—Why wouldn't I approve, Mama?" Or why would my approval matter? she wanted to ask. It had not occurred to her until much later that Emily's sense of responsibility was so deep that she felt she needed permission from anyone who might be affected by her actions.

Emily had touched her hand, grateful, saying, "Thank you, dear. That's very generous of you."

Lilly suddenly realized what her mother was trying to say. She was *keeping company!* And Lilly had to hold back her giggles. She liked Mr. Padgett. He was most entertaining with his stories about the West, and there was no question but that he was an unselfish man. But Emily had always rejected suitors! Better looking and more established suitors than the cowboy.

"That would be so nice for you, Mama. You do actually like Mr. Padgett, don't you?"

"I do like him, Lilly. That doesn't bother you, does it?"

Lilly had laughed, causing her mother's complexion to take on a slightly darker hue. "Oh, Mama, I trust you'll mind your manners."

"Yes, Lilly," she promised, poised and maternal once again, "I'll mind my manners."

"Have a fun time," Lilly said, turning to leave the parlor where

131

their conversation had taken place. "Oh, and Mama," she said in an afterthought, "don't ask Patricia if she minds."

"Why not?"

"Well, for one thing, she'll barely notice you've gone. And for another, she minds *everything*." Again Emily had smiled. In the end, however, she had told Patricia of her plans. And Lilly was correct—Patricia minded.

"I said to her, 'My goodness, Mama, you don't mean to say he *interests* you!' " Patricia reported.

"You didn't really! Poor Mama finally has something to do besides work, someone to talk to besides Sophia, and what do you do? You discourage her! Shame on you."

"What if she were to marry him? I would be mortified! He's so awful looking! And he's not even from the city!"

"And I suppose Dale Montaine is such a prize by comparison?"

"This has nothing whatever to do with anyone else," she said.

"Who is handsome and correct for Mama, Patricia?" Lilly asked, and asked sincerely.

Patricia stuttered. She stammered and opened her mouth several times, uttering little sounds but no answer.

"No one," Lilly said. "Isn't that right? You don't think Mama has any right to a beau."

Patricia's eyes narrowed. "Papa was right."

"How do you know? Do you remember him?"

"It doesn't matter. She loved him and married him. He was the right one, then."

Lilly looked at her sister with level and solemn eyes. "Who is right for you, Patsy?" she asked quietly.

"I'm not sure yet," she said, tossing her head in a dismissive fashion. And Lilly suddenly knew that Patricia, for all her flirting, had not yet met anyone she truly liked.

"I would think you'd be very grateful to Mr. Padgett for rescuing you from the party."

"I thanked him. That doesn't mean I'm offering up Mama."

"Patricia, you are too selfish. And if you dare say another word to Mama to discourage her from having a good time, I'm going to tell about Dale being, just by chance, at the theater every Thursday afternoon."

Patricia had fixed her with a glare that chilled her through and through.

But Emily had her picnic. Lilly, being very interested in watching all of this romance happening right under her own roof, had waited for their return, eager to hear all about it. When she opened her mouth to ask, Sophia had interrupted with chores for her to do and said, "Why don't you, jes' this once, mind your own business."

Lilly noticed at dinner that no one asked, as though they had agreed beforehand. There was a comical strain on all the faces, as if an unfurled peacock sat in the middle of their dinner table but must not be mentioned. They seemed to be ignoring this courtship. Eyes darted about to meet fleetingly, and lips curved in little smiles of knowledge. No one would risk embarrassing or discouraging Emily. Lilly, too, remained silent. Patricia was the only one who had a different reason for not asking about the picnic; she was sullen, disapproving, and possibly jealous. She did not want her mother to be seen with that frightful cowboy. He seemed so odd, even if he did have important friends.

A few days later, late in the evening, Patricia and Lilly were getting ready for bed. Patricia sat before the mirror and brushed her hair. She rarely spoke except to complain. Lilly sat cross-legged on the bed, her pen flying over the pages of her journal.

"Something wonderfully secret is happening in our house and it has to do with love. I've never known Mama to be unhappy—I've never seen her cry, not once—but she is showing a new, glowing brightness. Her steps are light, her voice is gentler than ever before, and when she looks at our cowboy-boarder, her eyes are filled with affection. Things that once threw Mama into a fit bother her hardly at all. For the first time she does not do so many evening chores, but sits on the porch swing night after night, talking with Mr. Padgett. When I remarked that we usually beat the rugs on Saturdays, she said it could wait a week, and Mama has never before gone off her schedule. She is in love with our boarder, and he with her. There will be a wedding."

Lilly was charmed by their exchanged glances, but Patricia was appalled. But then Patricia was hard to please, and it was doubtful that any man would quite do for Mama. Still, even Patricia seemed to cheer some when Mr. Padgett announced after dinner that he had a surprise for the entire household. His business was with the Centennial Exhibition, and he brought passes for everyone. Both the admission and the ferry tokens were passed around, but for Emily,

Patricia, and Lilly there was an even greater gift; he wished to escort them, treat them to dinner at a foreign restaurant on the grounds, and buy them souvenirs. Lilly had to physically struggle to keep her seat, her excitement was so great. And Patricia actually smiled. So plans were made for the next Saturday.

"What are you going to wear to the Exhibition, Patsy?" Lilly asked.

"I don't know," she replied absently.

"I'm thinking of my yellow chintz with the Chambéry lace. We'll carry parasols, won't we? Do you suppose we should suggest packing a lunch? He's spending a frightful lot, isn't he? Do you suppose he's very rich?"

"I'm sure I couldn't care."

"But he was at the senator's party—and wearing a formal suit. Don't you like him, Patsy? At all?"

Patricia sighed and put down her hair brush. "I think," she said carefully, "that he's an atrocity."

"But what if he's rich?" Lilly said, smiling, trying to tempt Patricia.

"Then he's a rich atrocity."

Lilly's smile disappeared, and she stared at her sister in disapproval before looking back to her journal, filling her pen, scratching on the page.

"I'm going to ask Mama something. I'll be right back," Patricia said. She took a robe from the armoire; she and Lilly shared one, and so the cut was generous. She was forced to lift it to go down the steps.

A lamp was lit in the parlor, and the smell of John's tobacco still hung in the air, although it had been some time since she'd heard John and Sophia depart. She heard voices, but the parlor was empty, and she grimaced as she imagined that her mother and Mr. Padgett were still on the porch. Night after night! Had her mother stopped caring what he neighbors or boarders thought? Their obvious courtship rankled Patricia. She lived in dread fear that they might actually marry.

She stopped short when she heard what was definitely her mother's giggle! Patricia felt her cheeks grow hot. Not really, she thought. Could that really be her strict and fussy Mama, *giggling with a man?* She listened more closely.

"I don't know that Mrs. Fairchild can manage the fair, but it was good of you. Nor Annie—she's well along now. The baby will come in another month, and she's had problems in the past."

"They have wheelchairs and carts for rent," he said. "But I aim to be with you. They'll have to find their own folks to push them around."

"You gave me no warning at all," she said softly. "I never imagined such a wonderful gift. And for them *all!*"

"For you," he said, his voice low. And she laughed lightly, *again!*

Patricia pushed through the screen door in a wide swirl of her nightgown and robe. She startled Emily, who jumped slightly. Patricia glowered at them, angry and ashamed. They were both on the porch swing, a change of venue. And his arm was around Emily's back, not quite embracing her, but it *was* behind her shoulders. They might have been *kissing!* Patricia wanted to slap her mother.

"Patsy?" Emily asked. "I thought you were in bed."

"Not just yet," she replied flatly.

"Do you need me for something?"

She is not even embarrassed, Patricia thought, glaring at her mother.

"I want to ask you something."

"All right."

Patricia shifted from foot to foot, letting outrage show all over her face. Emily should extract herself, go inside, and let Patricia ask her question privately. But it was obvious that Emily had no intention of moving.

"The lectures are finished," Patricia said. "But I need some kind of outing. May I go to the lending library on Thursday?"

"With Lilly?" Emily asked.

"Oh yes, ma'am," she replied quite sarcastically. "I will be properly chaperoned."

Emily frowned slightly, but didn't budge from the porch swing. In fact it appeared that she settled in more solidly, as if there were a contest of sorts. "Very well," she finally said, but by the sound of her voice she was displeased with Patricia.

Patricia didn't say anything else. She turned away as dramatically as she had arrived, letting her nightgown and robe swirl wide, storming into the house, although she was very careful not to let the door slam. She let her feet strike the stairs much harder going up than she had coming down, and she wasn't nearly so careful with her bedroom door.

"Good grief," Lilly said, looking up when the door shut hard.

"They were *kissing*," Patricia hissed, her eyes sparkling with rage.

"For heaven's sake," Lilly said. "Do you feel that Mama isn't *old* enough? What *is* the matter with you?"

"How *dare* she tell me how to live my life when she's found kissing on the porch swing in full view of the neighborhood every evening!"

Lilly glanced toward the window. It was completely dark. This was hardly full view. But she said nothing. She did not, however, understand Patricia's intense anger.

They had attended the lectures together for six weeks, every Thursday afternoon. Every time Patricia talked quietly with Dale Montaine while Lilly read the bills at the theater. Lilly was not confused by Patricia's desire to go to the lending library at precisely that time of day.

"I don't suppose Mr. Montaine will be waiting outside the theater?" Lilly asked Patricia as they walked across Rittenhouse Square.

"If that were any of your business, I would reply."

Lilly stopped walking. She touched Patricia's arm to halt her. Lilly's voice was low. "Patricia, please. Please tell me why you're so angry. Please tell me what you want and why you're so unhappy."

"It would be silly of me to try to talk to either you or Mama. Don't even pretend you understand me. I *know* you don't! It is perfectly all right for you to go where you like and do as you please and even skip school, but I am confined for the whole summer because I went to a very important social event! Mama can sit on the porch swing kissing, but I am punished because Mama thinks I am too flirtatious. Do you think that's fair, Lilly? Do you?"

"Patsy, it's not the same thing at all! It's very diff—"

Lilly was unable to finish because Patricia gave her head a furious toss, a groan coming through clenched teeth. She turned and stomped across the square. Lilly lagged behind, watching her sister's dainty but purposeful step, her narrow but rigid back.

They all think themselves so much smarter than I, Patricia thought angrily. They are so much smarter, so much more *proper!* She slowed her step and allowed a smile to replace her grimace as she recognized Dale, standing at the edge of the square. It was a smile she didn't feel inside. She let her eyes fill with him; no, she did not consider him appealing. He was handsome, confident. But she surveyed him in a way that might mislead him into thinking she found him desirable. She looked over his gray lined pants, narrowly fitted, his silk shirt, his shiny and narrow patent-leather shoe, his stickpin, his gray flannel hat. His clothing on this very afternoon cost more than all the full armoires in their house! They thought her a fool, did they?

When she reached him, she let her ungloved hand rest lightly on his forearm. She leaned close enough to whisper, "Saturday."

7

*A*manda, Lady Nesbitt, sat behind the huge mahogany desk in her late husband's study. It had been only two weeks since she buried her third husband, William. Most of the household goods were packed, and she planned to stay in an inn until her ship left the Port of London. She held a letter from her granddaughter in her hand; she had read it twenty or thirty times.

The door creaked open, and Amanda looked up at Bertie, short for Beatrice, her maid of thirty years. "What is it now?" she sighed.

Bertie straightened indignantly. Amanda was in a mood that was wearing down everyone's patience. "The coach is here, unless you'd like to walk off some of your huff and puff."

"Well, is Fletcher here?"

"Downstairs. Waiting. Like everyone else."

"Well, call him up here. I've decided to take the desk."

Bertie rolled her eyes. "That now. Do you plan to leave a stick of furniture in the place?"

"I might need it."

"There's a rumor going 'round that they build desks in Philadelphia—"

"I think they're in trouble," Amanda said, holding up the letter. "I can feel it. Lilly has told me things about their poverty that Emily never mentioned. And how they've gotten by! Cooking, cleaning houses, taking in boarders, and sewing! Lord above! And the older girl, Patricia, is determined to get herself a rich husband."

"Now there you go, thinking so much. Who could understand the girl better than you? How many rich husbands have you had?"

"I loved them all. Well, I didn't love John as much as the others, and not William so much as Richard, but— Oh hush up, this is quite different. The girl needs advice, and Emily . . . Do you think . . . ? Ah, she might not speak when I see her again."

"You worry too much. She'll speak. She's long past foolishness by now; she has her own silly girls to raise."

"I've missed her," Amanda said quietly. "So have you, though you don't say so. I can't imagine how they've lived, what they've gone through."

"Come along then, and you'll ask them soon enough. It's good she wrote to you, the girl. That should make it easier."

"Have you packed my ledger books?"

"Yes, yes."

"And you supervised the kitchen? And the contents of my fur armoire?"

"All of it. I'll tell Mr. Drake about the desk. Now let's leave before you think of something else you can't part with."

"I want to go by the cemetery and say a proper good-bye to William."

"And a thank you, if you please," Bertie said.

"I'm through with marrying," Amanda said. "I don't know if I have the worst luck, or the best. Three husbands in forty years—all good enough men, but I would have settled for one."

"The coach is here, as I've said."

Amanda stood, but she was weary. Her joints were stiffening up. Fifty-eight was not such an atrocious age, considering that with hair coloring she could pass for fifty or less. But she was feeling it.

140

"Are you up to this?" she asked Bertie, who was ten years her senior.

"No, I'm not up to spending a voyage with you, if you please. But then, what else am I to do? I never did like this country—cold and damp as a tomb. It's time we got home to Miss Emily." Bertie sighed heavily. "That ship doesn't appeal much; it won't be any warmer than this old house."

"Well, pack your pipe and brandy. I have the playing cards."

Bertie smiled at her oldest friend and employer. "You're not deep enough in debt to me, eh? Well, I'll prosper on the way over then."

"At least William left me money when he died. At least—" She stopped when she saw Fletcher Drake, her personal solicitor, appear behind Bertie. Fletcher had worked for her for fifteen years; his legal expertise and financial acumen had helped her to more than replace what Richard had lost. Fletcher was completely devoted to her, and she was completely dependent on him to supply her with investment information and the advice she needed.

"Lady Nesbitt, the coach—"

"I've decided to take the desk, Fletcher," she interrupted. "Take care of it for me, will you please? And have my bed shipped. I've decided I need it after all."

He smiled indulgently and nodded. "Perhaps we can float the house over?"

"I never liked this house much. Cold and damp, like everything else here. You'll like Philadelphia, Fletcher. It's warmer in summer. There's a lot of money there."

"Yes, so I hear. The coach, Lady Nesbitt."

But what if she's not happy to see me? Amanda wondered. What if she hasn't warmed at all, but is angrier than ever? She had decided it was best not to write to Emily or Lilly. She would surprise them. She hoped it would be a pleasant surprise. "Very well, let's go. It's time I got home to my granddaughters. Are you sure? Both of you? You're going with me?"

"Try to leave us," Fletcher challenged.

"Oh, Patsy, *no*."

Patricia moaned and rolled over, her hair a tangled mess

from sleeping. "There isn't anything I can do about it," she complained.

Emily, who had been summoned, came into the bedroom. It was still very early. They were rising at dawn for the most important day of the summer. Lilly had only just awakened, and Emily, the earliest riser in the house, still wore her wrapper. "Patsy?" she questioned. She put a cool hand on her daughter's forehead.

"I can't go," Patricia said sullenly. "I have the most terrible pains. It's my monthly."

"Are you sure? Can't you make yourself extra safe? Double slips? I can't stand for you to miss the fair. There might never be another chance."

"Oh, Mama, I couldn't enjoy myself. I feel terrible and I'll be an awful mess. I just couldn't."

"But Patricia," Lilly implored. Lilly thought it silly to give the thing so much importance. "If you're walking around a great deal, you'll get to feeling better. And there will be some sort of powder rooms where we can freshen up."

"Never mind, Lilly, I can't do it. My flux is much worse than yours. I'm always ill with it. Mama, will you make me some tea?" She pulled herself up in the bed. "I just want to stay in bed with a hot pack."

Emily frowned in concern. "Are you sure that's the trouble, Patricia? I hadn't thought your monthly was due now. I thought," she began, glancing away and putting a finger to her lips as she tried to remember the last time Patricia had complained of menstrual pains. She and Lilly were not so plagued, but Patricia did seem to suffer quite a lot.

"Yes, I'm sure. I'm sorry, Mama, I don't want to ruin your day. Can't you just tell Mr. Padgett I have a sick headache and can't go along?"

"Maybe we can change our plans. Perhaps there's another day—"

"After all the excitement? Oh no, Mama, you can't! Everything's arranged. Mrs. Fairchild is going to her son's house and the others are looking forward to it."

"There will be no one to fix dinner for you," Emily said. "There will be no one here. You'll be completely alone."

"That's just as well. It's so embarrassing to huddle in my room and have everyone always asking. I'll just rest."

"I could stay with you. Lilly would be in good hands with Mr. Padgett and the others."

"Oh, Mama, don't fuss so. What could you do for me? Go on, I'll be fine. I'll find something simple for dinner and drink tea. Then tomorrow you can tell me all about it."

"Are you quite sure, Patsy?" Emily asked.

Patricia settled down into the bed once again. "Will you make me some tea before you go?"

"At the very least," Emily said.

Lilly stood over the bed looking down at her sister for a long while. "I think it's the whole way you look at it, Patsy," she said. "Try to ignore it. We'll go slowly and stop quite a few times. You could try a seltzer for the cramps and the exercise of walking—"

"Never mind, Lilly. My head aches so that I can barely see. And I wasn't as excited about going as you were anyway. I don't care very much about inventions. Not really."

Having Patricia miss the excursion dampened everyone's mood, and Emily was reluctant to leave her. But the group, excepting Mrs. Fairchild, departed at seven in the morning.

It was nearly ten when Mrs. Fairchild tapped lightly on the door to say good-bye to Patricia. The sound of the old matron's cane on the floor tapped closer to the bed. "You're looking quite pale," she observed. "Sassafras will help."

"I'll be fine. If I can just have a quiet day, I'll feel better by evening. Go on to your grandchildren, Mrs. Fairchild."

"Is there anything I can put out for your dinner?"

"Not a thing. I'm going to make myself some honey and bread and a cup of hot tea. I'll be going to bed quite early. Before you're returned I'll be sound asleep."

"That's a good girl. Pity you have to miss the fair."

"Oh, better I stay here than to go and ruin everyone's fun by moping and complaining."

Patricia heard the sound of Walter Fairchild's carriage, his knock at the door, the door being closed, and the distant, mumbled voices as he helped his mother down the porch steps and out to the coach. And then, the blessed sound of creaking wheels pulling them away. She lay still for a long moment, listening to a quiet she had never before heard in the house. A smile grew slowly on her face. There was no flux today. And she had never felt better in her life. But she had purposely been stoic during her usual cramps all summer, ever since Dale's suggestion that she could beg off when her family went for an outing. It had given her the idea. She had just never thought the whole household would *ever* go for an outing. Emily had been putting pennies in a jar for a year, saving for the fair, but the jar filled with aching slowness.

She threw back the quilt and put her feet on the cool, wooden floor, stretching her arms up over her head. She loved staying in bed until late in the morning. She made a waking sound, ending with a little whoop that seemed to echo in the empty house. And then she let go with a robust laugh.

The group started out sullenly. How like Patricia to spoil the day one way or the other, Lilly thought. She would be the least enthusiastic were she along, and by staying behind with a sick headache, she had cursed the event in absentia.

Lilly guessed from the expressions on the faces around her how each felt about what Patricia had done. Sophia was frowning when she looked at Emily; Sophia had always thought Patricia a little too spoiled, though she did not remark on it often. John Giddings was disappointed; he looked down at his feet. Likely John had hoped to impress Patricia. Lilly had noticed how John's eyes brightened when Patricia was near, but he was too painfully shy to say anything at all to her. Annie and Jamie, though they held hands affectionately, looked toward Emily with pity—perhaps they were really concerned about the girl. Only Mr. Padgett seemed unaffected.

Perhaps Mr. Padgett had a reason for his indifference. Having already been to the Centennial Exhibition, he knew what they would see and do; he knew that even Emily would not be able to keep the excitement buried for long.

They took the horsecar to the wharves in the city where Mr. Padgett helped them all board the ferry that ran loads of visitors up the Schuylkill River, a new boat departing every ten minutes. They made plans to meet for lunch at the Dairy building at noon where they would take free buttermilk to the banks of the Wissahickon and spread a picnic blanket. At seven in the evening they would meet again, at the Horticulture building in the center of the grounds, to go together to the fireworks display. And the eight-thirty ferry would take them home.

The enthusiasm was contagious among the ferry passengers. Children were difficult to control, and young girls nervously twirled their parasols. The fairgrounds came into sight; buildings and tents rose in the distance at Fairmount Park. Excited spectators poured through turnstiles.

It was like stepping into the next century. There was too much to be seen in a week and Lilly's excitement and sheer wonder were hard to rein in. The Corliss engine was like a moving monument. There were fountains everywhere, some scented with cologne. The chief building, Main, was the largest structure in the world, with the Hook and Hastings organ at the east end, the Hilborne L. Roosevelt organ in the north transept, and the Electric Echo in the English tower. Music was scheduled so that the organs didn't compete with any of the many bands.

Exhibits numbered in the thousands, from buildings erected by foreign countries to depict their lives, their clothing, their foods, music, and art, to inventions and products never before seen but soon to become available in America. There was a floor covering called linoleum that intrigued Emily. And Lilly, who had never been on a train, stepped inside the displayed Pullman Palace car. The Norwegians showed their silver. There was an invention called the telephone, through which people could talk to one another without ever leaving their homes, but Lilly didn't quite believe it would ever catch on. There were guns, safes, clothing, glassware, inks, jewelry, arts, books, lighting fixtures, kitchen appliances.

The life-size grouping, art in the most realistic sense, called *The Siege of Paris,* caused Lilly to imagine herself abroad, caught in a tremendous political conspiracy. There were tropical gardens filled with rare flowers so overwhelming that Emily's eyes actually filled with tears.

As Noel had predicted, their group had separated as different interests dictated. At lunchtime they exchanged experiences to help each other decide on the afternoon activities. Annie wanted to hear the sixty-piece band at Operti's Tropical Garden, and Mr. Padgett heard from John how terrific was Theodore Thomas' beer and concert garden. Even Emily had to relax her standards so that her escort would not be deprived; she muttered *brew* with a smile.

145

Lilly laughed and ran; she ate pastry at the Vienna Bakery and was gifted with a souvenir parasol from the Japanese pavilion. Mr. Padgett was generous, inviting them to enjoy flavored seltzers and a new drink called root beer, over which Emily hesitated until she was promised there was no liquor in it. They decided on a French scent as a gift for Patricia and had their supper at the Kohn pavilion where the waiters wore Hungarian national dress.

Her eyes were full and her spirit soared. The streets of the Exhibition were overflowing with foreigners wearing their native garb and dignitaries from the United States identified by ribbons. Governors chatted with senators; Japanese smiled and bowed toward Swedes. Lilly had not known how much world existed beyond her mother's boardinghouse.

When she thought she might explode from all she'd seen in one single day, they rested under a generous tree in the Lansdowne ravine and looked upward toward splashes of color against the darkened sky. *Fireworks!* Noel said the display was nothing to what had taken place on the Fourth of July, two weeks earlier, but Lilly had a hard time imagining anything more grand than this.

Fatigued, gritty, but full on experience, they moved to the ferry, and on the ride home the passengers behaved like a well-acquainted group, singing popular songs—"*I'll Take You Home Again*" and "*Rose of Killarney*." Then they wearily transferred to the horsecar, their necks almost too weak to hold up their heads. John and Sophia separated themselves from the others so he could walk her home. Annie and Jamie lagged behind. As the boardinghouse came into view down the street, Lilly hurried toward the light, her arms heavy with packages—her own treats plus surprises for Patricia.

The front door stood opened, and the light from the parlor poured through the window onto the porch. Lilly heard her mother, just behind her and on Mr. Padgett's arm, wistfully comment, "I wish Patsy could have seen it. It would have filled her with such possibility—just what she's needing now."

Lilly thought Patricia was on the porch, waiting up. She hurried up the steps, and Mrs. Fairchild dragged herself out of the chair with the help of her cane. Lilly and Mrs. Fairchild stared at each other. Worry met surprise. Had Patsy become very ill?

Emily stopped behind Lilly and looked up at Mrs. Fairchild.

"She ain't here, Emily. The girl. Gone."

146

When everyone had gone to the fair, Patricia moved about languidly, enjoying the luxury none of them ever had: solitude. She went downstairs in her nightgown, fixed herself tea and bread, and dragged out the big wooden tub from the pantry.

She wished she had scents and someone to help her with her hair. That will come later, she thought, smiling to herself when, at nearly noon, she sank into the warm water. She longed for perfume. That would come later, too, when she was rich. Then she would bathe in French perfumes in her own bath closet. Some maid would worry about her hair, not her.

She envisioned her future maid as harried and frightened, sensing that was the way of it. Wasn't everyone frightened of power? Wouldn't she be powerful as the rich lady of the house?

She indulged a long fantasy of how her family would respond to her wealth, for she would share it. She leaned back in the tub, closed her eyes, and saw her mother nicely clothed in bright colors and Lilly entertaining gentlemen callers in Patricia's parlor. She saw them coming to her for advice. She imagined them asking her opinion of the gown they chose for her party. She believed that their superior attitude would shift quickly to respect—and not grudging respect, but deferential awe, for she would do what she had set out to do. They would shake their heads in amazement for only a moment, then shrug, smile, and say, "Imagine! How clever of her!" Most important, they would eventually be both repentant and grateful.

There was no vision of any man in her fantasy, until a picture of the cowboy, wearing boots with a formal suit and standing beside Emily, made a surprise appearance into her thoughts. She extracted herself from the tub. I won't allow it, she thought. I simply won't allow it to happen.

She patted herself dry, dressed in her camisole, slip, and bustle, and disposed of the bath water. Then she dragged a chair across the bedroom to sit before the mirror and began fixing her hair. She was going to the four o'clock performance of *Richard III* at the Academy of Music. She'd rather music than Shakespeare, for she wasn't certain she could discuss what had happened on the stage afterward. Then there would be a nine-course dinner in a fancy restaurant called Tiffin's. *Nine courses!* And she would not be able to eat a bite, certainly.

Still, she had not considered Dale. It was as though he was irrelevant to what was really happening. It was not until she cautiously pulled the fancy gown over her head that his face came into her mind. Dale. All this must be done through Dale. He was the benefactor.

She acknowledged, privately, secretly, that she disliked him. In fact, of all the young men she had known since she had first become aware of young men, there were several she found easier to abide. For one thing, he was difficult to fool and tease; he made her work so hard to entice him. But he wanted her. For the sheerest sliver of a moment she wondered whether she should sacrifice so much potential wealth for a man who was a bit easier to like. And she decided quickly against it. She could be civil to any beast of the jungle if it meant she would never again have to worry about money or social status.

Dale called for her in a hired trap, a decent, closed coupé. He did not come to the door for her, but waited within the coach while the driver knocked, escorted her to the road, and lifted her in. Just as he was handing her in to Dale, he leered at her, and she noticed he had a front tooth missing.

Dale received her with his hands. "Even with all this trouble, we'll be found out eventually," she said.

He kissed the cheek she turned to him. "It won't matter after tonight, darling."

"How can you think that?" she asked, somewhat annoyed.

"As we said, we'll show Mrs. Armstrong what a lovely man I am—how courteous and responsible."

"Yes. Yes, indeed."

He reached up and touched her bare shoulder, playing with the lace ruche and silk flowers that made for a thin strap. Today she wore the tulle wrap around her shoulders.

"Dale—"

"Come now, Patricia. If I begin to think you don't want to be with me—"

"I do, you know. Haven't I risked everything for this day? You must be polite. You must not compromise me. Dale?"

He dropped his hand to her waist and smiled into her eyes. "I certainly don't want to muss your appearance before we even get to the play or to dinner, but don't you have a kiss for me? After all this waiting, all this trouble?"

"A small kiss," she said, hoping her eyes twinkled.

"A meaningful kiss, I should hope."

"How will I know it's meaningful?"

His lips were nearly on hers; his hand squeezed her narrow waist. "Simple," he whispered. "Kiss me in a way that makes me believe you are as tempted as I. I want to believe your desire matches mine, that you will desire me this way for the rest of your life."

Just as his mouth, hot and wet, pressed down on hers, she felt her pulse begin to race. My God, she thought wildly, he means it. He wants me for his wife! Forever! And she allowed him, without rehearsed abandon, to push open her lips with his, to penetrate her mouth with his tongue. She raised her arms, drawing him closer. She became suddenly feverish, hot all over, damp and prickly. She opened her lips wider, hoping he was poisoned by her, hoping he was drowning in her. She would have to endure so many of these awful kisses in a lifetime . . . but it didn't matter!

His hand began to glide up her rib cage toward her breast, and she felt herself stiffen. She tried to pull away, but one arm was around her waist and held her too firmly. "You shouldn't," she managed softly, against his wet mouth.

"Let me," he begged. "Let me just once. Please. I'm dying for want of you."

She relaxed as much as possible, feeling his hand slipping inside the gown and his thumb grazing her nipple. She sighed, or hoped she sighed. If she wasn't terribly, terribly strong with herself, she might pull away. She hated being touched this way. She forced her mind to go to a cold, dark place while she squirmed slightly, enticingly, with her body. It was going to be far worse than this, she knew. He was going to claim his conjugal rights one day, lay atop her, get himself right inside her, whenever he liked. She hoped she would not faint. But she wouldn't. She wouldn't. She couldn't.

"Please, Dale. You promised." She whispered it, as if it was as difficult for her.

"But you like it. You want more."

"You must be a gentleman," she said, not denying it.

"It will be right with me." But he removed his hand and shifted a bit on the seat. Then he looked at her. His eyes were commanding. "You know it, don't you, Patricia? That it's going to be me?"

"Yes," she said, breathless with the wonder of how all this had worked.

The only way she could console herself was to remember that all women paid such a price. The bargain was simple: a woman yielded to the physical demands from a man in exchange for her keep. And if one must be kept, one does well to choose a situation that is at least luxurious.

The theater was not well attended, and Patricia's dress was too fancy. Women wore afternoon toilettes of somber colors and more sleek design, but of course Patricia had no other clothes she could wear to such an event. And when she asked why the audience was so sparse, Dale reminded her that there were not as many performances in summer; it was not *the season*.

The play bored her; she barely understood it. But she thoroughly enjoyed observing the people. It served well as instruction on how she would do as a rich and influential married woman. She spent her time watching the behavior around her and was relieved to see that even the best-dressed women there did not concentrate on the play any more than she, but rather flirted and chatted during the performance. How simple—it was to be able to attend *what*ever one liked, *when*ever one liked.

During the intermission, she wanted to go into the foyer where drinks would be served and people would chat. Dale did not want to leave his seat, but she persuaded him. Several people in a group passed Dale and nodded, paused, said hello, but he didn't introduce them to Patricia. He stood as if he were alone, shook hands with well-dressed young gentlemen and kissed the backs of ladies' hands.

"Why didn't you introduce me?" she whispered when they returned to their seats.

"Because they're clods," he said, looking straight ahead to the empty, curtained stage. "Just forget about them."

She frowned her confusion. "You're not paying very much attention to me," she complained.

He dropped his arm around her shoulders, toying casually with the tulle strip. "I'm sorry, darling. I'm finding it's harder than I thought to be a gentleman with you. You're so damned desirable!"

"Oh, Dale, is that all you think about?"

"With you," he said, nuzzling her ear.

"You would be a difficult husband to keep happy," she said, testing, teasing.

"Not for you, love."

Patricia thought of wedding gown patterns and fabric swatches.

The waiters at Tiffin's knew him, bowed to him, and escorted them through a crowded room. She tried to observe without staring. There didn't seem to be very many people here, either, and again, their dress was not nearly so ostentatious as hers.

But the room itself was magnificent. Waiters in starched white jackets carried trays to mahogany tables covered with linen cloths. China, crystal, and silver sparkled, and wine in ornate decanters decorated tables. Men wore jackets with ascots and women covered their shoulders with shawls. Patricia felt outrageously bare but held her head up high as she walked across the multicolored woolen carpet with Dale.

Their table was one of a few in the rear of the restaurant and there was a curtain drawn almost closed around them. It cut them off from the rest of the patrons and Patricia felt at once privileged and deprived. She had taken all these risks to win Dale, but also to see and be seen.

"Why don't we dine in the open with the others?" she asked.

"I don't like anyone to watch me eat," Dale replied. "It's something you should get used to, Patricia. When you're well known people stare. It's uncomfortable."

"I don't mind if people look at me."

"I'm sure you don't, dear, but quality people like to keep an element of mystery and secrecy that is more tasteful and better for their reputation," he advised. "There isn't anyone in the restaurant of consequence, in any case."

"Who, then, is in the restaurant, Dale?"

"No one of importance. Businessmen and parlor girls. Working-class people who have saved for a year for a meal here. The like."

"Don't your friends come here?"

"Before nine?" he asked, laughing. "Don't you like being alone with me?"

"Of course, darling," she said, trying out the endearment on him for the first time. What a clever word, she discovered by the way his eyes lit.

"That's a relief. I can hardly consider a lifetime with you if you're reluctant to share my company."

She lowered her gaze and looked up at him through her thick,

151

dark lashes. "All this talk," she said. "When are you going to come right out and ask me?"

His fingers caressed her neck. "At just the right moment, darling." And for that she rewarded him with a kiss that was interrupted by the opening of the curtain and the appearance of a waiter.

Dale discussed the champagnes with the waiter and made their dinner selection. It was all brought too quickly after that. There was cream soup and watercress with almonds and tomato wedges. Then came oysters and snails, though she simply could not touch them, which amused Dale to a great degree. She would have thought he was laughing at her had he not leaned over and affectionately stroked the inside of her upper arm. Next came a pastry and meat pie, then a slice of beef cooked in its own juices and side plates of exotic-looking vegetables: carrots cut strangely and ornately, pea pods, and miniature corn cobs. The bread was fresh from the oven and aromatic; the butter was whipped. Finally there was a chocolate mousse topped with whipped cream. The courses came so rapidly and efficiently that too soon they were finished.

Patricia, of course, didn't eat much. Her stomach was tense from pretending. She wasn't enjoying herself at all. She had expected so much more of the evening: introductions, much fuss over her beauty, playing and flirting and having fun. She was left standing alone while he chatted with his friends in the theater and was hidden behind a drape while she dined at the fancy restaurant. When, she asked herself, will I be with all the others? For parties and games and festivities? When will I be one of them?

"I'd like to show you my house," he told her.

"But Dale, I'm supposed to be home early!"

"You do want to see it, don't you?"

"Maybe it would be better if we did it another time," she attempted. "I should be home before Mama—"

"Have you had a good outing, Patricia?"

"Oh yes," she lied. The hired coach lurched into motion. She knew he had directed the driver before she accepted.

"You should go to plays and dinners every day."

But Patricia was aching with disappointment. She would not be marrying Dale to be with *him*. "I thought we'd meet people you knew," she said. "I thought you would be taking me to places where your friends gather."

"I'm afraid that will have to come later, darling. It's impossible with the hours you're forced to keep. If I could call for you earlier in the day for afternoon gatherings, there would be a group involved in something. As for parties, plays, and dinners, nothing much happens before seven. Never."

"Dale," she nervously asked. "What are parlor girls?"

"Don't you know?" he asked, astounded.

"No."

He laughed loudly at that and put his arm around her as the coach rattled along at what seemed a high speed. "Well, they're beautiful women," he said, a ripe chuckle in his voice. "You could be a parlor girl, Patricia. A good one."

"But what do they *do*?"

"Just what you do best, my dear. Adorn the arms of prosperous men and entertain them, make them feel important and pampered."

"And is that what I do?"

"Indeed, darling. Better than anyone. It is exactly what every man wants. Believe me. Now, I want to show you how a rich man lives. You should know exactly what it's like. I want to show you where Father figures his fat accounts, where dinner parties for seventy are held, where the finest books money can buy are shelved, where imported and exotic flowers surround our breakfast parlor."

His description of his mansion went on through the ride, and she fell silent and listened. She had imagined it all, but had never set foot in a wealthy home. She thought she had, visiting Mary Ellen Jasper, but that house was nothing to what Dale described. Sixty rooms made up his home. She indulged in more daydreams. Quiet and solitude while she took her tea and toast, surrounded by orchids and ferns even in the coldest month of winter. Bath closets with brass tubs for every member of the household; no more outdoor conveniences. Glittering men and women surrounding the largest dining table ever built, Patricia at the head.

She was so tired of Dale—so tired of pretending to like him. She had not had a fun day. Dale was solicitous, but greedy. He pawed her while he described his house. She wanted either to go home or to move quickly into the mansion and become its mistress. As the hour grew later and she remained at Dale's disposal, so diminished her chance of slipping back into the boardinghouse and acting as though she had never left. She hoped her mother would defer, profess understanding, accept Dale and his courtship graciously.

"My mother will be furious by the hour of my return."

153

"We can deal with Mama, Patricia," he said patiently.

Gas lights lit the gate and the mammoth front doors of the mansion. The ride itself had taken thirty minutes. It might take as long as an hour for her to get home. It would be after ten.

"Please wait," he told the driver. "We won't be long. We're just going in for a few moments."

She was so encouraged by his instructions to the driver that she went with him willingly. He took her hand, which had become cool and damp, and pulled her up the ornate, curving, walnut staircase.

"Where . . . where are we going?" she asked, expecting a tour of sorts, but not beginning upstairs.

"There's something I want to show you," he said.

"There doesn't seem to be anyone here."

"No one. We're completely alone."

"Dale, should I be here when there's no one at home?"

He pulled harder, hurrying her up the stairs even though she resisted. "But you are. Are you worried? I thought you were ready to spend your entire life with me. How can you be ready for the one thing, and not the other?"

"It's just that—"

"Here we are," he said, stopping before the door at the top of the stairs. "This is what I want to show you. Look," he said, opening a door. "This is the room that will belong to my wife. I've had it made up. I want to know what you think."

Patricia knew, as she had never known, the special moment had arrived. Now he would propose marriage. The room was lit, ornately furnished, a huge raised brass bed in the center with the satin drapes pulled back. There was a desk, table, dressing table, window seat, even a bowl of fresh flowers.

"It's beautiful," she said, envy causing her legs to feel weak. "Beautiful."

"Come here," he said, leading her into the room and opening an adjoining door. "Mrs. Montaine's sitting room," he said, showing her another luxurious setting. "And here," he said, leading her away to the other side of the bedroom and opening another door, "Mrs. Montaine's bath closet and dressing room." Within was one of Patricia's most earnest desires—a bath closet with tub, toilet bowl, large wooden sink with marble bowl.

"Oh, Dale," she breathed.

154

He turned again to the bedroom. "Are the colors to your liking?" he asked, his fingers toying with the tulle strip.

"Dale," she said, her voice wheedling and silky, "don't you have something you want to ask me?"

His eyes became smokey, intense. He lowered his lips to hers and softly kissed her. He leisurely played with the tulle strip until it fell away. He embraced her gently, toying with the buttons at the back of her gown, opening one, the next, the next. "Yes, darling, I have something to ask you. Will I be happy with you? Will you always desire me as you do tonight?"

"Yes," she breathed against his mouth. "Yes."

Suddenly her gown slipped over her arms, exposing her camisole. She gasped, and he chuckled softly. He moved her backward toward the bed while she struggled in vain to raise her gown over her breasts. "Dale!" she protested. He forced her to sit on the bed. "Dale, you shouldn't—"

But his lips were on hers again, and she was pressed so firmly against him she couldn't resist.

"You wouldn't pretend to want me, would you, darling?" he asked. "Do you know how it is with a man? A man can't be teased, can't be put off again and again. The urge in a man is so much stronger than in a woman—"

"But, Dale—"

"You do want me, don't you? Forever?"

"Of course, but—"

"Show me," he said, his voice husky. "Show me that my touch pleases you."

Patricia swallowed, but gave herself to his kiss. She endured his fondling, not attempting to distract him even though his hands on her breasts became rough, squeezing. When he pulled down her camisole, she pushed at his shoulders, but he was as immovable as any rock. Then he moved, putting his mouth on her, sucking at her nipples, and she pushed at him harder, an urgent plea escaping her.

He pushed her back on the bed, kissing her mouth to stifle her panicked cries, fumbling with her plentiful petticoats and his breeches. Her mouth and neck were wet from his tongue. She squirmed beneath him, but more for a breath of air, which she gasped greedily when it was possible. She pushed at his shoulders, pushed him away, but hardly a sound escaped her. His shoulders seemed to be pointing downward, his chest pressed against her so hard that she couldn't move, and her flailing arms could not free her. He let go of her breast and his face was buried in her neck. Her shock was so great that all she could do was utter his name, and his name came like a question, faint and disbelieving. *"Dale?"*

"Ah, Patricia, what would you give to show me you want to be with me forever? If you give this," he said, his hand on her upper thigh beneath her abundance of clothing, "it would be like a pledge. A pledge."

Then she felt it, his hot, hard, and bare penis, thrust there between her thighs. She knew it was too late. She had not given an answer, a consent. She had not even been forced to pretend, he was so oblivious to her. Her eyes, huge and astonished, saw only the dark hair that surrounded his ear. But then he raised his head as he poked at her again and again and she began to cry silently beneath his grunts of determination. And then the dam broke and he plunged into her. His expression became dark, flushed, detached. He was using *her,* yet seemed completely unaware of her. He smiled. His eyes glittered in victory, in conquest. He was *in* her! Her pain was blinding, searing, and she could not even scream. Her breath was gone. He thrust and pumped. Once, twice. Twice more. It tore her apart, and a small whimper of loss came from her as she turned her eyes away from his face. But that was all for him. It took hardly a moment for him to have his fill and become still. She turned back to look at his face. He held himself above her with hands on each side of her. His head was thrust back, as if he looked at the ceiling, but his eyes were closed, and the hot pink drained from his cheeks. There was sweat on his forehead and upper lip.

Then he pulled himself out of her and stood beside the bed. There she saw it, through eyes that smarted with anguished tears that wouldn't quite flow. His wet and bent cock hung out of his open pants. He touched himself there, stroking it with his thumb and forefinger, up and down, groaning softly with eyes still partially closed, as if consoling his injured member. Fluid dribbled from it, and she saw that her blood stained it. Patricia stared at it in horror, could not take her eyes away as it seemed to lose its power slowly. And Dale's face relaxed, softened, just as his awful cock did. She felt the sticky wetness that he'd left in her run out between her sore thighs. Her disgust was so intense that she tasted vomit at the back of her throat. And then Dale stuffed his now flaccid weapon in his pants and buttoned them. He turned away from her as he finished doing this, and she willed herself to be strong.

When he turned back to her, his eyes had lost all the fire she had seen moments before. "I'll give you a few moments alone," he said. "Use the water closet if you like."

She drew herself to a sitting position and pushed her skirt down. The threat of tears caused her throat to ache but she valiantly held her dress, a burdensome bundle of clothing around her waist, and went to the water closet. She washed her face, attempted to smooth her hair, which was a hopeless mess, and found her pantalets torn; they had not even been pulled off but rather ripped aside. All she could consider was that Dale would have to go to the door with her and beg her mother to let him marry her. She struggled to keep her composure. If she let him think she had been nearly destroyed by this event, he might doubt her.

When she finally left the water closet, she found him seated in a chair in the bedroom. His shirt was opened, his hair tousled, and he held a glass of clear liquid. He spoke without looking at her. "I seem to have lost control," he said, not apologetically.

"It will be impossible for me to conceal this from my mother. You'll have to come with me and talk—"

"The driver is waiting for you, Patricia. Go ahead."

"What?"

"I said, you can go now. And thank you for a pleasant evening."

She stood, stunned, looking at his profile, watching as he leisurely lifted the glass to his lips and sipped.

"What?" she attempted again.

He turned to look at her. "You'd better be going. Wouldn't want Mama to worry."

"Dale?"

"You can find your way out, can't you?"

"Why? What have you done to me?"

"You acted as though you wanted it, Patricia. Did I misunderstand?"

"Are you . . . do we . . . are we to marry now?" Her shaking hand moved, and she touched her hair, as if checking her coiffure. Confused and still anguished by the burning pain that lingered, she didn't know what to do next.

"I think not, Patricia. The coach is waiting for you."

"Dale! Dale, what have you done? Why have you—"

"Parlor girls, Patricia, are whores. You dined with whores this evening. They pretend to like rich men, act as though they enjoy their company, and then when the evening is paid for, the trinkets dispersed, there's a nice little moment of pleasure for the man, the money changes hands, the parlor girls go home, and the men go back to their wives. Their wives, by the way, never pretend to love them."

She stared at him in astonishment, staggered by the impact of this affront. He stood from his chair and watched as the meaning of this evening settled over her. Finally, outrage winning, she shrieked and flung herself at him. But he quickly grasped her wrist before she could slap him. The drink fell, and he had her easily under his control.

"There is no one home, darling. No one to hear your temper or screams. We can tussle a bit more if you like, but frankly I think you'd be better off taking advantage of that coach before the driver gets tired of waiting."

"You," she gritted out. "You lied to me! You tricked me!"

"Actually, no," he said patiently. "I never pretended to want anything from you but what I just got. You made yourself believe I wanted marriage—I never said so. I only said, 'What if?' and 'Perhaps.' But you, Patricia, you lied to me. Over and over. Do you honestly think a man doesn't know if a woman really wants him?" He laughed humorlessly. "You could hardly take your eyes off my diamond pin long enough to watch the play."

"How can you—"

He released her abruptly. "I'm serious, darling. That driver won't stay all night. If you are stranded here, I might develop an appetite for you after a bit."

She moved limply toward the door.

"Be careful whom you tell about this," he said.

"But you forced me," she said in a breath, her voice small.

"Not exactly. You came here with me. A nice girl wouldn't. You led me to believe you desired me—I asked you over and over. You didn't resist until it was far too late. You were playing for a trade, Patricia. Your virginity for a life in this house, spending my money."

Tears ran down her cheeks, but she couldn't be in the same room with him another minute. She opened the door, tripped twice going down the stairs, and was momentarily relieved to see the coach waited. The driver jumped to attention, holding the door open. She had not been in the Montaine mansion for even an hour.

The driver hurtled her within, slammed the door, and clicked at his horses. She was underway instantly, still hardly knowing how this had happened. It was as though the coach had dropped them, she had been dragged up the stairs, been ripped open, and disposed of in moments. Tears continued to flow down her cheeks, but she made no sound. It was as if some scratchy, brutal instrument had been left inside her. Her insides ached and burned painfully, hurting more from every rut and bump the coach hit.

Her mind returned to the cold, dark place to which she had retreated in the past when she had to endure the slobbering kisses of some young man. There hadn't been very many. Dale was the most demanding. She couldn't think about what was happening during the pawing and petting, and she couldn't think about it now. It was as though she wasn't really here; this was only a nightmare and she would wake up. At some point in her journey she leaned over and vomited her dinner. She retched and choked and then pulled her cherished gown away from the mess. Her fingers trembled and her throat ached, but the tears remained soundless. The coach made a careening turn and then stopped. The door was yanked open, and she was snatched out. She stood looking at her house, the open door, the parlor light flooding onto the porch. She saw her mother come suddenly into view as though she had run to the door at the sound of the coach. And then the conveyance behind her lurched away.

Emily rushed out the door and toward her. She lifted her skirt to get down the porch steps and called Patricia's name, over and over again, but Patricia's ears were not working very well. It was as if they were stuffed with cotton. And her mother's face blurred before her, as though she were looking through a veil. She felt Emily's hands on her shoulders, but she couldn't move.

"Mama," she whispered. "Mama . . . I never even saw the largest dining table ever built. I never even saw it."

"I know who it was, Mama," Lilly said. "It was Dale Montaine."

Emily blinked her eyes hard; tears squeezed through, but she willed herself to be strong. The very man she had warned her daughter to avoid, and for this very reason. She refused to give in to useless tears now.

The Swiss clock chimed the twelve bells of midnight, the kitchen door was closed, and the fire in the stove heated the room. The teakettle steamed, and Lilly lifted it, filling the teapot a second time. There was nothing for the boarders to do but go on to their beds and let the Armstrong women deal with their trouble alone. Little examination or explanation was necessary; the virgin stains and the tear-marked face told Emily more than she could bear to know.

Lilly and Emily heated the water and filled the tub.

They brewed tea and helped Patricia wash herself. Lilly twice lathered and rinsed her hair, and Emily examined her daughter's beautiful young body for further damage. Patricia soaked while Lilly, positioning a stool behind the tub, tried to pull the brush through her sister's damp hair. The tears had stopped. So had the look of proud defiance disappeared.

"Patricia," Emily said as gently as possible, "was it him?"

She nodded, lifting her eyes to look at her mother. "He said he wanted to marry me," she whispered. "But . . . but I didn't know he would . . . I couldn't stop him, Mama. And then he . . . he told me to go home."

"Where did this happen, Patricia? In the coach?"

"His house. He wanted me to see his house, and he showed me a room, a room he said was made up for his wife. He asked me if I thought the colors were right . . . as if it was to be my room. And then he . . . he . . ." She didn't cry anymore, but just looked down into the murky bath water.

Emily felt as though she had been kicked. *His house! My* house!

"Was his family at home?" Emily asked, the words nearly curling her lip. That household, those people! She had always thought them horrible creatures, but she had never imagined Wilson Montaine so ghastly as to allow a young girl to be raped under his own roof.

"There was no one at home . . . at least I saw no one. He said terrible things to me. He told me I had dined with whores, that I should be a parlor girl!"

Emily's face grew crimson with rage. Her hands shook as she lifted the sponge from the bath water to scrub her daughter's arms and shoulders.

"It hurts, Mama. Down there."

"Yes, Patricia. That will pass."

"Why do women marry if it hurts so?"

"Patricia, it is not meant to be like that. It is not meant to be *forced*."

"I'm *ruined!*"

"No, Patricia, not ruined. Bruised and hurt. Women survive even worse, though I don't know how we do."

"Mama, what will we do now?" Lilly asked.

"Now?" Emily repeated. "We'll dry off our girl and go to bed. Sleep in my room tonight, both of you. We'll have to rely on each other to get past this."

"But can nothing be done?" Lilly asked.

"What would you suggest?" she angrily questioned. "It cannot be undone. I know of no man ever made to pay. I know of no woman to escape the accusation with her dignity. And you can be sure that *Mister* Montaine is unconcerned!" She took a breath to calm herself. "We'll go to bed and do whatever we can to put this behind us. Pray that there is no pregnancy."

Patricia lifted her stricken gaze to her mother's face. She had not even considered that. Her mouth moved over the word *Mama*.

Emily met those terrified eyes with calm. Inside she felt a gut-wrenching hysteria, but she knew she was helpless against this monstrosity, and her only recourse was to behave as though she felt strong. For tonight her concern was that Patricia recover from the fear, the disgust, and the shock of it all. Later she would consider a confrontation with the Montaines, but only if she could think of a way that would not sacrifice Patricia in the process.

Both Patricia and Lilly looked to her for a solution, but in reality there was none. Emily wanted to slap her daughter for her foolishness, for her refusal to listen, to be helped. Yet she wanted to embrace her, cuddle her close, for every eighteen-year-old woman thinks she has more power than her mother's advice, more wisdom than the women who have been scarred before her.

At least, Emily thought, Lilly will be spared because she has seen first-hand what her sister was always too silly to believe.

"It is too soon to worry about a baby, Patricia. And even that can be survived."

"Mama, I would *die!*"

"I wish I had the strength to *kill* him," Lilly muttered.

"Vengeance will only make the price we pay for this higher still. Do you think we're the first women to tread on this ground? Come to bed. All we have is each other. We'll put this behind us. Somehow."

"Mama," Lilly said pleadingly, "don't you want to do *any-thing?*"

"*Yes,* Lilly! I want to do terrible things to make him pay! But tonight all I can do is what I've always tried to do—take care of my daughters."

Deep in the night Emily was awakened by urgent knocking on her door. Annie's time had come. Six weeks more should pass before her labor. All Emily's skill in midwifing, learned so long ago from Old Mary, was not enough. Lilly was called on to help, John was sent for the doctor, and Emily sat beside Annie through the early morning hours.

At dawn the child was delivered and pronounced stillborn. A son. And the doctor, who was paid from Emily's penny jar, told Jamie MacIntosh that his twenty-two-year-old wife should not attempt childbearing again, unless he wished to bury her as well.

The morning was lost in the chores of death. Lilly sat with Annie; Sophia and Emily cleaned the dead infant and dressed it in swaddling; John accompanied Jamie to the carpenter to have a tiny coffin made. The preacher was called to give solace to the household. Patricia did not rise from her mother's bed, but no one noticed until late in the morning that Mrs. Fairchild had not been heard from.

Sophia and Emily stood on opposite sides of the kitchen worktable, the tiny body lying in the center, when Emily looked up, suddenly aware of the missing boarder, and breathed her name in panic. The two women ran up the stairs and burst into the old woman's room.

They found her barely conscious, rasping and drooling. There was a blank look in the old dowager's eyes and she couldn't move herself. The doctor was called again, and Lilly was sent to fetch Walter Fairchild from his shoe-repair business.

"She has suffered a stroke," the doctor whispered in the foyer of the boardinghouse. "There is little we can do but make her comfortable. She is seventy-eight years old, Mrs. Armstrong."

"Can she be moved to her son's house?" Emily asked.

"I can't take her home," Walter Fairchild exclaimed before the doctor could even answer. "My wife couldn't—"

Wouldn't! Emily thought in anger. Even as she dies, they can't tolerate her presence!

All in a day. Her daughter defiled. Annie's child lost. And Mrs. Fairchild, troublesome and cantankerous, yet still beloved to Emily, lay dying. Slowly and terribly. The old eyes that stared up at her, not recognizing her, were filled with pitiable confusion. There were tears caught in the rivers made by old skin, and Emily was not sure whether or not there was pain.

Every hand was called upon for help, except the hand most

willing: Noel's. Emily nursed Mrs. Fairchild night and day. Sophia and Lilly and even Patricia were needed to do all the cooking and cleaning that accompanied a funeral, an infirmary, and daily living. John Giddings was the only help for the bereaved MacIntosh couple, the one to arrange for their priest, the funeral procession, and a decent plot so that the child need not rest in pauper's ground. The only sleep Emily had was the little dozing as she sat through the night by her dying boarder's bed. Dark circles hung under her eyes and she ate little.

"Tell me how to help her," Noel whispered to Sophia.

"Ain't no help fer all this, Mistah Padgett," she said, shaking her head sadly. "You help enough by being as quiet and kind as you is. You jes' go 'bout your business and if I thinks of something you can do, I sure will say so."

Emily sometimes thought of those nights on the porch swing as she tended her patient. It seemed as though it all had happened many years before. When she was near exhaustion, the faces of Noel and Ned blurred together in her mind. Had there been passion and intrigue? She must have been mistaken. Never again would she allow herself to be so distracted.

John Giddings dug into his own purse to bring food to the Armstrong household. Sophia noticed his generosity, but no one else knew. Emily was not completely without money, since Walter Fairchild guiltily paid more than the usual board for his mother. But John knew that there might be money problems ahead, for the MacIntosh couple had decided to leave as soon as Annie was strong enough to travel. They could not tolerate the tiny room where three children had been lost; they needed their families, and their money was gone. All that they had saved for their own tenement was still not enough to bury their child. Jamie had purchased the coffin and paid the priest. John bought the burial plot so that they wouldn't have to see their child taken away by the Sanitary Commission.

He noticed that Patricia was getting around the house more, doing more chores, but he knew she was a long way from recovering. No one had been told the circumstances, but John thought he knew them. He didn't have the vaguest notion who had done this thing to her, but he didn't care. He had known for a long time that the men who pestered her would only hurt her.

The household was in turmoil; there was no time to take a stroll or find Patricia sitting alone in the parlor. He did the only thing he knew how to do. Although he was afraid she might rebuff him, he could not delay another day. He wrote her a letter and passed it to her late one night before he took his evening walk with Sophia.

> *Dear Patricia,*
> *Forgive my presumption. I find my pen easier than my voice. I do not always suffer from shyness, only when confronting someone I so admire. In all these years in your household, watching you grow into a beautiful and graceful woman, I have wanted to compliment you, but I could never find the courage. And I have wanted to warn you; your beauty should be your greatest gift, your greatest attribute, but it will create envy in others, and vengeance and cruelty. Few will know how to admire you in ways that you deserve.*
> *Now, I must somehow find the words for you. I know you've been wronged. I do not have the physical strength to avenge you, but you need not be alone in this troubled time. Your grace and charm have given me years of joy. Whatever pains have been placed on you, I am still your willing admirer, your servant, and in any way I can, I would help you overcome your trials. Just to be allowed to sing your praises would fill me with joy. Just to see you happy once again would be my greatest reward.*
> > *Humbly,*
> > *John*

When his shaking hand passed that letter, he did not know that Patricia kept a journal and shared a rare trait with John. Her words and feelings also came more easily by pen. The next day she passed him a letter, but she did not meet his eyes.

> *Dear John,*
> *I had always thought that I wanted so little from life. I only want to be happy. I trusted all the wrong people, and I never will again! Your letter gave me solace. How could you know that I cannot meet your eyes or speak of*

166

the horrors I have suffered? Some sense deep inside you prompted you to know the way to soothe my injury with your pen, and I am so grateful. No one has understood as you seem to. I need a friend who truly admires me and does not wish to hurt me. Write to me again. I will write to you. In secret. You might be the only friend I will ever have who does not ask more of me than I have to give.

P.

John's heart nearly exploded with relief and turmoil as he sat down at his desk to pen another letter, longer and more flattering. He knew better than to speak of love, for Patricia had been hurt by a man and would be a long time in trusting another. But he believed time would heal her wounded soul and he would be there, close at hand, to offer himself as the only man who could love her properly, worship her as she deserved to be worshipped.

Notes became letters; letters became long cathartic essays of hopes and dreams. John admitted his writing ambitions, told her that a novel, partially written, had been inspired by her beauty. Patricia lamented her future and all that she had dreamed she would one day possess. She never did tell all that had happened to her, but John encouraged her toward her desires. He believed he was leading her calmly toward choosing him.

One night, near midnight, a strange and acrid odor filled the house. He pulled on his pants and went in search of a dangerous fire. Emily left Mrs. Fairchild and was ahead of him on the stair. In the kitchen they found Patricia, standing in front of the stove. She had secretly lit a fire when she was alone, and in the belly of the stove her lavender satin, fashion plates, and swatches burned.

Emily embraced her daughter. "Patricia, why are you doing this? It has never been said that marriage is no longer possible!"

She looked between her mother and John. "I'm starting over, Mama," she said stoically. "All that is from *before*."

John felt a hope that left him feverish with desire.

On the tenth day of August Emily reported to the household that God had mercifully taken Mrs. Fairchild. Another trip was made to the carpenter. Mrs. Fairchild was taken by an undertaker's cart to the cemetery to lie beside her husband. Food was prepared for Walter Fairchild's family and the neighborhood and congregation. Emily thought it only right that those who loved her even when she was at her worst provide her final passage. She did not trouble Walter Fairchild much with his mother's burial, nor did she present him with a bill for her nursing care. She accepted his envelope containing money and put it in her armoire without counting it. She bid him a tight-lipped farewell, almost unable to look at the young man who took all that his parents had to offer, yet turned his back during the final days.

The MacIntosh couple remained long enough to bid farewell to Mrs. Fairchild, then packed their meager possessions. Annie wept on the morning of their departure. She promised to visit, but Emily doubted that she would find the strength to return to the place where her fondest dream had died.

"Life is harder for women, Annie," she whispered. "Try to remember that there were glad times here as well."

Glad times! When her devoted husband made love to her, a thing that she would risk her life to enjoy again. Emily had no doubt Annie would remember the glad times, the love, hope, and joy of sharing that tiny room with her handsome young man. And no doubt she would weep from memories, or die trying vainly to bring them to life.

Through it all Emily never released her own tears. If the ache in her throat threatened to spill over, she reprimanded herself; she had been through worse and would rely on her strength, discipline, and faith. At least Patricia's monthly flux had brought their family one final relief. But ideas and desires did not light the girl's eyes anymore. In her eyes now there was a cold and frightening rage that Emily not only understood, but remembered.

Work was all Emily could depend upon. John and Noel were the only boarders left, and Susan Pendergast had decided to board with her friend rather than return to the Armstrong household. The funds had been so depleted that Emily was prepared to discharge Sophia to find other work. The thought of not seeing her dearest friend almost every day caused agony, but she could not be selfish now. She could not survive with an empty house and had instructed the girls to move their belongings back into her bedroom to make even Susan Pendergast's empty room available. Mrs. Fairchild's room had been scrubbed down and tidied. It was late, and she was tired, but she filled a bucket and prepared to scrub the MacIntosh's empty room.

"Emily," he said.

She turned away from the sink tub and looked at Noel. She briefly considered all she had lost.

"John has taken Sophia home, Emily. Your daughters are upstairs. Come onto the porch."

"I have work to do, Mr. Padgett," she replied stiffly.

"Why won't you let me help you?" he asked. "Whatever you ask, it's yours."

"There is nothing you can do to help me. Just let me do my work. We'll have boarders in this house again."

"Damn the boarders. Emily, you need rest, not more work. You need a strong arm, a—"

"I *do not!* I cannot rely on someone's strong arm now! I have daughters to see to, a house to manage. Let me be!"

He moved toward her and grasped her upper arms. "I love you. Why do you turn me away now?"

"Love?" She laughed humorlessly. "Your love, your courting and tempting and all these girlish notions it brought on caused me to glance away from my daughter long enough for her to be ruined! Haven't you asked yourself even once whether Patricia would be spared had we not skipped off to the fair without her? Lord, it was not the fair! It was my foolishness! And after all I should have learned!"

"Good God, Emily! You can't blame yourself for that! That girl was bound for it! If it hadn't been the fair, she would have run off some other time."

"I knew she was troubled, angry, defiant. Yet all I thought about was sitting on the porch, as fanciful as she! I don't blame you—they aren't your children. But I am long past these notions of romance and should have paid closer attention to my responsibilities. This is *my* fault."

"No. No more than it was your mother's fault that you married badly." Shock widened her eyes, and she stared at him in confusion. "I heard the story you told your daughters, Emily, I heard and I know why you feel like you do. I can make it right for you. Let me."

She stared another moment before she gave a huff of laughter and shook her head. "Make it right for me? No one can ever make that right for me—no one will ever remove that stain from my past. All I can do is carry on, take care of my children, manage my—"

"I'll marry you. Let me take care of you, and them. Emily, I want you. You don't have to carry these burdens alone."

"But I *am* alone! Marry? I can't *marry!*"

"I know you love me, Emily. You're tired, maybe sick. But you're not—"

"I can't marry!" she whispered furiously. "I'm not *widowed!*"

Noel actually withdrew slightly, though he continued to hold onto her arms. He looked into her eyes for an answer and saw tears well up there, the first tears she had shed since all the trouble began.

"Widowhood is a story," she said quietly, two uneven streams running down her cheeks. "Only a story. Ned Armstrong plied me with promises because he thought my family had money. He *left* me. He never even knew I carried Lilly!"

Noel rubbed the back of his finger along her cheek, wiping away the wetness. "He's been gone eighteen years, Emily. He isn't coming back. No one ever needs to know—"

"It's too late for all that, Noel. Don't you see? There is no room in my life for a man. Only twice in my life have I given in to such emotion, and twice it has cost me dearly. It's buried in me; I won't let that happen again."

"You can't blame love for this misery. Emily, you're a clever woman, sensible and strong. You don't have to be alone all your life. You don't have to give up any happiness you might have just because *he* wronged you."

"What do you suggest, Noel? That we marry in a lie and live out our days worrying that someone will find out I was never widowed? Would you make me an adulteress just to satisfy yourself?"

"I'm suggesting a decent life, a chance to be happy, to have a strong arm to lean on."

"Here? In Philadelphia? Or out in the plains of Wyoming, where you have your business, your land? Noel, we can't—"

"Emily, if you can't leave here, I won't make you go. But we were meant to be together, you and me."

"No. I made my choice many years ago, and it still holds me. I can't borrow any more sins. I'm still being punished for the first ones. I won't pretend a marriage that is not true, and I won't let romantic notions divert my eyes from my responsibilities."

"Emily, you love me. I know you do!"

"I thought—"

He wouldn't let her finish. He covered her mouth with his and held her tightly against him. He was forceful—he never thought he would embrace Emily like this. But his mouth was hungry on hers, desperate. His arms tightened around her. He was aware of how frail she had become. When he realized that she didn't resist him, when he finally tasted the salt of her tears, he slackened his hold. He whispered against her lips. "I know you love me. Let me take care of you."

"You said you only wanted me to be happy," she replied.

"Would you be happier without me?"

"I *can't!* No matter how much you offer me, no matter how sincere you are, I would be compromised. I could let you take care of me, pretend to be your wife when I know I am not, and live knowing only my shameful weakness. Is that what you want—that I should admit how weak I am and find solace in sin?" She shook her head. She pushed his hands away from her. "It's not our fault that it can't be."

"Why do you hurt yourself with pride? How can you punish yourself for feeling love?"

"Pride is what I used to survive! A good and decent life was mine because I was stronger than these feelings! It isn't love that hurts us—but letting love convince us to live immorally never stops hurting! Men can't understand because men never pay the price!"

She turned her back on him and continued to fill her bucket.

"You don't believe that. You're just confused, hurt."

"I think you'd better leave my house, Noel," she said, not looking at him.

"Why? Because if I stay you'll discover something stronger than all these ideas that keep you alone? Because if I stay you'll find out you can't turn your back on your feelings forever?"

She turned back to face him. Anger welled up inside, but she was unsure at who or what. "Ned did this to me, though he had other reasons for trying to wear down my resistance, but it's all the same. Give in, he begged me, for *love.* For *love* to make it right! If you stay here, I might only learn to hate you for showing me every day how incapable I am of making my own choices!"

Had she slapped him it would have been less painful. He backed

171

away a step. He looked at the fury in her eyes and the determination of her raised chin. He knew he was no match for all her suffering and self-blame.

"I'll go," he said, his voice soft. "I'll go and let you have all your hardship. You can tell yourself it's the only way if you want to. You can blame yourself for every misery in the world if you want to. I'll go so you can't think of me like you think of him. I'm not someone who's trying to wear you down for my own purposes, and maybe you'll remember that later. If I'm guilty of trying to tempt you, Emily, I only wanted to tempt you to share happiness with me."

He turned and went to the back stairs, to his attic room. She stood, her back against the sink, looking at her empty kitchen. It was getting harder and harder for her to collect herself, to ward off fear and loneliness. She turned back to the sink pump and worked it up and down, filling her bucket. She took the scrub brush, rags, and lye soap and climbed the stairs.

She knelt on the floor of the little room and thought of Annie and Jamie. Their joyful nuptial bed was naked of even the straw tick, and there was no sign of all the love and hardship that had happened here. She applied the water, soap, and brush.

Dear Father in Heaven, she silently prayed, if I could be given one understanding in all my lifetime, I would ask to know why You gave women enough strength in their bodies to bring forth a population, enough love to nurture nations of young, enough faith to carry them through the worst of times, enough wisdom to keep teaching them long after they've ignored the lessons, enough vigor to keep believing in life . . . and so few rewards. Can we not have love? If there is enough love to conceive them, feed them, even bury them, is there none to spare for a moment of peace and comfort?

She scrubbed tears into the floor with her brush. The only sound in the boardinghouse long after everyone had gone to sleep was the soft swishing of Emily's scrub brush.

Noel Padgett had writing paper in his satchel. He penned out the street address where his aunt lived so that he could be located if there was ever need and his gratitude for the room and board. He folded the paper over a considerable stack of bills and tied it closed with a string. He printed Mrs. Armstrong's name on the outside and left it on the worktable in the kitchen. The sun was not up when he crept out of the quiet house and went to the carriagehouse to retrieve his saddle. He made his way down the muddy road, his carpetbag heavy with all that he had accumulated in the way of clothes since he had arrived. His heart was heavy, too. He hoped Emily would change her mind. He would have stayed to convince her if he could bear the thought that she might only end up thinking of him as she thought of Ned.

He wanted Emily in ways so powerful, so final and desperate, that in the end, if he stayed, he might prove himself no better than Ned.

*W*hen Lilly heard the sounds of birds through her opened window and woke to the soft pink of early dawn, she sat up and jostled Patricia. "Wake up, Patricia. Mama is already awake and working. Come on, we have to help."

"Ohhhh," Patricia moaned. "It's so *early*."

"Come on," Lilly said, already out of bed and pulling off her nightgown. "Mama needs us. We have to help her. Don't be lazy now."

Lilly found her blouse and skirt and quickly dressed. She pulled the brush through her hair, but didn't bother with morning washing or braids. Emily had been going to bed very late, long after both the girls were asleep, and rising early, before dawn on most days. Fatigue and grief were showing on her: she had lost weight she could ill afford to lose and her radiant complexion had become sallow, her eyes weary. Lilly knew her mother would not rest until she had her house under control again—until there were boarders, a full table, and money in her jar for emergencies.

She was confused when she didn't find Emily in the kitchen. She saw a packet for her mother on the worktable, but the stove was cold. She went through the back door to look in the yard, then checked the parlor to see if she sat there with her sewing. Emily was nowhere to be found.

"Mama?" she called as she went back upstairs. The door to Susan Pendergast's room was closed and she opened it. She opened the door to the room in which Mrs. Fairchild had died. And then she went to the smallest room. "Mama!" she gasped, rushing in.

Emily lay face down on the damp floor, the scrub brush still gripped in her hand. Lilly knelt by her, turning her over and lifting her head. "Mama? Mama, are you all right? *Mama!*"

Emily's eyes opened, but her head lolled listlessly. She stared at Lilly for a moment, almost unseeing. And then she whispered, "Oh, Lilly . . ." Her voice was weak. Lilly felt her brow; she was feverish.

"Mama, what's the matter? Did you fall?"

"Lilly," she whispered again, helpless.

A million fears rushed through Lilly's mind. She was afraid her mother was dying. Some illness had attacked her in the night, and they hadn't even known she hadn't come to bed! Or had someone hit her, leaving her unconscious on the floor? Had she slipped on the soapy floor, lying injured and insensible through the night? It took a moment for Lilly to gather her wits enough to gently lower Emily's head to the floor and rush out of the room to get help. First she went for Patricia who was just dangling her legs from the bed. "Come quick, something's happened to Mama!" Then she went to John's room, banging on his door. "John, help me. Something's happened to Mama!"

John was quicker into his pants than Patricia was getting the robe to cover her nightgown. Lilly and John lifted Emily and carried her into her own room, to her own bed. Lilly was struck by how light her mother was in her arms. "What is it?" Patricia asked over and over. "What happened to Mama?"

Emily opened her eyes long enough to see that John was helping to place her in the bed. "Oh, John," she sighed, "I'm sorry."

"Mrs. Armstrong, can you tell me what's wrong? Did you fall? Are you ill?"

"No . . . no . . . it's nothing," she whispered, but she didn't seem able to lift her head.

"Lilly, get Mr. Padgett and send him for the doctor," John instructed. "Patricia, fetch Sophia. I'll sit with Mrs. Armstrong."

Lilly's confusion only mounted when she saw that Mr. Padgett's room was empty of his belongings. She couldn't imagine him just leaving. And then she remembered seeing the packet on the worktable and dashed down the back stairs to open it. She saw the money and read the brief note. She didn't understand why he had gone like this, but her mother was her first concern, and she stuffed the packet into her deep pocket and set off at a run to Dr. Olson's house. She prayed all the way that he would be there, that he would know what to do, and she was near tears by the time she was rousing the doctor's household. He answered the door himself in hastily drawn-up breeches. They did not bother with the carriage but rushed back to the boardinghouse on foot while Lilly breathlessly explained how she had found her mother.

Sophia had arrived and was sitting with Emily by the time Lilly returned. Patricia was sitting in the parlor, twitching and fretting. John Giddings was holding her hand, comforting *Patricia*. "Did anyone think of lighting the stove?" Lilly asked.

"Lilly, is Mama going to be all right?"

"Sitting there jittering about it won't help. There's plenty to be done while the doctor is with her. Let's don't just sit and—"

"But I don't know what to *do*," Patricia exclaimed, her voice trembling and her eyes watering.

Lilly whirled away from the parlor and went to the kitchen. She pumped water and started the fire. Her hands moved like lightning over bowls, pots, plates. She began biscuit dough and tossed a large hunk of bacon in a skillet. She steeped tea and broke open eggs. She alternately prayed her mother would survive and cursed Patricia's delicate helplessness. It was nearly an hour before Sophia came to the kitchen.

"Well, girl," Sophia said gravely. "Your Mama's used her last bit o' strength on this house, and now it looks like it's gonna be up to you."

"What is it? What does the doctor say?"

"It's the consumption, child. He say she don't take care of herself—she can't keep up without food and rest. She's down to bones and weak as a kitten. There comes a time when the good Lord

177

demands you take a rest. Dr. Olson says she's gonna be well, but I says it's more."

"What more, Sophia? What do you think it is?"

"I think that poor girl's heart's been ripped out every way it goes, child. First, Miz Patsy. Then the baby and Miz Fairchild. And then—" Sophia pursed her wide lips and shook her head. "She says he's gone, Mistah Padgett, but I don't think it likely he jes' *gone*. I think she sent him on his way."

Lilly was stunned. She touched the pocket that held the sizable amount of money and his short note. "Why?" she asked, a long way from understanding. "I've never known Mama to be happier than she's been since Mr. Padgett—"

"If she has her reasons, child, you let her tell about it. Right now she needs caring for. And I don't think Miz Patsy's gonna be the one, do you?"

Lilly wondered how Patricia had become so lazy, self-indulgent, and helpless. They had been raised by the same strict, energetic mother. They had been taught the same, been given the same chores, the same disciplines, had the same model. Yet Patricia had none of the virtues Emily had stressed.

Lilly searched her memory and realized that Patricia had always glided effortlessly through life by using her ineptness or her delicacy as a tool. She fell ill easily, had many complaints, and was always excused for no good reason except that it seemed more expedient to leave her alone than to insist, over and over, that she improve. Lilly and Patricia cleaned up supper dishes on alternating nights, but Lilly frequently cleaned up messes that Patricia had overlooked. If she forgot to dump the dishwater, Emily or Lilly would do it rather than call her back. If she was given a task of sewing, her stitches would invariably have to be torn out and redone, until it was hardly worth the bother to ask her in the first place. She made the biscuits taste bad by not measuring the ingredients, and Lilly or Sophia would be sure to do the next batch. If she was asked to wash clothes, it took her hours and hours and she would forget the soap; then they would have to be washed again. When Lilly asked her to help while Mama was sick by taking the wagon with rolls or pies to the brownstones to market them, Patricia would have trouble keeping up, or her legs would be sore from walking, or ultimately she was so unenthusiastic that she hindered rather than helped in sales.

Because Lilly felt she was on her own to care for her mother and manage the house, she was less inclined than ever to feel sorry for her sister. Even considering all that Patricia had been through at the hands of Dale Montaine, Lilly had lost all sympathy. That had been just another example of Patricia doing as she pleased without a thought of anyone but herself, yet Patricia thrust her burdens on them all when she had proved foolish. Now, in the aftermath of her devastating ordeal, John Giddings had taken the task of cheering her, spoiling her, and acting as her protector. He brought Patricia flowers, wrote her notes, held out her chair, opened her doors. But Patricia did not rally, even while Emily was ill. She only felt sorrier for herself and complained of how unjustly she had been treated.

Within a week of being put to bed, Emily began to improve. At first she slept nearly through the days and nights, waking just long enough to take a few bites of bland food. Another week saw her able to sit up, protest all the fuss that was being made over her, and eat heartier meals. Her color was coming back, but she was still too thin and weak to walk far without Lilly's help.

By the third week in bed, Emily was feeling strong enough to complain about being confined. But Lilly had a scare like never before in her life, and she would not allow Emily out of bed. She had spoken to the doctor and Sophia about this, and she had a schedule planned for her mother's recovery that would begin with sitting in a chair in her bedroom for a week, meals in the dining room the next week, short walks outside after that, and, when she was absolutely certain Emily would be all right, she would allow her to do a few light chores. It would be the end of September, another five weeks, before Emily could help around the house.

Lilly hid the fact that she was tired. Nor would she complain about Patricia, no matter how angry she became. She stopped to wash her face and smooth out her hair before entering Emily's room with a tray of food. And she concealed household problems as best she could.

The first problem was the absence of boarders. Lilly had decided they could take no new boarders before Emily was fully recovered.

Another problem arose. Although Lilly visited the same brownstones that her mother had frequented, she did not sell her jams or baked goods. When she delivered the sewing to Emily's customers, she was given very little more to do. Everyone, it seemed, preferred to wait for Mrs. Armstrong's recovery. Lilly's mending and baking was not lacking, but she did get an idea how difficult it really was to build up business.

She jealously counted the money that Mr. Padgett left and saw its limits. She had told her mother that he left his payment and an address so he could be contacted, but Emily had only looked away in discomfort. Lilly didn't mention there was more money than was due; she was afraid Emily's pride would forbid her to keep it. But, because even that generous sum was destined to run out, she had to release Sophia to seek other employment. That was the hardest news to keep from Emily. "There just wasn't so very much for Sophia to do, Mama, with no boarders other than John."

"But Lilly, we may not be fortunate enough to have Sophia come back to us after she finds other work; she's so skilled, so—"

"Don't worry, Mama. She'd rather be here than anywhere. And I don't want boarders before you're well."

"Oh, Lilly, I'm well enough. You've got to stop pampering me so much."

But Lilly thought it was high time someone pamper Emily. She was sorry she hadn't thought of it much sooner. Had Emily not been so exhausted and worried, she might not have become so ill.

"Mama, don't you want to read the note that Mr. Padgett left?"

"No. You did tell me everything it said, didn't you?"

"But I think he would want to know you've been sick, Mama. He was so fond of you."

"Never mind that, Lilly. He's gone about his business, and we don't want to bother him."

"But, Mama, he— Oh, Mama, did he just leave? Did you quarrel? Did you send him away?"

Emily reached for Lilly's hand. "No Lilly, we did not quarrel. It was time for Mr. Padgett to go."

"Mama, I believe he loved you . . ."

"What you saw, Lilly, was an unmarried man who wants a family of his own. I already have a family, one I'm very proud of. And this house to manage. There is no room in my life for more.

I'm content. And Mr. Padgett must look elsewhere for his companionship, for a family."

Lilly had heard Emily say many times that she had all she wanted, but this time she knew it wasn't true. This time she had seen for herself how radiant Emily looked when she felt loved. But all she said was, "I'll take care of you, Mama. I'll always be near."

During the last week of August Emily was getting up during the day and had even ventured downstairs twice. She was still far from her former strength. The evening meal was so different than it had been in the past. Lilly preferred to have her meal with Emily and left the dining room to Patricia and John. She began to hope that John would marry Patricia and take her away, but she wondered who would clean his house, mend his clothes, or cook his meals.

The first week in September brought dreary skies and occasional rain. Lilly was down to the last ten-dollar note. Emily was steadily improving, but even an hour or two on the porch left her exhausted. Lilly did nearly every chore—all the cooking, shopping, cleaning, washing, mending, and frequent trips to her mother's customers to request sewing jobs or offer the sale of foodstuffs. Patricia read or wrote in her journal or simply stared off into space. Lilly could barely conceal her anger.

After a very full morning of baking and cleaning, Lilly went into the parlor to check on her sister. She had given Patricia a light chore; she was to hem a skirt, a job that would pay fourteen cents. Lilly had been very specific about small stitches, about pressing the hem flat with a hot iron, about how carefully the job must be done so that more sewing jobs would be given to them. But when she went to the parlor, she found that Patricia was writing in her journal and the skirt lay untouched beside her.

"What are you doing?" she demanded of her sister. "You haven't even begun! I promised to return the skirt, finished, this afternoon!"

"I was meaning to . . . but, well, if you must know, I was feeling troubled again, and John says the best way out of a dreary mood is to write about it. I'll do it in a little while, Lilly."

"Do it now! Put that silly book away. It won't do you any good to work out your troubles if you starve to death because there's no money."

"Oh, Lilly, don't fuss about it. I'm not very good at it anyway."

"You're not good at anything! All you're good at is accepting

181

flowers and compliments. You don't *try!* You don't care that everyone must do your chores while you sit and worry about your *troubles!* You bring them all on yourself!"

"How can you say that to me, Lilly! How cruel of you! You know perfectly well that it wasn't my fault!"

"I know that if you'd gone to the fair with your family, or if you'd been too busy with chores to flirt, you wouldn't *have* these troubles!"

"Are you saying that . . . that . . . I—"

"I'm saying that you're lazy! And selfish! And you've hardly lifted a finger to help me since Mama's been sick! You don't care about anyone but yourself, and you *never have!*"

Patricia stared at Lilly. Her mouth was open in shock, and her eyes grew round before they filled with tears. She gasped back a sob and then burst into tears. "Lilly! You're so *mean!*" Clutching her precious journal book, Patricia fled from the room to hide in one of the empty bedrooms and pursue her problems in pen, in private. It had been a long time since Lilly felt curious enough to want to read those private pages.

Lilly stood in the parlor, seething. How had their mother endured Patricia these many years? How long would the entire household be left without any assistance from her because of her *troubles?* It was so plain to Lilly: despite warnings, lectures, and more careful explanations than a moron usually required, Patricia still dangled her virtue before a man just horrid enough to take it. And she played the wronged woman very well, while making no effort to change herself.

She lifted the skirt. She had promised it for today, and there was no way she could prepare an evening meal and get that done, too. Tears smarted in her eyes. She would stay up late again. She could apologize to Patricia and plead with her to fix the supper, but Patricia would only make it terrible and the most important meal of the day would not be enjoyable for Emily.

Lilly felt the tears run down her cheeks and wiped at them impatiently; it took so much to make her cry. She had never been this tired or so lonely. Anything for relief; she missed Mr. Padgett's stories, Annie's bright Irish tunes, even Mrs. Fairchild's testy complaints. Their house was quiet and dreary. The unseasonal September heat was muggy and unbearable. She went to stand on the porch, praying for a rain shower or even one brief, consoling breeze. She knew she must collect herself, not give into this self-pity. She'd never finish her chores if she couldn't—

Her eyes widened at the sight of a coach. Had Mr. Padgett come back? Surely Dale Montaine would not— The coach stopped in front of their house and she stared. Mrs. Wilcox from across the street leaned out her front window to watch. The driver jumped down to open the door and help someone out. Lilly couldn't help but tilt her head and frown as a woman approached. There was no question the woman was rich. She wore a bright yellow frock that had a low décolletage, despite the fact that she was much older than Emily. Her hair was a rich, thick auburn, and her hat was flamboyant, a large yellow feather bobbing over its wide brim as she walked. And she used a white cane with a gold handle and gold tip, although she was rather spritely and didn't seem to rely too heavily on the help. She smiled as she approached Lilly, looking up to the porch. Then she stopped walking. "Patricia?" she asked.

"Lillian Armstrong, ma'am," she replied in confusion.

"Lilly!" the woman exclaimed, then gave a short and pleased laugh.

"Ma'am?" Lilly questioned.

"Well goodness, girl. I came as quickly as I could after your letter! Aren't you going to greet me properly? Will it be a kiss on the cheek, or—"

"Grandmother?" Lilly asked quietly. "Grandmother!" she shrieked, bolting down the steps to embrace her. She nearly knocked her over in her excitement, but she found that her grandmother withstood her enthusiasm very well. She was tall, strong like Lilly. The first thing she noticed and delighted in was her grandmother's formidable frame; here was a woman of substance and sturdiness.

"I hope this means you're pleased by my surprise visit," Amanda said.

"Pleased? Oh!" Tears came to Lilly's eyes and began to spill over. "Oh, Mama is going to be . . . Oh, Mama is sick. She *has* been sick, but I'm taking good care of her."

"Well, take me to her, girl. Come now, if she's ill—"

"She's getting better every day, Grandmother, but before you see her, I should tell you all that's happened. So much has happened since my letter—more has happened since I wrote you than in my whole life!"

"Then, Lilly, tell me. Tell me quick so I can go to my daughter."

Amanda went back to the coach that waited in front of the boardinghouse. She had left Bertie sitting there for well over an hour. She opened the door and spoke to her servant. "Well, Beatrice, our girl is sick and needs our attention. Their household is in a dither. They've had nothing but problems. No," she said when Bertie made a move as if she would get out of the coach, "I want you to take the coach back to the city, collect a few things to see us through the week, and tell Fletcher to get about the business of finding us larger accommodations. We'll stay here and get things under control before moving everyone to a better place."

"Here, mum? Here?"

"Don't grouse. We've had worse. As Lilly tells it, Emily is quite proud of this and won't give it up easily."

"How bad is she?"

"I haven't seen her just yet, but my granddaughter has been telling me about the events that led to this present disaster. Lord above, Bertie! When I tell you all that's gone on, you'll think you've revisited the past! Bring something stout—you'll be wanting a tipple later. Get on with you."

By the worry in Bertie's eyes, Amanda knew it took discipline for the servant to go off to fetch their belongings. Bertie had helped tend Emily when she was a child and had been nearly as disappointed as Amanda when they all lost track of each other.

Amanda returned to the house where Lilly waited. "I think it would be nice if you brought us tea," she told her. "We'll need a little time alone, I think."

"I'm so glad you're here," Lilly said with relief.

"I've brought you a desk, Lilly. You did say you wanted to go into business?"

"Yes, but—Well, I don't have the first idea *what* business."

"Go about the business of tea, for now. I hope you have decent tea." She patted Lilly's cheek. Then she began to master the stairs. She was afraid, but had never let fear stop her before. She opened the door to Emily's room and looked in. Emily slept. Amanda took the liberty of studying her while she couldn't look back. Tears collected, and her chest heaved with emotion. How she had changed! Her golden hair had darkened, and she was so frail. Her hands, folded over the quilt, were rough and hard used; her cheeks were sunken.

Amanda wanted to embrace her and hold her to her breast. My child, my love. My daughter, grown old!

She sat gently on the bed and pulled the hat pin out of her wide-brimmed, feather-studded hat, removing it and laying it aside. She touched Emily's hand to rouse her. Her eyes opened, and she gazed sleepily, trying to acclimate herself, and then stared in surprise.

"Mother?" she questioned. "Mother?" She tried to sit up.

"I'm here, dear. Don't excite yourself now."

Emily reached out a hand to touch Amanda's cheek, then her hair, her shoulder. "Mother, it's you! How in the world—"

Amanda helped Emily to sit up, and they embraced. Emily clasped her tightly and cried. Long, tired, grateful sobs. Amanda felt relief flood through her. All through the years, through the guarded letters, she had feared the reunion. Their parting had been so angry; they had made such unforgivable pronouncements to each other. *"You'll pay in the worst possible ways for this foolishness!" "I'll believe you never loved Father if you marry again!"* On and on those angry battles repeated themselves in Amanda's memory. There were times she thought she would never reconcile with her daughter, yet now she held her in her arms. The joy of being received melted away the fear.

"There now, Emily. I'm here . . . and I'm not leaving you again no matter how stubborn you are."

"Never again, Mother. I have never stopped regretting those angry days, those awful, punishing things we—"

"Hush. We have years to discuss our many regrets. I understand you have a speck of trouble." Emily pulled herself out of her mother's embrace. "Lilly told me. She was very thorough."

"About Patricia? The boarders?"

Amanda nodded and touched Emily's cheek. "And the cowboy," she added.

Emily smiled in spite of herself. "A speck of trouble? Oh, Mother, all my life I've tried to face things the way you do. As if they're mere inconveniences, little nuisances to be tidied."

"Now I'm here to face it with you, darling. I know there are greater concerns, but what of this Mr. Padgett? He didn't hurt you, did he?"

"Lilly couldn't have told you everything, Mother. She barely knows the half of it. But now you're here, and I will tell you. Everything. As I've wanted to do for years and years."

Amanda spent the afternoon in Emily's bedroom, sipping tea and listening with amazement at all her daughter had managed in eighteen years, and all she had been through in a few short months. It was four in the afternoon before she heard the sound of the hired trap bringing Bertie back to the boardinghouse. She put her teacup aside and rose to look out the window.

"Well, here she is, the mean old thing. She'll help us put this house in order again. She's been saying the same thing for years, and she's right—the woman in this family carry on a legacy of stubbornness, contrariness, and perfectly miserable luck with men."

Emily smiled. "Also strength, Mother. We are strong, all of us, you can't deny that."

"But has it ever occurred to you, dear, that if we weren't those other things, we wouldn't require so much strength?"

10

*L*illy stood reading the bills outside the theater. She wore all new clothes: a silk blouse with thirty-five tiny buttons that went up to her throat, a deep green velvet skirt, a dark, fully lined cloak, and slip-on leather shoes with brass buckles. She wore a hat and four-button gloves, and carried a drawstring handbag. For the very first time in her life, she wasn't just reading the bills because she couldn't afford the price of a ticket. Now she could afford several.

"Lilly? Is it *you*?"

She turned excitedly. "Andrew! Oh, Andrew, it's been *months!*"

"Look at you! You've grown up five years in just weeks! Let me see you!" She turned for him, her smile wide and confident. "Good Lord," he said, nodding appreciatively. "You're a whole new person!"

Her eyes danced, and she knew it. She had pleased him. "For the past two weeks I've been to the library, the square, up and down these streets from morning to afternoon, *looking* for you! I don't even know your last name, Andrew!" And now, she thought with great pleasure, I'm not afraid to know.

"It's Devon, Lilly. Andrew Devon." He offered her his arm. "The square?"

She gladly took it, happy to stroll with him. "I always believed that when I finally knew who you were, I'd learn that you were some millionaire or royalty and would—I don't know why I tell you every thought that drifts through my mind! I always mean to guard myself better. My grandmother says that I'm painfully blunt. Oh, you should *know* her! She is incredible."

"Just so it never changes—your frankness. It's like a breeze. You've never mentioned your grandmother before."

"I've only just met her. She just returned to Philadelphia from London, England. *London, England!* Imagine, I didn't even know I had a grandmother, and here she is, home, and she's made everything so wonderful. There I go. I should start at the beginning, shouldn't I? The summer started out so badly, I wondered if we'd get through it."

She told him about the deaths of the MacIntosh baby and Mrs. Fairchild. She explained how hard her mother had had to work through that, only to fall to consumption. Then of how the boardinghouse had emptied of boarders, of how there had been no customers for their baked goods or sewing, and how she had been down to the last ten-dollar note when a hired coach had come up the drive and out stepped the most beautiful, formidable, confident woman she'd ever met in her life.

"She's been with us for a month, she and Beatrice, her tire woman. That's what personal servants are called in England, and Bertie complains that she is tired indeed!" Lilly laughed. "She also has a hired man, Mr. Drake, who does business on her behalf, and she took over the boardinghouse like that," she said, snapping her fingers. "Although she's used to having servants do most of the work, she is not shy of work herself. She had Mama up and about in no time, moved out our last boarder, and has found a buyer for the boardinghouse! We're moving into a hotel next week, all of us. *A hotel!*"

"This sounds like a guardian angel, not a grandmother," he laughed. "I see she fixed you up with new clothes. Lovely."

"She brought her desk all the way from England because I had written to her that I wanted to go into business. Imagine that! Now I have a desk, but I have no idea what business I'll pursue."

"Study, Lilly," he said. "Keep up your studies. You'll think of something special. You'll be buying all your books now, I suppose. Are you terribly rich?"

"I'm not quite sure," she thoughtfully replied. "Yes, I suppose we must be. Well, Grandmother is rich. She says that we needn't be worried about money anymore. She is a lady . . . I mean, a *lady*. Her last husband was a *lord*. She says we should forget all that since we're not going to England where it all matters. But when Bertie gets aggravated with her, she calls her *Laidy* Nesbitt. The two of them can tangle like snakes over the slightest thing, both of them bossy as hens, but every night they play a card game, bet against each other, and—oh, I know you won't believe this, but it's true—Grandmother has her brandy, and Bertie takes a *pipe!*"

Andrew laughed at her. "You're happier than I've ever seen you! You know, I worried about you—our last meeting . . ."

Lilly stopped walking and turned toward him. She was filled with hope and excitement. She grasped both his hands and looked longingly into his eyes. "Our last meeting was wonderful," she said in a soft voice. "I'll never forget it!"

His expression grew serious. "Lilly," he began, frowning slightly. "Lilly, I took advantage of you, of your youth and inexperience—"

"Oh, Andrew, no, I—"

"Let me finish, Lilly. I should not have done what I did. I found you desirable and vulnerable. You'd become very special to me. I didn't intend it."

"Andrew, I want to be special to you. You're special to me. Before . . . when I felt so far from your social status, when my family had so little, I knew it was foolish of me to be so taken with you. But now—"

"Lilly, nothing has changed. If it were possible for me to court you, I would, and believe me money would have nothing to do with it. It's not possible, Lilly. We can't even be friends now that there are romantic feelings between us." She stared at him, speechless and confused. "I'm married, Lilly. I have a wife."

189

First the shock of it drained the color from her cheeks. She was frozen, looking up into his bright green eyes in amazement. The pain in his expression finally nudged her into awareness, and she lowered her gaze and dropped his hands.

Andrew lifted the hand that hung at her side and put it in the crook of his arm, walking again. "I'm sorry, Lilly. I beg your forgiveness."

"But why—?"

"I was not a gentleman. I have no excuse worthy of what I did. Kissing you that way was . . . impetuous and foolish of me. I let my strong feelings for you override my good sense. In fact, I've had a long struggle over what, exactly, I should tell you. I finally decided you deserve the truth. I felt desire for you that I had no right to feel. A gentleman would have walked away from such feelings without taking any liberties. And now being with you at all is dangerous."

"But don't you *love* your wife?" she asked.

"Lilly, my feelings for my wife are not important. Facts are facts. I was attracted to you. I didn't intend that, but neither could I prevent it. Perhaps I shouldn't be telling you this, but I can't have you thinking I go around seducing young girls at the library. I don't want you to think I'm a rover."

"It just seems to me that if you really *loved* her, you wouldn't be tempted by such feelings."

"No," he said, laughing humorlessly, "that wouldn't make any difference. I'm still married. I'm not going to plead an unhappy marriage or any other excuse. That would only make the whole situation we face much worse, it would tempt us both to begin something with no happy endings."

"You won't be in the park anymore, will you?" she said, beginning to get the gist of this.

"Not deliberately. I was before, you know. Looking for you for God knows what reason. Intrigue at first, you're fascinating. Brilliant, full of life. I lied to myself for a while, I believed I could talk with you, walk with you. Be your friend."

"But Andrew . . . we can be friends . . ."

"Lilly, darling, we can't. Don't you understand the power of what you felt in the coupé? My God, Lilly! Did you think any man can pretend a kiss like that?" He looked at her. "You're all that much more beautiful because you don't know how beautiful, how desirable you are. I don't trust myself with you."

190

"Andrew, I want you to want me. I never thought—" She stopped abruptly. She didn't think it possible that he could feel that way. She had hoped to win him somehow, now that her family was improved and not so common.

"To what end, Lilly? You have your whole life ahead of you; this will pass into a memory. Let go of it. Try to think of me along with other unmannerly rogues."

"Andrew, I don't want never to see you again," she said, tears coming to her eyes. "It's all I've thought about for weeks—seeing you, riding in the coupé."

"That will never happen again. Lilly, don't cry. When you think about this, you'll understand. It's dangerous for you, for me. I came very close to keeping you in that coupé for hours . . . for days, had I been able to manage it. You deserve better than what you'd get from me."

Tears slid down her cheeks and he gently wiped one away. "I wanted to stay," she said, a little gasp coming from her.

"I know," he said, turning her again to walk. "That's why we're saying good-bye today. Because I can't trust myself, and I can't trust you. You're a passionate woman, Lilly."

"Andrew, if I promise that I—"

"Promise to hold in all those feelings that are so natural for you, so beautiful and real? No. It would be an empty promise that you would break too soon . . . to your heartache. If I were not a married man, I would snatch you up and never let you go. What you have is wonderful, Lilly. Give it to a more deserving man."

She hurt inside, more deeply than she imagined possible. "Don't leave me yet," she said, not looking at him. "Give me a little time to recover . . . I don't know whether to hate you or beg you to meet me in the park and . . ."

"It would be better if you hated me. Believe me, there is nothing we can do but part company. Your tears will dry."

"This whole summer has left me upside down. Do you know why I never asked your name? I was sure I would find out how rich and influential you are! I thought I'd lose the courage to talk to you!"

"I'm just a working man, Lilly."

"But I've never even seen you wear the same suit of clothes twice!"

"Now, you must be mistaken. I haven't any complaints about my status, but I don't have *that* kind of wardrobe."

"But you're a patron of the library. You have your own coach. You have time to stroll around the square—"

"I have more time than a lot of working men do, that's true, but my patronage at the library has to do with my own beginnings. I was born to a poor existence. I now work for a successful man and have studied on my own, the way you're doing. I was determined to make a success of myself, and the books I could borrow made some of that possible. It was that, in fact, that awakened my curiosity in you. We have that in common, you and I. I endow the library, but more conservatively than you might think—it's just a way of passing on good fortune."

"And if your wife had seen us strolling through the square together?"

"Mrs. Devon isn't seen loitering around the library or the square. Believe me."

"Do you have children?"

"No, we haven't been blessed. But we haven't been married all that long. Perhaps one day—"

Lilly shook her head in confusion. "I'm a long, long way from understanding men! I never will!"

"Someday, Lilly. I keep telling you—you're too beautiful and clever to be left alone for long. Some young fellow as clever as you will come along and—"

She put her hands over her ears. "Oh stop! I've heard enough of that kind of talk to last a lifetime! My grandmother says the women in my family are better off doing some sort of work because we're born to have terrible luck with men!"

"All the women in your family must be cursed with the same great beauty."

"Bertie says we're alike in three things—stubbornness, contrariness, and bad luck with men. Grandmother has buried *three* husbands and she's through with marrying. Mama won't even discuss the possibility of marrying ever again, and Patricia . . . Patricia's bad luck has only begun. She gets worse every day!"

"Patricia," he said. "She's the one determined to marry, though she dislikes all her beaux, children, and domestic work. Correct?"

"That isn't half of it. She ran into trouble with a rich young man, although Mama tried to warn her. She suffered for weeks through the summer. All the while Mama was sick, she just felt sorry for herself. It was perfectly horrid. But do you think she's given up

192

all her notions? Now that she thinks she has money, Grandmother's money, she's talking about parties, balls, and the like. She is determined to live among the very people who abused her. As if what happened to her wasn't awful enough."

"What happened to her?" he asked.

"She used some excuse to sneak away with her rich young man, though Mama had *strictly* forbidden her. Mama said that it was the misfortune of many a poor girl to be taken in by rich young men who never intended to marry them, but Patricia was absolutely determined that her beauty would win her a wealthy husband. She was courting danger from the start. And it was a mighty dangerous end."

"Your mother is right. I hope she wasn't hurt."

"She was hurt, as a matter of fact. He tricked her from the start, pretending to be in love with her. He was always tempting her with his riches, the wonderful events he would escort her to, even marriage! His final trick was to take her to his house when there was no one at home and—" She stopped explaining. She had already said far too much. She stole a glance at Andrew. By his eyes she could see that he didn't need to be told any more.

"I hope she's all right now," he said sympathetically. "You see, don't you, that completely unharnessed desire, whether for wealth or for love, can lead to despair? That's why, Lilly, you must be wiser than your sister."

"But Andrew, she never loved him or wanted him. It was his fancy life she wanted. It wasn't desire that got her into trouble. It was greed."

"It's just a lot of wanting something you can't have."

"You're wrong, Andrew," she said. "I can have what I want. I'm not like Patricia—I'm not greedy and selfish. I've thought about it all summer and I know what I want—I want work and love. I don't have to be married, I don't have to—"

"You know better than that. There is no love that works when its foundation is dishonest. You'll end up like your sister—angry and troubled and far from happy."

"And plotting revenge? Do you think so? She wants to be rich as sin and get even with that awful Montaine wretch!"

The moment the name was out of her mouth Lilly stopped dead in her tracks. Her face colored.

"Montaine?" Andrew asked.

"Oh, promise me you won't ever repeat what I've said! I was

193

ordered to keep quiet; Mama says there's no way a woman can accuse and keep her dignity—no way to make a man responsible for what he does to a woman. Oh, Andrew," she said pleadingly, "I never meant to say the name!"

"It's all right, Lilly," he said, glancing away uncomfortably. "I won't ever let on that you slipped. Don't worry."

"I suppose you've heard the name?"

"It is the name of Philadelphia. The young man has something of a bad reputation as it is. What did he do to your sister, Lilly?"

She shook her head. "I've said enough about her. She asked for it."

He lifted her chin. "And now you are." She began to shake her head, but he held her chin still between his finger and knuckle. "Say good-bye, Lilly."

"No, Andrew. Not after—"

"Good-bye. I'm sorry I hurt you. I won't hurt you any further, whether or not you like it."

"No," she said again, the tears beginning anew. But he turned away abruptly. His pace across the square was hurried, almost jaunty, and he did not look back. How many times, she wondered, had he said this kind of good-bye? How many women had felt this helplessly in love with him?

The tears dried after a while, but she stayed in the park the whole afternoon, thinking and seeking composure. The anger came, but slowly. Hate might actually be possible, if she thought about her dashed hopes long enough. Had that really been she? Proud, stubborn Lilly, begging a married man to pursue her despite the fact that he had obligations? She had lost her mind . . . over one passionate kiss. He should have known better; he had not forgotten he was married.

Perhaps it was his plan all along to make her his mistress. Perhaps a sudden attack of conscience stopped him. She had almost let it happen. She would almost have welcomed it, so wild had her day-dreams been since that kiss.

Married. She thought about that all the way home. He was married—a status that did not change. But there was another thought that she could not suppress; he wanted her. Somehow, through all her fantasies about him, she had never dared hope that he felt as strongly as she. She wasn't sure whether this knowledge made her feel better . . . or worse.

Lilly was unusually quiet during the dinner hour. The evening meal at the boardinghouse had become so interesting since her grandmother had arrived, the table so plentiful, the conversation so stimulating, that Lilly was usually the most animated. Tonight she was only half listening to the voices of her mother, grandmother, and sister. Her usually robust appetite was gone; she pushed her food around. She couldn't forget him. Had she found him an available young bachelor, her happiness would be complete. Her greatest hope had died, and she was miserable.

"Only four more meals at this old table, Emily," Amanda said. "Can you bear it?"

"The table isn't so old, Mother. And I still think we should keep the house if possible. I've always loved it—it's been my security."

"If we keep the house, you'll be tempted to come back here, and I want all this *behind* us! You worked so hard it nearly killed you!"

"Nonsense. It was consumption, not work."

"I can't wait to leave," Patricia said. "But when are we going to move into our own house? How long must we live in a hotel? And when are we going to meet all your old friends, Grandmother? When do you plan to tell them we're back?"

"We're not back, dear," Amanda said somewhat testily. "I'm back. You've been here all along."

"I wouldn't say so," Patricia replied. "I'm just anxious to get back into society!"

"I'm at my wit's end," Emily said, lying down her fork beside her plate. "Mother, please try again. Explain this business of society to your granddaughter. I beg of you."

"Your last voyage into society did not go smoothly, Patricia," Amanda chastised. "At this point in your young life you should be pleading with me to hide you from the people who treated you so badly."

"I want them all to see they haven't cost me a thing!" Patricia exclaimed. "I'd love to have Mary Ellen Jasper groveling for a kind word and Dale Montaine begging for forgiveness!"

"It won't go that way, Patricia," Amanda said. "We've been

over this a hundred times. You're expecting all the wrong things. You're being silly, and it will cost you far more than it already has. I honestly don't know how you've come by your notions! I have a mind to set you adrift in your precious society and see if you don't learn the merits of humility."

"I've been humbled enough," she said in a pouting voice. "Now I'd like to enjoy myself."

"Surrounding yourself with fancy people and things is not nearly as enjoyable as you might think—"

Patricia laughed. "Maybe not when you don't feel good enough for them, but when you can outdo them in every way . . . When you have twice their money and heritage, I imagine it's great fun!"

"Are you certain you gave birth to this child, Emily? You didn't find her abandoned—"

"Oh, it's easy to criticize me for wanting nice things when you've already *had* them! Is it so wrong, Grandmother, to want luxury and leisure?"

"Wanting, Patricia, should be balanced with a little common sense and style. I have a full purse, dear, not a magic one. It has a bottom. I don't plan to find the bottom of my purse through indulging your whimsy."

"Grandmother?" Lilly asked. "Do you actually know any of the Montaines?"

The room became stone still. Emily and Amanda looked at each other, and Patricia's eyes burned brightly, almost glittering in rage.

Amanda sighed, her fork poised over her plate. "You are the only one in this family who has not been given a full explanation, Lilly. I meant to tell you sooner. Wilson Montaine, Dale's father, was the man to relieve me of my family home after your grandfather's death. He virtually stole it, my circumstances were so bleak. So, there you have it. Dale Montaine soiled my granddaughter in my house —possibly in my room. I have spent a great many years resenting Wilson Montaine. I find little relief from that resentment now."

Lilly looked at her mother. "Mama, why didn't you *tell* us?"

"I was afraid Patricia might make the mistake of being encouraged by Dale's aggressive attention. I was afraid she would get it into her head that I would be grateful, somehow, to be restored to that estate." She glanced at Patricia. Patricia lifted her chin. "Afterward, it hardly mattered what that house once meant to me."

196

"Don't you want to get it back?" Patricia asked her grandmother in a shrill voice.

"I'd be glad if I didn't have to ever set foot in that house again, my dear. The happy times we had there can never be restored, and I am not eager to revisit the memories of the painful days when we were leaving."

"Well, you should *want* to get it back! He *took* it from you, didn't he? And after what Dale did to me, wouldn't it be justice to oust him from his fancy house!"

Amanda slammed her fork against the table. Her mouth became rigid and her eyes narrowed, her unusually smooth and youthful skin crinkling into angry lines. She reddened, and Lilly stared in wonder at her grandmother's gathering rage. How exciting she looked, how powerful. Patricia actually sat back farther in her chair. "I have half a mind to punish you with all your selfish desires!" she barked. "For a sixpence I'd toss you to the little monster, force him to marry you, and let you wallow in your luxury! I don't know how you manage to hear my money jingle when you're stone deaf!"

Patricia's mouth stood open in surprise. "Grandmother," she said in a breath, "could you actually *do* that?"

Amanda's eyes closed in complete exasperation. She groaned and let her head fall back slightly. It took a moment for Amanda to collect herself. She took several deep breaths before leveling her furious gaze on Patricia. "Excuse yourself," she said in a whisper that seemed to take effort. "Go to a nice, quiet place and remember every detail of your terrible experience and ask yourself if you could bear to relive *any part of it!*"

Patricia exercised a rare bit of wisdom in silence. She quietly got out of her chair and left the room. Amanda glanced at Emily.

"Oh, Mother," Emily said wearily. "What have you done? You don't suppose—?"

"Beatrice!" Amanda barked, her voice loud and biting. When Bertie showed her startled face at the dining room door, Amanda said, "Bring me a brandy! Before I faint!"

"Bertie," Emily quietly requested, "bring two brandies."

11

$\mathcal{I}$ find this distasteful. Abhorrent," Amanda told Emily. "I don't pretend I haven't done a nasty piece of business here and there, but this is the worst. Still, I can not think of any alternative that is not an even greater risk than this."

"Nor I," Emily said quietly, her eyes misting. They were discussing Patricia, a subject that could be counted on to make Emily's eyes tear and Amanda's ire rise.

Amanda had been able to secure a suite of rooms in the city. Their new address was the Grafton Hotel, at Twenty-One Rittenhouse. They could view the square from many windows on the fifth floor, occupied seven luxuriously furnished rooms, and paid handsomely for this privilege in an Exhibition city. Since their stay would be long and the close of the Exhibition would leave the city with many vacant rooms soon, Mr. Grafton was not reluctant to allow them the rooms. Even Emily had relented to the comforts, though she had secretly cried in her pillow the first few nights she was away from her beloved boardinghouse.

They had been in residence for three weeks, time enough to spruce up their wardrobes and argue with Patricia. Lilly was ignored during this time, but that was very much to her liking. She made herself busy with books, sights, plays, and generally getting acquainted with a higher style of living. And trying to forget girlish dreams of love and passion, which took a great deal of private introspection.

This business with Andrew brought her closer to her understanding of Patricia, for Lilly had met something she strongly desired, something it was not practical to pursue. The difference was that she did not feel the desire was larger than her will.

Patricia had become unbearable. The idea that she could be married into the Montaine family—into the Montaine mansion that had once been her grandmother's—had taken root and was growing thick, strangling vines of obsession. Patricia had never been more determined. Their discussions, those among Emily, Amanda, and Patricia, had been rife with emotion. Lilly had eavesdropped devotedly, when she was near enough.

"How can you endure the idea of more physical treatment the likes of which you've already suffered from Dale Montaine?" Emily had asked her, aghast at the suggestion that he be forced to marry her.

"Tell me, Mama, what man I will not have to lie beneath when we're married? *He's* the one who spoiled me—let him be the one to support me."

"And how do you propose to enjoy that support, however glamorous, living with a man you despise?" Amanda had pressed.

"What makes you think I can love any man now?"

"Time, Patricia, time. When your grandfather died . . ."

"What poor wretch should I take my used body to? My husband hasn't died. There has been no husband to explain my lost virginity! All I want is a pleasant life! He should be made to pay for what he's done to me. He only did it because he was certain he would never be forced to pay."

"Marriage for revenge, Patricia, is a—"

"Marriage for *wealth*, Grandmother. I don't want to go to another man when Dale Montaine's mark is on me!"

"You will have his children!"

"*My* children! Who will inherit!"

"Unloved wives can be treated like paupered cousins while their husbands—"

Patricia laughed cruelly. "Do you think my heart will break if he leaves me alone and goes whoring? Do you think he would strike Lady Nesbitt's granddaughter? Or perhaps refuse me food?"

She persisted for three weeks. The unlikely character to give in, relent, was Emily. She finally said to Amanda, "Do it, Mother. If you can."

"Emily!"

"I don't like it. I hate it, as you must know. I also remember very well what I did to myself when you refused to let me marry Ned Armstrong. Oh, Mother, I don't know what terrible thing Patricia might do to have her way. I know only two things for certain. She can never be happy in that marriage, and . . . and at least we will not be far away. At least we will be near enough to bring her home if it becomes dangerous. That is a greater advantage than I had."

"Aren't you afraid he'll hurt her? Hurt her in horrible ways that she hasn't even imagined yet?"

"Yes," Emily said in a shuddering breath. "And I have warned Patricia as well as I can. I only pray that if this comes to pass, Wilson Montaine proves to be a man who will not tolerate his son's further abuse of my daughter."

"I wouldn't put much hope in that," Amanda had replied.

Now, as she tugged on her gloves to go to the Montaine house, they gave it one last consideration. In answer to Amanda's written request, Wilson Montaine would see her. Amanda had come to acknowledge the very thing Emily spoke of. Patricia was determined and greedy. Amanda was not optimistic that she could convince Wilson Montaine to help in this; Wilson had never appeared to be a man of conscience. The young man, however, was rumored to find society and prominence important. He could therefore be tricked.

"I dread seeing it again . . . the house," Amanda said.

"You will have to see it one day, I imagine."

"Where does this trait come from? Why is she like this? She doesn't resemble any member of our family. No Chase or Bellmont would aspire to this kind of marriage—we were always proud and unshakable. Ah, I recognize the stubbornness, but where in our family tree—"

"Ned Armstrong," Emily said softly, looking at her mother. "If

201

Ned had stayed, he might have suggested this to Patricia. He would have delighted in her defilement. The greed and foolishness are his. Mother, he did this to me—he was very purposeful. He didn't value love or happiness above wealth any more than Patricia does."

Amanda considered for the first time that the loss of her family wealth had saved Emily from a lifetime with Ned, for he would certainly have stayed with her while there was something to spend.

"What will you say to Wilson Montaine?"

"Oh," Amanda began, positioning her hat on her auburn hair while looking in the mirror, "just that it is good to see him prosper, and it is nice to see the house in such good order." She looked over her shoulder at Emily and made a face. "I hope to save my most persuasive words for young Mister Montaine."

"Don't be too clever, Mother. I'm still a little afraid."

"Women can't be too clever, dear. Most especially the women in this family. I had begun to think it was good there wasn't a man among us. Men suggest marriages like this—an expedient remedy. It's medieval, barbaric. In times of yore queens have been the victims of the sins of men. I thought we four together could take the issues of our bodies and happiness seriously. Men treat such issues with absolute consternation. Even your father, good man that he was, courageous as he could be in politics, was baffled by the trials women presented. He might have suggested that the man who forced Patricia wed her. I could have saved her from that."

"Mother, she won't let you save her. Just as I wouldn't let you."

"Bertie!" Amanda called.

Beatrice opened the door to Amanda's bedroom. "Ready, mum?"

"Yes. Is Fletcher waiting?"

"Patient as a statue."

"And sturdy as a rock. I wish he were a little older, and I'd consider marriage again. What a good friend I've had in him."

"Mother, you're incorrigible."

"Yes, yes, so I'm told. Do you wish me luck?"

"I'm afraid to do that. I'm afraid to hope you fail. But I've considered that if you put your efforts forth and can then report to my foolish daughter that it can't be done, perhaps she will change. I pray."

Amanda grinned at her daughter. It was a tolerant grin. "Good, Emily, you pray. I'll negotiate." And she went through the door.

Fletcher Drake kept rooms in the Grafton as well, but did not reside with the women. He stayed on a lower floor in far less ostentatious surroundings. Amanda made sure his fortunes increased along with hers, and she accused him of being a miser. He needed comfortable quarters and a large enough study to manage all of Amanda's legal and investment affairs, but he insisted he was so busy in this capacity that little besides a bedroom, sitting room, and servant quarters for his man, Michael, was required. He was always available to Amanda, as he had been for many years.

Though the coach the women used was a hired trap, Fletcher had assumed the need for prestige and had brought a gold Nesbitt crest from England that could be transferred to whatever conveyance they used. When Amanda stepped out onto the busy Philadelphia street with him and saw the waiting coach complete with escutcheon on the door, she felt a pride that came frequently when Fletcher anticipated her. "Very nice touch, Fletcher. Do we own the coach and driver?"

"We have full-time use of both, but I haven't purchased one for the family as yet. I wouldn't without discussing it. Perhaps in the next few weeks . . ."

"But the family arms is such a good idea. How fussy you are about details."

Fletcher kept his chuckle under his breath—of course, Amanda was the fussy one. While she might not have thought of the crest before leaving London, she would have remembered it as soon as her journey was complete and would have groused about forgetting it for some time. He began to guess these things only after several years of listening to her grumble and complain.

"Do you think this is the right thing to do?" she asked him when they were underway.

"No. But I don't know anything about daughters or wives and was a little shy of alternatives."

"I should pay you to marry the little twit."

"Oh, thank you, madam, no," he laughed. "You don't leave me enough time for marriage, and I'm not sure the young lady would be relieved in any way."

"Hogwash, you have a sterling social life and are too set in your ways . . . too much a rover to be married. Have you found the women in Philly to your liking?"

"I've only met a few, and they're as charming as any British women. But, this marriage—"

"It's absolute foolishness, but the girl won't listen to me. No matter how many times I tell her! It's quite clear she doesn't believe me, for which she's going to pay a dear price if I'm successful today. However many pretty dresses the child gets out of this, they will do her little good. My greater concern is Patricia herself. Her reasoning is cold and calculating. I'm a little afraid of her sometimes."

"Afraid for her?" he asked.

"That, too. But those things she will do to have money and power ... frightening. If she would live in society for just a little while, she would understand. She is blind and deaf." Amanda grunted. "Would that she were mute as well."

Amanda had tried to explain society to her granddaughter, but Patricia seemed to think one buys a ticket to it as if society were a concert or play. In the end those she sought to be among would turn their backs on her. They would all attend her wedding—the Drexels, Biddles, Logans, Pembertons, Lloyds, Sinclairs, Wisters, Lancasters, the bulk of the assembly rolls—in deference to Amanda who was one of them from old days and continued among them by route of her dowager nobility. They would whisper about Emily, who had fallen from grace when she defied them all in her foolish marriage. And when it was over and Patricia was the young Mrs. Montaine, they would have none of her. Amanda told her this, thoroughly and frankly. "The Chestnut Street ladies will not speak to the Arch Street ladies because the fathers of the Arch Street ladies made their wealth, while the Chestnut Street ladies' fathers inherited theirs. Patricia, they will shun you. You'll be perfectly miserable." And her reply had been, "But will I have my own private water closet, my own monogrammed coach, and my own couturiere?"

More compact than New York's, more extreme and lavish than Boston's, Philly society maintained the longest record for exclusiveness. The soil beneath the Philadelphia elite would not nurture any wayward seed. They were tight as a drum skin.

"I have explained to Patricia that I might be able to buy her a fancy wedding, and that's where my abilities end. I cannot buy her a happy marriage, friendship, or even a list of social events. They will snub her."

"But she doesn't care," Fletcher said.

"She thinks she doesn't care. She isn't dying of loneliness yet. I won't rescue her from this when it all comes to nothing."

"Oh?"

"For God's sake, don't tell the girl the terms of my loyalty! I

204

would bring her out of that dungeon if she is physically abused, but if she gets wind of it and becomes desperate, she'll throw herself down the stairs and blame them! She's devious, Fletcher. An absolute liar! Do you understand me?"

"Would she really go so far as to—"

"Oh, Fletcher, it's unlike you to be naive. Yes! Don't you know why I'm doing this?"

"Yes, madam. The lesser of evils."

"In a way it appears to be the safest measure, considering her character and her demands. I've had scarcely more than a month to observe her. Her energy and single-mindedness are nearly a visible thing. I'm not sure that she wouldn't sell us all to have what she wants. She's already busy spending my money, begging me for influence on her behalf, and plotting and planning every second. If I can settle her where she thinks she wants to be, however terrible her choice, she will pester someone else. It is my fondest hope that she will mature, come to her senses, and learn some enduring lessons about what to value in life. But if she doesn't, we're all in for trouble.

"I hate allowing Patricia to sacrifice herself in this scheme," she told him. "But I won't hold firm against her and watch the rest of my family sacrificed while she struggles to achieve her prestige and wealth. Lilly and Emily are too good, too valuable, for me to stand by and let them be further victimized by Patricia's selfishness."

"Mister Montaine will have his hands full."

"Yes," she said, "and I hope Patricia does not pay too great a price for this insanity of hers."

The ride was long, the house being a pleasurable distance out of the city. When Amanda saw it again, unchanged on the outside, her thoughts took her back in time. Memory was peculiarly selective: there was no particular event that she had always associated with her life here. But if she closed her eyes, she saw something like a family portrait; Richard, handsome and tall as he stood against the mantle in the upstairs sitting room watching Emily, age seven or eight, playing in front of the hearth with her many dolls. Amanda would spend her Sunday afternoons lounging on a daybed with a book, feet propped up, her family near and content. It was a period in her life long ago, when there was the kind of serenity in being settled in a happy marriage with a bright and beautiful child, past all that newlywed passion, prior to that time of trouble around Richard's death and Emily's rebellion. If she could have stopped time anywhere in her life, it would have been there, on a Sunday afternoon in her sitting room when she was just under thirty years of age.

"It's going to be a struggle not to let them see how sentimental I am," she told Fletcher.

"You've had plenty of practice at that, madam. And I'll be there."

"I wonder if he's the least curious about my visit?"

"Don't expect anything, madam. It will be difficult for you to react when he does something unexpected if you prepare yourself too well. Keep yourself fluid—keep your mind wide open to any possibility. People like Montaine succeed by doing the unexpected."

The coach slowed in front of the mansion. "You must have been hell in the courtroom," she said to her personal solicitor.

"Ah, yes," he replied, jumping out ahead of her. "But as I told you, it takes it's toll after a time. This is much better work."

Amanda had prepared herself for a feeling of nostalgia when she entered her old home and used all of her conscious energy to cover it. The maid who answered their knock curtsied and said, "Good afternoon, Lady Nesbitt," and Amanda was impressed with the mannerly greeting. She remembered Wilson as uncouth. This was an improvement. "Mr. Montaine is waiting for you in his study. If you'll follow me."

"As if I don't know the way," she whispered to Fletcher when the maid preceded them.

As they walked through the house, she looked through open doors to see the mark of the parvenu. Gilt and possessions. The house had become cluttered with crystal, china figurines, gilded tables, filigree fixtures, gilded picture frames and too much art, linen and lace and gold and gold plate. It would be difficult to pass through any room without upsetting the gimcracks that littered every shelf, table, and mantle. Rather than tasteful, quality items in an orderly design, Wilson had crushed too much of what he owned into the rooms. It was not an uncommon sight in the homes of the *nouveau riche*. Although the maid walked ahead of her, Amanda did not stare. She had learned how to observe without moving her head or eyes very much. To notice wealth was to give away a yearning for it. She was practiced in this mien of *noblesse disdain*.

Despite her efforts to follow Fletcher's advice about remaining fluid, she knew why the study had been chosen. Wilson wanted to confine her with the portrait he kept and find out her business. He must have already surmised this was not really a social call.

She had forgotten to warn Fletcher. "Don't look at the portrait," she whispered just in time. The maid tapped lightly on the study door, opening it.

The study was cloudy with cigar smoke, possibly a deliberate attempt to make it unpleasant, but Amanda did not react. This was easier for her because of the years of Bertie's pipe. Wilson stood from behind his desk as she entered. He had put on pounds. She remembered his gluttony for all things. It looked as though his table had recently become more alluring; the buttons on his brocade vest were strained.

She held out a hand in greeting. "Hello, Wilson."

He placed his cigar in a crystal dish and bowed slightly rather than taking her hand over the expanse of the desk. "Amanda, Lady Nesbitt," he said. "You've hardly changed a bit."

Looking at him, little changed as he was, she nearly exploded into laughter but caught herself. He had always had the most horrid bunch of hair on his face and head. Black and silver, it was bushy and unkempt. His long sideburns fluffed out of his cheeks, his mustache was out of control, and his eyebrows could stand a combing. "You've always been such a pleasant liar, but never a good one," she said. "Your continuing prosperity is quite well known, Wilson. Congratulations. Please, meet my solicitor, Fletcher Drake."

Wilson extended his hand to Fletcher, man to man. "Why bring a solicitor, Amanda?"

"Fletcher serves many purposes, not just legal. He's been with me for so long that he's almost an appendage. I hardly go abroad without him."

"Sit down then," he said. "Tell me what you want."

"It's good to see the house in such fine order, Wilson. It brings back memories."

"I'm sure it does. Shall we proceed?"

"Is my visit badly timed? Are you busy with something? I could—"

"This is not a visit, Amanda, and we both know it. Let's get straight to the point, and then maybe we'll have a brandy."

Amanda relaxed in the chair in front of his desk. It had once been Richard's. She wanted to caress it . . . and could not. Would not. Nothing that Wilson owned that had once belonged to her would experience her touch of longing. She was determined to forget all that.

"I thought it was reasonable to come here first, Wilson, to tell you personally that I am reestablished in Philadelphia. I wanted to tell you so that you won't be surprised by the fact. I have already contacted some of my old friends, and we might encounter mutual acquaintances. It seemed prudent to be sure we're on agreeable terms."

By the way his eyebrows lifted, she believed he found this lie impossible to believe. She proceeded just the same.

"There are no hostilities," she added.

"I never did anything wrong," he said.

"When I left this house . . . at our last discussion . . . I swore revenge. I want to tell you myself that I have long since given up that notion."

"In the end, I was more than generous," he said.

"In your own way." He had discovered Richard Bellmont's posthumous financial calamity, Amanda's desperation to pay the debts, and bought the house for almost exactly the amount Amanda needed to clear her name. Then, at the last moment, he had offered her ten thousand dollars for her portrait. It hung in the study still. "Why?"

"Why have you never asked me before now?" he countered.

"Perhaps I was afraid of the answer." She let her head turn for the first time to regard the painting. Amanda at age thirty. She had almost forgotten how flattering it was. Fletcher, loyal to the last, did not look.

"You were afraid I kept it because it's beautiful? Because I thought you beautiful?" Wilson asked. She did not react. His voice was deep and scratchy from many years of cigars. "I had to know I could beat you, always been as much a game to me as a way to make money—getting the best price. It gave me no pleasure to see you suffer, and there was no other buyer at any price. When I think about a sentimental investment, I look at that face and remember what happened to you. I give a second thought."

"You could have saved me some dignity by giving me a little more for the house and letting me keep the painting. Richard had it done."

"You can have it now if you like. Free. I think the lesson ran its course."

"No, thank you. I frankly like my face better now. It's less pretty

208

perhaps, but it is to my liking just the same. Why did you think I came to see you?"

"To ask to buy the house."

"Would you have given me a price?"

He laughed loudly, leaning back in his chair and picking up his cigar. "Oh, yes! A price that would amaze you!"

Amanda smiled with every ounce of charm she could muster. She could not dredge up a scrap of liking for him, but there was a grudging respect. He was a tenacious old devil. Never bested by emotion, never disadvantaged by affection. She had wished, quite often, that she had had some of those qualities when it mattered, before Richard Bellmont had exhausted her fortune. Before he died. She had been in a difficult place for a woman; she had admired him so thoroughly, it had never occurred to her he had had flaws. Even now she would not change those things she respected about him; he was a powerful abolitionist, a great advocate of free education, a staunch proponent of laws to protect women and children—but what she would have given for a little financial sense, a little healthy cynicism!

"Are you ever fair?" she asked him.

"Fair? Always," he answered. "But I am no fool."

"Wilson," she said, leaning toward him, "I'd like to meet your son. Is he here?"

Again he put aside his cigar. "I'd like to know the reason before I call him. When your letter arrived asking if you could visit and meet my son, I asked him what he knew about you. He'd never heard of you except from me. I suppose he's asked around, but he doesn't understand your curiosity."

"I'm sure he knows nothing about me. He has a passing interest in my granddaughter, however. I would like to introduce myself."

Wilson's face became expressionless, a quality that had proved good in business. But Amanda had a good eye; she noticed the shrinking of his pupils. He knew a few things about his son. Now, she wondered, where did he stand? She would know shortly if Wilson thought it prudent to be as much an opportunist in romance as in business. She had heard he once divorced a wife.

He rose rather clumsily because of his bulk. The man must fill a Pullman car, she thought, his size was so formidable. Not just wide, but tall, and with that monstrous hair he presented a wild and awesome figure.

209

He sent the maid for Dale and went back to his chair, waiting silently, brooding. He was too clever to be fooled any longer; he must have guessed her business. She had to remember what Fletcher had advised because she couldn't imagine Wilson's position on an issue like this. Wilson took what he wanted. Why not his son?

When the young man arrived, Amanda was momentarily relieved to discover his appearance was far more bearable than that of his father. She judged him: he was handsome, well groomed, but his eyes, narrow and deep set, looked a little conniving to her. But she smiled very pleasantly as he kissed the back of her hand. Fletcher stood from his chair, shook Dale's hand, then positioned himself against the bookcase behind Amanda's chair. No doubt he stole a look at that painting now, but Amanda couldn't see his face. "Please," Amanda invited, "sit down. I'd like to get to know you a little bit."

"I'm flattered, Lady Nesbitt, but a little confused," Dale confessed.

"Oh, I'm sure you are. But don't worry. Philadelphia was once my home and will be again from now on. We have many mutual friends here. I'm sure your father has told you how he acquired this house and land. I'm afraid my husband, poor Richard, lost all our money, and I was forced to sell. Your father got a good bargain. But I've been fortunate enough to more than recover from that sad circumstance. Unfortunately, I'm widowed again. I think I will have to be done with marrying."

Dale laughed lightly, stealing a glance at his father. Wilson did not move. He observed shrewdly.

"My husband left me enough to reestablish myself here, with my friends. I've missed them. I am home, finally, for good."

Dale nodded, waiting. He grew up with the story of this house. He knew painfully well that the Bellmonts were once the richest, most prominent in society, then were suddenly deposed. If she had *more than* recovered, he was chatting with one of the wealthiest women he'd ever met. The Bellmont name was, in its time, better known and more respected than any.

"I'm well acquainted with the Sinclairs, the Lancasters, the Towerys. You have some young friends in those families. In fact, I've been told that you might be accused of aspiring to Dorthea Lancaster's hand in marriage."

Dale laughed in good humor. "I'm afraid you put me at a disadvantage, Lady Nesbitt. I've been keeping company with Dorthea, but we haven't made any agreement about marriage."

"Good, good. Then I'm not too late! I'd be honored if you would consider my granddaughter."

His eyes brightened slightly at the prospect of a family even more prestigious than the Lancasters.

"She's very beautiful. Very charming. You could not be embarrassed to have her on your arm. She could do you credit."

"I don't know what to say," Dale said. "You must understand that Dorthea—"

"Dorthea will understand, Dale, I assure you."

"Oh, Lady Nesbitt, I'm not certain she would. She has come to expect me to play escort—"

"Say you'll consider this, Dale," she said, her voice wheedling and persuasive.

"Certainly I would be honored to make the acquaintance of your granddaughter, my lady, however—"

"But you've already met." A flicker of doubt crossed his eyes—just what Amanda was looking for. He would not have missed a young woman more beautiful, more prominent, and even richer than Dorthea. "Her name is Patricia Armstrong."

There was momentary shock as she hit her mark. It took him a long moment to recover. "I'm sorry," he said, less agreeable now. "Again, you have me at a disadvantage."

"I'm sure I don't, Dale. It was in July, I believe. The day her mother and sister attended the Centennial fair and you had convinced her to steal away with you. You took her to the theater to see Shakespeare, then to dinner, and finally to tour your home. Specifically, I am told, to see the room prepared for your wife."

Dale decided, wisely, to lean back in his chair, lock his fingers together across his waist, and say nothing.

"It took a little doing, but I was even able to find a person or two who saw the two of you together. I dine at Tiffin's myself, quite frequently."

"What do you want, Lady Nesbitt?" Dale asked.

"Fortunately there is no hurry. The holidays will soon be upon us and we will all be terribly busy. My family will be doubly burdened—we have so many friends to visit. And of course I want Patricia to be gracefully introduced to all our mutual friends. It

211

needn't get around how well the two of you already know each other. I think a wedding . . . perhaps in the spring, should do."

"You don't think things are as simple as that, do you? You don't really think you can—"

"Dale, what I think is this; I think my granddaughter has made a despicable choice for herself. Even to consider accepting marriage with a man who tricked her, took advantage of her, and then dismissed her as you did seems the worst horror to me. But you are the man to stand responsible if Patricia is willing to accept you."

"Father? Father, I—"

Wilson stood from his chair, cutting his son off. "Where can you be found, Lady Nesbitt?"

"The Grafton Hotel." Fletcher had an embossed calling card ready to flick toward Wilson as quick as a magician. "You may call on me, or Lady Nesbitt, depending on your preference. Madam?"

Amanda stood. "Once again, Wilson, it is good to see that you continue to prosper." She turned to Dale. "Do give my regards to Dorthea. I'm sure you'll be talking with her soon."

She turned to Wilson. "My earlier declaration stands. I want only goodwill between us. If possible."

"We'll have a brandy another time," he said shortly.

"Perhaps, Wilson. Good day." She left the study, Fletcher close beside her, and they found the maid ready to hold the door for their departure. When they were in the coach Fletcher asked, "When do you imagine we'll be hearing from the Montaines?"

"It shouldn't be long," she said, beginning to feel exhausted. "Unless Dale has cuts and bruises to heal before he can show his face."

"How do you feel?"

She was quiet for a moment. "Stricken," she said at long last. What a dirty piece of business that was.

Lilly was fond of looking out the window into Rittenhouse Square for many reasons. One of them was Andrew Devon. She watched his clothing change from thin wool to a dapper overcoat with a leather collar as the weather became colder. She knew why he was there.

He was looking for her. Her grandmother had explained the Montaine family quite thoroughly.

Andrew Devon had been taken under Wilson Montaine's wing when he was an orphaned boy without resources. Montaine himself had been an orphan who made good in property by way of determination, cleverness, and a few inside clues to property values he had learned while sharpening knives in the kitchens of rich Philadelphians. Andrew Devon, it was said, had become a protégé of sorts, though he now owned a factory, a carpet manufacturing business. He was married to a beautiful woman who brought this business to their marriage. Wilson Montaine regarded Andrew as one of the family; the old millionaire appeared more proud of Andrew than of his own son.

Lilly never let on that she knew Andrew Devon.

Lilly did not rush into the square the first time she saw him there . . . or the tenth. A new snow, swirling lightly around the square, gathered on his shoulders and hat. Her mother, grandmother, and sister sat before the hearth making lists for holiday parties to which old family friends would be invited. Lilly let the drape fall and turned away from the window. "I'm going for a walk," she told her family.

"Don't you want to help plan?" Patricia asked.

"No, thank you. Just tell me what I'm to do and I'll do it."

"Lilly," Amanda asked, "are you all right, darling?"

"Yes, Grandmother. Only bored."

"Don't worry, love. We'll be finished with all this nonsense soon."

"Nonsense?" Patricia asked hotly. "It's only my entrée to society and my *wedding!* Why, if you all think it's—"

"If you shriek one more time, Patricia, I will wash my hands of this entire—"

Lilly left them. She walked across the street to the square, her hands in her fur muff, her hair tucked into a fur cap that almost covered her ears. Her cheeks were pink, but this time it was from the cold. Lilly had almost completely stopped blushing. She walked toward him and stopped when she stood in front of him. "Hello, Andrew," she said.

Those days in the park were so long ago—all that talk of philosophers and mannerly women. His eyes did not brighten with playful enthusiasm now. The Dublin green darkened, and his smile was

213

melancholy. The thing that had confused her last spring was a little too obvious in the cold winter light. She no longer had trouble distinguishing friendliness from desire. She remembered when she would have been so happy to see desire in his eyes. "Lilly. I wondered when you'd come."

"I've seen you."

"Of course you have," he said, offering his arm, and she accepted his escort, as she had before. It was all so different now. "We'll be seeing each other often. Now that there is to be a marriage."

"He doesn't want to marry her, does he?"

"No. Nor does she want him. But then there's a lot of that. And he doesn't seem too displeased with the prominence of your grandmother's good name. His father hardly had to threaten him at all."

"I won't be able to pretend I don't know you," she said. "My grandmother is shrewd, my mother can mask almost all her true feelings, and Patricia . . . well, we know how capable Patricia is in acting. I have never been able to lie."

"Don't lie, Lilly. Go upstairs today and tell them you met me in front of the hotel. I've done a little business in this neighborhood, and my presence wouldn't be amiss. Tell them we talked for a while in the park."

"If they should ask me if I've ever met you before—"

"They won't ask you, Lilly. You're clever and daring. It's all going to be quite a challenge. It was easier for us before, when—"

"Before, when I was poor and our families would never come together under any circumstances? Is that why, Andrew? Is that why you told me how you felt, how wrong it would be for us to want to be together . . . because you thought you'd never see me again? Maybe that's why you took liberties, kissed me the way you did? Because it was safe, and if you scared yourself you could run away home— to your wife and your mansion?"

"Lilly, I take all the blame. I know how wrong that was. I thought I would never see you again, and I couldn't have you think I purposely seduced you and had no feeling for you. I intended to relieve your mind, not place a burden on you."

"And if the next time you had seen me had been at my sister's wedding? Would you have lied? Would you have pretended to feel nothing?"

"Yes," he said.

"Was it some kind of gift—your declaration of *desire?*"

214

"You're so young. You've always wanted the truth. You are desirable. Tempting. It never occurred to me it would do more harm than good."

"You should never have spoken to me in the first place! Never!"

"I didn't mean for this—"

"If my grandmother hadn't come home, if Patricia had not forced Dale Montaine into this farce, this marriage, would you have eventually tried to make me your mistress? Would you—"

He turned her toward him abruptly, his hands gripping her upper arms, his eyes narrowed in anger. "Stop it! Do you think because I am that much older than you I have fewer feelings? So much more restraint? Hell, Lilly, what were you counting on—my lack of devotion to my wife?" He laughed harshly. "You'll meet Mrs. Devon soon, Lilly. Then you'll know what kind of fool I really am."

"Why did you marry her? Because of her money? Because of the factory she brought you?"

He looked away and laughed bitterly, not answering her question. "You'll find yourself thrust into parties soon, Lilly. Surrounded by the rich and haughty. See if you can find yourself a nice young man among them. There must be *one*. Someone to give you a family, a home. Forget all this. I can't ever be alone with you. We both know it."

"I've tried to forget you, you stupid fool. Why did you come now? Why would you stir it all up again?"

"We won't be able to avoid each other. You're going to have to change what you feel. You will never see any kind of invitation in my smile, I promise you."

"Oh . . . so simple. Is it so simple for you, Andrew? You can make a resolution about what you feel, and it's done, is it?"

"Yes, Lilly. And until you can change what you feel, you must not let it show. It would ruin us all, but you more than anyone."

"And what do you expect of me? How am I to—"

"We'll be courteous. We'll dance at your sister's wedding. We will never be anything more than friendly acquaintances. I want you to know it, believe it. I will avoid you if I must, and I will be cruel if it's necessary. Don't make it necessary. Live your life. There is nothing between us. There almost never was."

"You've been cruel enough," she said. "You should have lied to me. Your honesty hasn't helped anything. Such a gentleman! Andrew . . . what am I to do?"

215

"Be stronger than this, Lilly."

"Oh, you'll never know how much I wish I'd never met you."

"Sooner or later we would have felt something . . . then faced the struggle to overcome it. When we meet next, there is nothing, do you understand? Nothing. Good-bye."

"Andrew . . . how many times are we going to say that same good-bye? Do you really believe it changes anything?"

"In time you'll hate me. The only thing I can give you would be so wrong for you. So cheap and dirty. Do yourself a favor and hate me now . . . for even thinking it."

When she turned away from him, the tears came. Hate him for thinking it? When she could think of nothing else? She was glad he couldn't see her cry. It took a good deal of walking for her to rein in her emotions and feel under control again. When she did return to her hotel, the women were having tea. Lists and notes were temporarily put aside.

"You've been gone a long time, Lilly," Emily observed.

"I met Andrew Devon in front of the hotel. I heard him give his name to the doorman, and I introduced myself. We walked for a while in the square."

"How odd. Was he coming here?"

Lilly tilted her head to one side, a look of confusion on her face. "Funny, I never did learn his business."

"Well," Patricia began, "isn't he the one who was the orphaned son of a chambermaid or something?"

"Yes," Amanda said, looking closely at Lilly. "Lilly? Did you like him? Is he polite?"

"Yes, Grandmother. He is polite, and I liked him. Excuse me."

"What's the matter with you? You haven't been very happy about all that's going on," Patricia complained. "One would think you're not the least bit grateful for all this good fortune, not the least bit excited about all the fun things that will be happening."

"One might think that," Lilly said, looking over her shoulder at her sister before leaving the room.

The Montaine family had never enjoyed popularity. Wilson Montaine was resented for his prosperity; he had taken advantage of more than one fine old family in trouble. Dale had managed some tenuous acceptance, but there was no possibility that Wilson Montaine was going to experience friendship among elite society. Fear, perhaps. Grudging respect among the most open-minded. Largely there was and would remain disapproval.

This was the reason for Amanda's calculating maneuvers. Dale Montaine was the only one who could betray this plan, and he would not. In his arrogance he did not realize that Dorthea had a secure position within the local aristocracy . . . as did Amanda. Married to a Lancaster in good standing, he would have the benefit of her friendships. Patricia was a mere visitor. Acceptance in society was important to him, but like Patricia, he didn't understand the rules. It was his only redeeming quality, Amanda soon decided.

The Sinclairs were the first to welcome Lady Nesbitt and her family home, as though Emily and her daughters had not lived in Philadelphia all these years. Emily was greeted politely and no one asked her about Ned. Patricia and Lilly were introduced, but there was no suggestion of enduring friendship. Patricia didn't notice, and Lilly didn't care. Only Amanda and Emily knew how this sort of thing worked. A party was given, a lavish evening affair to include dancing. To this function Dale Montaine escorted Miss Lancaster and danced twice with Patricia Armstrong. It was widely observed.

At the next party, given by the Dresden family, Dale Montaine arrived alone and gave almost all his attention to Patricia. Only the immediate families knew it was contrived affection, but Patricia was not at all discouraged. Her new gown was admired by many.

During the week of Christmas Lady Nesbitt presided over a reception in their large gallery at the Grafton Hotel. Old friends and even some new ones attended her event. It was catered by a staff of twenty waiters and a kitchen staff of nineteen, and a twenty-eight member orchestra played. She was careful to invite judiciously; there were bankers, politicians, and business owners as well as socialites from old families. Amanda's parties had been missed; she had been known as the most original and experienced hostess in Philadelphia, and since her departure she had entertained nobility in Europe as the wife of a well-known and rich baron. Many of the recipes she used had come from Queen Victoria's kitchens. She even managed exotic flowers that had been shipped in ice from the Caribbean Islands and fruit that came by railcar from Florida. Her hors d'oeuvres trays and wine collections were incomparable.

Nearly two hundred of Philadelphia's most wealthy, most well known were in attendance. Dorthea Lancaster was not. Her mother apologized—it seemed she was taken with a winter sniffle. Dale Montaine never left Patricia's side.

On New Year's Eve at the home of Wilson Montaine, there was a rare gathering of one hundred guests. Six months earlier Wilson would not have issued invitations to these people, and had he done so, they would have sent their regrets. But Amanda Chase Bellmont Campbell Nesbitt had put her mark on the Montaine family. One hundred lifted glasses of champagne when the engagement was announced.

"I don't know how you could have resisted this idea," Patricia told her grandmother and mother. "It's all going beautifully, and I've never had such a wonderful time in my life."

There were no friends to call on Patricia, and she had not been invited anywhere without her grandmother, but there were many new faces, and a few familiar ones, to smile at her and ask her who had designed her gown. When she noticed women whispering and staring, she assumed they either admired or envied her.

"Well, Patricia, enjoy it while you can. There will be few occasions like this after you're married."

"I will, I am. Thank you, Grandmother. I've never been more happy in my life."

Amanda watched Patricia dance and could not help but acknowledge her beauty, her public grace. These people did not know how she could shriek and complain. She did look well suited for this role she played in her pale, virginal pink satin. Hers was such a perfect, frail femininity—all lace, sparkles, flounces, demitrain to swish around behind her. Now that she had snared the one she meant to have, she did not expose so much of her figure, but she still preferred to have her gown cut low. Patricia was as alluring as any princess. There was not a girl in the room who was prettier, Amanda silently relented.

But there was Lilly. The young people did not notice her much because they were distracted by Patricia's flamboyance. But Lilly was noticed. She stood back from the crowd and had no preference for flouncy dresses, for lace or puffs or bothersome trains. She had refused all the designs that were presented to her and selected a deep, royal-blue velvet gown with a high neck, long fitted sleeves, and a modest gathering of cloth around her bustle. The gown was top-sewn with silver thread in straight lines a quarter inch apart from the neck to the hem; it was sleek, flattering, and seemed almost to give off light. The style did not conform to anything in the room. She pulled her hair back into a clutch of natural waves that fell below her shoulders—no suggestive ringlets for Lilly—and wore a single pair of diamond stud earrings that her grandmother had insisted upon.

Lilly was too confident for frivolous games, for flirtation or vying for popularity. She mocked traditional fashion and defied custom. She danced only with Fletcher Drake, with whom she had developed a comfortable friendship, and one or two other mature gentlemen. She was not giddy, though she had good humor and would smile or laugh when something genuinely funny had been said.

Amanda kept an eye on Lilly. The girl had no idea how she was regarded. Though only seventeen years old, she was mature in both behavior and appearance and could easily pass for a woman in her twenties. Amanda noticed desire in the eyes of men who were intimidated by her powerful, clear, intelligent eyes. Women, suspicious of her refusal to flirt, to dress like the rest of them, to take notice of the grandeur that surrounded her, regarded her through narrowed eyes. She was shockingly, stunningly beautiful. More than pretty, she was magnificent—sensual and formidable. Her almond shaped, blue-green eyes were arousing; her finely arched brows were rarely raised in confusion. She was of potent size, nearly five feet, eight inches, and perfectly, deliciously proportioned. She had natural command —a scepter would not look out of place in her hand. Amanda saw more than one man walk toward her, lose his nerve, and turn away.

Amanda had not felt such pride in years. She wondered if Emily noticed. But Emily was made nervous by all of this; she suffered some embarrassment during this reentry and continued to worry about Patricia. She was evading possible questions about her last twenty years. She could avert her eyes, pretend, fail to answer quite well, but she fretted just the same and longed to have it all behind her. Emily had long since given up any attachment to this haughty group.

Amanda went to Lilly. "What are you thinking, darling?"

"Oh, I was thinking how warm it's becoming in here. How long after midnight will we stay?"

"Not long. Are you enjoying yourself?"

"Yes, ma'am."

"Come, Lilly. You needn't lie to me. You know that."

"Do you really want to hear the truth, Grandmother? Be sure now."

Amanda smiled with pleasure. "The truth, darling."

"I think this is silly. And quite boring."

"Yes!"

"You needn't worry about going through all this for me. I wouldn't have it."

"But what do you think of my friends?"

Lilly looked around, smirking slightly. "I find it hard to imagine how they entertained you. They lie like wretches and are the least genuine people I've met in my life."

Amanda laughed. "Indeed! But Lilly," she said, whispering conspiratorially, "there is more money in this room tonight than you can find in Washington, D.C."

"How pleasant for them. But there aren't as many brains in this room tonight as you're likely to find in a thimble on any day."

Amanda loved her. Instantly and ferociously. "You are too brilliant. You will be bored, searching for your match."

"Why would I search for a man? Hasn't that been the downfall of my family? This is nonsense. I hope you don't expect me to become attracted to all of this. I think the idea of having good clothes is very comforting, and I don't miss mopping up the kitchen, but in all honesty, Grandmother, does this ever become fun?"

Amanda leaned toward her. "Never. But if you have a lot of money, you should be nice to these people."

"Why?"

"Well, first of all, you should be nice to everyone, no matter how you feel. And secondly, there is also power here. If you must protect, preserve, or earn money, you don't want enemies among them."

"I hope I won't be expected to pretend to love this."

"You're doing fine, Lilly. I'm sorry this isn't particularly appealing to you—but I'm quite relieved it's not. There will be more substance to your life in that case."

"I should hope so."

"Ah, here comes Mr. Devon at last. And, I suspect, his wife. Have you met his wife?"

"No, Grandmother. But I—"

Andrew was upon them before she could say she'd rather not, and she could not have come up with a reason. Naturally she had seen them enter and dance. She had watched Mrs. Devon all evening, trying to conceal her observation. Lilly was terribly disappointed to see that the raven-haired, china-faced woman was beautiful.

Andrew bowed over Amanda's hand. Mrs. Devon made a slight dip and opened her fan. And then it was Lilly's turn.

"Miss Lillian Armstrong, may I present Mrs. Devon."

"Lovely to meet you, dear," the woman said. "And if it were not for you and your wonderful family, we might not have so many

221

people in this old house again. Lady Nesbitt, it must feel wonderful to be home. Have you missed Philadelphia terribly?"

"Of course, Mrs. Devon. And it's good to be home. Do I detect a slight accent?"

She laughed musically and fluttered her fan. "Why, you do indeed. I hope it's not much of an accent anymore. My mother and I came to this wonderful city in sixty-six when I was just a girl. I hail from Atlanta. After that silly business."

Lilly's eyes widened. The Civil War, a silly business. Dear God.

"Ah yes," Amanda acknowledged. "The South."

"I'm so warm; I do believe I should sit down for a spell. My darling Andrew has danced me to death! Lady Nesbitt, I can't wait for you to meet my mother. She will be so thrilled to make your acquaintance . . . we came from one of the finest families, but the war, you know, so devastated Mother. She longs for delicate society again . . . and your homecoming is surely a sign that—"

"Why don't we find a chair and visit, Mrs. Devon. If you don't have people to see, that is. Perhaps Andrew could ask Lilly to dance. Andrew?"

"I would be honored," he said smoothly.

Lilly barely heard. She couldn't take her eyes from Mrs. Devon. She stared. Her grandmother and Andrew's wife had turned their backs before Lilly could pull her eyes away.

"Lilly, would you like to dance?"

"Ah," she said, her attention back. "Ah, no, thank you, I'd rather not."

"I can't stand here chatting. Nor can I take you to a corner to talk. I'll have to say—"

"I've heard enough of that. Good-bye, isn't it? Becoming almost a habit for you, Andrew. For the sake of appearances. Very well, let's dance then. Otherwise I'll have to find someone to talk to or appear conspicuously alone, and I don't feel like either."

Andrew scowled at her sarcasm and led her to the dance floor. "Are you enjoying yourself?" he politely asked.

"Of course not. She's very beautiful, your wife."

"Brenda. Yes, she is."

"Fresh from that little trouble in the South. That trifling little war that killed five hundred thousand."

"Lilly—"

"Are you in love with her? Is she a convenience to keep you safe from all the young girls who desire you?"

"Lilly, stop it. Don't let what I've done to you turn you into a bitch."

"What was it that attracted you to her? Just tell me that. Her beauty, or her factory, or her ability to be polite in society by over-looking little inconveniences like wars?"

His eyes burned into hers. "When I married Brenda, I was deeply in love with her. Helplessly. It would have amused even you. Her factory, her deceased stepfather's factory, was steeped in enormous debt because of her mother's failure to manage the inheritance prop-erly. It required substantial loans from the Montaine estate to run again, loans since repaid. They would have been reduced to poverty—Brenda and her mother—had they not found a gullible husband. It is now very profitable. And my wife has since found my virility tragically lacking. She no longer desires me, but she will not ever willingly let me go. Unless I fail and become poor. She likes money, you see. And she has a healthy appetite for physical pleasures—an appetite her mother helps her carefully control, know-ing how fussy I can be about scandal. She knows that I can divorce her for adultery and fears I would. And of course I can divorce her for failure to meet her conjugal obligations, but she has a way of managing that, too. She's perfectly willing, you see, if I—It becomes fairly disgusting. Do you want to hear more? Is there anything else you wish to know?"

Lilly dropped her gaze. "Andrew, I'm sorry."

"Oh, but Lilly, the best part is yet to come. I'm Catholic; Brenda is a Catholic. But that's not the half of it. My mother died when I was only seven years old, leaving me orphaned. As she died, she begged me to honor the faith to which I was born. That's one of the reasons I did not immediately shed the coarse overcoat of an unloving wife. Even if society one day learns to be more tolerant of divorce, you can be sure the church won't."

"Andrew, please, I—"

He moved her around the dance floor. His hand on her waist felt secure, even when he was angry with her, with himself. Lilly was ashamed of herself, but her disappointment in him would not leave.

"It's not common knowledge. You might keep it to yourself. I find it rather embarrassing . . . and one of the few predicaments of my life I am unable to change. I am far better in business than romance. But you wanted to know. Now you do."

"She's hurt you. How terrible of her."

"Yes, well," he laughed, "perhaps you could use the argument that I've only hurt myself. And I'm the one who's sorry. I shouldn't have let you goad me into such a blatant explanation of personal difficulties. It doesn't matter, you see. It makes no difference whether this is a good marriage or bad. It is very legal."

"I don't understand why you endure it."

"Don't pity me, Lilly. Hate me, but don't pity me."

"If she were a good wife, you wouldn't have—"

"But, you see, that's not necessarily true. Don't go assigning me virtues that aren't really mine. I haven't proven that I wouldn't look at you, desire you, if my marriage were good. Marriage is marriage, and I don't know of many happy ones. Some men are rovers, some are not. What if I had a good wife, but fat and ugly? What if I had a wife who loved me, but had an accident that left her paralyzed? How many possibilities can you come up with that would pardon adultery? It's not worth it, Lilly." The music stopped and he released her.

"One more dance, Andrew," she asked softly.

He bowed as if to depart. "I don't think so, Lilly."

"Please. Besides the wedding, I'm not going to attend any more of these foolish parties. I don't plan to be seeing you often."

People were milling around, waiting for the orchestra to begin again.

"If I excuse myself, you will be free to accept a dance with some—"

"Andrew, please. No one has asked me yet. My grandmother forced a few of her old friends to . . . I'm . . . Oh, damn it, Andrew, I'm *lonely*. I'm not trying to seduce you or tempt you, but I don't have anyone to talk to or anything to do!"

The music started, and Andrew put his hand on Lilly's waist. "One more," he said.

Lilly had not been instructed in the art of dance as so many young women in this room had. But in Andrew's arms, dancing came easily. She liked the way she felt when he directed her.

"Andrew, have you ever thought about running away?" she asked him.

"Meaning? Escaping this bondage of work and marriage to flee with you?"

She laughed. "I suppose you should expect that of me. No, not run away with me, Andrew. Patricia is so thrilled by all this—she really is happy. I've never been so bored. I think I was happier when I was skipping the young ladies' school to tangle with the librarian over forbidden reading. I don't like this kind of society life."

"Find something useful then. If you're very bored for very long, you'll get sick."

"I'm never sick."

"Then you'll get fat," he teased.

"What do rich women do?" she asked him sincerely.

"Have dresses made. Go to parties. Supervise the cleaning of the house and oversee the cooking of the meals. Have children. Travel on cruises."

"Well, there you are," she said unhappily. "I think I had better make use of that desk."

"You could write stories and publish them. Or teach. Or go to some godforsaken island with a Bible in your fist and—"

"I know this sounds uncharitable, but I'm not so much for good works. And I'm not fond of fairy tales." She looked into his eyes and smiled. "Anymore."

When the music stopped a second time, Andrew released her, bowed over her hand, and escorted her to where her grandmother and Mrs. Devon sat. There was a flurry of excitement in the ballroom, and someone shouted that it was almost midnight. Everyone stood waiting. Andrew reached for his wife's hand to draw her to her feet, and Amanda used her cane.

When the hour struck and the clock began to chime, people in the room cheered and began to embrace each other, wishing friends and family good health and good fortune. Lilly saw Dale Montaine grasp Patricia's waist and give her a very platonic kiss on the cheek. Andrew embraced his wife, and she turned her face away with a poorly concealed grimace. He frowned and touched her cheek with his lips.

Amanda put an arm around Lilly's waist. "You'll be eighteen years old this year, darling. Think of something you want for your birthday. Something wonderful."

Lilly could not draw her eyes away from Andrew. "I don't think you can get me what I want, Grandmother."

"Then think of your second choice," she said, following Lilly's eyes. "And make sure it's something that will do you good and make you happy."

Lilly looked at Amanda and smiled gratefully. Then she said a terrible prayer that Brenda Devon would be run over by a horsecar. Soon.

The wedding date was set for the middle of May, to be followed by a wedding trip to Saratoga for the bride and groom. The Grafton apartments were turned into a sweatshop of sewing, writing, interviewing maids for Patricia to take with her to the Montaine mansion, discussions with caterers, choosing patterns for silver, china, and crystal.

January dragged by slowly for Lilly, who could hardly stand to be in the same room with this activity. She escaped frequently to the library and the square.

There was a Valentine's Day ball given by some fancy family, but Lilly declined. Then, on the first of March something happened that would change everything for Lilly.

When she was returning to the Grafton Hotel from an afternoon of music at the Academy she noticed Andrew leaving the hotel. His coach waited, and she hurried across the street, waving and calling his name.

He could resist a smile. "Lilly," he greeted, "I haven't seen you in months. You're good to your word—you don't intend to go to many parties."

"Well, don't give me too much credit for discretion, Andrew. I'm not doing it for you. I don't think they're any fun. Have you been circulating?"

"Now and then. Upon demand, I should say. And I was away for a while—business in New York. Are you keeping busy?"

"No. I'm bored as a dead horse. What are you doing here? Were you visiting the family?"

"No, not this time. I was speaking to Mr. Grafton. Just a little business."

"What kind of business?" She noticed he carried a business satchel.

"It's fairly routine. I stop in to talk to any number of business owners when the word gets around they might be willing to sell."

"And is the hotel for sale?" she asked him.

He laughed at her. "Lilly, if Mr. Montaine waited for the hotel to be for sale, he wouldn't own so much Philadelphia property."

"I see," she said, first in some confusion. Then suddenly she understood. That was what had happened to her grandmother and until this very moment she had not quite understood. Wilson Montaine had managed to learn, somehow, how much debt encumbered the estate and then cleverly offered to pay that amount. Far less than the actual value, but an amount that would salvage a reputation or give a troubled owner escape from total poverty. Her eyes widened with knowledge.

"Does Mr. Grafton want to sell his hotel?" she asked.

"No. You have to have patience in property, Lilly. I have to run along. There's a lot on my schedule today."

"Of course. Yes. Good-bye," she said, turning away with a new kind of excitement beginning to rise in her.

The first thing Lilly did was rummage through boxes from the boardinghouse that the hotel stored for them. There were many things that Emily wouldn't part with, but had no real use for. Lilly found her mother's accounting books.

She roamed through the hotel daily, becoming a familiar face in the dining room, kitchens, hallways, linen closets, and spent a great deal of time in the lobby observing the arrival and departure of guests. She began to read the newspaper daily, looking for all available financial and society news. Society had suddenly, thrillingly, begun to hold meaning for her.

She went to visit Fletcher Drake in his small clutch of four rooms when she knew that her grandmother was busy with one of Patricia's many fittings. His servant, Michael, took her to his study where she found him buried under mounds of accounting ledgers, letters, and other paraphernalia. The sight of so much work filled her with a kind of heat.

"Lilly, what a surprise. Let's go in the sitting room and have Michael bring us tea."

"No, Fletcher. Please, let's talk right here. I have a lot of questions to ask you. Questions about business."

He looked perplexed, and Michael, a quiet man in his mid-thirties, stood in the study door with a confused look on his face.

227

"Would you like tea in here?"

"Never mind tea." She turned and smiled at Michael. "Thank you, Michael." He left in total bewilderment.

"Fletcher, I want to ask you some questions without Grandmother knowing."

"Now, Lilly, what sort of—"

"Don't worry, you know I wouldn't hurt her for the world. But I have to know, does Grandmother actually *earn* any money?" She pulled a chair that was positioned against the wall toward the front of his desk and perched on the edge of it.

"In a way. She has some very good investments."

"What kind?"

Fletcher sat down uncomfortably, folding his hands over a mound of paper and looking at Lilly closely. "Well, she had a lot of money in a Vanderbilt shipping company, which we sold a while ago for a nice profit. There is steel, a coal mine in northern Pennsylvania, and more recently petroleum—"

"Yes, petroleum will do well. I've been reading about it, it's said to be a popular investment."

Fletcher smiled suddenly. "We have money in several New York banks, a variety of bonds, a factory that promises to start converting part of its operation to the development of the floor covering linoleum, and I am trying to convince her that we must closely watch any company that attempts to develop the telephone system."

"The telephone machine? Oh, Fletcher, that will never catch on. Why would people want to talk through that thing rather than meet people face to face?"

"People like being busy—they want to be everywhere at once."

"Has she lost money? Ever?"

"Here and there. She got a notion to invest in a peacock farm at a time when she was very infatuated with plumes used in fashion. It was all right for a while—a short while."

"Fletcher, I have an idea. I need some help developing it, and I don't want to talk to Grandmother about it until I'm sure. Will you help me? And keep a secret?"

"Well, Lilly, I can't be expected to keep anything from Lady Nesbitt if it would put her at a disadvantage. My job is to keep her informed and growing richer."

"Yes, indeed," Lilly said, grinning broadly, more enthusiastic than she'd been in months. "I see that as my job too. I think we'll make a formidable team."

Fletcher leaned back in his chair and studied her delighted face. He picked up a crystal paperweight and tossed it lightly in the air, amused and a little intrigued. "Do you now?"

It was nearly impossible to hold Lilly still long enough to have her dress fitted for Patricia's wedding. She was constantly on the run, spending whole days at the library studying city maps, country maps, world maps and reading every newspaper she could find. She spent hours with Fletcher learning about accounting, investing, and building. If her grandmother had not been so busy with the wedding and various parties for Patricia and Dale, she might have asked more questions. The one question she did ask was, "Have you thought of anything for your birthday, Lilly? It's only two weeks away."

Lilly kissed Amanda's cheek and grabbed her coat. "Yes, Grandmother, I think so. But I don't want to tell you about it before. On the day I'm eighteen, I'll tell you. Be patient."

"Can I get whatever it is on your birthday if you wait so long?"

"Don't worry about that, darling," Lilly said. "I have to run off. Fletcher is going to take me on a tour of the First Banking House to see where all the figuring is done and where the money is actually stored in the vault."

"I see," Amanda said, somewhat miffed. "You're taking up quite a lot of his time. I think he's begun to work more for you than me."

Lilly laughed happily. "Oh no, Grandmother. He's very busy with all your accounting, I promise you."

On the eleventh of April, nearly a month before Patricia's wedding, two days prior to Lilly's birthday, Fletcher and Lilly went to see Mr. Grafton at his home. They spent the entire afternoon and all of the next day. On April thirteenth Lilly awoke an eighteen-year-old and asked Amanda if they could have a family dinner to include Fletcher.

"Is there a special dish you'd like me to have made?" Amanda asked her.

"It doesn't matter in the least. But may we have champagne?"

"Lilly, wouldn't you like to go out to a restaurant? Shopping? Have a party?"

"Mercy, no! Just the family and Fletcher. Patricia needn't come if she has something she'd rather do, but please make Bertie put on her good dress and sit with us . . . no matter how stubborn she is about it."

The hours dragged until it was time for Lilly's birthday dinner. She bathed, dressed, pulled up her hair, and waited impatiently for the hour to arrive. Finally Fletcher knocked on their door, and Lilly almost overturned a table as she rushed to let him in.

His eyes sparkled appreciatively as he looked her over. "Are you ready, Lilly?"

"Oh yes! Do you still intend to do your very best to help me?"

Before he could answer Amanda came into the room; she had overheard. She looked at the two of them together. Lilly's incredible excitement and Fletcher's knowing smile. "There is a conspiracy here. How much is it going to cost me?"

Fletcher made a half bow. "An impressive sum, madam."

"Well, let's have it. The suspense is too much."

"Be patient, Gran," Lilly said. "When everyone is together and we've had dinner."

A Grafton Hotel waiter in formal attire lit the candles and supervised the serving of the table. By Lilly's request, Bertie sat with them, stiff and uncomfortable in her best starched dress. Patricia was bored and testy, but kept mostly quiet. Emily was intrigued. But Lilly made them wait until the meal was finished, coffee and dessert served. Then she excused the waiter. "I'll ring for you when we're finished. We'd like to have a private discussion now," she said, as confident as any experienced hostess.

"Grandmother, I've finally found a purpose for the desk you brought me. Weeks ago I happened upon Andrew Devon leaving the hotel. I thought he had come for a visit, but I learned that he was here doing Mr. Montaine's business. It seems he frequently comes around to certain businesses rumored to be having trouble and offers to buy them at a bargain. Just as he did to you."

"How well I remember. He's an experienced predator."

"Fletcher and I have spent the last several weeks studying this hotel. We've even been to see Mr. Grafton. He was good enough to share the offer with us. It's just about all he's worth. It leaves him very little . . . but the hotel is losing money, and he's going to be forced to sell eventually."

"Lilly, should you have done that? Gone to visit Mr. Grafton to ask such personal questions?" Emily asked with concern.

Lilly virtually ignored her mother. "Grandmother, this hotel could be made profitable. Fletcher and I have taken a hard look at it. First of all, Mr. Grafton has inherited this hotel from his family and doesn't have very good help. They waste a lot of time and money. It needs improvement—it needs to be made more like the guest houses that are becoming popular among the rich, but Mr. Grafton dislikes change. Single rooms are losing fashion and are only used by businessmen and a few travelers. Walls should be knocked down and rooms joined, converted into suites like this one—apartments that can accommodate whole families and their staffs."

"Have you ever been in another hotel?" Amanda asked.

"I have now," she said proudly. "Fletcher arranged for us to tour some of the hotels in Philadelphia, and we studied a blueprint of the Astor. Grandmother, do you read the columns in the newspaper about all the things people are doing? Where they travel, what parties are given, all that society hogwash? Have you noticed what they're up to? They hardly stay home. They go to New York for the winter season, to Paris in the spring, to Newport in the summer. Some of them have discovered it isn't prudent to keep houses at each place. They stay in *hotels*, Grandmother, but only if they're grand enough for all their social affairs and fancy diversions. The chief reason we are the only residents of the Grafton Hotel who can afford to give parties and dances is because there is only this one, single suite of rooms. Mr. Grafton thinks it a waste of money to convert it because there doesn't seem to be much of a demand for its use. And the reason there isn't much demand is because many of the better families like to be among their friends. At the same time they go to New York, where there are many fancy suites and stay at the Astor together. They are all in Paris or the South of France at the same time. And when Patricia and Dale go to Saratoga, they will stay at an inn that will specialize in serving people with a lot of money."

She paused and took a deep breath. She looked around. Bertie waited. Patricia was not listening. Emily's eyes had grown wider in anticipation. Amanda's narrowed shrewdly, with interest. Fletcher had a half-smile playing on his lips and gave a slight nod of approval.

"Grandmother, there is not a single fancy hotel in Philadelphia. There are only two hotels with ballrooms, and neither of them has many suites. The hotel dining rooms are not as fine as the restaurants, but they could be."

Amanda lifted her coffee cup to her lips. "You suggest?"

"Let's buy it."

Patricia looked up in amazement. "Lilly, have you gone mad? What would you want with a—"

"Patricia, if you say a single word to Dale Montaine about this, I will make it my sole purpose in life to *ruin* your reputation, do you hear? I mean it!" She turned back to her grandmother. "Let's buy it and run a hotel. Mama would love to have her business back—there isn't anyone more efficient. You would have a fine investment for your money, you're known as the grandest hostess in the world, and I would have something to do. We can all learn a great deal on this hotel, making it profitable . . . and—"

"Lilly," Emily argued, "a hotel with so many rooms, such a big kitchen, it's hardly a boardinghouse!"

"Oh, Mama, it's not really much more than a boardinghouse. You would just need a few more people, that's all. You can point, direct, order food, inspect the cleaning, greet the guests. Mama, it would be perfect for you. You can hire Sophia to help you . . . What are you going to do with yourself after this silly wedding is over?"

"*Silly* wedding! Lilly, how dare you speak of my—"

"Oh, Patricia, shut up. For heaven's sake, are we supposed to gather around and watch people stick pins in your sides for the rest of our *lives?* You'll get married, move into your big fancy house, and be on your own. Have all the stupid parties you want, but I need a little something—"

"Mama! Are you going to let Lilly talk to me like that? After all I've been—"

"Patricia," Amanda sternly warned, "I think this hotel could not set me back as much as your wedding and all its accompanying frivolity. Now hush. I want to hear what Lilly has on her mind."

"Mama! Lilly, you are so selfish!"

"Said the pot to the kettle! Grandmother, we can learn on this hotel and then . . . if it goes very well, as it should, we can build one! A huge, grand, wonderful hotel with hundreds of rooms and lots of diversions!"

"*Build* one? Good Lord, you've carried this whole idea a bit far, haven't you? I don't know that I'm quite that eager to lose all my money."

"I wouldn't even suggest it if it were not sound. Fletcher and I have spent *weeks* studying this. We've looked at the costs of improving this one. We've ridden around the countryside looking for attractive sights. Fairmount Park is ready for a large hotel. We have a plan to draw people from all over the world by, inviting a few prestigious families to be guests for their first visit. We'll impress the devil out of them! Sorry, Mama. Dickens." Fletcher smothered a laugh. Amanda could not resist a smile. "We'll spend the next year working on this building, do a bit of rehiring—some of the waiters and maids are lazy and often absent—and when we get this hotel on its feet, we'll begin the foundation for the newer, larger one. We could be set to open in the spring of eighty-one! Maybe sooner!"

"She's mad," Patricia grumbled. "May I be excused?"

"If you breathe one word—"

"Why would I discuss this idiocy with anyone? You're out of your mind."

"Go ahead, Patricia," Emily said. "You're excused." She looked at Lilly. "Lilly, I think you might be thinking a bit too extravagantly. I certainly don't feel qualified to run a hotel. Or even help."

"Don't worry, Mama. I do."

Amanda lifted a brow and peered at Fletcher. He took that as a question. "I was as stunned as you, madam. And no less skeptical. But, after a closer look, I see Lilly is onto something here. I can spend some time reviewing the plans and figures with you—but frankly, there seems a reliable solution to every possible problem. And she's right about one thing for certain. Grafton has managed very badly. His heart just isn't in it."

"Grandmother, Wilson Montaine would *not* be interested in this hotel if it couldn't be profitable! Will you consider it?"

"I'll look at Fletcher's numbers, Lilly, but I'm not promising any—"

Lilly shrieked and bounded from her chair, running around the table to embrace her grandmother. "Oh thank you! You'll see! It's perfect for us!"

"I said I wasn't promising," Amanda persisted.

"But you'll see! Oh thank you, Fletcher," she said, turning to him and throwing her arms around his neck. Fletcher, so proper and businesslike, was thrown off balance by Lilly's enthusiasm, and it caused him to blush and laugh uncomfortably. "I told you we'd make a good team, Fletcher."

"So you did, Lilly." He looked almost apologetically at Amanda, shrugging. "She's had the time of her life, madam. And so have I."

"Happy birthday, Lilly," Amanda said, peering at her closely. She had never brought up the subject of Lilly's gaze toward Andrew Devon and his chilly bride. "Tell me, darling. Was this your first choice?"

Lilly smiled. "It is now, Grandmother."

13

$\mathcal{P}$atricia wore white satin complete with a fourteen-foot train designed especially for her by Madame Thérèse Boulliazau. She covered her head with a white veil that canopied her shoulders and reached her bent elbows. She carried an elaborate bouquet of silvery pink Jacquesminot roses. Orchids and white satin ribbons decorated the church. Dale Montaine arrived at the altar in a white formal suit with tails. A small string group played the music to which she walked down the aisle on the arm of Fletcher Drake. At the altar rail stood Lilly, resplendent in blue satin. Behind Dale stood Andrew Devon. In the pews sat sixty special guests. Three hundred had been invited to the dinner and party to follow the early afternoon ceremony.

Patricia, serious and calm, quietly spoke her vows. Dale repeated his in a firm and resonant voice. It was a polite ceremony carefully planned and executed by Amanda. Emily wept as her daughter became Mrs. Dale Montaine. Lilly and Andrew tried not to look at each other.

A string of open carriages decorated with ribbons and flowers carried the wedding party and guests to the Montaine mansion where a large party awaited them. At four o'clock on a bright May afternoon an elaborate buffet was opened in the garden. Patricia and Dale and their families occupied a long, linen-covered table and presided over the many guests. Their gifts were on display on long tables in the foyer and considerable champagne was drunk. When the plates and tables that held roast beef, squab, curried ham, and a wide variety of complementary dishes were cleared away, the orchestra set up to play for dancing in the Montaine ballroom.

Dale and Patricia led the dance, and after a few moments and brief applause, other couples joined them. Lilly waited through four very long waltzes before Andrew approached her, bowed, and led her to the dance floor. His eyes twinkled in amusement, and she carefully held her lips still to keep from smiling.

"Have you been busy, Lilly?" he asked.

"My yes, Andrew. Busy as a bee."

"Have you done quite a lot of reading lately?"

"Certainly. And other things."

"Other things . . . like buying hotels?"

She grinned, pleased with herself.

"You believe you got the best of me, don't you?"

"Indeed I did, Mr. Devon. You'll be more careful with your business secrets from now on, won't you?"

"You naughty girl. Mr. Montaine is very unhappy with me. And, I suspect, you."

"Naughty, clever, and quicker than you, Andrew Devon! And soon . . . busier than even you!" She squeezed his hand while they danced. "Tell the truth—you envy me!"

"Yes," he said, his voice husky. "And I'm proud of you. Do you think you can make it go?"

"I know I can. *You* know I can! I know perfectly well that Wilson Montaine would not look at that hotel twice if he didn't think—"

"What makes you think he wants to own a hotel, Lilly?"

Her eyes widened and her mouth stood open despite the fact that Andrew whirled her effortlessly around the room.

236

"How do you know he didn't plan to gut the building and put a factory or bookbinder or clothing manufacturer in there? You see, you haven't done all the studying necessary."

"Tell me," she demanded seriously. "What did he plan?"

Andrew smiled slyly. "Wilson doesn't plan. He never tells what he's going to do—only what he's done. He remains ready, at all times, to make whatever change necessary to make a profit. Don't worry. That hotel can work," he said. "But you see, you must look further than your nose, Lilly. If you're going to succeed in business, you have to think like those who have been successful before you— look at what they did and how they did it."

"You beast," she accused, then laughed in delight. "You frightened me half to death! I wish we could have talked about it. You would have had all kinds of advice for me, advice I needed. But I can't confide my business in you—you would race ahead of me and win the game!" She laughed. "I did it, Andrew. I actually did it! I had some help from Fletcher and Grandmother, but I have a business!"

"You haven't done it yet, darling. Be careful, go slowly. And if you want my help, you have it. No one wants to see you succeed in this more than I. Especially if it makes you happy."

"That's a lovely sentiment, but I can't accept help from you. It would not only put you in a bad position with Mr. Montaine. I mean to do this on my own—though with Fletcher and Grandmother, of course. I hope to be a veritable viper in business, terrifying to every other investor and predator."

"I have a hard time picturing you taking advantage of people."

"Unlike Mr. Montaine, I don't mean to be purposely unfair. Mr. Grafton is far happier with my offer than he was with yours. But when it comes to the types who would quickly disable me in any way possible to get the best of me, don't look for charity. With those types . . . you and your sponsor, the illustrious Philadelphia Landlord, you will find me a formidable opponent."

"I think I'm starting to believe you."

"As well you should! Oh, Andrew, I don't know when I've had a better time! Tell me you admire me!"

"You know how much I admire you. Don't fish for compliments. And Lilly, do yourself a favor. Don't discuss business within earshot of the new Mrs. Montaine. I already know about your plans for Fairmount Park."

"What?!" She nearly stopped moving her feet. Andrew almost stumbled and had to urge her into motion again.

"Don't worry, Lilly. She mentioned some madness about a grand hotel in that area. Fortunately, only Dale and I were within hearing, and, given the fact Patricia is unimpressed with your plans and Dale is a dunderhead when it comes to business, you may consider it done for now."

"You didn't tell Mr. Montaine?"

"No. And I've decided not to."

"Why?"

"To avoid a war, perhaps. With you. I'd rather not put any little traps in your way, and that would be one of my first assignments, I feel sure. And, I'll share a secret with you, to make our terms equal—I'm getting out of his business. In two years I'll be completely on my own."

"And he doesn't know?"

"Oh, I think he knows. It's always been my agenda. Since Dale has failed so miserably to take over his own interests, Wilson can't even bring himself to discuss the prospect of not having me at his beck and call."

She lifted a brow. "Well, what do you think of the Fairmount Park idea?"

"I think," he said, smiling, "it's splendid. Genius. But now, before you become vain, let me tell you something. You'll have to provide a lot of fancy activities to draw the kind of hotel guests you want. Riding, lawn tennis, croquet, bicycles were very popular at the Centennial fair. You'll have to be sure to include fine dining, parties, and a fully trained staff—complete with women who can attend ladies and valets who can take care of gentlemen. If you're going to be out that far, you'll have to copy the Centennial committee's decision to provide transportation—but yours must be more elegant than ferries and horsecars. To make people feel at home outside the city, you should consider coaches that will get them to the theater, the musicals, the homes of their fancy acquaintances . . . not to mention delivering them from their private railcars and yachts to your friendly abode."

"Yes! Of course!"

"Plenty of pampering and fussing. The price matters far less than the luxury—that's why Grafton's wasn't working. Grafton was al-

ways more interested in being among the privileged and not concerned enough with serving them. He considered himself above that.
It cost him in the end."

"Why are you doing this? If Mr. Montaine ever found out—"

"He won't, Lilly. Unless you tell him. He has his fist around
enough property in Philly. Even Dale won't be able to run through
all the Montaine money in his lifetime. And I assure you, that's about
all Dale is capable of."

"Wouldn't he be quite angry to know you're giving me free
advice? Especially since he had his eye on Grafton's?"

"You know him a little now, Lilly. Do you think he could create
the kind of establishment that you intend? After today, do you think
he'll be included in all the social activities of Philadelphia society?
Do you think he'll care?"

"No, he seems a little lost around all this hoity-toity nonsense,
probably the sole quality for which I can admire him. But why will
we succeed where he would fail?"

"One reason. Only one. Amanda, Lady Nesbitt . . . at the helm.
She is the best and most well known hostess in Philadelphia. She
remains in the good graces of this group because she hasn't dishon-
ored herself by divorce or silly marriages. Mrs. Armstrong will be
tolerated politely because of her mother, but I'm afraid she lost your
access to the *haut ton* in her marriage. The new, young Mr. and
Mrs. Montaine will be out. Poor Patricia. The truth will come
slowly."

"Oh please, what a bleak picture!"

"*Chronique scandaleuse*," he said. "A dim view of society, but
a true one. The aristocrat is born, Lilly, never made. Nothing can
make Patricia a true aristocrat."

"And you? Are you not seen as one of them? Isn't Dale?"

Andrew chuckled. "Dale and I share two traits . . . and I hope
only two. We are seen as young men with a lot of money and are
occasionally tolerated because of that. Dale nearly won his entrée
with Dorthea Lancaster—the Lancaster fortune could use a little
bolstering. Now he's lost it completely. But then he's always been a
fool."

"And the other trait?"

"We have no friends."

"Oh, Andrew, surely you *could* have friends, if you chose."

"I don't think so. Those who have less suspect me. Those who have more fear me. And those of like fortunes and methods are wary, as well they should be."

"I will never have friends then," she said sadly.

"You have family, Lilly. And you will have a good business. Take my advice and use this society to finance your own fortune. Don't pretend to be one of them. Let your grandmother keep her acquaintances—they will be careful with her. Let her bring you the rich and influential and give them your rooms. In time, God willing, you will establish the best hotel and be in much demand before she is gone. I want you to be a success."

"Oh, Andrew, how I *adore* you!"

"Now, what have we decided? None of that! You are not allowed to adore me, and I am not at liberty to accept adoration."

"But we *can* be friends, you see! We *must!*"

"Ah, Lilly! An occasional dance at a family gathering, a glance over the heads of other guests, perhaps a raised glass at the opening of your hotel. The rest of our friendship is too tarnished."

She tilted her head and gazed at him. "Andrew Devon, you're too young and too handsome to be such a horrible prude."

The music stopped and he released her. He bowed and she curtsied. They laughed together as he escorted her to the edge of the dance floor, bowed over her hand, and turned away. She let her eyes follow him for a moment. The longing, she decided, would be her lifetime curse. But she would stay busy and challenged. She looked away.

While Lilly danced, her eyes had been so securely locked into Andrew's, her conversation so animated, so *familiar,* and their dancing so natural, neither noticed that the other dancers gave them room and many interested parties closely observed. There was a commonly held conception in society that strangers never argue or overexplain. People not well acquainted do not shock each other or laugh deeply together. The intensity of their conversation, the laughter, the frowning, widening eyes, and serious discussion had created some suspicions.

Amanda locked her arm into Lilly's. "Have I told you, love, how much I approve of your birthday request?" Lilly looked at her in confusion. "I was afraid you wouldn't show such wisdom."

"What do you mean, Grandmother?"

"Never mind, sweetheart. Let's see now—are there any young men you would like to get to know better? Look around now."

"Oh Grandmother, don't be ridiculous! I haven't time for young men!"

"I wouldn't want you to become lonely."

"I haven't *time* to be lonely! I simply can't wait to get moving again. Now this silliness is finally over!"

"I see," Amanda said. "I see."

When the bride was finally ready to retire to the third-floor suite that had been prepared for the couple, Amanda and Emily accompanied her to say good-bye. Lilly remained behind with Fletcher, who would escort the women back to the city. The guests began to request their cloaks. The day had been long, entertaining, and exhausting.

Mr. and Mrs. Devon said their farewells to Wilson Montaine, his young wife, Deanna, who was slightly tipsy, and to Lilly and Fletcher. Their coach waited, and Andrew helped Brenda up. When they were seated on opposite sides and the driver jolted them into motion, she spoke.

"You seem to have more than a passing interest in young Miss Armstrong."

"Don't be ridiculous. She's a clever girl, and entertaining."

"And attractive. Tell me, Andrew, have you slept with her?"

His eyes moved to her face, leisurely appraising her. "Would you honestly care if I slept with most of the women in the city?"

"Ah, yes, adultery! The male privilege! The male prerogative! Of course not, darling. Not if you could be discreet. My reputation is very important to Mother."

"Does Mother know about the blacksmith? The grounds-keeper?"

Brenda laughed at him. "That was all so long ago, Andrew. Don't be cruel—I've been so good!" Andrew looked away. His hands rested on his knees, and he clenched them. "You know I have. Mother told me you had me followed. There was nothing to report!" She laughed again.

"Shut up, Brenda."

"Oh, darling, how it must upset you not to be able to get rid of me! Especially now that there's a lot more to interest you. I saw the way you looked at her. You were never very good at concealing your—"

"Shut up, Brenda!"

"I don't think Lady Nesbitt will allow you to dally with her granddaughter. You'll have to be very secretive if you plan to continue your seduction."

Andrew looked coldly at his wife. "Nothing could be further from my plans. I assure you."

"Well, then neither one of us has had much . . . amusement lately."

Brenda had been his wife for four years. When he met her and fell in love with her, he had been overwhelmed with passion, adoration. Brenda amazed him as no other woman had. This demure little southern belle who could charm the skin off a snake and appear to have almost nunlike chastity in public could do things to him in bed that left him shaken in the cool morning light. She was more than most men dared dream of: a lady on his arm, a vixen in his bed.

A few months after their wedding he had sensed something was wrong; Brenda had become less passionate, more irritable and morose. He witnessed odd behavior—wheedling and seductive one moment, she would show an evil temper the next. She became so unpredictable he found himself worrying what he would find when he went home each evening. He hoped pregnancy caused these bizarre changes; a son would make him happy and fulfill a long-held desire. But when he happened home earlier than usual one day, the truth changed everything. He overheard his mother-in-law scolding her daughter. "I don't *care* if you can't stand it! *Pretend!* And if you ever go near that actor again, I'll whip you myself!"

Andrew left his house without ever letting them know he had overheard. He learned how shockingly unfaithful Brenda was—she had liaisons all over town. He confronted her when he should have divorced her instantly. Drugged by her physical allure and shaken by what he felt was a personal failure, he merely threatened divorce—a divorce he knew would be difficult for him to pursue, given the strong convictions of the Catholic church on that issue.

Completely fooled by her tears, her begging and promises, he gave her another chance. He soon found himself with a wife who did not wander, but met his advances passively. By the time he realized the futility of their marriage, the complete absence of affection, her adulteries were behind them.

242

Brenda's behavior was difficult for Andrew to understand, she seemed to sweep suddenly from lethargy to wild energy. He rarely knew what to expect of her; she was seldom balanced or affable. He left her disposition to her mother, Mrs. Waite, who seemed to have no trouble controlling her. Sometimes weeks would pass without Andrew and Brenda speaking a sentence to each other. The tense arrangement he had made, not with his wife but with her mother, was that if Brenda would behave as if she were a good wife, Andrew would publicly and economically act the part of the husband, and they would not attempt intimacy.

For at least three of the four years of his marriage, Andrew had welcomed any reason to be away from home.

Patricia was left in the bridal chamber. Fresh flowers surrounded her, and she wore a long satin dressing gown of muted gray trimmed with pink piping. Midnight had come and gone and as the hour grew later and she was still alone, she climbed into the bed. Amanda and Emily had escorted her to the bedroom and left her. She remembered, as she rested her head on the pillow, that Emily had tried to comfort her and Amanda would not allow it.

"Patricia, darling, if—"

"Emily," Amanda sternly reproached. "Patricia is on her own now."

"But if . . . if something should . . . oh, darling," Emily had said, embracing her daughter, "I do love you. I hope you can be happy."

She had listened to the large house slowly grow quiet, but Dale did not join her. Perhaps he wouldn't, she thought. Of course that was her preference, that he ignore her, so long as he behaved himself in public and managed to get them a lot of invitations. She dozed, uncomfortable in this bed, this house. A loud crashing sound startled her, and she bolted upright. The lamp was turned low but still illuminated the room. She heard four chimes on the gold and crystal clock that sat upon the mantle. Her husband stood unsteadily at the foot of the bed. His hair was mussed, his shirt partially unbuttoned and askew, and he held a glass in his hand.

"Well, pretty bride," he slurred, "are you ready?"

"Dale, you're drunk!"

"What did you expect? You thought I couldn't wait!" He laughed, the sound fading into a boyish giggle. "A little gin will make this easier. Get undressed. And hurry. I don't want to spend too much time."

"Dale, just go to bed," she said, lying down again.

He weaved toward her, lifted his glass, and drained it. He made an attempt to place it on a bedside commode, but it slipped to the floor and lay on the thick carpet. He pulled at his shirt, ripping the buttons off, and began to undo his breeches.

"Dale, if you think you're going to assert yourself in this condition, you—"

He reached down and flung back the satin quilt. "My father wants a grandson, Patricia. And you decided to be the one to give him one." He grabbed the neck of her nightgown and ripped it. She shrieked at his violence and attempted to cover herself. But Dale flung himself atop her and began to squirm around. He tried to free himself from his breeches, and she struggled against him.

His face was buried in her neck, and he grumbled unintelligible words. Raped, night after night, she thought. She forced herself to lie still and quiet. She hoped he would be quick at least. She steeled herself against the inevitable pain while Dale made clumsy attempts to fondle her and get himself out of his pants.

Suddenly he was still. It would be too much to hope he was dead. She remained motionless; it was hard to breath under his weight, but she willed herself to take shallow breaths and wouldn't move. When several minutes had passed, he snored. She eased herself out from under him with great difficulty. She stood at the side of her nuptial bed and looked down at him. He sprawled across the bed, arms flung wide, feet hanging over the edge, completely gone to drunken stupor.

She slipped into her dressing gown and began to ease off his shoes and stockings. His breeches were a much more difficult matter and took a long time, but she finally had them in her hand. She tossed them down on her rended sleepwear on the floor. Dale lay naked and unconscious on their wedding bed. She picked up the glass and sniffed it. Then she gathered two pillows and dragged the quilt to the daybed. She curled up there, quite content, and made a resolution to always be sure there was plenty of gin stocked all over the house.

Emily, Amanda, and Lilly went to the railroad station on the Monday morning following Patricia's wedding. Wilson Montaine's private car, complete with sleeping compartments, would carry the newlyweds to Saratoga where they would enjoy two weeks at a pleasure resort. Emily had hardly slept the past two nights, anxious to see how Patricia had fared her first two days as a wife.

When the women all came together, Emily was amazed by Patricia's confidence and apparent happiness. They all embraced on the platform while Dale, quiet and sullen, supervised the loading of their trunks. Patricia embraced each one, kissing their cheeks. "Grandmother, darling, thank you so much for the wonderful wedding! Lilly, my dear, how wonderful you look; I adore your new hat! Mother, Mother, you're tired . . . you mustn't work so hard now that Grandmother is here to take care of you!"

Emily pulled Patricia aside. "Patsy, are you well? You feel all right and you're happy?"

"Mama, everything is going to be just fine . . . as I knew it would," she whispered. "Dale hasn't bothered me in the slightest. Oh, he means to, but actually he becomes so roaring drunk that he . . . well, drops off to sleep!" She giggled conspiratorially.

Emily frowned. "Do you think that will go on for long?" she asked her daughter.

"I imagine for some time, Mama. And from what I hear about Saratoga, he will be far too busy and too drunk to pester me!"

"Oh, Patsy, what kind of life have you gotten for yourself?"

"Well, probably the closest to perfect I could ask for." She kissed her mother's cheek. "Now promise not to worry about me anymore. I know what I'm doing. After we've returned, we'll have a grand summer party with food in the garden and dancing in the ballroom, and we'll invite everyone we've ever met or heard of! Good-bye, darlings. I'll send you a letter packet soon! I'll bring you all presents!"

The women waved as the private coach pulled away. Emily wept all the way back to the Grafton Hotel.

Lilly did not try to change the Grafton Hotel in a day. The first order of business was to supply the place with a better staff. She knew within a week of her grandmother's ownership that she could not change the attitude and energy of the existing group of bellmen, waiters, maids, and kitchen staff. But when she had discharged fifteen of the worst, the others were a mite more eager to please.

The next thing she did was to improve the dining room. She had it enlarged, refurnished, and carpeted for the very first time, and she purchased all new table appointments. Reorganizing had to be done on the ground floor of the five-story hotel in order to accommodate the expansion. The office of the proprietor was eliminated so Lilly and her grandmother shared the large desk in a room converted to a study in their suite. The ballroom was reduced in size, and the kitchen area was extended into the alley. The project took nearly three months of constant work and the price per room had to be temporarily reduced to account for inconveniences suffered by the guests.

The cost of providing each suite of rooms with a water closet was too high so Lilly satisfied herself with refurnishing, enlarging, and fixing up dressing rooms complete with tubs, china basins, dressing tables, and portable pots. The work was done one floor at a time.

Lilly was pleased not only with the progress, but by the effect all this work had on her family. Emily had insisted that a traditional New England breakfast be served every morning, despite the work it required of the staff and the expense of the food. Oysters, eggs, potatoes, sausage and ham, a variety of baked goods, gravy and biscuits, whatever fruit could be found was prepared daily, supplemented by Emily's own jellies, jams, and preserves. Emily rose early to supervise, and her own recipes were used. The color on her cheeks became robust again, and her skin took on a healthier glow than ever before. She visited with guests in the dining room, eager to see that each table was pleased, and worried about Patricia much less. And the enormous breakfast became popular. Whole families arrived on weekend mornings to partake, and the restaurant business alone was quickly becoming successful.

Amanda was rapidly infected by the business. She approached sixty years of age and knew only too well that there were two choices for her daughter and granddaughter: to exist on whatever fortune she could leave behind, or establish a legacy of business they could maintain after she was gone. Having been dependent on men, having been made poor or rich according to the skills or absence of skills of a certain husband, she found the decision simple. She made a routine of having her driver take her all around the lush green hills surrounding Philadelphia in search of the perfect landscape for a large luxury hotel. She invited businessmen, politicians, and old family friends to the new restaurant to dine, had the ballroom carpeted and furnished like a large parlor for afternoon soirées, and studied building plans.

Lilly asked her mother and grandmother to reserve time for her one afternoon so that she might bring a guest to tea. Emily nearly lost her composure and openly wept when she was reunited with Sophia Washington. They embraced like long separated sisters.

"It took some doing, Mama, but Sophia is willing to work for us again. I had to promise her the moon."

"And all the stars!" Emily quickly agreed.

Sophia became Emily's right arm, just as she had been in the boarding house. Within two months of following Emily around the hotel, Sophia made rounds on her own. It didn't take more than a single test for the staff to learn that Sophia's praise or chastisement carried all the weight of Emily's. Sophia, in fact, was still more demanding of perfection. Having had Sophia as her best friend for so many years, working side by side with her for so long, Emily was never fooled by a worker who blamed Sophia if the task was poorly done. Emily *knew* how good Sophia was at managing.

The fifty-year-old black woman was hard to convince, but she soon relented to afternoon suits with blouses and more attractive shoes, but she would not part with the colorful turbans that covered her woolly gray hair. And, finally, she moved into the hotel, although giving up her garden was a terrible loss for her.

When it became apparent that Sophia was taking a supervisory role, some employees became disgruntled. Lady Nesbitt was visited after tea one afternoon by three chamber maids, two of whom were mature women. Lilly and Emily happened to be in the room, and the boldest of the three asked for a private conference.

"I'm afraid not," Amanda said. "In fact, the most responsible for your job is Miss Armstrong," she said, tilting her head toward Lilly. "So, state your business or leave."

The spokeswoman, a stout, grandmotherly woman in her fifties, wearing a crisp white apron and eyelet cap, separated herself from the other two. "We don't like taking orders from a colored woman," she said, matter-of-factly.

Emily's face became pink and her lips tight.

"I see," Lilly said. "Is Mrs. Washington too strict? Hard to please? Abusive?"

"Yes, she's all that and more."

"More?"

"She's a Negress. It don't sit well with some of us to take orders off her."

"Ah, I see. How many, would you say, have trouble working to please Mrs. Washington?"

"Mostly all," the woman said, straightening her back, the others doing the same behind her.

"Well, that can be easily resolved. If you'll tell each one who cannot happily work to satisfy Mrs. Washington to simply come to Mr. Drake's office tomorrow at two, we'll take care of the matter."

"You'll be getting rid of her then?"

"Certainly not," Lilly said with conviction. "Mrs. Washington is not only the best supervisor available, she is a trusted and valued friend. But at two tomorrow I will be prepared to give final pay to each maid, cook, or waiter who dislikes working to please her. I don't think I'll have a great deal of trouble finding willing staff in a city that is plagued by joblessness. Good day."

When not one appeared, Amanda whispered to Emily, "I think our young King Solomon will enjoy great success."

One day while Sophia stood in the women's suite looking out the window into the square, Emily asked her if she mourned her garden. "Well, Miz Em, I do miss that little plot was all mine, but my thoughts were more 'bout that newspaper office yonder. Seems to me this would be a good spot for a newspaperman to live . . . save a mite in horsecar fare."

"Yes," Emily said, smiling.

By the time eight months had passed, the hotel was refurbished and redecorated. Amanda was busily socializing, but for an entirely new reason: to increase the numbers of influential people who would pass through her doors and enjoy her hospitality. Emily had Sophia with her again, and John Giddings had taken a room with them.

The first of February arrived, a little more than nine months since the women had begun. Fletcher and Lilly sat on opposite sides of his large desk, more burdened with paperwork than ever before. It was after nine, and Fletcher's man, Michael, brought them each a brandy.

"It's official," Fletcher finally said. "Your first profitable month."

"Thank God!" Lilly said, tired, drained, and elated.

"Many debts remain," he advised her.

"But they can be paid by the hotel itself rather than Grandmother's savings if we continue to carry this number of guests?" she asked, pointing to the ledger he had opened.

"Yes, the hotel can pay for itself now; we shouldn't require any more loans from the estate."

"Oh, there were times I wondered if we could do it. You did it, Fletcher. You, more than any of us."

"I believe you called it a formidable team. None of us could have done this alone." He stood up. "Forgive me, Lilly. I'm tired."

She stood as well, lifted her glass toward his, and took a sip. Then she held out her hand to shake his.

She used her own key to open the door of the suite she shared with Amanda and Emily and found what had become a typical scene within. Emily worked on a sampler, no longer sewing for pay. Sophia knitted something for a grandchild. Bertie and Amanda sat at the table with their cards, a cloud from Bertie's pipe hanging in the air.

"If I called my debt now, I could live out my days in fashion," Bertie said.

"You wouldn't know what to do with fashion," Amanda accused.

"Hello," Lilly said. She raised up the heavy, bound ledger book when they turned toward her. "It's happened. We're making money."

Lilly did not spend as much time at the lending library as she had in years past, but when she did go, she had a purpose. She spent every afternoon there for two solid weeks, browsing, looking over the newer books, examining the newspapers. And the patrons. She followed a woman out of the library and watched her find a bench near the horsecar stop.

"Excuse me," Lilly said. "I've seen you in the library a few times now. I'm Lillian Armstrong."

The woman looked up at her in surprise. Lilly's coat, hat and gloves gave her a status the young woman did not share. Though they were approximately the same age, the woman said, "How do you do, ma'am."

"And your name?"

"Elizabeth Hartly, ma'am."

"I'm pleased to meet you, Elizabeth. May I sit down?"

"Oh . . . oh yes, ma'am," she said, pulling her gray wool coat against her thigh and sliding over on the bench.

"You must be very fond of reading. Have you gone to school?"

"Primary school, ma'am. But I'm a working girl, ma'am, and I don't have the . . . means. But I do love books, when I can borrow them."

251

"What are you reading?"

"Oh, ma'am, it's . . . it's—"

Lilly presumptuously lifted the book she held in her lap and the woman's cheeks grew pink. Lilly smiled. "*Amelia!* Elizabeth, you're romantic!"

"Ma'am, I—"

"I loved *Amelia*. I have no intention of ever being as patient and long suffering, however. Elizabeth, you're wearing a uniform. Do you work as a maid?"

"Yes, ma'am. A kitchen maid. A residence kitchen maid, ma'am. I begin very early in the morning and am free before dinnertime most days."

"Do any of your family rely on your income?"

"Yes, ma'am, why—"

"You don't wear a ring," Lilly said, lifting her hand, which was quickly becoming bright red from the cold. Lilly released her hand and began slowly to remove her hand-sewn leather gloves. "You're not married."

"No, ma'am."

"Elizabeth, I am planning to hire an unmarried woman as an attendant. Some of the chores will be maidlike, but I'm really not accustomed to having anyone besides myself take care of my personal things. I was not prosperous while growing up, and my mother owned a boardinghouse. I always fixed my own bath, my own hair, and mended my own clothes. I'm far busier now and could stand some assistance. Someday I will need a very capable assistant who can write letters, make travel plans, and even balance some simple accounts. Here," she said, handing Elizabeth Hartly her first pair of expensive gloves. "Take these. You need a pair of good gloves before your fingers turn blue and fall off. If you think you might like to work for me, come to the Grafton Hotel tomorrow afternoon at four, and we'll discuss the possibility over tea. And bring along a list of your favorite books!"

Elizabeth's lips were parted in amazement, and her eyes were wide. "Ma'am?"

"Yes?"

"Is your husband a wealthy man, ma'am?"

"No," she laughed. "I am not married. I have a business. Do you think you'll come to see me tomorrow?"

"Yes, ma'am . . . if—"

"Oh, I'll pay you more than you're earning now. We can talk about that tomorrow."

"But, Miss . . . Miss . . ."

"Armstrong, Lillian Armstrong."

"How did you . . . why did you . . . ?"

"Do you realize in two weeks of afternoons at the lending library I saw only four women borrowing books to read? Oh, there were house girls borrowing books for their mistresses, not for themselves—I asked Mr. Wendell about the withdrawal cards. But of the four women I saw, three were elderly! There it is—a building filled with books to be loaned, and who borrows them? Schoolchildren and men! Well-to-do women send someone from their staff! You were the only young woman interested for herself. I never thought it would take so long to find a woman with initiative. I fancied I would be able to interview several young women. It appears, Elizabeth, you're the only one in the city suitable!"

She smiled shyly. "My mother says I waste my time."

"But you knew she was wrong!"

Elizabeth Hartly was eighteen years old, shorter than Lilly by three inches, heavier by a few pounds. She had a pleasant round face, alert eyes, honey-colored hair that had a springy quality she attempted to control. She was the second of three daughters, and her father worked long days as a clerk in a banking house. Elizabeth's older sister was married, her younger sister helped their mother at home, and the family occupied a humble two-story house in South Philadelphia. Over tea Lilly discovered that Elizabeth was patient, good natured, somewhat shy, and not very confident. But she was hired.

Elizabeth rode the horsecar to the Grafton Hotel every morning and departed every evening. She was instructed to follow Lilly around through her routine, unless she was given a specific chore that had to do with mending, pressing, tidying, or adding a column of numbers. Lilly found she had to take some time to make Elizabeth more proficient, but she improved steadily and responded very well to praise.

Lilly, always purposeful in what she did, had taken this time to be sure Elizabeth would be a competent assistant so that she could travel with a companion and helper. She told her grandmother that now that there was a profit at the Grafton, Sophia and Emily had control over the daily operation of the hotel, Amanda had a number of eager builders begging to draw up plans, and Lilly would have to start traveling. Patricia approached her first anniversary, and though she didn't exactly thrive, she wasn't in need of constant help.

Lilly presented her grandmother with an itinerary. She meant for the hotel to be better than a profitable operation; she wanted a fantastic success. She planned to tour Bath, Baden-Baden, Aix-les-Bains, the Riviera, the Gastien Valley, Lake Balaton, and finally all the best and largest hotels in the northeastern United States. "It will be expensive, Grandmother, but I promise to test their abilities to the limit and bring home every scrap of knowledge."

"But Lilly, I've already visited many of these places."

"I know, but not with your attention focused on the operation of the hotels. You were a guest, not a spy! I mean to look closely at how every single hotel pleases and displeases."

Her plan would take over six months. She refused a farewell party and made her grandmother promise there would be no fuss. She said good-bye to the staff, to Fletcher, and John Giddings. She had tea with Patricia, an unavoidable formality that left Lilly feeling cynical and cold; there was hardly anything they had in common. And once again Lilly and Amanda stood at the station to say good-bye.

When Lilly had been gone three months, a large area in Fairmount Park was cleared to begin the construction of a five hundred–room hotel to be named the Armstrong Arms . . . for Lilly.

Patricia rarely got out of bed before one o'clock. There was no reason to get up early. She would rise, have her tea and toast, take her bath, dress for the afternoon, and occasionally she would have the driver take her into Philadelphia to the Grafton Hotel for afternoon tea. She did this less and less often as her mother and grandmother were too busy to idle for long; they were far more interested in their stupid hotel than in her. On rare occasions she had the company of the Devons at dinner, only because she begged Andrew to bring his wife along when he dined with Wilson Montaine. But Patricia did not like the woman or her mother, Mrs. Waite. Both had a syrupy sweetness that Patricia immediately identified as wholly deceitful. Mrs.

Devon always made such a fuss over Patricia. At first that had been fun, but her experience made her aware that it was false.

Patricia had invited Mary Ellen Jasper Markland to her home for tea, not to watch her grovel as had been her original intent. She wanted a friend, any friend. But Mary Ellen declined as she was near confinement for childbirth and was not being seen in public.

The Montaine household was either quiet as a tomb or trembling with quarrels—between Dale and his father, Wilson and his wife, Dale and Deanna, or Patricia and any one of them. Wilson Montaine liked his work, his meals, his cigars. Amassing a fortune was a game; he was friendless but for Andrew Devon and did not care. His anxiety to grow rich had obsessed him since childhood. He would far rather beat someone out of property than have a dinner guest. Patricia quickly saw the futility of trying to convince him to have parties. Deanna Montaine was a brassy, rough-mouthed woman in her mid-thirties who seemed to be in a constant poor temper. Sometimes she tippled all afternoon and fell into bed early, missing the evening meal. And Patricia never sought Dale's company, though it was occasionally forced on her late at night.

Patricia kept wondering where the three hundred who drank at her wedding had gone. She attended fewer social gatherings every month, largely because her grandmother hostessed fewer. The only invitations she received came from Amanda. She discovered something unexpected and unfortunate: she was disliked. People tolerated her, even complimented her, but they never even pretended they would be inclined to include her in their events. Wilson Montaine would never be accepted, and his son had been grudgingly tolerated because there were a few socially prominent, financially distressed families who could profit from a clever marriage. But Dale had nothing to offer now. He spent his days and nights holding off boredom with riding, hunting, gambling, drinking, and his favorite pastime of sporting young girls. When Patricia realized Dale was still victimizing women, she did not feel the relief she expected. Rather, she encouraged his jaunts to Saratoga where gambling and drinking could keep him out of trouble. Dale favored the races and gin.

Patricia had been married over one and a half years. Christmas approached and Lilly would soon be home from her long tour, but Lilly would be less inclined than ever to socialize. It was Lilly's fault, Patricia believed, that her life had become so dull, so boring. If Lilly had not begun this insanity of hotels and businesses, there would be parties to attend.

Patricia felt ill and tired all the time. Her anger with the farce her life had become gnawed at her. She wanted it behind her. To that end, she went to see her grandmother at the Grafton Hotel. She had never been so lonely.

"Grandmother, I want to come home," she said.

"Ah, do you?" Amanda replied. "I'm afraid it's too late for that, dear."

"Grandmother, I'm unhappy! Please!"

"Tell me, darling, what makes you so unhappy?"

"Everything! I have no friends! My family is too busy for me! My husband is a drunkard! My father-in-law is a ghastly, smelly, sloppy jobber-done-good! All those people who gave me gifts for my wedding snub me! I have nothing to do!"

"You've been married how long?" Amanda asked, knowing almost to the day how long it had been. She had been ready for this much sooner, a fact she would not be sharing with Patricia.

"One and a half years. I can't *stand* it!"

"And what would make you happy, Patricia? What would *finally* make you happy?"

"I want to divorce Dale and live with you again."

"And do what? Work with us to establish a hotel? Where do you think you could be most useful?"

"Well," Patricia began, falsely encouraged, "I don't have all the skills Mama and Lilly have, but I can be a good hostess, I know I can. I know you wouldn't be ashamed to have me come to your parties and teas. I know I could—"

"That's what I expected, Patricia. I'm sorry, there is simply no such chore . . . therefore, no place for you here."

Patricia's mouth dropped open, and she stared at her grandmother in complete horror. Her eyes began to well with tears.

"I wish you would have listened to me, Patricia. I truly did put your happiness first. But you see, you are still expecting to be indulged—to be the prettiest, most popular, best gowned and to have perpetual fun. I warned you quite explicitly; I told you you would not find society to be the grand and friendly group you envisioned. I told you they would be cruel—"

"They're not cruel to *you*," she said, tears sliding down her face.

"I haven't betrayed them."

"How did I—"

"You crept into their secure little world and selfishly snatched the richest bachelor there, and worse, you only wanted his money. You tried to best them all, for greed and . . . for revenge. You wanted not only to be accepted by them, you wanted to be the best among them. You wouldn't believe me, would you? I told you a hundred times, you can only be born into their world—"

"But you were born into society . . . and I'm—"

"The unfortunate daughter of Ned Armstrong and a working class owner of a boardinghouse."

"But *your* granddaughter!"

"It won't do you any good. They are somewhat careful of me, they accept my hospitality graciously, and I have a few friends among them . . . but Emily and Lilly understand only too well the limits of my name, a name long since removed from their lives. That's the reason for the hotel, Patricia. Because when the name is gone and the money runs out, there must be work. There must always be work!"

Patricia put her hands over her face and cried. "Oh, Grandmother, how terrible of you! Won't you let me come home? If I promise to work?"

"Do you think you can?" she asked.

"Yes!" Patricia promised, looking at Amanda with her tear-stained face and desperate eyes.

"If you think you can work, darling, go home and see if you can mend something with your husband. Perhaps you can build some kind of family with him. Perhaps you can remove the liquor rather than stock it to keep him docile and unconscious. Perhaps you can improve that dark house and fill it with the laughter of children. Failing that, perhaps you can put your new fortune to good works. There are hungry people in this city, children who cannot read, orphans who have nowhere to live. But I am telling you this, Patricia, as long as you think the world was created for your amusement and requires nothing of you but your willingness to attend, you will suffer this unhappiness. And it will only get worse."

Patricia swallowed her tears and fixed her grandmother with a cold, angry stare. The tracks of tears marked her face, but despair was no longer what she was feeling. "Betrayed," she finally said, "by my own family."

"No, Patricia," Amanda said calmly. "You betrayed us . . . and

257

yourself. You used me, my money and influence, to buy yourself the sort of life you think you deserve. I told you long ago my purse has a bottom that will not be reached by indulging you, and you were foolish to doubt it. Now go home. See if you can make something useful of your life. You have greater means to do that than anyone I know. Happiness or misery is entirely up to you; you cannot buy it, steal it, or have it bequeathed to you."

Patricia took a handkerchief from her handbag and dabbed at her eyes. "Is it divorce you find so abhorrent? Do you know that my husband, when not drunk, continues to play the ladies?"

"Oh, Patricia, you knew he would."

"Help me get free of that place! Must I beg?"

"No amount of begging will change my mind, Patricia. This was what you wanted. You have it. Make use of it."

"Why is it that Lilly can do whatever defiant, mad thing in the world she desires and she is *admired*? Send me traveling then! Send me away on a long, long trip—"

"Patricia! Lilly is about business! Visit when you like, but you have taken on a marriage, and I will not be a party to your changed whim!"

"I hate her. She's always been the lucky one. No matter how outrageous she is, she is approved of. Praised."

Amanda sighed. "And now I suppose you hate me as well, and your mother."

"No," she said sadly. "But I am hurt by your refusal to help me."

"The pity is that I tried to help you. The greater pity is that you would find in Lilly more compassion for your predicament than you will ever find in me. You can still change your dreams, Patricia, into something that will give you satisfaction. It's up to you."

"Is there nothing to change your mind?"

"Nothing! It breaks my heart to see you suffer, but as long as I help you, you will never help yourself. I know Wilson Montaine; I know that household. There are things you could do to turn it right. You must make an effort."

"How in the world can anyone make anything out of—"

"By not becoming one of them! By giving your husband some encouragement to perform as a good son, good man. Put yourself to work! Do something with yourself!"

Patricia angrily stuffed the handkerchief in her purse. "You don't understand," she said.

"Yes, I do. More than you think."

She returned to her monogrammed coach without another word. When she had left the suite Emily opened the door of her bedroom and looked at her mother. "I heard what you said to her," she confessed.

"You certainly had to listen quite carefully to do so," Amanda said without a hint of surprise.

"I'm so afraid for her. I'm so filled with pity for her."

"Yes, I'm sure. So am I. Patricia will have to suffer a great deal more before she will change . . . and perhaps she never will."

"You know exactly what I'm feeling, don't you, Mother?"

Amanda laughed humorlessly. "Oh yes, darling. There is nothing to compare to the pain and fear involved in releasing a child into her own maturity. I envy you one thing, Emily. I had only one daughter . . . and the circumstances were far worse."

"Mother, I could not have changed Ned. Do you really believe Patricia has a prayer of changing anyone in that household?"

Amanda shrugged. "You tried to make a marriage with that fraud. Although I always knew it was useless, I have to give you credit for the effort. My marriages were not always blissful—they all began as tense, burdensome liaisons. I had to work, compromise, struggle. Patricia has not tried anything but to force parties on Wilson. I'll have a better answer for you if I ever see her do something for herself rather than asking people to make her happy."

Patricia returned to the Montaine household at dusk. Wilson Montaine had finished his dinner and was having a provocative argument with his wife behind her closed bedroom door. The sound of bickering, shouting, ridicule, and whimpering often plagued the upstairs halls in the evenings. Dale's coach was out. A young maid, one just as she had imagined so long ago, harried and worried, approached her. "Can I bring you a plate in your room, ma'am?"

"No. Just sherry and a biscuit," Patricia replied.

She shrugged out of her afternoon toilette of heavy velvet, tossed her hat and gloves on the bed to be put away by someone else, and dressed comfortably in a satin dressing gown. She sipped her sherry at her writing desk. She remembered what had saved her from despair once before and sought that comfort again. She dated the top of her page and wrote:

"Dear John . . ."

15

*L*illy returned to Philadelphia just before Christmas, making her tour nearly nine months long. She had done far more than examine hotels abroad; she had lived a lifetime of experiences in a few months.

Lilly had visited some of her grandmother's acquaintances, attended social events, made purchases and placed orders. In London she viewed the Gilbert and Sullivan musical *H.M.S. Pinafore,* saw a lawn tennis championship played at Wimbledon, and ordered a huge crystal chandelier to be shipped to Philadelphia for the new hotel foyer.

In Paris she bought and shipped paintings, a Corot, a Delacroix. She visited Charles Frederick Worth on the Rue de la Paix and was measured for a complete wardrobe that would be shipped to the States as she continued her travels. She had her portrait done by Emile Auguste

Carolus-Duran. It was there that Lilly met one of her grandmother's oldest friends, the former Mary Newbold Singer, whose son, John Singer Sargent, promised to be one of the finest portrait painters of all time.

The hotel, slowly growing while she was away, was always foremost in her mind, and she selected crystal, china, silver, art, bric-a-brac, statuary, and linen. Furniture, carpet, draperies, tiles, and fixtures would be purchased at home, where they were less expensive while of higher quality. Items she ordered and had sent home were arriving before her journey was complete.

Lilly was noticed by a few gentlemen. She, however, never paid them much notice.

When she finally returned to Philadelphia, tired but full in experience and richer in knowledge, she could barely be still long enough to tell all she'd seen and done. She was desperate to see the new hotel. Although it was little more than a short foundation, to Lilly it seemed like the beginning of a castle.

The Armstrong Arms grew slowly through 1879, floor by agonizing floor. Construction was often abandoned during the winter months of 1879, beginning again in earnest in the spring. By the spring of 1880, after two years of construction, Lilly was able at long last to begin the decorating in the interior and the landscaping of the grounds. The construction of the building itself was a four-year project that had been pushed into a little over two years because Amanda was impatient, spent top dollar for the work, and hired the very best. Lilly celebrated her twenty-first birthday in a very special manner; she moved with her immediate family into the apartments on the top floor of the new, unfinished hotel. Although the hotel would not be able to accommodate guests for another year, she had gone to great pains to make their living quarters ready.

Except in their apartment, all the decorating, landscaping, furnishing, and hiring were still left to be done, but the shell of the hotel was complete, the elevators operational, and the spacious apartments that Lilly had overseen for months were livable, if not perfect.

The seven rooms at the Grafton Hotel had seemed luxurious, but the twenty-one rooms atop the Armstrong Arms were magnificent. The apartment resembled a house in itself. The family had access through their own elevator and two open staircases that reached from the foyer outside a grouping of fifth-floor offices. A locked door on the fifth floor insured their privacy. Their living quarters held a large, marble foyer that opened into a front parlor forty feet long and twenty feet wide.

Three private sections, each containing one or two large bed-chambers, a dressing room, a water closet, a sitting room, and a study surrounded a central living area. Each of the three women would have her own spacious quarters for solitude and sleeping; to share there was a large formal sitting room, a formal dining room that could serve thirty seated guests, a gallery, the spacious parlor, a library—at Lilly's insistence, a kitchen separate from the hotel cooking rooms, and a conservatory. Outside the quarters was the awesome width and breadth of what remained of the hotel's roof, some of which Lilly envisioned she could decorate with vines, potted trees, garden furniture, and wooden boxes of flowers to resemble garden areas. For this reason Lilly, with the help of her mother and grandmother, had designed their rooftop home so that it was tucked into a corner of the roof. Each bedroom–sitting room area had a portion of rooftop and doors to the outside, which accounted for three sides of the apartment, each side with a good view of the countryside. The fourth side contained the staircase and windowless wall of the front parlor, because from there one could only view the rooftop devices such as water tank, pipes, and other necessary equipment.

A portion of the hotel's first floor was finished into temporary quarters for those servants whom the women needed daily. Amanda found it necessary to hire a secretary, and there were a cook, two drivers, two maids, Elizabeth, and a new steward by the name of Cleaves. Sophia, Fletcher Drake, and John Giddings did not move with them. Sophia was well established in the Philadelphia hotel and needed there, John required the convenient location to his newspaper, and, although Amanda offered quarters to Fletcher, he had decided to purchase his own property in the city.

Lilly was too busy to be impatient about the opening. However, she often encouraged painters, carpenters, smelters, and gardeners to hire additional help to hurry her project, just as she offered more money to textile weavers, ironworks factories, and glass blowers to get her orders filled ahead of others.

The work thrilled her. She was close enough to watch every drape hung, every pot polished, every blade of grass clipped.

Lilly interviewed many applicants to the hotel staff herself, often deferring to the wisdom of one of the other women or Fletcher. She had a long list from her travels and wrote to some experienced personnel, and she stole a few—stewards, chefs, domestics, a stable master. She routinely put on sturdy clothing and comfortable shoes to walk through the huge, vacant structure to inspect work that was being done. She could be found anywhere on the property—in the loading area to inspect furniture or building and decorating materials as they were delivered, in the stables where Armstrong Arms coaches and horsecars were being built, painted, polished, upholstered, and made generally ready, in the kitchen where large cooking stoves and ovens were being installed. She judged the hanging of every portiere, eighteen different woods were used in the mantels and wainscoting, and George Kemp himself supervised the installation of carpet from his factory. She chose delicate colors—primarily blue, silver, and muted rose—and observed the completion of frescoes and friezes.

When the hammering and sawing ended each day, Lilly did not stop. That was when she strained her eyes over long columns of numbers or read newspapers from all over the country.

"Everyone works," Fletcher told Amanda, "but Lilly works too hard."

"You try to stop her," Amanda challenged.

"She's only twenty-one. She should have a life apart from work," he argued.

"I suppose you think that hasn't been suggested? Poor Elizabeth! She hasn't had time for *Amelia* or any other novel since that fateful day she visited the library!"

Lilly would accept only financial advice; the only suggestions she would hear had to do with menus or wallpaper or furniture. When it came to her personal life, she would not be distracted from work long enough to have one. "I have a very satisfactory life," she said, sounding remarkably like Emily not many years before. "I have work, family, and never a moment without challenge."

The hotel was taking shape beautifully, with remarkable speed. A large portico in front led into the hotel foyer. The chandelier Lilly had purchased in Europe dangled from the thirty-foot ceiling. The first floor held the dining room, ballroom, a large gallery, and several small parlors that could be used by guests for entertaining, plus the massive kitchens and wide hallways that led to the four corners of the enormous structure where elevators were conveniently situated. Although there were staircases throughout, the largest and most magnificent led from the second-floor balcony into the foyer: it was fourteen feet wide at its base and sported grand brass banisters.

Patricia was among the first to visit the new apartments above the unfinished hotel. The women had been in residence just a few months. The summer was growing warm and bright, and recently planted flowers were beginning to spread around walks and partially constructed gazebos. Amanda and Emily had gone to the city to make fabric selections for coverlets and upholstery, and so Lilly gave her sister a tour of the apartments. Patricia walked from room to room, observing the rich decor, the quality furnishings, the novel arrangement. Only the patio areas were still unfinished.

"I must admit, Lilly, you have fashioned quite a little kingdom for yourself."

"It's not very different from living above one's shop," Lilly replied, though she felt the differences, and the feeling of power it brought.

"And if the hotel is not a success? Will you have no home?"

"We always have the Grafton. The name will be changed now, however. The hotel will become known as the Nesbitt House, for Grandmother."

"Is there a guest room?" Patricia asked.

Lilly smiled proudly. "Yes, Patsy. Five hundred at last count."

"Oh, Lilly, how jealous I am. I wish I had a talent of any kind at all . . . but I—" She stopped abruptly. She looked away from Lilly, and Lilly reached out to touch Patricia's arm.

"What is it, Patsy? Is something wrong?"

"Ah, there is always something wrong with me, isn't there? Well, have you the means to serve tea?"

Lilly sent Elizabeth to get them tea and took Patricia into her own sitting room.

"Are you so unhappy?"

"Well, didn't you expect I would be? It seems everyone knew how miserable I would be except me. You don't have to pretend to be surprised."

"Oh, Patricia, you have always been so determined about what you wanted."

"So have you! Would that God had given me a yearning for a business rather than a marriage!"

Lilly knew that was the core of the problem: it wasn't marriage

Patricia had wanted at all. Marriage was simply the only means Patricia could imagine that would make her rich and pampered. It had seemed for years that Patricia was the only person not clear about the terrible illusions she had created. She could never be made to understand that what she wanted didn't exist. "Is he terrible to you? Does he . . . ?" When Lilly couldn't finish, she waited for Patricia to make some response.

"Beat me? Rape me? No. You'll be glad to know he is not physically brutal. He calls me names—everyone in his family is good at that. They're all so nasty to one another. He invites me to leave him. 'Run away,' he tempts. 'I'll give you a little pot of money and a divorce.'"

"Oh, Patsy."

"Where would I go? Grandmother says I may not come home in disgrace, she won't support me if I leave my husband."

"You asked her? And she said she wouldn't?"

"She said she tried to save me from this misery, and since I wouldn't listen to her, I have to try to make something useful of my life in my present circumstances. She says no one has greater means than I. But Lilly, I haven't had a useful idea in my life!"

"Patricia, why don't you take Dale's offer? Why not accept his little pot of money and—"

"And what? Live in some tiny house with chintz curtains and sew hems?"

"There's more dignity in that than in your current situation. You could—"

"Stop it, Lilly. You know perfectly well how it would be. Everyone says it—you don't have to pretend anymore. Everyone tells me I'm lazy and spoiled and not good at anything. I may as well be a failure in style! At least I don't have to pull my tub out of the pantry!"

Lilly felt her cheeks grow hot. She had a sudden, pitying understanding. She had always hated Patricia's laziness and self-indulgence. What if she couldn't help it, no matter what? What if she hated having no interests, no discipline, no desires of any kind save the desire to be constantly attended to, but couldn't change?

"Grandmother told me to *try*," Patricia said. "Everyone has always been telling me to try harder. I have never understood how they're all so sure I can!"

"Patricia," Lilly said, "no matter what Grandmother says, I would have you home."

"I'm afraid it's a little too late for that now. Dale has finally been successful at something, you see. Just before Christmas, while you are all very busy with your hotel, I will be confined in childbirth."

"Patricia! You're pregnant!"

"I'm afraid I am," she said, sitting back in her chair and looking a bit pale.

"You're not happy? Even knowing you're having a child of your own?"

"*My* own? Good Lord, Lilly! Can you imagine bringing a child into that dreadful family? Can you imagine what kind of father Dale is likely to be? I did everything I could think of to prevent it—I even found a doctor who would give me a pessary, though it was only peach pit, but he swore it would prevent a baby."

"A *what?*"

"Oh never mind. There are ways. I would have an abortion if it weren't so dangerous and painful. But if I was found out, then I'd be in deep—"

"But you'll be a mother! You could be a good one! Mama raised us without a father!"

Elizabeth brought a tray of tea and cakes, and Lilly dismissed her, serving Patricia herself.

"*You* could be a good mother, Lilly. You're good at everything, but I simply dread it! I don't feel well, I'm losing my figure, and I hate Dale for this!"

"You have to stop that!" Lilly said, suddenly desperate. "You have to make yourself try to be a good mother! You have to simply force yourself to make this one thing the best thing you've ever done!"

"That's all fine and good, Lilly. What if I fail again? What if I'm simply not able to *love* this baby?"

When Patricia finally left, Lilly stayed in her sitting room. She had never had such a depressing afternoon. She told Elizabeth she was finished working for the day and didn't want to be disturbed. The temporary quarters Elizabeth used were functional and little more, and she could have stayed in the apartments for the evening, but she was invited to borrow any books Lilly possessed and went happily to her little room downstairs, out of harm's way, in case Lilly changed her mind and thought of a project.

It was not uncommon for Lilly to take a tray in her room or, for that matter, to have to be interrupted in order to be fed. When Emily and Amanda had returned from the city, neither wondered about Lilly's whereabouts. Since Elizabeth was not in evidence, both assumed Lilly had duties outside or somewhere in the hotel and had her employee with her. A place was set for her in the dining room, but as was often the case, the place remained vacant. It was nearly nine in the evening when Amanda finally became concerned—it took considerable concern to pull her away from her card game with Bertie.

When she knocked at Lilly's bedroom door, there was no answer. She opened the door and peered in, calling out Lilly's name, but still there was no reply. A lamp, turned low, was lit in the room, so someone had been there. Amanda walked through to the adjoining sitting room. There she saw a figure sitting in the dark, the chair usually situated before the hearth had been dragged to the window, and the draperies were open, revealing the star-lit sky.

"Lilly?" Amanda called.

"Yes," she said softly.

Amanda felt instant relief when Lilly spoke; she had begun to imagine terrible things—accident, illness, worse. The way Lilly was fond of tromping through the big empty innards of a hotel still under construction, Amanda was never completely at ease. She had worried Lilly would trip, fall, have a bucket dumped on her head, that some catastrophe would come of her gallivanting around men's work in women's dress. She went to her instantly, but in the dark she could only make out the silhouette of her granddaughter. "Lilly, may I light the room?"

"Not too much light, darling," Lilly said, her voice quiet and solemn. "Please."

Amanda did as she was told, placing a candle on the hearth, not too close to Lilly. Then she went to Lilly, brushing her feet off the footstool and carefully lowering herself onto it, despite her bad knee, and looked up at her granddaughter. "Lilly, you're crying!"

"Shhhh. Please, don't upset the household. It's quite an event, I'm sure. Lilly crying."

"But what is it, love?"

"Oh, you won't be very pleased with me, Grandmother. I'm afraid it's only self-pity."

"Bah," Amanda scoffed. "You, of all of us, has the least of *that!*"

"I suppose that's what people think. Busy Lilly! Active Lilly! Lilly, who insists on a business, insists on challenge!" Tears began to free themselves in rivers from her eyes. "I don't know when I last cried." But Lilly did know; over three years before. Twice in the space of a few months. When Andrew said good-bye, when he said good-bye again. Since that time she had successfully staved off loneliness by hard work. "Did you know Patricia was here today?"

"I was in the city with your mother. What did she do to make you feel so terrible?"

"Oh, nothing, Grandmother. Truly, Patricia was as decent as I've ever seen her. Terribly unhappy, but she wasn't unkind."

"That girl! She wears her unhappiness like a banner! She accuses us all of being part of it!"

"No, you mustn't blame her. Really, Patricia has never had a spot of sense. I'm sure she can't help that. And she has rather startling news. She's pregnant."

"Oh?" Amanda said, watching Lilly. "Well, it was bound to happen. This will surely please Wilson."

"Even Dale. Patricia said he doesn't take a fatherly pride, but he does assume a manly arrogance that he finally got her caught. Did you know she'd taken steps to prevent it? Ah," she said to Amanda's shocked expression, "of course she wouldn't tell you that. I'm sorry."

"Lilly, what is it? Are you worried about her?"

"I've long since given that up, Grandmother. Patricia is beyond hope and therefore beyond worry. Poor thing—how can one be beyond hope? But she doesn't want to have a baby. She's afraid it will be impossible for her to love it. And I can't understand how that can be." Again her tears spilled over.

"Lilly, Lilly, she will surely change her mind! When she feels the baby move. When she holds the baby."

"Perhaps. I hope you're right. Oh, Grandmother, she said she envies me. She said she hasn't had a useful idea in her life. She will never know how I envy her, even in her dreadful marriage, in that awful old house. I would love to have a child."

"But you will, Lilly! One day—"

Lilly was shaking her head. "There's something terribly wrong with me," she said, brushing the tears from her cheeks. Amanda braced herself. She had lived in Europe, spent many months that would add up to years in Paris. She was fully prepared to struggle with the acceptance of her granddaughter's sexual peculiarity. "I was entertained by this bachelor or that during my tour. I remained completely immune to love. It is far too easy for me to be consumed in work."

269

"Now, Lilly, surely you didn't—"

"I assure you, I took a very good look at the available men. I felt no affection for any of them!"

"But Lilly, have you never been intrigued? Interested? In the very least way—"

"Oh, years and years ago, before you were home to us, I fancied myself madly, wildly in love. What a reckless girl! He was very forbidden, and I knew it—perhaps I thrilled in it. He even treated me to a ride in a closed coupé and a most exciting kiss . . . just before he vanished. But Grandmother, I have not felt anything nearly as pleasant since!"

Amanda sat quiet for a moment. "Lilly, when did this happen to you?"

"I was only seventeen. Long before Patricia's troubles, before all the trouble in the boardinghouse, before—"

"But Lilly, did some man—"

"Molest me? Oh, hardly. I had been talking to him at the library for months! I admired him. Adored him. I never thought he could feel the same way. I was just a poor working-class girl, and he was so handsomely dressed, so brilliantly well-spoken. He was a worldly, older, intelligent man, Grandmother, who kissed me and then told me frankly he had better never kiss me again. I ran for my life, like a good girl. Sometimes I regret it. Am I never to find another such kiss?"

Amanda nearly breathed an audible sigh of relief. Then a chuckle escaped her. "You fancied yourself in love, did you?"

"Oh, desperately. I've never told a soul!"

Amanda squeezed her hand and then gave it a pat. "Lilly, you're not immune to love—you simply won't make room! You work too hard, you keep yourself to much removed. Why, these workmen and bookkeepers can't be very tempting. My dear, you mustn't declare yourself an old maid at twenty-one!"

"But that's what I am. Most women who will marry do so before they're my age."

"Ordinary women, Lilly. Ordinary women marry early. You mustn't grieve the loss of something that has yet to arrive."

"I'm afraid I will never have that feeling again, Grandmother. He admired me so. All those things about domestic life that troubled me, troubled him. He said my questions caused him to raise questions of his own."

"Lilly, darling, he seduced you! Don't you understand that he—"

"What I understand is that I want too much! I want work and a family too! I want a husband who is proud of all I can do! Grandmother, I dined with a viscount in Germany. I told him I was building a grand hotel with my mother and grandmother, and do you know what he said? He said I would need a strong man to manage such an enormous enterprise!" She made a derisive sound and waved her hand. She added, "I didn't stay long enough for the fruit and wine."

Amanda made a sound she hoped Lilly would not be able to identify as smothered laughter. And pride! What a stubborn, marvelous girl!

"I'm afraid if I talked myself into marrying a man who thinks I'm not capable just so I could have a family of my own, I would hate myself."

"You don't have to do that, Lilly. The right man will—"

"Grandmother, you married three times. How were you able to do that?"

"Lilly, I loved my husbands. None of them was a perfect man, and marriage to the finest man is never as easy as women think, but they all had such sterling qualities. Richard had such visions of the world. He was a brilliant man. I could listen to him for days on end and never be bored. John, God rest his soul, was the most handsome and entertaining man I've ever known. He was so filled with adventure—adventure killed him eventually. How he loved his horses—how he loved travel. He was a trifle younger than I, but I think he died not knowing how much. I wish I had told him, but . . . And William, poor William. A gentle, giving soul. He was so all alone, and so— Oh well, they were all good enough men. None of them ever complained that I was a bad wife. You will meet a good man one day, darling."

"Patricia could have had any man of her choosing. She's beautiful, and she can be charming. If she hadn't been in such a panic to get rich . . . Well, she made a mess of things. And now she's to have a child, and she's angry about it. I would think it would fill her with joy, especially since the rest of her life has so disappointed her."

"Sometime, Lilly, you must talk with your mother about that. Bringing a child into a terrible world can make one despair. Patricia sees her world as terrible right now. Perhaps when the baby is born, she will see her child as a kind of reward for all she believes she has endured."

271

"If only Patricia had been in love with Dale," Lilly said wistfully.

"Being in love feels rather like food poisoning," Amanda pointed out. Lilly let a little laugh come through her tears, knowing the truth to that only too well. "And being married to a solid, dependable man can be a wonderful thing. But being in love, darling, is no guarantee of marital happiness." The temptation to mention Ned Armstrong was difficult for Amanda to resist. "Will you come and have something to eat?"

"Not tonight, Gran. Let me sit here and feel sorry for myself a while longer. Please, don't bother Mama about this. There's nothing anyone can do. This will pass soon enough—tomorrow will be a very busy day."

"She'll want to know what's troubling you."

"Tell her that she'll be a grandmother—that will surely distract her."

Amanda nodded and used Lilly's assistance to stand from the low footstool. She kissed Lilly's forehead and gently squeezed her shoulder. "Don't give this too much time, Lilly. It's not like you to suffer envy."

When Amanda had gone, Lilly remained in the dim room, looking out at a dark, clear sky. She had seen Andrew twice during the winter: at Christmas dinner at the Nesbitt House and once just prior to moving into the new hotel. Both times she had invited him to view the construction of the Arms. Both times he had said Mrs. Devon would certainly like to see it.

There was a tune she often hummed; it popped into her mind when she felt lonely. It was the music that accompanied her last dance with Andrew . . . years ago. There had been no parties or balls since at which they had both been present. She wanted another chance at private conversation. Has your marriage improved? she would ask. Is there any hope for a child for you? Is there any hope for . . . us?

Oh, what dangerous pleasure I crave! she thought.

"Lilly is in her sitting room, all alone, feeling sad," Amanda told Emily. "Patricia visited today to tour the building and apartments. She has a piece of news: she is pregnant."

"Oh! When will she deliver?"

"I'm sorry, dear, I didn't think to ask. I was worried about Lilly. Poor thing, she has herself upset because Patricia is unhappy about having a baby."

"But does Lilly find that surprising? Surely Patricia will change her mind."

"Emily, maybe you should tell them about their father. Although I hadn't thought about it much, Lilly has as many illusions about love and marriage as Patricia. Not so dangerous, perhaps, but—"

"Mother, what could it help, their *knowing?*"

"But he's not dead, Emily. That we know of."

"One can only hope!"

"You've managed to avoid the subject well enough, dear, but it's already come up. He's been seen since the war. People suspect you simply left him. Someone whispered divorce."

"If only!"

"Emily, will you go to see Patricia? Wish her well and talk to her? If I'm to be a great-grandmother, I'd like to know the child is desired by someone."

"Now Mother, don't be feeling sorry for yourself. If that baby is not welcomed by its mother, I'm sure its grandmothers will compensate nicely!"

"Well, I hope it's not a boy. The women in this family have the worst damn luck with men."

Andrew Devon looked at the same stars, the same moon as Lilly. Some of his thoughts were the same; some of his desires could not be driven away by the worst distraction. He had his driver take him past the site of the growing Armstrong Arms several times, and he had even seen her at a great distance. But she had been busy talking with carpenters and brick layers. He wished to stop and praise her achievements, but did not. The risk was too great, the longing too strong. More so now than before.

The tense quiet that surrounded him was the sound of death. Brenda's mother lay dying in their house. His wife, whom he had so completely misunderstood, had become even more confusing to him. One moment a terrified child in desperate need of consolation and affection, another, a raging banshee in the mood for murder. Andrew was well aware of the close family ties between Brenda and Josephine Waite; they were closer than sisters, thicker than thieves. But until this fatal illness entered their home, he had not known the depth or power of this relationship. Brenda was losing the only person she had ever loved. The only person who could control Brenda was unconscious.

"My God, Andrew," she had pleaded, her voice desperate, terrified, "she's *dying!* I know how you've hated me! How you've refused to forgive me! I know what a fool I've been. Won't you forget that now? You have no idea what my mother's been through in her life—her husband and son lost in war, her home burned, her person assaulted! Surviving all that, she fades away from me while I watch. Won't you pity me? Won't you hold me . . . even . . . now?"

Josephine Waite had been the widowed mother of a fifteen-year-old daughter, paupered and ravaged by war, when she married a carpetbagger from Philadelphia and came North. She sold herself into marriage for survival, having buried both husband and son, and having lost her grand and gentle life on a plantation. And this bitter yet determined woman had buried a second husband, claiming his factory and then manipulating her daughter into the best marriage that could be found. Josephine helped Brenda know which lies to tell, which seductions to employ, and which man to pursue. They had lost their aristocratic lineage to war; they could not merge with northern society. Yet they could conspire to trick the clever young protégé to the richest man in the city.

Andrew had known for a long time that he had been used. But until grief and fear overtook Brenda, he had not known the tragic history that led both Brenda and her mother to such dishonest, destructive attempts at survival.

Weeping, clinging to him, she told him. "I cowered behind a bush with my mother watching my house burn down when I was ten years old. I helped her bury my father, then my brother two years later. We walked to Richmond—*walked*. And there were whole days we had no food. Our clothing was nothing but rags. We were both assaulted. I was raped by a soldier! When it was over and everything gone, the entire South gone, it was a Yankee, a man who had worn a blue coat who offered to marry her. 'Blue!' I shouted at her. 'Clarence Waite could have been the very man to kill my brother!' But she said that hunger made her blind to color!"

274

Pity for her caused him to reach out, and he had given whatever comfort he could. Tenderly holding her, he told her he understood.

Andrew was not a stranger to hunger, despair, fear. He was also acquainted with shame, for he had concealed a secret all his life. He had a vague recollection of a large, burly man, the man he believed was his father. He came with his mother to America, a little boy. Where had that man gone? he asked her frequently. It was when she lay dying that she told the truth, the reason her family would have none of her, none of Andrew. The man he recalled was his father. He visited Maureen and his son in the stone cottage outside Dublin. He didn't live with them because he was a priest. It was when the church sent him to Rome that Maureen left Ireland with her child.

Andrew had balanced allegiance for the church with contempt. "You are a part of the church, whether or not you like it," his mother had told him. "The church bred you. You are the seed of the church." Since that time Andrew had felt simultaneously drawn to the church and repelled by it.

Perhaps just as Brenda felt drawn to the South, horrified by it. He did understand. While he comforted the woman who had wronged him, used him, he had a flicker of hope that she would, in her grief, depend on him and be changed.

Mrs. Waite only worsened, as did Brenda's grief and fear, and, having been invited to console her once, he reached out to her again. She turned on him like a tigress.

"Bastard! Bastard! Don't touch me! Do you think you'll find me in a weak moment and satisfy yourself? You've kept me living in this dungeon for years with nothing but threats! You think you'll seduce me now? You don't know the indignities I suffered at the hands of Yankees! A girl, a child, abused, starved, raped! I will never, never have the stomach for a Yankee touch!"

And later, mewling and whimpering, Brenda came to him begging forgiveness, comfort. More tales of her traumatic childhood . . . followed by another rage.

"If you so hate Yankees, why did you marry one?" he had asked her.

"Why, Andrew, there were no gentlemen present!"

Brenda had periods of sleeplessness that stretched out for days, leaving her face dark and her eyes looking hollow. She talked to her dying mother unceasingly, though Mrs. Waite could not reply. Her sleeplessness was followed by long slumbers; she had a bed moved into her mother's room where she slept through almost whole days. She alternately paced and wept, raged and muttered to herself, or fell into unconscious slumber. She asked him to pluck a flower for her out of the hearth and then railed at him when he tried to explain there were no flowers there. She was sometimes so delirious he checked her for fever, but she was cold. The mania had stretched on for weeks. Brenda was being driven mad while her mother lingered at death's door.

The doctor said Josephine would not survive the night, something he had already said several times. Brenda sat with her mother, and Andrew looked at a sky he shared with Lilly. He wanted the same things as she: work, love, children. For Lilly those things were still possible. For himself, he thought, it all seemed more impossible than ever. He made a decision that when Mrs. Waite was gone, Brenda recovered, he would set her handsomely free. Whatever the cost, he would shed this burden. Brenda would punish him . . . but only financially. She couldn't want to stay with him.

There was a knock at his bedroom door. The housekeeper faced him. "Mrs. Waite has passed on, Mr. Devon. Mrs. Devon can't be convinced to leave her. I'm afraid you're needed."

"Thank you, Jenny. I'm coming."

Lilly had written to every newspaper around the world. Since they could not possibly attract enough guests to fill up their hotel in the first months they were open, the women had decided to stage the opening when the ground floor and two guest floors were finished. So long as snow covered the mess of still-incomplete grounds, they should make use of what they had.

She had spent weeks on the correspondence, announcing the opening of the Armstrong Arms before Christmas. Finally she began to see small mention of the hotel in various newspapers, but it was not nearly what she had hoped for. Still, she knew that the true popularity would come from the lips of guests and from mention in society columns of their accommodations at the Armstrong Arms.

She clipped the small articles and shared them with Emily and Amanda. She showed them the correspondence she had just finished, mentioning the names of those people who would attend the opening of the hotel in hopes that newspapers would repeat the gossip in print and reservations would be forthcoming.

"It's going to have to be done differently, Lilly," Amanda said. "You'll have to omit the names of the Wynnes, Cadwaladers, and Wisters. Mention artists, writers, politicians, and—"

"But Grandmother, we have to pull the fine families closer."

"No, no, they'll know, believe me, but tact is essential. In society you must be more than a little sensitive to privacy. The Vanderbilts like to see their name in print, the Astors despise it. They are two very different types of rich—you must know the difference. They will know you understand their special and peculiar tastes when you mention the right names at the right times. To come here, to live here, they have to believe they can trust you."

"If we aren't able to speak of our guests in residence, then—"

Lilly was interrupted when Cleaves knocked at the sitting-room door and opened it. "There is a gentleman asking for Mrs. Armstrong."

"Who, Cleaves?" Emily asked.

"He won't give his name, madam. He describes himself as an old friend."

Emily's eyes widened briefly. "Bring him up," she said.

"He has requested a private meeting with you. He's waiting in the offices downstairs."

"Mama, it could be Mr. Padgett!" Lilly exclaimed. "Maybe he's read about the hotel!"

Emily's cheeks became rosy. "Tell the gentleman I'm with my mother and daughter and he's welcome to join us."

"And if he isn't inclined?" Cleaves asked.

Emily lowered her gaze to a letter she held, pretending to read it. It trembled slightly. "If he isn't inclined, he can't have been a very good friend, although I suppose he could as easily be old."

When Cleaves closed the door, Lilly laughed. "Mama, you make everything so hard for him!"

"Who, Lilly? I have no idea who calls. I have more than one old friend."

"Oh?" Amanda asked. "Perhaps we should discuss the vast number, dear?"

Both Lilly and Amanda grinned at Emily. But Emily tried to ignore them. In her heart she was preparing herself to be calm when faced with the longed-for eyes of Noel Padgett. This left all three

277

completely unprepared for the man who entered the apartment sitting room.

"Emily?" Ned Armstrong said, holding his hat in his hands. "Patricia?"

*E*mily's shock was so extreme that she slowly rose from the sofa on which she had been seated and stared at her estranged husband, mute and nearly helpless. Amanda stood as well, but hardly helpless.

"What the bloody hell are you doing here?" Amanda demanded.

"Let Emily speak," he said. "I knew you wouldn't be glad to see me, but she—"

"Cleaves!" Amanda barked. "Cleaves!"

Bertie came from another room, the distress in Amanda's voice an obvious alarm. Cleaves, fifty years old, large, and strong, came to the door through which he had just led Ned Armstrong.

"Is this my daughter? Surely a man has a right to see his daughter?"

Lilly looked between her mother and grandmother, stole a glance at Bertie's dark scowl, Cleaves's confusion.

"You gave up that right long ago," Emily said.

"I had a spot of trouble, Emily. I tried to find you. I—"

"*Liar!*" Emily shrieked, a sound that Lilly had never heard before in her life. Emily's face seemed to change color before Lilly's eyes— starchy white, pink, red. Lilly instantly knew—this man was her father. Yet the fact was not acceptable; it contradicted everything she had been told. "You lying *jackel!* I went looking for you and you'd scoured! Don't you dare—"

"Mama?" Lilly asked, finally standing as the other women had.

"Don't be shouting, Emily. I'm back, that's all. You should be glad to see me. I can explain where I've been, but—"

"Get out! Get out! Don't you dare come around here. Don't you dare talk of being *back*. I swear before heaven—"

Cleaves understood why he was needed and grasped the shoulder of Ned Armstrong's coat, but Ned writhed loose, shaking himself free of the steward's grasp. Before Cleaves could repeat the move and eject him, Ned joined the shouting.

"Get out of a hotel named for me? No, I'm not going anywhere. I have name rights, father's rights! We haven't had an easy time of it—but we *are* still married!"

"You filthy—"

"Mother!" Lilly said, frantic, grasping the sleeve of her mother's blouse. "*Mother!*"

Emily whirled and fled. She ran into the nearest room, Amanda's suite and slammed the door behind her.

"Get him out of here, Cleaves," Amanda said. "Take him downstairs and keep him there. Quick, before I do something terrible."

"Wait a minute, Amanda. You can't do that so easily. I have a right to speak to my daughter. Is this beautiful young woman my daughter?"

Lilly's face had lost all color, and her eyes held the greatest shock she had experienced in her lifetime. Her mouth stood open as she looked at this man. She judged him to be approximately fifty years old. His silver hair was mixed with coal-black; his stature was tall and slender; his face was still handsome; his clothing was decent if not rich.

"Yes, this is your daughter," Amanda said, her voice shaking.

Lilly felt herself begin to tremble. "My father is dead," she said weakly.

"No, Patricia," Ned said, advancing a step.

"Not Patricia, Ned," Amanda said, stepping close to Lilly and putting a supportive arm around her waist, more than conscious of what Lilly could be thinking, feeling. Ned stopped moving toward her, and now the look of astonishment was his. "Lilly," Amanda said. "Your second child. The one you didn't even realize you had given us."

Ned slowly accepted this possibility. He began to smile but the door through which Emily had disappeared was jerked open. Emily stood in the frame and slowly raised a pistol, the pistol that Amanda kept in a locked box in her bureau. She clutched it with both hands and the look on her face changed her whole appearance. Her mouth was twisted in distraught lines, her eyes narrowed in almost demonic rage. "Get out!" she screamed. He took a step backward, shocked. "Get out and never show your face again!"

Cleaves was no longer needed. Ned Armstrong did one or two clumsy dance steps in his rapid retreat, leaving the door open behind him. His quick moves suggested it wasn't the first time someone had leveled a pistol in his direction.

"Follow him," Amanda shouted at Cleaves. "Don't let him out of your sight!" She turned toward Emily and took quicker steps than she had in some time. "Good Lord! Put that thing down!"

Emily slowly lowered the heavy pistol and turned to her mother. "Oh, Mother!" she cried, shaken and desperate.

"Give me the damned gun!"

"It isn't loaded," Emily said, her voice sounding almost familiar again. "I don't know how."

Amanda took it away from her and quickly passed it to Bertie. "Well then, I'll teach you how later. The next time you aim it at a scoundrel like that, you might as well fire it!"

"Oh, Mother, what is he *doing* here?"

"Forget about yourself for a moment," Amanda whispered harshly. "There's Lilly!"

Sanity slowly returned to Emily's eyes as she and Amanda turned toward Lilly. Lilly was far from recovering. She had just been visited by a ghost. She slowly backed up to a chair and lowered herself, her shaking legs no longer able to hold her upright. She swallowed once, studying their faces. "Is what you're about to tell me going to change my whole life? Again?"

"Oh, darling," was the way Emily began. The story took the rest of the afternoon and continued into the evening. This time Emily didn't keep portions to herself; she told everything. Lilly was numbed by it, stunned, amazed, and crushed. She could seize on a variety of feelings, each one more confusing and debilitating than the last. Relief that she had a living father after all. Rage that he had been a miserable son-of-a-sod who had abused her mother. Fear that he would create trouble for them all. Grief, for all her life she had thought a good man died and now she thought a beast lived only to haunt her. *Name rights!*

"Lilly, I didn't want you to ever know," Emily said. "I always thought a dead father with a decent memory better than one who would abandon you and your sister. I made it all up."

"But you've guarded it all this time? Suffered alone? Told no one at all?"

"No one. I confided in Sophia, but I was afraid to tell her everything. Mother didn't know until she returned to us. Bertie knew . . . and, well, I was forced to tell Mr. Padgett."

"Oh, Mama, is that why Mr. Padgett left?"

"Lilly, I sent him away. There was simply no way to accept his good intentions."

"You *did* love him! Mama, you should not have sent him away. Not on account of Ned Armstrong!"

"What should I have done, Lilly? Entered into a marriage that would not be legal? I hoped your father really was dead, to my shame, but I had no way of knowing. It wouldn't have been fair to any of us if I had selfishly created more lies."

"It's the hotel," Lilly said. "He's read about it, that's what. That's why he was here. Name rights, he said. Good Lord!"

"Most definitely," Amanda said. "A leopard can't change his spots. He's after money."

"What are we going to do with him? I'm not letting him near Mama, that's sure. I'm not letting him in this establishment. Dear God, he's my father—what am I supposed to feel? Do?" She looked at her mother. "Mama, we'll change the name of the hotel. You can go away for a while, if you like. Grandmother and I will—"

"Negotiate," Amanda said, cutting Lilly off. "We'll manage some terms with Mr. Armstrong."

"I'm not going anywhere," Emily said. "He's not driving me away from my family. Patricia is about to give birth, and our business nearly ready to open!"

Amanda asked Bertie to serve up something stout and have a message sent to Fletcher asking him to come to the hotel first thing in the morning. After a generous brandy, it was decided that Emily lacked the nerves to deal with her estranged husband and Lilly lacked the experience. "And Patricia is not to know about this," Amanda added.

"Doesn't she have every right to know?" Lilly asked.

"Yes indeed, but I'm not concerned with Patricia's rights, not at all. She is continually balancing plots against gains and plans against requests. As long as she is safe, well cared for, and in decent health, I want it kept that way."

"But Grandmother, it isn't fair! She wanted to come home, she told me that! And you refused—"

"Lilly," Emily interrupted. "Your grandmother wouldn't refuse to take care of Patricia under all circumstances. You must understand, if she were in desperate trouble, we would bring her here in a moment. But the troubles she has, her loneliness and boredom, are troubles of her own design. If she is rescued time after time, her appetite for having her way will only become insatiable. And Lilly, if she ever meets Ned Armstrong, she will find the other sleeve of her coat!"

"She is her father's daughter, Lilly," Amanda said. "What I was forced to do for Patricia I had once been forced to do for your mother. The difference between those two situations is that in the first case it was Ned's lies and schemes; in the second case it was Patricia. Patsy, God bless her, was never really a complete victim. She did not believe Dale because she loved him. She despised him . . . before and after he assaulted her. She, like her father, is a user."

"But surely—"

"The two of them together would be impossible. And you and your hotel would not be immune."

Lilly laughed in disbelief, not amusement. "But what in the world could they do?"

"Even though I have a rather canny imagination, I don't dare guess. Both Ned and Patricia have a remarkable talent for putting people at a severe disadvantage to get what they want. And their wants are astonishingly alike."

"But this is a business! Patricia can't abide work, and he—"

"This is a business that will rely heavily on reputation. Remember that. We haven't yet had a chance to show we're above reproach and maintain the highest standards. I'd hate to have that threatened before we've even begun, or this great, brick monster could stand vacant forever. Do you think those who can afford these services will visit us if it's thought we behave scandalously? Think, Lilly! This is delicate!"

When Fletcher Drake arrived at the hotel, Amanda took him into her study. It took a very long time to inform him about Ned Armstrong, who he was, the shabbiness of his character, and the reason he was to be feared.

"The first order of business is to buy his silence. I'm sure that will come at a high price, but convince him somehow that I'm willing. And next, let's find out what he's been up to for the past few years. There has to be something in his past for which he can be prosecuted and put away. And he must not know where his other daughter is."

"If he can be found guilty of some crime, to prosecute him will create quite a stir—a lot of talk."

"Don't be a ninny, Fletcher. I won't prosecute him. But he'll open his mouth at the risk of prison. I hope and pray!"

"And Lilly?" Fletcher asked.

"What about Lilly?"

"She knows about this? Your plan?"

"Of course. More or less. What are you getting at?"

"It's her father—" he began.

"He's a scoundrel! Jackass! Devil of the—"

"Her father," Fletcher added, quietly.

"Well, what the hell would you have me do?" Amanda demanded impatiently.

"I don't know, madam. My own father was a ruthless bastard, and I hated him." He shrugged. "I wept at his burial . . . just the same."

"Oh, Fletcher, for God's sake, you're nearly fifty years old! Surely you recovered from—"

"Amanda," he said, stopping her with the use of her name. Although he was an old friend, he rarely presumed unless the matter was personal and sensitive. "I don't mean to tell you how to deal with Armstrong. But does one ever recover from the abuse of a parent? I'm not sure. We'll do what has to be done. Comfort Lilly

284

as well, that's all. This can't be easy for her. Harder for her than all of you."

Amanda slowly softened, the angry turn of her mouth relaxing. "Perhaps you will comfort her?"

Fletcher smiled tolerantly. "I feel affection for Lilly. Not passion. Yes, I'll comfort her, if I can."

"That's good," Amanda said, picking up her pen again, composed. "If it were passion, Fletcher, dismissing you would be only the beginning."

He laughed loudly, enjoying her threat, knowing she was completely dependent on him. "Ah, to see the two of you tangle, what a rare treat that would be!" He stood to leave.

"I hope you never do," Amanda said to his back, her voice small. She had taken pride in Lilly, she loved her more than anyone else. She suddenly visualized a battle with Lilly and knew she would lose it . . . probably by choice. Her love was too intense.

Fletcher turned to see her sitting at her desk, her thoughts far from the hotel. "Madam," he said. "I'm forty-six."

"Ah. Well." She shook herself. "Lilly is twenty-one. If your touch is ever more than avuncular, I'll probably have to shoot you." She looked again at her papers.

"Yes, madam," he said, laughing.

When Lilly awoke on the morning of November 25, 1880, she bolted from her bed and pulled back the curtains. A shriek of sheer delight escaped her. The clouds had gathered in the previous days, and she had nearly fainted from the intensity of her prayers—she asked God in desperation to send snow to cover the grounds, the gently sloping hills surrounding the hotel. The area surrounding the hotel was still patchy, dirty; there were deep rivets and gullies from construction, half-finished flower beds and lawns—a sight she hoped to conceal during her opening. And not just any kind of snow, she prayed, but a perfect, gentle snow. A storm would paralyze them.

The opening would constitute a three-day celebration of food, drink, diversions, parties, music. Fires were set to blaze in hearths around the hotel. An orchestra played for three hundred guests, over two hundred of whom would stay at least a few days in the Armstrong Arms. Magnificent dinners were served: squab, duckling, porterhouse steak, fabulous pastries, a variety of breads, soups, and puddings. Musicales were performed by singers. There was a formal ball and dancing, a great deal of champagne, and complimentary sleigh rides through the hotel grounds. Skating on the nearby frozen pond entertained some guests while others were content to take tea and cake in one parlor or another.

From all Lilly could tell, it was a success followed by a modest but not disappointing number of reservations. Reporters from various newspapers had been invited, their meals and accommodations provided by the hotel, and the stories about the opening that followed were glowing. The Armstrong Arms, it was written, was more luxurious than La Pierre House or the Nesbitt House, the two luxury class hotels in Philadelphia. More than one reporter suggested that the Armstrong Arms could easily, over time, develop a reputation as the finest hotel in the United States.

Patricia was not seen publicly during the opening because of her advanced pregnancy. Lilly did not admit to any member of her family that she was relieved not to have to endure Patricia's presence among so many prestigious guests.

Patricia delivered a daughter, Katherine Amanda Montaine, on the first of December. Emily moved into the Montaine house for the entire month to try to coax her daughter into becoming a good mother. Emily had a powerful hand when it came to creating a home; she pulled open draperies, lit lamps, and had cozy, welcoming fires blazing in every hearth; she brought out her recipes and covered the table with good food. The Montaine mansion had been a house full of closed doors, each member of the family and staff hiding his or her unhappiness in a study, bedroom, or sitting room. Emily opened doors, made rooms cheerful, and praised all those she met for attributes they hardly knew they possessed.

She re-created the home she had known as a child, a home filled with not only love and laughter, but tolerance and mutual respect. Rather than avoiding the residents, she sought out each one. She ignored Wilson's terrible table manners and asked him questions he was pleased to answer, about his childhood, his businesses, his travels. She taught Deanna to sew, encouraged Dale to hold his child.

"Despite your many complaints, Patricia, I don't find this place to be the terrible dungeon you've described," Emily said, contentedly rocking her granddaughter, the hotel far away from her as she mended fences with the Montaines.

"They are on their best behavior," Patricia sulked.

"But what is wrong with this family? How is Wilson any more trouble than Mrs. Fairchild ever was?"

"Oh, Mother, he's smelly and arrogant!"

"He's quite taken with the baby and generous with his money. I suppose he's proud of what he's accomplished, which is understandable. He even asked very nicely if he could hold Katherine. And for a man like Wilson, who doesn't bother much with manners or—"

"When you leave, he'll act like a mule again. He hasn't had a single fight with Deanna since you arrived!"

"Dale has been a gentleman, and—"

"Mother, don't be naive! He is always sober when his father is here. He's afraid of being disinherited if he creates too much trouble!"

"And Deanna, poor thing, is only lonely. I spent a large part of the afternoon with her and—"

"She is *terrible*. She tipples all day and all night and—"

It seemed to Emily that Patricia could not be convinced of any virtue among them. While Emily couldn't say she would choose any of these people for close personal friends, it was obvious Patricia could be more effective in her relations with them if she could only learn to sense their needs, understand each character, as Emily had learned to do when operating a boardinghouse. Wilson blustered, but was civil in her company because Emily's behavior was not only decorous, but invited decorum. She did not respond to the old devil's ranting, but faced him calmly and without judgment. She gently disregarded his worst habits. Dale was sullen but polite, and Emily found that he responded to praise as well as any man. She thought he had the potential to be charming and even productive, given the least amount of encouragement and affection from his father and others in his family. Wilson criticized him, Deanna avoided him, but Patricia was the worst—she actually sneered at her husband, the father of her child. And Deanna didn't tipple at all when she had someone to talk to. Andrew Devon, who happened by once to view the new addition to the family, was as pleasant a young man as Emily had ever met. However unfortunate, there was good reason Wilson favored Andrew over his own son.

Because Patricia was confined and because Emily saw more potential in the Montaine household than anyone else had, Emily had a talk with her mother. Amanda consented to participate in a quiet Christmas in their old family home, an event that would unite the Montaines and Amanda's family. "This is the last thing I ever thought I would do," she groused.

"Come now, Mother, like it or not, we're all family now. It's time for forgiveness and charity—perhaps something can be salvaged. I'm actually beginning to enjoy some of these people. Why, when you encourage any one of them the least, each one can be quite dear."

"Humph," Amanda returned, "each one except our very own."

Lilly had become even more serious, but it seemed reasonable she would be. The hotel was not a quaint hobby, but an enormous obligation. She behaved like a professional spinster, long before her time. Only her grandmother, mother, and Fletcher knew that she had been more quiet than usual since the sudden appearance of her father. But no one knew that one of the chief reasons she was solemn could be attributed to her anxiety over the prospect of seeing Andrew Devon for the first time in at least a year.

Christmas dinner came and went without him; no place had been set. She could hardly contain her disappointment, but the fuss around little Katherine kept the worst of it under control. Patricia was in her element because she was being indulged and praised in her new status of motherhood. But a wet nurse had to be found; Patricia was unable or unwilling to nurse her own child.

The sun was going down in the sky on Christmas day when Andrew arrived, carrying packages for every member of the extended family. For Amanda, he had a broach from India, carved from the finest ivory; for Emily, a silver tea service; for Wilson, a terrible looking pipe that made everyone laugh; for Dale, a watch chain; for Lilly, a gold-plated fountain pen; for Katherine, an engraved silver cup.

There were gifts for Andrew and Brenda, but Brenda had been unable to join him. Lilly noticed that Andrew had become haggard, thinner. She tried to hide the fact that she saw this, but the urge to reach out to him was strong. She was afraid he had become ill.

After sharing a late evening libation with everyone, he excused himself. When the question was on Lilly's lips, Amanda preempted her. "Wilson, what is the matter with that young man? He looks dreadful!"

"You hadn't heard? His wife is ill."

"My goodness, no! We'll have to call on her," Emily said.

"That's not a good idea, Mrs. Armstrong," Dale cut in. "She's not exactly sick, but rather off her rocker."

"What?" Lilly asked.

"Mad as a hoot, Lilly," Dale said. "Her mother died last year, and Brenda hasn't recovered."

"Oh, Wilson," Emily said, concern for everyone and everything ever being her focus. "How terrible for him. What can be done?"

"As long as he is unwilling to have her confined, not much. It's going to kill him before long. He hasn't confided a thing to me except that Brenda is indisposed, the servants can tell a tale or two that's interesting. Word is that unless she's given a goodly supply of laudanum, she's up stomping around creating disturbances all through the night—seeing her mother and hearing voices. You can see the boy hasn't had much sleep lately."

"He isn't a boy, Father," Dale said, jealous and miffed.

"He ought to do something with her, that's what," Wilson went on. "But he's so damned private in his affairs—won't open up about her. I've had to find out on my own. Had to know what was starting to keep him from working. Never known the boy to neglect work before."

"Oh no," Dale said sarcastically, "Lord knows Andy loves work as much as you, Father."

"Ahem, yes, well, as I wish you did, son."

"Dale loves gin," Patricia muttered under her breath so that only Dale and Emily heard. He shot her an angry glare, which she returned in kind. Emily sighed wearily. The battle between them raged on and could be attributed in equal parts to each.

"Wilson, what if I called on them?" Emily offered. "What if Deanna and I went together to their home, visited, and tried to convince Andrew to get some special help for her?"

Despite the fact that Lilly was consumed with sudden worry for Andrew's well-being, she could not help but notice the effect her mother had on this household. It could be her old boardinghouse, filled with people who had special needs that Emily could sense, reach. Deanna's face brightened hopefully, as if she could be useful to someone at long last. Wilson's harsh, wild appearance softened into a dear, St. Nicholas face as he smiled and nodded toward Emily, thanking her softly and kindly for her concern. Even Dale, comfortable sitting beside Emily, the only person who found redeeming qualities in him, reached across a short distance to stick his finger in his baby

289

daughter's fist. Emily passed the infant to her father, saying, "Be useful, Dale, and rock her for a while. She loves it so when you hold her."

When Lilly and Amanda rode together back to the Armstrong Arms, Lilly had a great deal on her mind. She wouldn't be discussing Andrew with anyone, of course. But what she had seen her mother do intrigued and fascinated her.

"Do you see what she does, Grandmother? Mother heals people with kindness. Before your very eyes."

Amanda smiled kindly, wistfully. "She has Richard's caring, generosity, and charity. Good Lord! Don't give her any extra money! She'll scatter it well!"

"Was my grandfather like that?"

"What a tender heart, Lilly! He could not be convinced to stop. His only reason for trying to preserve our money was so that he could be charitable!"

"The apple doesn't fall far from the tree, Gran," Lilly said. "Mother has a line of hungry, jobless men forming at the back of the Nesbitt House."

"Oh dear God!"

"You didn't know? She has given Sophia the strictest orders that if there's anything to spare, they will be given food."

"Lilly! The guests won't tolerate it!"

"Never mind that. Can Mother help them? Is it possible that just by being in the Montaine household for a while, things might change for the better?"

"Well, love, I—"

"She can! Don't tell me otherwise. She *can*. It's what she is. Oh, it's all so evident, suddenly! Who we *are!* Why, Mother's naturally so good and generous, so tolerant of people's quirks and so understanding of what they need! Why, she'll be perfect in the Arms. She's always been perfect at taking care of people. Small wonder she spent so many years trying to get Patricia and me to understand hard work, propriety, and generosity! They worked for her. And you—"

"Be careful, Lilly—"

Lilly laughed. "Well, you *are* a bit bossy, but easy enough to tolerate when you have your grip on fortune. As long as you never have to answer to anyone, you're quite tractable. And what about Patricia? What is her special force?"

"Would that I knew, dear . . ."

"It seems to me that if we could get her a position as a princess . . . She played princess all the while we were growing up. All she has ever really wanted is to sit on a throne and be worshiped. If I could think of what would make her finally, completely content, I would get it for her, no matter what the cost. How simple it all becomes! You are happy with power and control. Mama is made happy by good works. Patricia is made happy by being indulged and admired!"

Amanda chuckled in spite of herself. "And you, darling?"

"Oh," she said quietly, "there's a lot I have left to do. And plenty of time to do it in, I suppose."

"You might give another look to the gents, dear."

"I have you and Mama and the Arms. That should keep me busy and content for some time to come."

Amanda reached across the coach and grasped Lilly's hand. "Lilly, work is good and important, but life must be filled with many things. You're too determined to be alone. I don't think you've left any room for pleasure."

"But I have great pleasure in my—"

"You won't have us forever, your mother and me. In a way difficult to express, we're all different from you, Lilly. We were created by men. For some reason you were not. My father and husbands formed my character, my mother taught me that a woman's life had to do with a man. I was raised to please men and be pleased by them. My greatest rebellion was to attempt to be in control of my own money—quite late, I admit.

"And your mother, bless her heart, is Richard's daughter indeed . . . and the part of her that added hard work and fierce independence to that generous spirit was contributed by that beast, Ned. Patricia can't seem to help being as selfish as her father was, and the moment a young man noticed her, she decided her womanhood was only useful as far as it could get from men what would serve her selfish whims. But you—"

"I am no different from the rest of you . . . in one way or another . . ."

"You are different, Lilly. I don't know how it happened, where you got your will, your spirit. Not from me—I was never around to influence you. Not from Emily, she worked to be a good mother and keep you fed. If you have anything of hers, it's that determination you don't need a man for anything. There was *never* a man in your life to create you. You're the only young woman I have ever met who won't compromise. Sometimes that worries me, Lilly. I don't want you to be lonely."

"Grandmother," Lilly began, her mind elsewhere, "I have a very important question."

Amanda made a face. Lilly had not been paying attention. "What is it? And make sure it's not as expensive as your last important question."

"Will you please approve Fletcher telling me whatever is found out about my father?"

"Oh, Lilly, we've been over all that—"

"Grandmother, please? There are certain things a woman must feel she's actually *finished*. Do you understand?"

Amanda grimaced unpleasantly. "I don't know," she said, shaking her head. "No promises."

"Oh thank you, Grandmother!"

"Stop thanking me before I've consented to anything!" Amanda virtually shouted, stamping her cane on the floor of the coach for emphasis. "I'm tired of being understood so well!"

The Armstrong Arms received its guests in a style unique and exclusive. Lady Nesbitt, the best hostess in Philadelphia, was seen in the large, marble foyer of the hotel every afternoon at four. There she would hold court in a manner only she could effect. The fine old families began to regard her as a noble dowager rich and refined; this business of a hotel was simply a means for her to occupy her days and allow her to entertain her guests more lavishly. At a time when working women were thought to be either sadly reduced to employment or of questionable character for actually seeking work, Amanda became known as clever enough to do something unusual with her time in her declining years. Goodwill followed Amanda; she was not thought foolish for refusing to discriminate among new money, old money, or lucky money but was regarded as gracious. She had had ups and downs; through the loss of her husband and family fortune she had kept her dignity and remained within the aristocracy through her subsequent marriages. She did nothing to invite envy and everything to provide elegance. She was not associated with anything so base as earning money. The Armstrong Arms, named for her granddaughter, made her appear sentimental and was regarded as Amanda's new home. No one ever suspected it was not her idea from the first.

Lady Nesbitt knew how to please each guest; her social training was of the highest order. She knew when a wealthy patron required some special treatment, ranging from exclusive privacy and catering to a formal gathering in one of her dining rooms, ballrooms, parlors, galleries, or, in the warmer months, the parks and gazebos. She held receptions for artists, teas for poets, dinners for politicians. She could bring couturieres with their designs from as far away as New York and supply fittings for fussy ladies. She could sense the time for a concert and whether it should be a formal evening affair or an out-door soirée. The Arms could manage anything from fox hunts to nuptial suites. And since Amanda didn't dirty her hands but simply snapped her fingers to bring an eager-to-please staff of chasseurs in gold braid and brass buttons to heel, it appeared that she was only doing what she'd always done so well—entertaining guests. In no time at all, if a guest couldn't gain the notice of Lady Nesbitt and have her hotel scampering to please, that guest was no one. The whole operation was considered a mere extension of society—society being a chiefly feminine achievement.

Emily Armstrong was much more a working woman, but in a special way that was Emily's alone and had nothing to do with society. The unspoken needs of guests could be answered with her warmth. She knew by instinct when the wife of a resident was lonely and needed diversion while her husband was working or riding. She could select the right personal maid to help dress hair or press gowns before a woman thought to ask. She could supply old matrons with a surprise visit and catered tea, admired children of all ages, and knew exactly when some sweet pastry would perk a lolling spirit. Emily knew whom to introduce to whom so that friendships would form, just as she knew when furniture should be moved around to provide some special form of comfort like a wider or lower bed. Although Emily had a fine Parisian chef at her disposal and a large kitchen staff, it was her face in the dining room and sometimes in the halls that gave guests a sense of comfort, home, and security. They came to the Arms looking for luxurious accommodations, but it was Emily's patience and sincerity that left them feeling nurtured at their departure.

Lilly's sharp mind might have been the seed from which the building and opening of the hotel grew, her uncanny insight the impetus that placed the older women in their most suitable roles, but she was taking on an identity new, different, and somewhat distant from what was understood by the people of her era. Lilly, twenty-two years old in the spring of '81, was not credited for her brilliance or hard work. She was, however, greatly admired.

Never one to worry over how others viewed her, Lilly did not hurry to correct assumptions or explain herself to anyone. She could frequently be seen descending the wide, open staircase into the foyer of the hotel to stand beside her grandmother while guests were arriving or leaving. She was often found walking with her mother through the wide hotel halls or offering good evening or good morning in the dining room. She was available to preside over parties, receptions, or formal dinners with her family. Aloof and self-assured, her preference for clothing that provided a slim silhouette, all bearing the labels of famous designers like Worth and far more elegant than fluffs and ruffles, began to set a standard for fashion. The wide, flouncy skirts and large bustles were never pleasant to Lilly, and she eagerly opted for the sleek lines, clean designs of the Aesthetes and dress reformers. Her posture was always excellent, and she was not self-conscious because of her height. Her eyes were clear and decisive, and she never fluttered her lashes. She was not shy, but not showy. There appeared to be a kind of serenity and control about her that presented the image of a new kind of woman to society. Failing to understand her type, most of the visitors to the Arms thought of her as a serious and responsible heiress to the vast and prestigious hotel. No one ever considered that she preferred work to play; rather all believed that she was a loyal granddaughter who took grave interest in her legacy. Lilly developed a reputation as a young woman who could defy tradition in style. And the men who passed through her doors were not blind to her many assets.

With Emily being middle-aged, somewhat withdrawn, and private, and Amanda being older still and too reserved for nonsense, it was Lilly who became a good prospect for marriage. Not long after introductions, invitations to social events began to arrive. It was a tenuous situation for her, for Lilly would not have anyone feel slighted when she declined, but she was not good at frivolity. She was perfectly happy to assist her grandmother with entertaining, but she didn't enjoy social events that had nothing whatever to do with business. She knew with absolute certainty that a number of people desired to see her married. If it wasn't enough that guests within the hotel saw fine marriageability in her and urged her to their dinners, parties, or receptions to meet this gentleman or that, some of her grandmother's oldest friends from the finest of Philadelphia families had discovered an enormous number of bachelors.

"Now, be a big girl, Lilly," Amanda urged when Lilly complained of no gracious way to refuse. "If you put your mind to it, you might meet a special gentleman—even make friends!"

"Don't be as bad as all the rest," she huffed. "I don't want to meet anymore special gentlemen! I don't have to be a wife to be happy!"

"No one said you did, Lilly. But we all know you would be even happier with all the right circumstances—a family of your own and your business!"

"I regret the day I admitted that!"

Emily observed with some concern, Amanda with amusement. An ordinary man was just not good enough for Lilly. She couldn't be attracted by looks without intelligence, by a foreign title without a sense of humor, by money without substance.

She dined with a British earl of reputation and charm, but returned to her suite morose. Emily was watching a card game between Amanda and Bertie. "He is so dull," she reported. "I nearly fell asleep in my dinner. With all his traveling and experience, isn't it odd that all he's read in his life is the face of a playing card!"

A young man from a fine New York family escorted Lilly to an evening of music at the home of the Huntington family. He was polite, attractive, had plenty of money, and political ambitions.

"He told me that women are born to create a gentle atmosphere for the men in their lives! He said the reason I am content living in a hotel is because I am doing what women do best—providing a home for others!"

"Oh, Lilly, you didn't hurt his pride—"

"I asked him if he had the first idea how much accounting, planning, hiring, and firing a hotel owner was responsible for, and he squeezed my hand! I swear he did! He told me he hoped we had a good solicitor to take care of our business!"

There was a miner from Minnesota who betrayed his need for money, an aristocratic gentleman from Boston who was recently widowed with two young children who missed their mother, and a young banker from Washington who assured her that he had great expertise in bookkeeping and had enjoyed success in the trading of stocks—he would oblige by trading some for her. She also had the unfortunate experience of being courted by a few men who neglected to mention they already had wives.

Lilly had reddened a few cheeks with her palm, although she usually tried to be polite and avoid creating a conflict that would hurt the hotel's business by behaving in a controversial manner or contradicting the notions of the many gentlemen who pursued her. She did become more and more convinced that there was not a man alive who could appreciate her just as she was. They all seemed to want prestige, money, a business, or a mother for their orphaned children. "Old fashioned," she would report in the evening. "Arrogant." "Boring." "Stupid." And more often than anything, "He seems to be in need of money."

There were also times, though fairly rare, when Lilly had nothing at all to report. She would enter the apartments shared with Emily, Amanda, and Bertie and slam the door. They continued their ritual of cards, pipe, and stitching on almost every evening, not quite admitting they waited up for her. If the sound of Lilly's return was angry, all three women would flinch, look toward the door, and observe Lilly's pursed lips and glittering eyes. Lilly would glare, then walk past them in a huff to her private sector, and it would be apparent that the suitor of the day had committed more than one of the usual grievances: undoubtedly he had diminished the possibility of her intelligence, all but asked for a money-making business, betrayed a houseful of children awaiting a new mother, and quite likely had placed one or both hands in an unwelcome location.

"My granddaughter has not stayed for the fruit and wine," Amanda would say to the others. "Again."

The Armstrong Arms' success grew through the winter and spring of its first year, and June of 1881 brought gardens more resplendent than Queen Victoria's. Compliments from guests provided a foundation of good reputation and brought many visitors for summer holidays, and the hotel enjoyed a larger number of guests every month. Lilly installed a bay of bicycles and had the work of clearing and cleaning the nearby pond begun so that small boats could be used there for the pleasure of the guests.

In this spring John Giddings finished his novel, a thing that should have marked the greatest achievement of his life. All the joy that could accompany that feeling of completion was diminished by an almost panicked concern for Patricia. For over two years letters had passed between them, letters that had begun as admiring poems and kind words and then had grown into passionate, erotic love letters. It had become a love affair of words, an affair not physical but a fictitious invention. John could not touch her silken flesh or give her exotic sexual pleasures, but he could write of these things. And she was safe from any caress because of her marriage and motherhood. But the letters had become powerful messages of love, sensuality, desire, and promise. "I know in my heart that you are the only man I will ever truly love, the only man who will ever truly love me," Patricia wrote to John. And to Patricia went the message, "If all I can do is worship the softness of your skin, the sweetness of your breath, and glow of your hair, then worship I shall . . . until my last breath."

This writing escalated into passion right up until the time Patricia delivered her daughter. Her opportunities to write to him decreased during her mother's long stay and the fuss over the new baby, but gradually she resumed her letters.

All the love and passion she wrote of and received was as intense as ever before, but something began to change. Their correspondence began to lose its fever and was replaced by Patricia's increasing unhappiness with her life and a strong desire to escape. John would have gladly traded any possession he had for a chance to be the one to take her away from Dale Montaine. John suspected Patricia didn't care for motherhood; she never mentioned her child. But Patricia's misery only increased, and then the letters had stopped suddenly on the first of May.

He tried every rational thing he could think of, but was left with only one option. Worry and grief sent him to Lilly. He hoped she would help because he lacked the courage to go to Mrs. Armstrong.

Lilly hadn't seen John in a very long time. She had only exchanged passing greetings with him during her few visits to the Nesbitt House, but even if she hadn't seen him in years, she would never have trouble recognizing him. He evolved only into an older version of himself; he became bald early and his little bit of wispy hair was overlong; his clothing, though of a decent cut and style, was perpetually wrinkled, and his spectacles slid down his nose.

"I need your help," he said nervously.

"Anything, John," she said sincerely, inviting him into her office on the fifth floor of the Armstrong Arms. "You have only to ask."

"It's Patricia. I'm sure something is wrong."

"Patricia? But I saw her just—" Lilly stopped to think. Patricia had joined them for tea a few weeks before, had attended a party for a portrait painter a few weeks before that. Patricia was not ignored, but then there were very few functions that could reasonably include her. "What's wrong with Patricia? And how—"

John edged along the seat of the chair. He held his hat so tightly that his knuckles were white. "Lilly, in order for you to understand, I must tell you something very private. Can you give your word to keep a secret? My telling could embarrass Patricia."

"I suppose," she said uneasily.

"We've been writing to each other," he began.

"Why, John—" she said, smiling, dismissing the importance of such an admission.

"Not innocent letters, Lilly. Very serious letters. Of course, Patricia being married and a mother, it was impossible for us to spend so much as an hour in mutual company. I could never compromise her in that way because I do care for her . . . But we did have the letters."

Lilly frowned; she remembered days of notes and journals in the boardinghouse. John loved Patricia, and apparently that love had never faded, but had become more fierce. "I'm sure it is a mistake, John, to correspond so personally with—"

"Oh, Lilly, that's not why I'm here. I didn't come here to make a confession! I thought I could make you understand why I know something is wrong. I would know because a letter came from her at least every week, except when she was lying in with her child. Then, when the letters began again, Patricia was not herself. She's been feeling terrible about her life, more unhappy than I've ever known her!"

"But John! When have you known Patricia to be anything else? She's determined—"

"No! No! Not easily contented, I know. She's never had everything just the way she likes it, but her unhappiness was getting worse and worse, and then the letters stopped. I waited. I wrote to her again and again, and finally I went to the Montaine house and asked to see her. I was told she was indisposed and couldn't be seen by anyone."

"John," Lilly entreated, "you mustn't take Patricia so seriously. You know how she is. You watched her grow up! She gets an idea of something she wants and . . . Well, if she's hurt you I'll never forgive her, but it's very likely that she just—"

"I know I don't look like the kind of man who can win the heart of a beauty like Patricia, but I tell you, Lilly, she's in some kind of terrible trouble. Maybe her husband found her letters? I think if he had, however, I would have been invited into his house and battered. But something's wrong. In the last letter I had from her, she said she had so thoroughly lost interest in living she wished she could go to sleep and not wake up!"

Lilly's eyes widened slightly, then narrowed suspiciously. She guessed that Patricia had led this innocent man on, letter after letter, using all his genuine affection and reassurance to buoy her spirits and distract her from boredom, and then had simply forgotten about him. Lilly quickly thought about the times she had seen her since Christmas. She was no more unhappy than she ever was. Even Emily had taken to visiting the baby without bothering much about Patricia's moods. A good nanny had been installed; it was as much as any of them could hope for.

"She's been very busy with the baby, John."

"She doesn't even mention the baby! Lilly, please go see if she's all right!"

"I'll go," Lilly said, standing. "I'll go today, if it will make you feel better, but really I think there's nothing wrong. Patricia is often thoughtless. She just became busy and preoccupied and—"

"No," John said. "I understand why you would think so, Lilly, but you're wrong. Patricia has very strong feelings. Not many people understand her as I do, she has always been criticized and accused of being selfish and lazy, and you don't know how much pain it causes in her. I know how she feels about me. I know she wouldn't forget to write to me. She's told me more than once that my letters keep her alive!"

Lilly's heart broke for him. She knew her sister had been unforgivably cruel. She would go see Patricia, and the first thing she would discuss with her would be the total disregard for John's feelings Patricia showed by expressing so much in letters to him.

"Today, Lilly!" he said, the nearest thing to a command she had ever heard from him. "Promise!"

"Yes," she said softly. "Today, John."

He turned and left her office, and she sat down again. "Oh, I'm so sorry, John," she muttered to herself.

It was simple embarrassment that caused Lilly to go alone to her sister's home. She might have spoken with her mother and grandmother about John's visit if she could have discovered a way to disclose the reason for his concern. Instead, she told no one and took a covered carriage and driver from the hotel stables and went by herself. Lilly was so angry, so enraged by Patricia's behavior, that all she could do was rehearse the tongue-lashing she would give her sister. Patricia's damned unhappiness! Her everlasting helplessness! She had hurt so many people with her need to be indulged and now it had reached so far as John!

John was a kind if misguided man who would not lash out at anyone, especially Patricia, to whom he was so devotedly attracted. Poor John, poisoned by Patricia's completely impossible encouragement, would probably never be able to find himself a nice young woman who could become his wife.

Lilly was momentarily confused when the housemaid gave her the same excuse John had reported. Mrs. Montaine could not be seen by anyone.

"Don't be ridiculous," Lilly said. "She's my sister. I can see her in any condition!"

"No, ma'am, my orders are very firm. She's not to be seen by anyone at all."

"Then I'll find her myself," Lilly said, prepared to force her way up the stairs.

"No, ma'am! Please, ma'am! Let me get the nurse, then, and let her explain. Please!"

Lilly stopped short. "The nurse? What the devil is going on here?"

"Please, Miss Armstrong, let me get the nurse. Stay here, please."

Lilly waited, looking around the foyer and into the front sitting room while she was left alone. The house looked the same—fancy and cluttered. The opened draperies made the place brighter, a custom Deanna had inherited from Emily. It was quiet, but no longer glum to her. Their Christmas together had made her feel much better about this place, these people. But how the devil, she wondered, could Patricia have a nurse and none of them know?

A woman about forty years of age came down the stairs. She wore a stiff blue dress, white apron, and a cap. She had pleasant features and smiled at Lilly, but the smile was too starched with formality to be sincere or caring. Something was not right.

"You're the nurse?"

"Yes, ma'am."

"I want to see my sister. Immediately."

"Miss Armstrong, I know you're concerned, but let me explain, and then you'll feel very good about all this, I assure you. Your sister is quite well, actually. She becomes a little agitated now and then, but Mr. Montaine had secured a specialist, Dr. Merlin Wissel. Mrs. Montaine is being treated for melancholia."

"Melancholia?" Lilly repeated with a laugh. "Miss . . . Miss—"

"Stewart, ma'am," she stiffly provided.

"Miss Stewart, my sister was *born* with melancholia! Now really, I insist you take me to her. Patricia doesn't need a specialist. She needs a good kick in the behind!"

302

Lilly made another attempt at the stairs and found her sleeve was pinched by the nurse. "I beg your pardon, miss, but I'm very serious. Mrs. Montaine is being treated by Dr. Wissel, who has made his schedule cure quite famous, especially among the finer families in the United States and Europe."

"I don't frankly care if he can raise the dead. I'm going to see my sister!"

Lilly snatched herself free of the nurse and glanced over her shoulder at a cowering, helpless housemaid. She would not be stopped. She went up the stairs to the second floor and opened Patricia's bedroom door without knocking. The room looked as though it had never been lived in. She quickly forgot her anger; her sudden conviction that Patricia had been misbehaving again was replaced by rising fear. She called out her name in the hall and began opening doors, finding each room empty of people.

She heard footsteps on the stairs and turned to see Dale and a gentleman with a dark, pointed beard and slick mustache.

"Where is she, Dale?" she asked, noting that his appearance was slightly more rumpled than she was accustomed to. Patricia had sworn that when he didn't have to be in the company of others, Dale would let himself become sloppy, drunk, and obnoxious, but whenever Lilly had seen him, he had been impeccably dressed and only sullen.

The gentleman stepped around from behind Dale to face Lilly. "Miss Armstrong, for your sister's well-being, it is imperative that you hear an explanation and leave quietly."

"I'll hear that explanation, believe me. But as for my quiet departure, that's unlikely."

"Let's go down to the library and—"

"Right here!" she demanded, stomping her foot. "Right now!"

The man sighed patiently. "I see. Then at least lower your voice. I am Dr. Wissel," he said, making a short bow at the waist. "I came directly from my clinic hospital in New York when Mr. Montaine wrote to me, describing his wife's symptoms. I'm supervising her recovery from melancholia. I have developed a method of treating the disease that has enjoyed wide success."

"Dale, this is nonsense! What have you done?"

"I couldn't let her get any worse," he said, shrugging. "Not after what happened to Andrew's wife! Don't you understand? She only gets worse all the time, just as Brenda did. I can't live with that kind of madness!"

Lilly knew as much as anyone about Brenda Devon. Emily had visited her and had heard from Andrew much of the story of Brenda's tragic life and then retold the story to Lilly and Amanda. Patricia's circumstances bore absolutely no resemblance.

"Miss Armstrong," the doctor attempted, "there is certainly no reason for hysteria. The treatment is very simple, very neat. A quiet, darkened room, no stimulus to excite the patient, no disturbances or distractions—no books, writing materials, paints, needlework. Complete, extended rest and absolute silence. It quiets the spirit and allows the mind an atmosphere of contentment in which to reappraise all former complaints and discontents. After a month of rest and silence, I provide a schedule that will slowly and carefully reintroduce the woman to her wifely domain, and I assure you—"

Lilly had to think only a moment to know that such a cure would drive her insane. Even Patricia, as unmotivated as she seemed to be, couldn't possibly benefit. "Dale! What the devil is he talking about? Where is my sister?"

"Lilly, she's upstairs, in bed, and quiet. She has to become quiet before she can—"

"Good God! Where is your father?"

"Father has been gone over a month. You knew that. He has taken Deanna on a tour."

"And you took that opportunity to bring this lunatic into your house to do this to my sister?"

"Madam," Dr. Wissel said, stiffening, "I assure you I have been in the finest homes, with the finest families, creating an entirely new—"

"Lord," Lilly grumbled in complete exasperation, whirling around and moving toward the stairs that would take her to the third floor.

"Miss Armstrong! You may *not* disturb my patient!"

"Lilly! Lilly! Please don't interfere in this!"

But Lilly was far ahead of them. She lifted her skirts and went up the stairs two at a time. Behind her the two men scrambled trying to reach her before she got to the door. When she tried to throw it open, she found it locked. She rattled it and pulled, but it was secure. Inside she could hear soft, distant weeping. "Patricia!" she called, pounding on the door. "Patricia!" But the crying did not become any louder, nor did Patricia respond to the sound of Lilly's voice.

She turned around, her back against the door and faced Dale and the doctor. "Two choices, gentlemen. Unlock this door now, or I will return with twenty men and the law. Don't put me off and don't argue with me. I mean it."

They looked at each other, Dr. Wissel sighing wearily. "You may well be making cure impossible with this interruption," he said, reaching into his pocket for the key.

"Lilly, you've got to understand, she is impossible to please, impossible to live with. She won't hold the baby, she won't take her dinner in the dining room, she locks her door against me. She constantly complains and— I wrote to the doctor because she's only getting worse. And Brenda Devon—"

"Brenda Devon is a poor, war-weary, abused woman who is sadly out of her mind!" Lilly ground out. She stepped aside so that the door could be unlocked. "My sister is a spoiled brat and no worse than you!"

The door swung open, and Lilly saw her. Patricia sat in the center of a four poster hugging her knees. Her sheets lay on the floor, torn into strips. There was no furniture in the room save a chamber pot, and the two small windows had been painted black. A few streaks of light came through, but the room was like perpetual dusk. She wore only a nightdress, her hair uncombed, her face pale without any cosmetics. She looked like a ten-year-old girl.

Lilly's steps toward the bed were slow, the shock so great and the disbelief so profound that she could hardly grab hold of anger. "Patricia?" she asked, hoping to find her sister still with a shred of sanity.

"Lilly," she said, her voice hoarse and her eyes spilling over tears onto chapped cheeks. "Lilly, they're trying to kill me."

"Miss Armstrong, of course that's absurd. We're trying to help her. It's a difficult process, true, but the results . . ."

Lilly pulled one of Patricia's hands away from her knees and looked closely at the bitten nails and the chafed wrists. "What is this?" she asked with calm that took effort.

"It sometimes becomes necessary to restrain and medicate the—"

"Come darling," Lilly said to Patricia. "Come now—you're coming with me now." She pulled her to a sitting position and helped her to stand.

305

"Miss Armstrong, you may not take the patient out of the room! That's the worst possible thing to do now! You must not defy her husband; he has absolute authority in this!"

With an arm around Patricia's waist, Lilly calmly walked her toward the door. She briefly considered leaving her sister's side long enough to fetch that chamber pot and hurl it at these men. She used enormous strength to contain her fury. "Please Doctor, Dale . . . resort to physical force against me. I beg it!"

"Never mind, Merlin," Dale said in frustration. "You did your best."

"I warn you, Miss Armstrong, you're making a terrible, terrible error. I have references! I have evidence of cures! Many fine families—"

"Lilly," Patricia softly entreated as they went down the stairs, "will you take me home?"

"Yes, darling. It's all right."

Lilly wore no cloak; the weather was too warm. She had not paused long enough in the Montaine house to gather even a wrapper for Patricia, but walked her calmly out the front door to her waiting coach. Barefoot, in a stained bedgown, her hair gnarled, Patricia looked as though she had escaped from Bedlam. Lilly instructed the driver to take them to the rear of the hotel rather than the portico or stables. The driver was then sent to the sixth floor for a blanket and Elizabeth. Patricia was wrapped up and carried to Lilly's apartment.

Lilly couldn't risk putting Patricia in one of the hotel suites where any guest might have access to her. She worried that Dale would find some legal recourse and remove her. She settled her sister in her own bed and left Elizabeth in charge.

Rather than looking for her grandmother and mother, Lilly quickly found stable hands and took them back with her to the Montaine household. They followed her carriage in a wagon, enough muscle to make her intentions very clear.

She was surprised but extremely relieved to find that Dale stayed behind closed doors and did not interfere with her when she arrived, as if he knew it was futile to argue. The nurse and doctor were not visible, and the maid stood aside, mute and nervous, when Lilly told the nanny to pack belongings for herself and Katherine. She then searched her sister's bedroom for clothing and accessories. The thing she was really looking for was difficult to find, but Lilly had past experience in nosing through Patricia's things. She found journal books and letters in the bottom of the armoire beneath shawls and scarves. Easily two hundred letters!

She packed a trunk and carpetbag and had them carried out. The nanny and baby were in the carriage, and Lilly was about to leave when she heard his voice.

"Everyone thinks I've wronged her," Dale said, his voice rather quiet and weary. She turned to look at him. He leaned against the sitting-room door frame some distance away, his shirt collar opened, sleeves rolled up. He held a glass of gin. At the moment he spoke, the maid skittered away, head down. "I did in the beginning . . . but—"

"Oh, Dale, don't even begin all this!" Lilly gritted out angrily.

"But it has to be said, Lilly. I took advantage of her flirtation— but it has been much the opposite since." He took a sip of his drink, closing his eyes. "She's refused me everything—she won't be my wife."

"Do you even bother to *pretend* you want Patricia as your—"

"I didn't want to marry her any more than she wanted to marry me! No, we didn't love each other—is that a surprise to you? Christ, Lilly, I was a failure enough before Patricia—but don't you know how hard she's worked to create a worse monster?"

"How can you blame—"

"She encourages my drink, my whoring—did you know? Then she laughs at my drunkenness and tells my father about my gambling losses. And of course the baby came only because I demanded she be my wife—my father was desperate for another heir," he said, his voice weakening at the end. He looked down into his glass. "Who can blame him for that, eh, Lilly? When all he's got is—"

"Don't do this, Dale. Don't—"

"Once she was pregnant, of course, she'd done her part. Since the day she told me about the baby coming, she's been damned if she'd so much as speak a word to me. She told me I can have her by force, or not at all. I tried to change, you know. Once I realized we were stuck with each other and there is no alternative. There isn't any tenderness or tolerance between us—never was. I know I was

307

the one who—Jesus!" He ran a hand through his hair. Tears seemed to be in his eyes. Lilly was astonished.

"You so deliberately molested her! Lied to her! *Raped* her!"

"Rape? Oh, you should have been there. Suppose it was, actually? Why did she force the marriage, hating me? Blaming me? And what do you think it is *now*? I stopped the drink after Katherine . . . I asked her if we could possibly treat each other humanely for Kath—"

He stopped rather suddenly. Lilly felt torn between what she'd found done to her sister and the sudden realization that Patricia had spent much of her time punishing Dale ever since that long-ago night.

"Go ahead, Lilly. Patricia and the baby are better off with you. No one can make Patricia happy. She'll be a constant burden to her family. And the baby can't be raised by a drunkard and a shrew." He finished his drink and turned the empty glass upside down. One drop fell to the carpet. "In the end I did her a favor, didn't I? I was only trying to get a wife, a mother for my child. But what she wanted was to go home to her rich grandmother where no man could touch her. So . . . now she can. It'll be my fault. Again."

Lilly said nothing. She looked at Dale's glassy, reddened eyes. She noticed he had developed a slouch and a paunchy gut. She turned and reached for the door handle.

"Take care of her," he said. She looked at him over her shoulder. "Katherine."

By the time she returned to the hotel, Emily and Amanda had discovered Patricia and were with her. They welcomed the nanny and Katherine, and Lilly had a hotel bed moved into her sitting room for herself while Patricia used her bedroom. It was evening before the household calmed down. Still, there was not much to be said.

"We took too much for granted," Lilly said. "We waited too long. Despite your good intentions, Mama, Dale is incompetent, and Patricia, I think, will always need a keeper. I suppose it's going to be me."

She never explained how she found out her sister was in trouble, but through the night she read the letters. Tears ran down her cheeks as she read page after page, but not tears of sadness. Shame, shock, bewilderment. She couldn't imagine what Patricia had written to John; John's letters were detailed, erotic, passionate descriptions of physical love. There were endearments aplenty, but far more plentiful were the promises of sexual acts that would be committed between them on some future day when Patricia announced that she was finally bedewed with the wetness of desire. "I know how he's hurt you, darling," John wrote. "How he has damaged your heart, your mind, your womanly parts. But I will gently kiss those tender, secret places, and you will feel the dew of desire. And what you will beg me to give you next will make that boy you are troubled with ashamed of his weak, blushing wick."

Lilly remembered the shuddering thrill of reading of Patricia's journal. Her first gasp had given way to intrigue—but this! In all her years of reading, all the forbidden books, she had never seen anything to compare with the obscenity! Yet perhaps even worse than the words, worse than the descriptions of body parts, the amazing acts promised, was the deeper message. This was what Patricia wanted. To receive the writings and herself write about these physical things between a man and woman—and at the same time extract a promise that there would be no actual touch against her invitation. "You have my solemn oath that my fingers will not graze your skin. You likewise have my oath that one day that part of you will be reborn and your invitation will become a scream of desire, pledge of pleasure! Oh my darling, that you humbly beg more of my pleasure words to precede our pleasure acts is all I live for! Your letters to me rob me of breath, give my heart pause, create in me an astonishing size."

By the time the sun rose, Lilly had not finished reading; there had been many times she had to set aside a page and breathe deeply, searching for composure. Lilly was not shy of the prospect of coupling—indeed, she longed for the day when she could indulge that deep affection that became a physical expression. It was Patricia who had always dreaded it! These writings, even with the endearments, did not remind her of love, but loveless lust. The things John promised to do with his manhood, the praise for her flushed, pink breasts, the exclamation that they might one day sweat, scream, and claw each other in frenzy made Lilly think only of assault. Many times their faces swam before her eyes: dowdy, small, rumpled John, who fearlessly described his own stiff, dripping manhood; prim, haughty, cold Patricia, who had obviously written him of her damaged pudendum.

She looked in on her sister in the night. Patricia cuddled a pillow and slept soundly, feeling safe with her family. Small as she was, her long yellow hair braided by her mother for sleep, she looked like a child.

In the morning Lilly was sitting in a chair before the hearth in her sitting room when Emily appeared, carrying a tray of breakfast to the bedroom to serve Patricia. "Lilly, isn't it too warm for a fire?"

"I felt a chill, Mama."

"But Lilly, close the window if you're cold! Heavens!"

"I will in a minute, Mama."

Emily put the tray on a nearby commode and walked over to the window, closing it. She paused beside Lilly's chair and touched her brow. "You're flushed! And chilled? I hope you're not becoming ill."

"I'm never ill, Mama, don't worry," she said, watching the fire burn. She had left at least fifty letters unread; in three full journal books she had read only fifty random pages. Now there was ash.

Patricia recovered quickly from her ordeal. It took only a few stout meals, leisurely tubs, sunshine, an unlocked door, and Emily's constant reassurance. Lilly was a long way from recovering from her sister's correspondence, a burden she carried alone. She did tell Patricia that everything was burned. "I don't know that we could expect Mama's heart to keep pace if she read one page of what you had saved."

"You read it then." It was not a question.

"Patricia, what purpose could that have served?"

"I was bored," she said simply, which wasn't half the answer Lilly hoped for. Still, she didn't have the nerve to question any further.

Quarters became cramped, even in so large a space. A room had to be set up for Katherine and her nanny and Bertie had to be temporarily moved from Amanda's quarters in order to accommodate them, which made both old women testy. Emily was happy to have greater access to her granddaughter, but was displeased with both Patricia's indifference to her child and the circumstances that brought them together. Lilly spent more time than ever in her fifth-floor office; she found sharing rooms with Patricia more difficult than ever before.

Lilly was not in the apartments when Dale arrived and was therefore surprised to find him in the parlor with Emily and the baby. Dale looked more beleaguered than Lilly had ever seen him. His eyes were dark and blank; his white, starched shirt looked slept in and had a large spot on it. Lilly could smell the liquor and assumed it must have been Dale's drinking. She had obviously found them in the middle of a conversation that was taking place over the top of Katherine's head. Emily balanced the child on her knees.

"It seems to be the most practical solution," Emily was saying very kindly. "So long as I'm willing and you're willing, our most important consideration should always be Katherine."

Lilly entered. "Hello, Dale," she said, as politely as she could.

He rose clumsily. "Lilly," he said, nodding and sitting again.

"Come in, dear. Dale's come to see the baby and Patricia. However—"

"She won't be in the same room with me," he said.

"Is that so difficult to understand, Dale," Lilly said. "After all you did—"

"Sit down, Lilly," Emily interrupted. "Dale has a very good explanation for all that. It was all done with the most honorable intentions. Dr. Wissel does indeed have a very strong following. It just wasn't the time or the cause for his services, but that isn't a mistake so extraordinary. I know you acted out of genuine concern, Dale."

"Dale, you were duped," Lilly said. "He probably isn't even a real doc—"

"Dale and I have discussed all those possibilities already, Lilly. We're trying to make some decisions about the future now. Dale, I don't think Katherine can do without you. You'll have to come often to spend time with her. She needs her father."

"Yes," he said. Lilly's eyes widened. She couldn't imagine what her mother was doing.

"It's sad the two of you couldn't come to some sort of agreeable terms. I'm hopeful that can still happen. At the moment, however—"

"It was a mistake from the beginning. If Lady Nesbitt hadn't threatened and insisted—"

"Well, that's all water over the dam. And if you'll remember, the problems started long before Lady Nesbitt arrived. I'm afraid I'll have to insist the two of you share blame for your troubles."

"You won't find my wife willing to share blame!" he contested.

Or anything else, Lilly thought.

"You're far too busy to give the baby all that she requires, and Patricia is not a doting mother. I am, however, a very interested

311

grandmother. If you tried to raise Katherine alone, you would find yourself too often giving up important matters to be sure she is being properly supervised, don't you think? But you must promise to come here often—she mustn't grow up not knowing how deeply you care for her."

"I won't," he said. "I will," he amended.

"I'm so sorry all this has happened," Emily went on. "And Dale, I *do* understand. You're looking weary. Get some rest, try to enjoy yourself if you can, and please don't be concerned about Katherine. I promise you I'll take good care of her."

"But, my father—"

Emily laughed very good naturedly. "Please, tell Wilson to come and see me. Such a dear man! I know if he trusts anyone with his granddaughter's welfare, he trusts me. And give my regards to Deanna—I miss seeing her."

Dale took a moment to absorb that. He frowned and then nodded. "Yes, he might approve."

"There really doesn't seem to be an alternative that works as well. I think no one will notice, actually. It's not as though all society stayed close enough to tuck you in at night."

"No . . . but don't you think they'll soon discover that I live at home and Patricia—"

"I doubt, under the circumstances, Patricia will be inclined to socialize. Don't you agree?"

Dale made a few lame attempts at conversation for a while longer and then left when Katherine became fussy and difficult to hold. Once the baby had been passed to her nanny for a nap, Dale lost interest and left. Lilly had said hardly a word. Emily sighed as though she was exhausted.

"Dear God," Emily said in a breath.

"What in the world—"

"Oh, Lilly, I had to convince him to leave the baby with me. I'm not usually one to give up hope, but the man is a drunkard, Patricia is completely self-centered and takes no notice of her child, and Wilson didn't take a hand even in raising his own son. There just isn't any other way!"

"You're just going to let it be? You're not going to make Patricia go back?"

"Who knows what kind of cure he'll try on her next," Emily said wearily. "Who knows what kind of condition she'll *invite*. Lilly,

312

I give up. Patricia is not going to make any improvements in her marriage . . . and I honestly think Dale has destroyed himself with drink."

"You knew he was drunk," Lilly said.

"I as much as invited him to go home and drink some more. I offered to keep his child for him so he can!"

"Is he gone?" a voice in the doorway asked.

"Yes, Patricia," Emily said patiently, looking at her daughter. "He's gone."

"He's not coming back, is he?"

"I've asked him to visit Katherine, but I don't think he'll bother you."

"Well, good. I'm not going back there, not ever. You do understand, don't you, Mama?"

Emily stood slowly, leveling her eyes at her daughter. "Patricia, I think it very likely I will die not understanding you." Emily left the room.

"Well, that's just fine!" Patricia said to Lilly. "What does a person have to endure beyond being stripped and tied to a bedpost before a little sympathy is in order?"

"Believe me, Patricia, we *all* sympathize," Lilly said. "In fact, I think there's not a person alive I don't pity more than you."

Lilly should not have been surprised when a letter arrived for Patricia, and she gleefully snatched it out of Emily's hands.

"Who is it from?" Emily asked.

"A young lady I met years ago in Saratoga," Patricia lied.

In the middle of July, when the heat was high and the air thick with humidity, Patricia requested a suite of her own on the fifth floor. "Since we're all so crowded here," she said, "and since it's understood I'm not returning to my former abode, I think we should do something a bit more permanent."

"And the baby?" Amanda asked.

"She seems very content here," Patricia pointed out.

It was done with very little fanfare. Katherine was left behind with her grandmother. Quarters were adjusted so that Emily could be nearer the baby, and Bertie, who was aging and not serving Amanda so much as living out a retirement, could move back with her friend. Patricia settled herself and two maids into a comfortable suite of rooms. There was no trouble about the arrangement until Lilly found Patricia standing beside Amanda in the foyer of the hotel,

313

taking the hand of a guest and smiling. Then something like an explosion went off inside Lilly's head. She waited, seething and nearly frothing, until Patricia finally took the steam elevator to the fifth floor and her suite.

Lilly was ushered into Patricia's sitting room by a maid and found her sister reclining on a daybed, sampling candies.

"Lilly, what rare honor is—"

"You are not a hostess here, do you understand me? You will not join the family in greeting guests!"

"Lilly, what in the—"

"You may have this suite, you may join us for dinner, you may occasionally attend a function here if I feel it will do no harm, but you *will not* be a part of this business! This hotel has nothing whatever to do with you! You are given accommodations out of the *mercy* and generosity of this family, and nothing more! You are a married woman who chooses not to live with her husband and chooses not to be a mother to her child, and I will not have you playing hostess as if you built the place!"

"How like you, Lilly. After all I've been through, you act as though you could be ashamed of me!"

"I am ashamed of you," Lilly said carefully. "I'll take care of you because you can't take care of yourself, but if you do anything to embarrass this family further, I will throw you out! Do you understand? You can go find your own place to live, your own income, and your own damned social life. You will not be here at Mama and Grandmother's expense."

"Hah! That's what you say, but when the whole story is told, I have been more a victim of this business than anything else. When I needed my family, where were they? Building Lilly's hotel, that's where! And they call me selfish!"

"I'm warning you, Patricia. I will tell them about your letters. I could probably *show* them. I know the two of you are at it again."

"Is that how you expect to keep me invisible, Lilly? By threatening to divulge my private correspondence? You will be sadly surprised in that case."

"Do you mean to tell me it's stopped, at long last?"

"I'm just saying that one day you will regret your accusations. Someday you will be sorry you treated me so badly."

"Patricia, if you do anything to hurt this family or the reputation of this hotel, I will get my revenge. Tread carefully. Very carefully!"

Flushed and trembling, Lilly left, slamming the door. She had never before felt the murderous rage she felt today. Through all that Patricia had done, through all her duplicity, it was not until Lilly saw her business compromised that she felt her anger turn to a hot rage.

When the summer passed and Patricia seemed to be following orders, something occurred to Lilly. Patricia was seen about the hotel frequently enough; she couldn't be expected to remain behind locked doors. But she seemed not to attract attention, certainly not the sort of scandalous chit-chat that Lilly had feared. When Mrs. Sinclair visited the hotel for a tea and was talking with Amanda, she saw Patricia in the room and clucked sadly. "What a shame," was all she muttered. That's when Lilly understood that each of the women was regarded differently. Amanda was the noble dowager, Emily was the hard-working, widowed mother of two daughters, Lilly was her grandmother's protégée, and Patricia had become, by her own hand, a problem to the managed. If Patricia created scandal and was evicted, women like Mrs. Sinclair would click their teeth with sympathy.

With all she had accomplished, this was the very first time Lilly had felt the power of a heavy hand. She knew herself capable of handling problems even greater than those her sister presented. She thought it was high time they got rid of Ned Armstrong. She had a plan she thought would expel him from their city, from their worries. She met with Amanda and Fletcher and informed her grandmother she would go with Fletcher Drake to the Philadelphia address to which money was sent every month.

"This doesn't appear to be a social visit," Ned said, looking at Fletcher.

"You don't have to invite us in," she said. "This will take no more than a moment. My grandmother has been giving you some money—is it fifty a month? It's going to stop immediately. You may do anything you like."

"Then you won't mind getting to know your father again?" he asked, puffing up and smiling. "I can move into the—"

"I won't be spending any time with you, and you won't be admitted to the Armstrong Arms under any circumstances. Mr. Drake, our solicitor, has discovered you have indeed had a spot of trouble here and there, although nothing too criminal. A little phi-landering, for which you've become well known. At any time you would like to make public the fact that you abandoned your wife

315

and children, we're prepared to withstand the embarrassment. In fact, we're prepared to help you spread the rumors. Mr. Drake?"

Fletcher pulled several folded papers from the inside of his coat and handed them to Ned.

"Keep this," Lilly said. "It's a list of addresses for newspapers in major cities throughout the United States. Have you visited any of these places? When you begin your siege, we'll write to them all. I have a very good friend who is a cartoonist and can make an excellent captioned drawing of your face. I think you'll get your wish at long last. You'll be quite famous. I do hope, for your sake, no one is looking for you."

"You would do this to your own father?" he asked.

Lilly shrugged. "Only because my mother doesn't know how to load a pistol and fire. Good day."

"Wait a minute, what about Patricia? I demand to know—"

"Patricia, sadly, was lost to us in seventy-six. I'm sorry, there was nothing we could do to save her. We did try, you may believe me."

For all the power she had exercised, all the poise she displayed, when she was in her coach again, she leaned against Fletcher and sobbed. "If you knew all the years I longed for a father!"

"I do know, Lilly, darling. I know."

"Oh, Fletcher, I don't understand that kind of evil! I can't bear the fact that I'm part of it!"

"Lilly, Lilly . . . do you think one inherits evil like one does hair color?" He put his arms around her shoulders, holding her. "No, darling, if you have none of his treachery now—you won't. Believe me. You weep for loss, not really for shame."

"For years when I was young I dreamed of this poor, tattered but honorable soldier, not really dead. All a mistake! he would say. I'm home to my loved ones! he would proclaim. Oh, Fletcher, how did this happen?"

"You wanted to be the one to send him away, Lilly. Something about feeling you'd really finished with him. You can't be finished with him . . . not ever. Long after he is dead, you will lament the truth."

As she wept, as Fletcher held her, she might as well have been returning from a cemetery and the burial of a loved one. But Fletcher, who had his own troubled youth and disillusionment, comforted.

316

"How I wish you were my father," she said as they approached the hotel.

He wiped her eyes with his hanky. "I wish it, too, Lilly," he said. He kissed her brow in a fatherly way. "Think of me as your father, if you like." A huff of laughter bubbled through her tears. "You'll have to behave, however," he added staunchly. "You'll have to be completely obedient."

She studied his face, as if for the first time. His thick brown hair, warm brown eyes, strong nose, and angular face gave him a soft handsomeness. He was the dearest, most sensitive man she had ever known. "How I wish I were in love with someone like you," she mused aloud.

"I am your loyal friend, Lilly. I would do anything but murder for you. Would you ask any more of me than that?"

"I suppose not," she said. "Thank you, Fletcher. You've saved me again."

Four days later Fletcher found Lilly in the foyer of the hotel at almost teatime. Emily was standing beside the desk, talking quietly with the clerk, and Fletcher reported to Lilly in a hushed voice that Ned Armstrong had taken a trunk and carpetbag to the train station. His destination was Chicago. Despite the relief, tears came to Lilly's eyes.

"Shouldn't I feel good?" she asked Fletcher.

"It can't be pleasant, Lilly. But you can't blame yourself."

"It's this feeling of being cheated, Fletcher. If it isn't terrible enough to never know a father, you can't imagine the strange feelings it creates when you discover one, and he is terrible."

"Have you told your mother?"

"No. Maybe I will, if the time is right. She says he can't do any worse to her than he did years ago, leaving her at a dockside shanty pregnant and with a small child. Mama is a strong believer in God's will. She accepts any burdens thrust on her and only worries about others. Her fear was more for Grandmother and me than for herself. She worried that Ned would create some sort of gossip and hurt our hotel."

"I think it might come as a relief, then, when you find the moment to tell her he has disappeared again."

"Have you heard Grandmother say we have the worst luck with men?" she asked him. "Not so with you, Fletcher. You've been the best sort of man. Do you think you'd change much if one of us decided to marry you?"

"You flatter me. If I could find a woman like any of the three of you, I would marry in a moment."

"The rumor is that such an event would break a hundred hearts." She cocked her head to look at him. He was so handsome a man, a man of such stature and charm. "You've escorted dozens of beautiful ladies to our various parties. None of them can keep your attention long."

"I assure you, Lilly, the rumors give me undeserved prowess. Perhaps I can't keep their attention."

Lilly was prepared to argue when she was distracted by a very unusual sight. Her eyes became large. "Maybe our luck is about to change," she told Fletcher. "Excuse me a moment."

She walked to the desk where Emily talked with the clerk and tugged on her mother's sleeve. "Mama," she whispered. "Look."

On the portico, just off the coach, stood a tall man with sandy colored hair, a cowboy hat, a limp, an untrimmed moustache. He was dusty; he looked as though he could have ridden a horse all the way to Philadelphia.

"Can it really be?" Emily asked softly.

He was arguing for his saddle, a huge, ornate thing that the coachman wanted to carry for him. A slow smile spread across Emily's face. She clasped her hands together at her waist as he entered the foyer balancing his saddle on his shoulder and carrying his overstuffed carpetbag. He lowered the saddle to the floor, put down his bag, and removed his hat.

"I didn't think it was possible," he said, "the name, and all."

"Carl," Emily said to a bellhop, not taking her eyes from Noel's, "Mr. Padgett will have suite five-twenty-three. That will be twelve dollars a week in advance, Mr. Padgett."

He grinned, but the poor clerk stuttered and stammered. "Twelve . . . Mrs. . . . Mrs. Armstrong, we—"

"You won't be needing a spittoon, I trust," Emily said.

"I reckon not, ma'am," he grinned.

"Welcome home, Mr. Padgett."

"Thank you kindly, Mrs. Armstrong. It's mighty fine to be back."

illy returned to the apartments one afternoon and was amazed to be told that Andrew was visiting with her mother. She quietly entered the sitting room, paid a brief, polite greeting, and sat down with them.

Andrew Devon felt a debt to Emily Armstrong. She was the one to influence him to find a special kind of help for his wife. It had taken many months and many visits from doctors before he came to the conclusion that a home away from Philadelphia, under the supervision of a very sensitive and kind couple was the best sort of life for Brenda. Andrew had come to inform and thank her.

"Her condition is described as mania," he explained. "There is no cure, and even though we might draw the conclusion that the harsh life Brenda endured could explain this illness, there is also no known cause."

"Does she seem content, Andrew?" Emily asked.

"Contentment may not be possible for Brenda, Mrs. Armstrong. There are asylums, mostly terrible and costly places. She's already in a kind of prison—she can't escape the grip of hysteria. There are times she can't sleep for days . . . also times when she seems to be all right and apologizes for creating disturbances, but she doesn't seem to remember what kind of disturbances she has created."

"Oh, Andrew, I'm so sorry for her . . . for you both."

"Now that I've learned a few things about her disturbance, what little is known, so much has become understandable. Before Mrs. Waite's death, Brenda was plagued . . . perhaps less severely, but plagued just the same. I was often confused by some of her rages that seemed to be caused by nothing at all. Or, those times she was sick in bed for days, but there was no real illness. The truth is that her mother could control her and hide her symptoms."

Lilly listened calmly, though whenever he was near her heart pounded. Freedom from Brenda's illness must be credited for his apparent health—he looked rested and refreshed. There was a new touch of gray at his temples, hardly more than a suggestion. Andrew, thirty-three years old now, grew only more handsome, more powerful. She watched him perform small habits she hoped to memorize: the way his strong hands gripped and squeezed his knees while he talked, relaxed while he listened; at times his smile lifted the left corner of his mouth more than the right; he frequently tugged his coat sleeves toward his wrists.

"How often do you see her?" Emily asked.

"I take the train to Reading at least one weekend every month, but there is no way of knowing in advance whether she will benefit from a visit—no way to know what condition she'll be in because it's all so unpredictable. I don't know where people think my wife has gone."

"Don't ever worry about that, Andrew. She can't help it, and neither can you!"

"Don't misunderstand me, Mrs. Armstrong—I'm not embarrassed. Brenda never did enjoy the kind of social life she wanted— she's not missed, sadly. I myself seem to be in more demand, but—" He stopped and looked down momentarily. Andrew had become richer; this was becoming a known fact. He had nearly separated from Wilson Montaine and pursued his own investments. He was, therefore, also pursued socially. "It's fortunate that my business does well. Brenda's care isn't as costly as it could be . . . but I have no encouragement from the doctors that this will be a brief ordeal. It's very likely she will suffer like this for the rest of her life."

"Can nothing be done to help? Nothing—"

"She must be kept safe from herself," he said, his voice quiet. "She might hurt herself."

"In her mania?" Emily asked.

"It's so hard to understand without seeing it yourself. She took scissors to her dresses one afternoon. She explained, angrily, that she was only getting rid of the spots. After a big fuss getting the scissors away from her, it actually appeared that she didn't think she held a scissors at all, but a rag. She didn't see herself cutting, but cleaning. The next day she was very upset that she was not allowed to wear her favorite green dress. Mrs. Sherman promised her a new one."

Lilly looked down at her hands. She fought the urge to cry. Tears did not come easily to Lilly; she wasn't fretful and seldom sentimental. And the tears would not be for Brenda, but for Andrew, locked in marriage to a mad woman.

"It must be like caring for a small child," Emily remarked.

"Which is why Mr. and Mrs. Sherman are perfect. They had a child who was severely abnormal and never could do anything for himself. He had to be carried until he died. He lived into his late twenties. Their finances are bad. What they do to keep Brenda isn't always easy, but far easier than what they had to do for their son. They now have a retirement. If anything happens to Brenda, I'll give them the—" He closed his eyes and rubbed his temples briefly. "I'm sorry," he said.

"It's all right, Andrew. You've done all a husband can do. Now you have to take care of yourself. Fortunately you have the means. I'm glad your business hasn't suffered."

"My own investments are fine. I'm trying to keep everything in order because as the business grows, I am less and less able to help Wilson. He has always known the day would come when we would only be friends and I would be working for myself. It was much easier for him to encourage me to be independent when I was twenty or twenty-five. But now—"

"Ah, Wilson," Emily said knowingly. "I know, I know. Home now and in a fit over the children. He's been here. Storming about and shouting. I'll visit him again. He's feeling his age, you know. He must calm down. He can't do anything about Dale, I can't do anything about Patricia, and he's going to give himself apoplexy."

"Mama," Lilly said, "you don't have to take care of everyone all the time. Mr. Montaine can take care of himself." And, she thought, let the old devil get riled up till he pops!

"He's all bluster," Emily said. "He never learned to show people he cares, that's all. It's the fact that he does care that makes him behave like an old bull."

"There's no denying all that I owe him," Andrew said.

"Andrew, have you ever had a tour of the hotel? Lilly, take Andrew around the hotel and grounds, will you please? And Andrew, I want to see more of you. Come for dinner. Are you still at the same address?"

"I'm selling the Philadelphia house, although I don't have a buyer yet. I find I just don't need it."

"Well then, when it sells and you're looking about for your next address, we'd be privileged to have you consider the Arms."

"That's very nice, Mrs. Armstrong. I don't know if I'll take you up on that, but I will at least visit."

"Yes, you must. And do give my regards to Brenda. Poor thing—I do think of her often."

When Lilly descended into the hotel foyer with Andrew, she said, "She means it, you know. Only Mama is such a tender heart."

"I know," he said. "There is nothing about Mrs. Armstrong that is anything but sincere. And kind."

"Would you live at the Arms?" she asked him as they walked out the door en route to the walks, gardens, gazebos, and stables.

"I don't think so, Lilly." He took a deep breath, inhaling the fragrance of summer flowers. "It all thrives so. As do you."

"It's been four years, Andrew. It hardly seems that long. Four years ago since the idea was born, and it will be a year come November since we've been open. It's a success, you know. I imagine Wilson is jealous as a fishwife. He makes Grandmother offers regularly."

Andrew chuckled and pointed his elbow toward her, inviting her to stroll. "He still doesn't suspect me of encouraging you."

"For the first time since that awful summer years ago, everything seems to be in order. It's all calmed. Patricia is fairly quiet, although I brace myself for her next prank. Katherine thrives in my mother's

322

care—she's crawling and trying to stand up in her bed! There's a gentleman who keeps company with Mama, but she is trying to pretend there is no romance. Did you see her face, how bright and beautiful she's looking?" Lilly laughed.

"Lady Nesbitt does well?"

"Grandmother has power and money and her family together. She had three husbands, all of whom she swears she loved dearly. There was hardly anything else she ever wanted. Everyone has what they desired." She paused. "Everyone but you and I."

"I have what I'm going to have forever, but you have no excuse. You could make some kind of happiness for yourself——"

"Don't start all that. For the past year I've been pestered by every bachelor anyone has ever met!"

"How terrible for you," he teased.

"You must do as Mama says, Andrew. You have to come around the family more. Visit. I know what you're up to. You're trying not to put temptation in my path, but believe me I've had time enough to become accustomed to the fact that you're a hopeless prude. And I am far too busy most of the time to spin fairy tales in my mind. I've become too practical for nonsense."

"Oh, have you now?"

"Unfortunately," she said in a sulking voice.

"Are you absolutely sure I'm protecting you?"

"Oh, absolutely!" she laughed. "Although I've come a distance since those afternoons in Rittenhouse Square, you still treat me like a reckless, naughty girl!"

"I'll have to watch that," he said. "You haven't been a girl in a long time."

"I think it's time you began to give me some credit for intelligence—no one has her life in better control than I." But the touch of his hand on her back when they approached the gazebo steps brought a familiar thrill. Lilly knew him too well. If he suspected she had any feeling for him at all, he would run away and never return.

She showed him the stables and the patios, the walks and the gardens that had been begun and explained what would be added. It was not unusual to see Lilly Armstrong showing a gentleman around the grounds, and when any employee of the hotel passed them, she smiled and said good afternoon. She encountered her mother and Mr. Padgett at nearly teatime as they were on their way to the dining room and paused long enough to introduce Andrew to Noel, claiming Andrew as an old family friend. When the tour and afternoon had been spent, he was ready to go. "I'm going to tell Mama that you've accepted an invitation to dinner next Friday, Andrew."

"Do you think that's a good idea, Lilly?" he asked her.

"Sometimes, when I feel sorry for myself, overworked or lonely or frustrated with the quality of suitors who bang at my door, I remember those days when we walked in the square and talked about books. About Mrs. Hale's manners. I realize I was just a girl . . . I know present circumstances discourage any romantic notions . . . but Andrew, it just isn't right for us to avoid each other any longer. Perhaps that was the best thing years ago, I won't argue that, but—"

"The forbidden," he said, laughing in a mocking way, "only becomes more delicious as the years——"

"I'm lonely, damn it! There aren't many people to talk to— about books, business, plans I have. Just Mama and Grandmother, Fletcher, sometimes Elizabeth, when I can interest her. You're lonely, too, Andrew. We *can* be friends. Mama and Grandmother enjoy your company. Say you'll come?"

"Well . . ."

"If you don't, I'll just plant the seed in Mama's mind and she'll pester you until you accept. So?"

"I'll come," he said. "And you had better be a good girl."

I'm not a girl, she thought.

"I wonder how I was able to convince myself to come this far," Emily told Noel.

He turned her around and began to unfasten the buttons of her dress. He pulled the shoulders over her arms and kissed her neck. "Maybe you just stopped borrowing so much trouble," he said. "I love you."

She turned in his arms and met his lips. Her dress fell around her ankles, and she stood against him, clad only in her chemise. "I don't know when I've been happier, Noel," she said at long last.

"That's all I ever wanted, your happiness. It don't hurt none that mine comes in the bargain. I waited a good long time."

"You always give yourself so much credit," she said. "As though I didn't wait as long!"

"Yes, ma'am, but you wanted to. I always knew it was a good idea. You still determined how it has to go?"

"Yes, Noel. I could never leave my family. It would be hard enough to leave my mother and Lilly, but Katherine? Impossible!"

"I could stay."

"Forever? Oh, Noel, darling, I know better than that. And if you did, it would never be more than this. A few strolls, an occasional dinner, now and then an hour in your room. I love it all! But you must believe me, when you become restless, go. Go happily. I'll be here when you return."

"And if I want more, Emily? What if—"

She stopped him with her lips. "There isn't any more, darling, but isn't this so much more than either of us thought possible? It's enough, Noel. If you can't come back to me, I'll be all right. If you come back to me, I'll be better."

"I can't get too restless when you tempt me all the time."

"You're such a wonderful liar! So we can't marry, but never mind! How is it any different for a married man to go off on his adventurous diversions of hunting and herding and leaving his wife behind with a bunch of little ones clinging to her skirt?"

"The thought of leaving hasn't hit yet," he said, running his hand up her rib cage and over her breast. His touch made her sigh and lean against him.

"But you will," she said, resting her head against his chest. "And you must believe me, I'll wait for you patiently, contentedly. When you're an old man and I'm an old woman, then perhaps you'll stay. The one thing I want you to know, to believe, is that this is no longer the kind of life I feel has been thrust upon me—not the kind of life I must endure. This is what I really want. I have my family, my work, pride in what I can do . . ." She lifted her head and looked up at him. "And you. There isn't anything more God could give me."

"You think it's a good idea to bring God into this?"

"I no longer think He begrudges me happiness. Did I tell you, Noel, that Ned Armstrong appeared?" He held her away and looked into her eyes. "Oh yes, he is alive. Sent on his way by Lilly, poor girl. The shock of seeing his face caused a remarkable thing to happen to me. I realized very suddenly that I could no longer punish myself

325

for what he did to me . . . to all of us. I tried to shoot him with Mother's Flintwood."

A big smile broke suddenly over Noel's face, and he laughed.

"Unfortunately, I didn't know how to load it, so I simply pointed it. The sight of him running away from me was the most pleasant thing I've ever seen in my life!"

"And he's gone?"

"Oh yes. Gone. Lilly informed me just after you arrived that she had visited him with Fletcher and threatened to expose him by sending a drawing of him to all the city newspapers in the country. What a good bluff she had! Although Fletcher had gone about the business of trying to find out if he had committed any crimes, nothing could be found. Still, Lilly assumed that there must be at least some angry women or fathers about. It must have been a good bluff."

He embraced her, holding her close. "You know how to load that gun yet?"

"I don't need it anymore, Noel. I'm not afraid of him. I don't care what he does or says. He can rot in Chicago—a great place for him to rot and far from here. I'm completely apart from him at last. Not free, but I have everything I—"

"But the hotel—"

"Impervious. It is Mother's hotel, not mine or Ned's. Lady Nesbitt will be replaced by Lilly. I am still what I have always been, what I want to be. I am a domestic woman. It is my love and my talent. I am found in the kitchen, in the halls, with the maids and clerks. It is Mother who greets the guests and bids them farewell, Lilly who labors over ledgers, newspapers, and correspondence. I visit Sophia at the Nesbitt House and she comes here, we sit and gossip and laugh over tea like old widows. I show young girls how to mop floors and wash sheets. What can Ned ever do to me?"

"Emily, there's something I have to tell you. I don't know how it'll sit."

She lifted her brows. "Do we need your tonic?"

"I don't think so," he said. He let go of her, and she backed up to the bed, sitting down, while he went to his carpet bag and retrieved a long, folded paper. He looked at it for a moment and then handed it to her.

She unfolded the paper and studied it, frowning. "It's a deed."

"The boardinghouse," he said. "Things were mighty bad when I left you that day. I didn't know what was going to happen to you.

I visited every bank in Philly till I found the one that held your mortgage. I wasn't even sure you had a mortgage. I told the banker to hold my offer to buy it, lock, stock, and barrel. I didn't let on that I knew you. I let them think I had money to invest and gave them a long list of property locations to check against their mortgages."

"Why would you do that?"

"You wouldn't let me help you. I got all stirred up and worried that you'd be in a snare—you'd need money, and the only thing you could sell would be that old house at a time when there weren't buyers. Emily, I wanted to rescue you right at the time when that was the last thing you'd let me do. I would have tricked you into marrying me if I could only think of a way."

"Oh, Noel. What a stubborn, wonderful man you are!"

"Keep it, Emily. Put it in your safe with your other papers. Maybe you'll never need it. Once it was your security—all yours and yours alone. If times ever get bad, you need a place."

She smiled at him, put the deed aside, opened her arms, and he entered her embrace.

The Armstrong Arms saw its way into 1882, a year filled with people from near and far and a growing peace at the center where Amanda hovered, queenlike, over her family. Katherine walked, Noel Padgett left Philadelphia in late October and was expected to return in May, and Andrew Devon was frequently invited to dinner, receptions, or musicales. Although Lilly was often obligated to accept the escort of some bachelor, she thrived on Andrew's presence. She had also constructed it. "Mama, you must remember Andrew Devon. At least when you feel it necessary to invite Wilson and Deanna Montaine. Remember, he has no family . . . no family at all." How easily done!

Patricia's behavior was similarly disciplined; she was given times and places and words to speak. Although her marriage to Dale Montaine was a hopeless joke, there were times that Amanda insisted the two of them stand together at a social event, or Patricia was not allowed out of her suite. "But we haven't lived under the same roof in a year," Patricia argued. "Why bother with any pretense now?"

"Since you never had many visitors, no one speculates much on where you live . . . nor does anyone care. But he is still your husband and will remain your husband, and I intend to protect the reputation of this hotel."

Lilly celebrated her twenty-third birthday with guests. There was food, dancing, and gifts in the Armstrong Arms ballroom. She was kept busy by dance partners, but the tune she hummed after her party was the music that she had shared with Andrew, in his arms. Two weeks later there was an afternoon reception for John Giddings; he was beginning the publication of his novel in monthly segments. A special edition was being financed by his newspaper, the *Philadelphia Inquirer*. The gathering was small—few would ever be personally acquainted with John Giddings; his novel was being published under the name John Patrick. The significance was not lost on Lilly.

In order to do a kindness to John and perhaps help the popularity of his forthcoming work, Emily had asked her mother to prepare this small party, introduce John to some of her old friends as an author, and announce the novel, *The Found Fortune*.

It was difficult for Lilly, for she had not forgotten the letters and knew they continued. Patricia was altogether too sure of herself, something that made Lilly very suspicious of what might be going on. John's admiration for her was distant but evident, his apparent shyness mere duplicity. They did not look at each other often, but when they did there was a kind of poorly restrained fever in John's eyes. That they never stepped nearer than twenty feet from each other only distressed Lilly; she found this peculiar romance of constant arousal without consummation bizarre. They had not been in the same room together since the boardinghouse, so far as Lilly knew. They did not touch, but what was between them, evident only to themselves and Lilly, was flushingly hot.

Andrew was present, as had become routine over the year. "Are you the least bit curious about this novel?" she asked him.

"I haven't had time for novels in years. I'm pleased for him."

"Do you notice anything between John and my sister?" she asked pointedly.

"No," he answered, glancing toward each one. "Is there something?"

"Yes," she answered, "but I don't know what it is. Exactly. Do you know there will be *real* people in this story? People who may not appreciate it. Ulysses Grant, Boss Tweed."

"The Boss is dead. He can't rise up and smite the author."

"Patricia indicated there could be others. *Found Fortune* has a familiar sound . . . I know a few people who found their fortunes in this city. And Patricia is very smug about something."

"I'll have to read it. Save the first portion for me, Lilly. I'll borrow it from you."

"When did you become so tight-fisted? Borrowing?"

"I won't be here for the first edition. I have to go to New York the first of May. I could be tied up there for two weeks."

Lilly's decision had been made. She thought the risk that Andrew would rebuff her far greater than any risk she might face as a result of her decision. She told her mother and grandmother that she was taking Elizabeth with her to New York to have dresses made and enjoy a brief holiday from work. That Lilly had never before taken time from work, even while touring Europe, did not raise a single eyebrow.

"Your loyalty is about to be tested as never before," Lilly told Elizabeth.

"That," said the assistant who had lost all her shyness over the past few years, "seems impossible!"

Lilly wrote only "Suite 511" on a note card she closed with wax. Elizabeth took it from her. "Lilly, are you absolutely certain?" she asked.

"I'm sorry, dear," she said. "I simply can't explain my feelings to you. You're going to have to let me have my way."

"Lilly, I've always trusted you about everything. I know something is going wrong with you now."

"No," Lilly said. And she thought, poor, poor Elizabeth! Taken along on a holiday and told, explicitly, there would be a man. She must not remember his face; she must pretend not to know his name; she must not hear a sound. Why? Elizabeth had asked. Why Mr. Devon? He's a family friend, a married man! But Lilly couldn't answer—the answer was six years long.

The sealed card was to be passed to an Astor bellman, who would put it in Mr. Devon's mail.

The May nights were warm. She could hear the sounds from the New York streets through her opened window. There were

329

horsecars, omnibuses, carriages, hawkers. Let one of those creaking wheels bring Andrew back from Wall Street, she silently begged. She believed there were women in his life, that he was routinely seduced as he went about a married man with no wife. Many would contentedly be a mistress to a man as rich and handsome as Andrew. Tonight, she thought, let there be no woman to whom he has committed his time.

She sat in her parlor, relaxed, comfortable in her white satin wrapper, her feet slippered and raised to the footstool. She held a book she didn't read and lit a lamp on the table beside her when the sun went down. Elizabeth said nothing to her this evening. Elizabeth had already harped and pleaded— Don't sacrifice yourself! Don't! But Lilly couldn't think of this as any kind of sacrifice. Lilly told her, "Don't stay with me then, if you can't trust me, if you can't respect me. I wouldn't blame you. You're a woman of high virtue. I am only a woman."

"I don't want you to be hurt," Elizabeth had replied. "Talk to your mother about this need you feel! Mrs. Armstrong would know what to—"

"Need?" Lilly had questioned, laughter lighting up her face. Oh Lord, Lilly thought, it is so far past that! So long ago was the curiosity of a young woman, a girl. Far behind her was that first flirtation with desire. Need? This was as filled with purpose as the building of the Arms. This was not something Lilly felt she needed. She had proved quite well she could do without a man. This was something she wanted.

She wondered if Elizabeth would fail her, compromise or trick her. But she did not. There was a knock, the door was opened, Elizabeth's voice said, "The sitting room, Mr. Devon," and Lilly's heart began to race.

He stood just inside the frame and Elizabeth pulled the double doors closed. He looked at her for a long moment. Finally she stood to face him. He made no effort to cross the eight feet that separated them. He had never seen her like this; her satin hugged the outline of her naked body and her thick auburn hair was loose and flowing over her shoulders.

"I want you to teach me that kiss again," she told him.

"You may have finally gone too far, Lilly," he said, his voice thick.

"I hope so, Andrew. I'm tired of trying to make do. There just isn't anyone else for me. Grandmother says I refuse to compromise."

"And in that, will be compromised."

"Then you know what is intended? But do you *understand?*"

"I've known you a long time. I know how you think. This is—"

"Victoria Woodhull said this problem of sexual freedom is the greatest to challenge the human mind, she said it is only decent when it involves reciprocal love . . . and I know of no marriage that does. Not yet."

"Woodhull," he muttered.

"And George Sand said that love outside of marriage is more lasting than—"

"Quote me Tennessee Claflin, Lilly, quick! 'Until we recognize the rights of nature, until we provide in a normal and proper way for every passion of the soul . . .' You *know* I am not free!"

"I am. I want freedom. I want my hotel, my family, my work . . . you. I think they're all right—they spoke of the hypocrisy of marriage and you're living it. They said that free love—"

"Free love? You little fool! The cost is so high that even you cannot pay it!"

She shrugged lamely. "Nor can I seem to meet the cost of not having you. That has become expensive in loneliness and emptiness."

"You stalked me. You played your seduction so carefully. All that business of having me come into the family—"

"You were less lonely when you did. I was less lonely."

"You spent so much time, Lilly. Did I appear that difficult to conquer?"

"Stubborn. Pig-headed. Will you come?" she asked him, opening her arms. "I could follow you, sit in wait for you at this hotel or that. Eventually . . ."

He walked toward her, tossing aside his hat as he went. He slipped an arm about her waist, and his mouth was just above hers. "What is it you hope to gain, Lilly?"

"Joy," she said, her breath warm on his lips. "Pleasure. Those things I can't find. That part of me that can't be complete alone. It's you I love. I always have."

"And what of heartache? Desperate, lonely nights apart? What of the pain of *lies?*"

"Worse lies than the ones we used before? Worse heartache than

331

trying, before the world, not to look at each other? Worse than those evenings I have to spend with bores who want my business or my money? Oh damn, I took your advice. I wanted to love someone else!"

He lowered his lips to hers, gently touching, tenderly tugging at her lower lip. "Lilly, Lilly, I'm more married than ever. Is that the kind of life you wish on yourself? On me?"

"No," she said, slipping her arms around his neck. "What I want for us is far greater—and far more impossible."

"But this?"

"Tell me you don't love me! Tell me you can find someone else and be happy. Tell me you're content to be alone—"

"I love you," he said. "That's why I tried to protect you from this."

"Don't," she said.

He kissed her lips, her neck, her ear. He slipped the wrapper away from her neck and teased the untouched flesh of her shoulder. His hands caressed her back and found her buttocks, pulling her hard against him. She could feel him; all the power of him pressed against her while she reacquainted herself with the rangy flavor of his mouth.

He released her enough to untie the belt at her waist. "You're settling for less than you could have," he said, kissing her now and then. He slipped his hands inside her wrapper, feeling her skin, her back, her hips. This was something she had dreamed, his hands on her—firm, decisive, strong hands. He trembled! She felt the same ache in her nipples that her fantasies brought, the same pulling in her secret place, a place she intended to be a shared secret.

She put her hands against his chest, pushing him away. She took his hand and led him to the bedroom. The coverlet was pulled back on the bed, the pillows fluffed, the curtains drawn. The lamp had not been lit; Andrew did so, but turned the wick low so that the room was shadowed, like dusk. Lilly stood beside the bed, her wrapper hanging loosely closed.

Andrew kept his eyes on hers as he pulled off his tie, tossing it. He began to unbutton his shirt, tugging it out of his pants. He had to sit on the bed to remove his shoes, which he kicked aside. Finally he stood before her, barefoot and bare-chested. Her eyes filled with the sight of his chest, pale and broad and sleek, a tuft of hair in the center and a few wayward sprigs around his nipples. His hands were on his breeches. "This cannot be undone, Lilly," he said. "This is another kind of life."

She closed her eyes, tilting her head backwards, silent. A kind of life she had been afraid to imagine. She didn't know what sort of secrets awaited, but she knew she was sorely, inconsolably unfinished. Any number of men would have been pleased by this invitation, but there was only one kind of man for whom she felt passion. It was hardly a coincidence that it would be Andrew—it could be no other. The circumstances that made him the worst choice also made him the only one: her equal in passion and intelligence; a poor-boy achiever, driven; a man married to a terrible woman whom he could not only forgive, but care for; a man tender enough of conscience to avoid her, discourage her, and refuse her.

His hands entered her robe at the waist, slowly moving upward separating the fabric, and she felt the satin of her cover sing across her skin as it flowed over her shoulders, down her arms, and fell behind her. Gone! Her breath came hard; his fingers were soft. She felt his body against hers. She pulled his head harder against her breasts when he kissed her there. Finally, he lowered her gently to the bed. It was while he knelt above her that she saw the naked body of a man for the very first time in her life, and at first the sight awed her. His legs, strong, bent, muscled, were covered with coarse black hair, and out of the thick batch below his belly had sprung that scepter that would soon be a part of her. She thought it a fearful, wonderful thing, and innocent as she was, wondered how he had managed to conceal it so well!

He made a study of her skin, each touch was the first touch. Lilly had tried the lips of others—unsatisfactory. She had been touched and grasped; she had slapped a few faces. But this was the thrill she had waited for. Passion is a thing of the mind. Andrew, though handsome and strong, was no more so than many others. For six long years she had wanted only him.

His lips were moist and tempting on the inside of her arms, at her breast, her belly. His hands on her were smooth, exquisite. His eyes, when they looked into hers, were a wilder green than she had ever seen. His features were hard as stone; it appeared he worked, and the strain was powerful. The longing she felt was intense, but nothing to compare to what she felt when he touched her inner thighs, her inner sanctum. His fingers, deft and clever, began to massage,

333

stroke, tickle and tease. The longing grew and grew, like a fire stoked, a flame fueled. She could not be silent; she moaned the incredible pleasure he brought her and felt herself grow soft and wet and hungry while his kneading grew more fierce.

He lay beside her, on his side, and kissed her deeply, consuming her with the power of a kiss so desperate, so strong, she became lost in its darkness, in a space of mindlessness that seemed to billow like clouds around her head. Her hands sought the muscle of his chest and arms and lower, finally daring to touch that wonderful thing. It pulsed, warm and firm in her hand, and a growl of pleasure came from his lips against hers. And then her world burst into a flame of light, and she shook from it. She imagined she was lifted from the bed and her body became suddenly, astonishingly tense. What wild, terrible, impossible pleasure! It almost hurt, it was so profound. "Andrew!" she exclaimed.

He murmured softly against her lips, his fingers yet experiencing the shuddering response of her flesh. "Yes, Lilly," he said, holding her closely.

She was not nearly recovered when he raised himself above her, his knees between hers. She locked her fingers into his thick, dark hair and drew his lips to hers. He lowered himself and began to probe. Her softness there, the slick invitation was still not enough. The resistance against his entry was tough. "Are you sure you want me to take this, too?" he asked. "I can make you happy without—"

"Please!" she insisted, clutching him.

"We have to have done with this, Lilly. Hold me." She complied, her arms around his chest, meeting across his back. She felt his hands on her buttocks as he tilted her up to meet him. Her knees bent to brace herself, and he made a quick, frightful stab into her. She felt the membrane that was called virtue burst and her eyes teared from pain that was burning and quick.

He held her fast and still. She sighed against his shoulder. Done. He was hers now. She was his. The fullness in her nearly caused her to cry. The pain slowly gave way to a minor discomfort; the discomfort was soon lost. Andrew kissed her lips gently, a tender touch. "Are you all right, darling?"

She looked into his eyes and saw what she'd dreamt of seeing: the glow of happiness was there. The fulfillment of this coupling was not hers alone. She smiled up at him and gently touched the hair at his temples.

He moved, a slight rocking that soon began to sweep her into that feeling she now understood; the longing would rise and build and explode. But when she would have seized it and ridden with him, he withdrew, lay atop her where his manhood throbbed and spilled. Lilly knew enough of coupling to understand what he had done. The tears that smarted in her eyes were of loss. She could not reasonably have his child. In her mind she had traded that possibility for this. To keep him, she must not hope for a baby.

19

*A*ndrew awoke in the morning to a strange humming. He stretched out a hand toward Lilly, found the bed empty, and opened his eyes. He looked through the posters to an amazing vision beyond the foot of the bed. Lilly hummed the tune from their last dance. Naked, breathtaking with auburn hair curling down her back, her hands held up to accommodate an invisible partner, she danced. Danced and turned and swayed, her hair bouncing, her long, slender legs carrying her around in a circle. He laughed—still there was the child.

Her eyes darted over her shoulder to see him awake, but she paused only briefly and continued her gliding dance. His eyes filled with the sight of her, just as he had filled the night with the texture and taste of her body. He sat up, the cover drawn to his waist, and rested his arms on his raised knees. "You're mad," he said, but he smiled as though he had been given a gift.

She twirled. Her eyes were half closed; her lips curved in a smile. Andrew had never seen a more beautiful sight. He threw back the cover, stepped out of the bed, and joined her. A chambermaid would have fainted dead: two naked dancers in the early, pink, light of dawn dancing to a woman's humming. And he held her at arm's length, the length he would employ in a formal dance. She made the music for their dance until she burst into laughter and embraced him, hugging him fiercely, joyfully.

"I have never really seen the morning before!" she said, her face bright from a night of passion.

"I have never had such a dance!"

"Do you think we'll be consumed by laughter at Grandmother's next party? Oh, Andrew, just think! Now these melodies have new meaning for me."

He ran a hand down her hair, free and wild.

"Are you happy, Andrew?" she asked. But he turned away from her. She reached out to his shoulder, turning him back. "I won't let you be unhappy! I won't let you spoil it! It's too late—you said so yourself!"

Reluctantly, slowly, his smile grew. "Oh, Lilly, I don't think you know how rare a woman you are."

"Don't I?" she asked, almost skipping away from him to pick up her wrapper from the floor. "What can you tell me about women, Andrew? Have there been many?"

"No," he laughed, "not so many."

"I'm sure this sort of thing happens quite often. What a clever secret was kept from me! But I am the one who is well known in the Astor—I can't have a strange man in my room when the maids come. You'll have to go. Now." She stopped, looking him over. She gazed over his body, from his toes to his nose. "Oh, Andrew."

"What did you expect? You know I'm not a eunuch."

She understood now, how it gained power, lost power, and it made her laugh to remember her first thoughts. "Not a eunuch, but you are certainly greedy. Dress. Poor Elizabeth may not have survived the night."

"What have you told her?"

"Hardly anything, and the poor darling doesn't understand at all. She is ordered to keep the secret, that's all. I'm sure she feels I'm a fallen woman at long last." She tied her belt and picked up his shirt. "Andrew," she questioned seriously, "is there another way? To prevent a baby?"

He took the shirt from her and tossed it aside, taking her into his arms and kissing her in the way that made her forget sending him away. "We'll talk about that. There is nothing quick we can do. Do you mean to promise me more such nights?"

"Enough to fill your life."

"Lilly, will you make me a promise? A real one?"

She tilted her head and looked at him strangely, finally nodding.

"When the time this is not a good thing for you comes, will you tell me?"

"Oh, Andrew! Do you have to spoil the morning?"

"Promise," he demanded.

"If that day ever comes, yes. Now dress. I have to visit the couturiere since I've come on the pretense of having dresses made. I'm staying in New York, you know. For as long as you are. I hope you're in no hurry!"

"Do you intend to keep me from work?" he asked, shrugging into his shirt and finally accepting his pants. She didn't answer immediately. The devil was in her eyes.

"If possible," she said.

"I can't keep you if I'm poor. You'll become weary of a man who clutches your wealth and lays about doing nothing."

"If I could keep you a prisoner, I would. I'll have dinner here at nine. That will have to do, for now." She walked to the small writing desk and opened a drawer. She pulled out a key. "You needn't knock," she said.

He took it. "How long have you known it would come to this?"

"Six years. I didn't know when or how." She put her arms around his neck. "Andrew, you tried to be wise. I tried to forget. I simply don't know what else there is. If we could be together—"

"Shhh," he said, the finger on her lips then replaced by his mouth. "Give me some time. Perhaps there is a way. Let me think about this."

"But you won't leave me?"

"I can't," he said. "I told you—it can't be undone."

Elizabeth's fork brought her eggs to her lips stiffly. She lifted her coffee slowly. She avoided Lilly's eyes. Finally, disconcerted, Lilly slapped her own knife onto the small breakfast table in her sitting room. "Very well, Elizabeth, get it out. Anything you want to know—ask it and be done with it. I can't take a lot of this."

"There's nothing," the woman said evenly.

"Oh hell, there's plenty. Is it because he's married? Is that it? Well, his wife is ill, you know, and will probably never recover—"

"And if she does?"

"If she recovers, he will divorce her! You just don't understand all the circumstances! I've been in love with Andrew since I was a girl! We've always wanted to be together. It was never possible!"

"Lilly, this way is wrong! I heard what you told him, about Woodhull, Sand. I'm afraid you'll be punished!"

"I've *been* punished, you old ninny! Elizabeth, I *love* him. Far too much! Don't you see," she asked more softly, "that this isn't really what I hoped for? Don't you think I'd rather marry him, have his children, sleep beside him every night? Don't you know how hard I tried to care for someone else—anyone else? Oh, Bethie, darling, I don't want to be a fallen woman! A mistress! I want to be a wife, a mother! What choices are there for someone like me—to pretend to love some poor man so I can have a family or to trade a family to be with the man I love?"

Tears came to Elizabeth's eyes.

"Bethie, I've thought about this for a long, long time. If Andrew thought I had surrendered, he would run. He loves me, he can't bear to think of my hurt. But I don't want to live my whole life with this one part empty. I tricked him, you know. Andrew is too good to let me sacrifice myself. This is all I can have of him, all there is left after . . . If I'm happy, can't you be happy for me?"

"If I could pretend he was your husband—"

"That's what I pretend," Lilly said softly. "Perhaps one day it can be true. I was simply too afraid to wait for him any longer. I was afraid I would hurt inside for the rest of my life."

"And all that business about free love and hypocrisy and—"

"Hogwash. I *do* know that what I'm doing isn't perfect. But what I had was less so."

"Oh, Lilly, can we keep everyone from knowing?"

"We have all this time, darling. We will a little longer." She reached for Elizabeth's hand. "Now don't worry. Andrew's a lovely man who is very kind to you and a great pleasure to be around. You'll see, everything will be all right. If it becomes too much for you, I'll give you whatever settlement you want."

"I could ask you for a fortune! I could threaten to—"

Lilly burst into laughter. "Oh, Bethie! Would I have brought you with me for *this* if I were unsure of your love? All I really have to do is keep you busy, make you laugh, and give you books! One day you'll build your own hotel and go to the lending library looking for a good assistant!"

Elizabeth reluctantly smiled. "Are you so sure?"

Lilly's eyes glowed. "That little bit of doubt and fear is gone, now. This is how it will be."

Elizabeth had heard those words before. When Lilly made a decision, there was no discussion. "This idea of being happy," Elizabeth said, "is reminiscent of Patricia's—"

"Patricia's quest for happiness? Lord almighty! Do us a favor, Bethie, make no final judgment on Andrew and me just now—and don't even bother to mistake an *affair* for happiness! Affairs can become hopeless, you know. Endless, dire, hopeless, dreary exchanges of love between two people not allowed to be in love. That's why I've done what I've done, will do what I will do. Because what I think would give me total happiness is completely out of my reach.

"Patricia will never be happy, you see, because she keeps thinking if one more person will do one more thing for her she will finally be happy! I want only what is possible—this is all that is possible. Before you decide I'm crazy or wicked or selfish or as impossible to please as Patricia, just consider that I might be taking the only joy there is and making it enough. I *do* love him!"

At nine that night, when Lilly was in her bedroom and dinner had been set up in the sitting room, Elizabeth heard the key in the lock. She waited just inside the door for Andrew to enter. He smiled, closed the door, put his key in his pocket, and stretched a bouquet toward Elizabeth.

"I'll put them in water for you, and then I'll—"

"They're for you, Elizabeth," Andrew said. "I should give you gems. I know what we're asking of you."

"You must not ever hurt her, Mr. Devon," she said solemnly. "Lilly is the most important person in my life. She is my dearest friend. I love her too much to see her hurt."

He made a half bow. "I share your feelings, Elizabeth."

Lilly did not lament those things she was without. She could not attend the theater with Andrew, nor dine in public with him without her entire family present to shield her from gossip. But she could have him in her arms, in her heart. Her eyes were brighter than ever, her laughter quick and joyful. Two weeks in New York put something of a strain on Elizabeth, but she endured bravely and slowly overcame her worries. It didn't take long for her to become a conspirator. Lilly grew radiant and Elizabeth was a witness to the good health and vitality that love provided.

In time even Elizabeth was converted by Andrew's charm and thoughtful gifts. After the first flush of passion had been spent and the lovers were not so desperate to be alone together, it was not unusual for the three of them to share a Saturday luncheon or a late dinner in Lilly's suite. It was impossible to ignore the fact that Lilly thrived.

In June Elizabeth accompanied Lilly to Saratoga for a week— a week spent enjoying days at the races, evenings of music, and every night by nine Andrew would arrive, and Elizabeth would excuse herself to leave Lilly and Andrew alone together.

In August Lilly returned to New York with Elizabeth, but this time the assistant was left in Lilly's suite at the Astor. Andrew had made provisions for a small, secluded house on a strip of beach near East Hampton where there would be no servants, no work, no distractions.

Lilly hired a trap and, following directions left for her at the hotel, was taken to the cottage on a Saturday morning. The driver was instructed to return a week later at the same time. The little stone cottage was surrounded by trees and flowers, water for cooking and washing came from a well. Smoke from a stove curled pleasantly from a chimney. Her bags were left on the stoop. No one was about.

She dismissed the carriage, unlatched the door, looked inside, and smiled. The interior was compact with settee, cold hearth, floral draperies. There were two chairs and a small wood table, on it a vase filled with flowers from the vine outside the door. A kettle sat on a wood stove, and through a doorway she could see a bed, a wardrobe in which some of Andrew's clothing hung, and a commode holding a pitcher and basin. The cottage was simple and quiet. Though far smaller, it was as homey and neat as her mother's boardinghouse. Sunlight poured through three small windows and an ocean breeze cooled her warm cheeks. She walked through the small cottage, touching the worn furniture, tugging off her gloves. She looked out the window to see the sea stretch before her to infinity.

How could he have known, she wondered, that this tiny cottage would please her more than anything? She had seen richer, larger homes as the coach brought her; she could afford a fancy house as well as Andrew. Yet he had chosen something modest and quaint.

She heard him whistling as he came up the path to the house and she felt a familiar, delicious anticipation that she knew would never go away. When he entered the cottage, his arms heavy with wood for their stove, she filled her eyes with him. His fancy shoes were gone; he wore gardener's boots. No starched shirt with studs, but a white flannel work shirt opened at the neck and rolled up to above his elbows. His breeches were snug and worn. His hair was tousled and a rough beard had begun to darken his face.

He smiled at her only briefly before carrying the wood to the bin, then turned to her. "Are we really, truly alone?"

"All alone," he said. "For a week. And for other weeks, whenever it's possible. I bought it, Lilly. It's ours."

For an instant it occurred to Lilly to send a message to the Astor, sending Elizabeth home. She briefly considered never leaving, staying forever, washing his clothes and cooking his meals and having his babies. Who would know? Would they come for her, carry her away, and lock her up, a mad woman, drunk on love and pleasure?

"I know what you're thinking," he said, embracing her and beginning the delightful task of unbuttoning her blouse, starting at the neck. "This might be all we ever have."

"Do you read my mind?"

"Our mind, Lilly. Don't let greed cause you to make bad choices for yourself. You can still have both—work and love."

"I wonder sometimes, how do lovers work? How do they stand

a few hours apart? Does this hunger ever cease? Is there ever a final, glorious moment that fills the cup forever?"

He laughed at her, opening her blouse. "The cup is filled again and again, Lilly. Every morning it is magically empty! Forever is in the mind." He kissed her deeply. "Forever is how I love you. Take this off. I want to love you in sunlight. I've been here for four days, waiting, aching with impatience."

"It's been two months, darling. The same amount of time for me as for you. If we could be together all the time, would we get tired of this?" she asked, scampering off to the bedroom, pulling at her clothing.

He followed, tossing his shirt to the floor, trying to balance well enough to tug off boots, unfasten breeches. He pulled the pins from her hair, tumbled with her on the bed, unmindful of opened windows and unlocked doors in a place he had determined was completely safe.

Lilly's pleasure was quick; he had but to touch her to bring her that blinding, amazing joy of fulfillment. Lilly did not know what kind of lover she was; she looked to Andrew for the instruction he was more than pleased to give. She felt as though the two of them had created this. She had no way of knowing that her abandon was rare, her freedom remarkable. She had talked to him of her sister's dread of coupling, a thing Lilly had decided was due only to the absence of love.

"I love to watch your face when that happens to you," he told her. "You just don't know, do you, how many women never feel any power, any satisfaction, anything like that? Look at me." She would then watch his face, his intense eyes, and her body would quiver like the strings of a musical instrument, her lips would part, her cheeks would flush, her eyes grow large just before they closed. He would smile, as thrilled by her achievement as she; her fulfillment caused her face to glow as if there were a candle within. There was nothing so great to him as making her feel all that could be felt. Before he would take his own pleasure, he coaxed her into many freeing, exhausting, shuddering orgasms.

Lilly had long ago spurned nonsense about false modesty, and no one had ever shared the secrets of the bedroom with her. Besides what she had read in John Giddings' letters to her sister, her knowledge was all at the hands of Andrew. She didn't know about taboos; she couldn't be shocked when she was filled with trust. Therefore, she didn't know that Andrew experimented himself, did things with her he had never before done, pushed himself farther than he had ever tried. This was the single danger here; it had nothing to do with pulling closed the curtains or locking the door.

When he opened her legs and put his mouth on her, it never occurred to her to resist or decline. He was only good to her. She moaned with incredible pleasure that was spontaneous, wild, convulsing. He lifted himself quickly, plunging into her. She saw his face taut with the work of control, his eyes pinched closed as they often were, taking in all the wonder of being bonded with her. But this time he had gone too far. He had never attempted to share that moment with her, but had always treated her first, many times, then finally himself. She was more than hot and deep to him; he was in her grip and felt her pulsing, throbbing pleasure surround him. He was too late. He lost himself inside her, and when he knew it was done, he could do nothing but push himself deeper.

Lilly felt not only the heat, but the beauty of it. She lost her breath for a moment; her body was damp and hot. He moaned deeply and lay his head down on her breast, trying to keep his weight from crushing her. When the trembling stopped, she gently stroked his hair.

"Damn, Lilly, I'm sorry!"

"Oh, Andrew . . ."

"I meant to be so careful with you." He began to pull away.

"It's too late, darling," she whispered. "Don't move now. You can't fix it. We'll be lucky this time. It can't be undone."

He touched her lips and lay with her, quietly, a part of her. There was no talk, only the tired breathing of spent lovers. He relaxed, and his body lost power. They might have dozed. Time was gone. After a long while, he lifted his head to kiss her lips.

It had been his privilege to teach her the kiss; he had taught her this erotic motion of lips and tongues. She touched her tongue to his mouth; she opened her lips and felt his heat inside her mouth. He regained his power while still inside of her. Her hands were firm on his back, moving slowly from his shoulders to his buttocks. She grasped him, pulling him hard into her. She opened herself more, bending her knees to give him depth. He moved, slowly at first, considering what they were doing. He looked into her eyes. "Oh, what the hell," he said. "Pray it's a good day for bad judgment."

345

And he proceeded to move, skillfully, slowly, quickly, slowly. Thrusting, rotating inside of her, until they could share the moment again. When her pleasure clutched him, he let himself go.

That one day he lost control, but not again. Still, the week was idyllic. They walked on the beach. Farther south there were more houses, but all inhabitants were strangers who might have thought them a newly married couple. They cooked their own meals, played in the surf, collected fresh berries, talked late into the night under clear, starlit skies, and slept late in the morning. Lilly grew lazy and content. "I'll stay here forever," she said, and he didn't argue with her.

Since they didn't have to separate and go to their own quarters, there was finally time to talk about many things. She told him of the letters she had read; he asked about John Giddings' novel. But since Andrew had entered her life as a lover and all troubles and curiosities had fled, she had forgotten about the novel and her sister. Nothing could disturb her. She asked him about Brenda, but what she ultimately learned about was the childhood that led him to his marriage.

Andrew had no self-pity, though his early years would have certainly given cause. Lilly was the only one ever to be told the truth—that the man he knew as his father had been the priest his mother loved. He remembered the giant, tender man to this day; he had loved him. Later, he thought he hated him. His mother took him to Philadelphia when the priest was gone. Andrew shared a room and a bed with his mother until the age of seven, when she died of a winter illness; she died as he held her hand and wept.

The stone beach house reminded him of the little cottage outside Dublin. In those early childhood years he had been happy, well fed, and loved.

Andrew's mother had been one of the Montaine maids, and it was Wilson who had buried her in a decent plot and let Andrew stay and work. He took an interest in the orphan and let him be tutored along with his own motherless son. Soon he took pride in Andrew's accomplishments and gave him more room to study, work, grow. Despite Dale's jealousy and frequent harassment, Andrew had a chance to be a success.

"It wasn't until Brenda became ill that I realized money wasn't the only thing I needed. I had been hungry, you see. My mother died in poverty. I had no food and thought I would have nowhere to sleep. It wasn't ambition that drove me, Lilly. It was nothing but fear. I was afraid to die hungry."

"What are you afraid of now?"

"Of dying lonely."

When Saturday morning came, she grudgingly packed her satchel and put on her good dress. Andrew planned to stay one more day to close up the house. When they heard the sound of the carriage coming up the drive, her eyes became glassy with tears.

"If you cry, I'll sell the cottage," he threatened.

"I only want to stay forever," she replied. "Don't be hard on me now . . . after this wonderful, wonderful week."

"You promised you could do this—take whatever time there is. Isn't this more than we hoped for? Lilly, if the pain is worse than the—"

"No! When can we come again?"

"I don't know. Don't make Amanda suspicious. We'll see each other. We'll think about the next time."

"Will you come to the hotel? Soon?"

"As soon as I can," he promised.

She spent one night at the Astor with Elizabeth, and they took the Sunday afternoon train back to Philadelphia. Lilly watched the countryside move past her. "I have discovered something, Bethie."

"Mm?"

"There is something more difficult than living without him." Tears came to her eyes. "Leaving him."

Lilly had always been strong, stronger than the fears that paralyzed ordinary women and bold enough to grasp desires that were treacherous for many. Her spirit perked the first time Andrew joined the family for dinner. She reminded herself that she had far more than she had dreamed of a few years ago. She had not known in the beginning that she would become desperate for Andrew, that the separations would stretch out for too long. For the first time in her life she struggled against greed. All the while she built the hotel that was fast becoming one of the most popular in the Northeast, she had been driven by ambition. But she was smart enough to know greed.

She had never before seen herself as susceptible, but she was greedy for her lover.

She sometimes thought she would faint from longing. It took every ounce of will, control, to keep from begging Andrew to take time, soon, for the cottage. Andrew came to dinner, and when the family had temporarily moved away from the dining room, he whispered across the table. When he admitted his own desire was as fierce, she was so relieved she laughed.

"I've taken a flat in the city," he told her. "I can't get away for long, I can't leave work, but if I'm not alone with you soon—"

An almost wild laugh escaped her.

"Lilly!" he said, looking around.

"I had been berating myself for being so wanton!" she whispered back. She grinned, her eyes sparkling with devilish delight. "You're insatiable!"

"I swore it would never come to this! A shabby flat in the city and disguises while—"

"Not a moment too soon!" she exclaimed.

The flat was not just a hideaway for illicit lovers, however. It was far more. They almost always made love there, but more important was the time they could be alone to talk, to touch without the danger of being seen. Almost twice a week, on the excuse of shopping, visiting the library, attending some lecture or tea, Lilly had enough of Andrew to build a very satisfactory love affair.

It seemed that she was not far wrong in seeing satisfaction all around her. Katherine had her second birthday and toddled about the apartments; Amanda entertained as frequently as she liked and enjoyed the hotel more every year; Mr. Padgett had returned to Philly from the end of May to mid-October; and guests came and went grateful for their treatment and the fine accommodations. Everyone, it seemed, was content. But Lilly had not looked far enough, for that small thing that remained a bristling irritant came into full rage in early December. Patricia. It was Dale Montaine who upset the tea cart.

It was on a quiet, late Sunday afternoon when the smell of roast beef permeated the apartments and all within were relaxed and happy that he burst upon them, waving a sheaf of pages in his hands.

"I've read it!" he announced, his face contorted. He stared across the sitting room at Patricia. "It's *you!*"

348

"Dale, what is it?" Emily asked, picking up Katherine and looking worriedly at her son-in-law.

"Dale, come in and stop all the commotion," Amanda said testily, dropping her newspaper on her lap.

"None of you has read it?" he asked.

Lilly was running figures up and down a tablet, a frequent obsession of hers, to determine the best charges for occupancy. She knew that Dale was holding John's novel and looked at Patricia. Her sister did what she had always done. She lifted her chin in a dare.

"John Giddings' book," Dale said. "At first I wasn't sure. Through four segments I suspected, but now I know for certain. Patricia is the heroine. Patricia, who has always been completely misunderstood. Patricia, the pure of heart and conscience who—"

"Dale! Come now, what are you saying?" Emily asked anxiously.

He threw the chapters that had been published monthly since the June before. "Read it for yourself!" he said. "Just have a look at what she's done to us all!" He turned angrily away from them and slammed the door as he left.

Lilly felt fear stain her cheeks. John could not successfully publish anything like the letters he had written to Patricia. She put aside her tablet and went to pick up the pages that constituted John's novel.

"Do you have any idea what he's talking about, Patricia?" Emily asked.

"Yes, Mama," she said sweetly. "The woman John used in his book was fashioned in appearance to look like me."

"In appearance?" Amanda questioned suspiciously, removing her spectacles.

"There are a few other similarities."

"Difficult ones for Dale to live with?"

"Perhaps," Patricia said. "But what's the difference? John's novel is becoming *extremely* successful. It's going to be published in New York, Boston, San Francisco, and Chicago. He's had offers to publish bound copies from every publisher in the country. He will soon be more famous than Mark Twain. He's becoming very *rich*."

Lilly ruffled the pages. "If there's a hotel in this novel, Patricia," she said, "you will soon be homeless." And with that she excused herself to read.

And there she was: Patricia. Dale couldn't possibly be more right, except about Patricia's character. The hotel had not appeared, but still could as the chapters continued. Here was a young, virtuous, beautiful woman, the daughter of a shrewish seamstress who could barely serve a table to her two fatherless children—a son and daughter—who was trapped into marrying a rich, impotent drunkard just moments before it was discovered she was really the daughter of an aristocratic man—an unknown descendent of an important family. But this poor, trapped creature was too late in her fortune to claim the man she truly loved and wanted, a large, muscled, handsome journalist who had been very attracted to her, but had failed to get up the courage to speak of his intentions until—too late! She'd been given to the beast by her terrible, insensitive mother!

Lilly might have laughed had the poor likeness not disgusted her. Many of the characters were based on fact, the impotent drunkard was the son of a parvenu who made his unscrupulous rise to a financial empire by eavesdropping in the kitchens of the wealthy when he was a poor orphan who sharpened knives. He took advantage of conversations he had overheard and cleverly learned how to buy property not yet for sale, preying on the disadvantaged rich. There was Boss Tweed, fictionalized, who took so much money out the budget for building government buildings that he was said to be the richest man in the world. The president of the United States, though not named Ulysses S. Grant, was a large, bulky, mustachioed man, stupid in government, greedy in personal affairs, who used the secretary of the treasury to earn millions in a fraudulent gold scam. Familiar families, well-known tales. But the most interesting were the tales of the heroine, Chloe Tillets, a woman of tender heart and solid conscience who constantly had to fight her mother's greed, her brother's ambition, her grand*father's* control, and whose poor baby was taken from her. She was often described as a victim of her own glorious beauty and sweetness.

The novel itself was good reading; Lilly did not doubt the reasons for its popularity. There was a strong current of sexual titillation so that even Lilly began to hope that poor Chloe could one day have her desperate would-be lover. She almost longed to see how poor Chloe survived, taken for granted, abused, and misunderstood as she was. Now Lilly knew what had been in Patricia's letters besides erotic passages and declarations of chaste longing—the story of her life as *she* saw it. The victim of a grasping family, the poor wretch was forced to make the best of her sad lot despite the cruelty that surrounded her. And of course this loving, kind, pure heroine was under constant threat of being homeless if she did not behave.

It was at breakfast the next morning that Lilly gave her review. "Besides Boss Tweed, our past president Mr. Grant, and Wilson Montaine, I can't really say for sure which characters we are. It's a rather remarkable story and very obvious that Patricia had shared her point of view with the author. You'd better read it yourselves and see what you decide. My opinion is that my sister's illusions are intact and monstrous. And John is poisoned beyond recovery. I'm sorry. It could harm us. If a hotel is constructed in the novel, our reputation could be doomed."

20

$\mathcal{T}$he hotel in the novel was called the Belvedere Palace. It appeared in the January 1883 installment. A newspaper publisher in New York began to serialize the novel, following John's home city of Philly in the publication. In February Boston and Chicago and San Francisco newspapers began. St. Louis was interested. The novel would run for three years in thirty-six installments. Then it would be bound and sold. The most interesting and least known fact about the story was that John and his publishers agreed to make changes for the second publication in New York based on Philadelphian reactions; interest had lagged in the chapter following the villain's death, and the character who strongly resembled Wilson Montaine was resurrected in New York, recreated in another similar type for Philly. In essence, different novels were appearing all over the country, and when John had determined the best version, it would be contained in the bound book. Chloe Tillets was adored.

Patricia's resemblance to the heroine was noticed by strangers, people who had never suffered the piercing wound left by her selfish acts. When she was abroad shopping, people stared at her. Sometimes a man or woman would sheepishly approach her and tentatively ask, "Have you ever heard of a woman named Chloe Tillets?" She would smile demurely, the gentle, subdued smile of Chloe, and say, "Yes, of course." They would then comment on the resemblance, and she would explain it was possible, as she was well acquainted with John Patrick, an old family friend and renowned writer.

This was much to her liking, of course, but all too often for Patricia that was where the personal questions stopped. The curious wanted only to know about the fascinating novelist. What was he like? Was he handsome and muscular? Why did he hide himself away, uncomfortable with fame? Where did he work? Was the story based on fact? Patricia became impatient the moment attention drifted away from her. Still, she was as close as ever she would be to fame and admiration for those precious moments she was confused with John's heroine.

Those who knew her and were still much in evidence as her grandmother's oldest and dearest friends, the Sinclairs, Lancasters, Biddles, et al., turned their backs when they saw her. They did not have starring roles in the novel, but what was said about their less than virtuous society had not settled very well. At the hotel she was forced to trade fame for solitude. Her family was not pleased with the whole event of the novel. And John, though he still wrote to her, was hard at work; he could not abandon the story. He had lessons in publishing that could not be learned in the simple writing—the important one being that Chloe did not get the sympathy she deserved when one of her chief abusers vanished. In order to fulfill his dreams of publishing a great novel, he was not at liberty to spend all his time in pursuit of Patricia. John was busily rewriting. And he was no longer welcome at the Arms.

Lilly was amused to be portrayed as a capitalistic man, Emily was upset that she was a villainous seamstress who wanted her daughter to marry into society, and Amanda was nothing less than enraged by her character—a blustering man who had plotted revenge against the society that had failed him, returned to take ruthless advantage of them all, and kept them in a merciless grip as the proprietor of the only fashionable luxury hotel in the country.

The installments came, twelve more in 1883. It reached its half-way mark. It was much talked about, and even newspapers reported on its popularity.

"Why should I bother to come up here for dinner if no one will pay the least attention to me?" Patricia had whined.

"Don't you get enough attention imitating a virtuous young woman?" Amanda had coldly returned.

Thus, Patricia was seen less and less. She was sometimes on the grounds, parasol protecting her ivory skin from the sun, but she was seldom in the company of the women in her family. Many meals were served in her suite . . . sometimes there was a meal for two . . . but if it was John, he was sneaked in through the back stairs. Her treatment of Katherine was heartbreaking. The little girl talked all the time. When she saw Patricia, she would grin, clap her hands, and cry out, "Mama!" But Patricia tried to avoid her child.

The novel created a startling change. As it grew in popularity and the owners of the hotel in the story became more and more terrible in early 1884, Amanda braced herself for a lull in reservations. Lilly figured accounts more frantically with Fletcher, concerned that her grandmother, the foremost authority on society, could be right. Emily, still working hard and often relying on Sophia for companionship, seemed to be gazing West in anticipation of the predictable springtime return of Noel, who left every winter and returned every spring.

March arrived with a few premature blooms and a full house. More guests than ever before.

Along with all the questionable characterization in the novel, John had inadvertently drawn attention to the pleasures to be had in a great American hotel. His poor Chloe was often abused or mistreated at a fabulous ball, compromised at an outdoor spring concert, locked away in an incredible, luxurious prison-suite. For twenty-one chapters, twenty-one months.

The women might not have known of this phenomenon, but Amanda asked a new guest how he became aware of the Armstrong Arms and he informed her that it became his intention to spend his spring in a hotel in the States rather than Paris because of a story he had read. She asked a few more. She learned that many hotels were enjoying more than the usual number of guests. Quite a few of their new spring guests seemed to have had their curiosity about hotel living aroused by *The Found Fortune,* the most formidable among them a Mr. Mark Twain.

"Very damn few seemed to think of us in connection to the novel," Lilly told her grandmother.

"And so your sister is damned lucky!"

"What would we have done had we been empty on account of it?" Lilly asked.

"Is murder still against the law?" the old dowager returned. "I should not have been surprised! It's the Quaker heritage coming out again. Remember *Leaves of Grass*—banned by those shamed Puritans in Boston while these Quaker Philadelphians suffered embarrassment as they read every page, a condition I assure you we all loved!"

"Explain New York," Lilly, intrigued, asked her grandmother.

"New York?" she asked, peering over her spectacles. "They're a lot of pirates; nothing shames or embarrasses New York!"

Lilly pleaded overwork and begged the month of April away. She hoped to spend much of that month with Andrew, but there was more reason for her going away. The hotel was busy, full all the time. Gone forever were the quiet evenings the women spent in their apartments while the hotel was being finished and the first few guests had begun to arrive. Their extended family had grown, and their seams bulged. Sophia was frequently at the Arms with Emily, Fletcher took many dinners every week with them, Andrew was a regular guest, Dale managed to drop in at least monthly, Wilson and Deanna came to see Katherine, and Katherine, a thriving four-year-old, created a daily havoc with happy noises and plentiful toys. Amanda had discovered that special guests with interesting lives provided great dinner conversation, and an invitation to dine at her private table was soon a greater compliment—more prestigious than her offer to provide a formal dinner in the hotel. Lilly, sometimes tired and in want of a deep bath and quiet evening, found herself listening to poets, writers, politicians, or foreign diplomats. With guests, friends, and family, quiet was impossible. And Lilly desperately needed some quiet.

Andrew had been her lover for two years. She had begun to take their time together for granted. There was not the least suspicion, not so much as a look askance. Becoming more brazen, she told her grandmother she was going to look for a house somewhere, a place where she could be alone and not be bothered to keep company with bachelors. She did not need to look, of course. She freed Elizabeth to travel or visit her family and went to the cottage.

This time it was she who arrived early, chopped the wood herself, and tidied the cottage for Andrew. He had business on Wall Street; he had opened his own brokerage house there. All that kept him in Philadelphia was Lilly. He was more sought after each year because of his brilliance with stocks.

Lilly had brought a large load of books to read that had nothing whatever to do with her. She discarded her shoes and pulled her skirt through her legs from the back and tucked it in her waist at the front. When he arrived, she was sitting on the beach, digging her toes into the sand. He still wore his jacket and tie; she had a shawl wrapped around her shoulders because the air at the ocean was still cold. He stood and looked at her, and she had the sudden urge to tell him the things she had discovered, things that had never before happened to her.

In her first days alone she had not known what to do with her time. Her work had filled so many hours, included so many people that solitude was something she had lost in the hotel. She hadn't been able to sleep the first nights. She was cold, and the wood was difficult to chop; it chafed her hands and her cheeks were burned pink. Her lust for Andrew had been eased by their flat in the city, and her anticipation was more for her dearest friend and lover than for the physical pleasure she craved. After four days the solitude had settled within her and she began to feel her own mind and body; she become reacquainted with her dreams and stubborn beliefs. She read and ate at odd hours; she would light the lamp in the middle of the night and read on through the whole day without stopping or cook herself a hot beefsteak at seven in the morning. She napped and walked and lay on the sand at midnight to contemplate how strangely God had arranged the heavens. She had *liked* it then—no schedule, no commitments, no one to listen to but the voice of herself inside her own head. She wanted to tell him this: how the cottage was more than a place for her to escape convention and enjoy her forbidden man.

As she looked up at him, all she said was, "This is the only place I have ever really been myself."

The urgency of their early romance had been replaced by a

constant and reliable togetherness that made their intimacy richer, more gratifying. And having weeks as compared to hours was something to be grateful for. She knew that if they could have each other publicly, they would not be like other couples. They were too closely entwined. They were a solitary pair, could predict each other's thoughts and needs, were dependent on each other for so much . . . for so long.

"How is she?" she asked him, a question that came very infrequently.

"The same. It doesn't change. Do you have trouble saying her name?"

"I have no quarrel with Brenda, Andrew. I never have."

"She's become so ugly, Lilly, you wouldn't know her. She's too thin, pale and sometimes wild-eyed, sometimes drawn and melancholy. Sometimes she has a rare reprieve and seems almost well, but it doesn't last. The most painful thing, I think, is that she always hopes she is getting well," he said, a hollow laugh following. "This pitiful creature who doesn't remember more than snatches of her behavior, who doesn't know what her illness is, is so excitable when she thinks she's recovering. When I married her, she was the most beautiful woman I had ever seen. For a while she was everything a man could want. She fooled me so completely; it was a few months before I knew I had been her mother's plan."

"Andrew," she said cautiously, "I couldn't love you if you were the kind of man who would completely abandon a sick wife . . . But this sickness—does it sometimes become your own sickness? Do you sometimes fear telling Brenda the truth because it might make her ill?"

"You mean tell her about us?" he asked.

She shook her head. "No, that would never do. But do you let her believe, whether she's ill or well, that you can have a marriage with her? You told me once that she didn't want to be your wife, that it was Mrs. Waite who controlled her."

"I spoke to her about—well, an annulment. We were married in the Catholic church and a dispensation can be made. I will always pay for her care. If the church would grant an annulment, the courts might."

"What did she say, Andrew?"

"She said it was absurd. I couldn't be her husband. She would never have married a Yankee."

"How long would such a thing take? Months?"

"Longer. Years, perhaps. I would hope for less, but I haven't been encouraged by what I've learned. Of course, my petition could be denied altogether. There is no other recourse."

"Do you ever . . . love her? It's all right to tell me the truth."

"Love?" This was the only facet of his life, he explained, in which he felt a complete failure. He had fallen in love so thoroughly, was duped so completely. A young man with plenty of money, destined to grow richer, had been completely seduced, coddled by a beautiful, twenty-year-old woman, a mad woman controlled by her widowed mother. Wilson had warned him against love; Wilson had told him that a wife was an exceptional idea, but love drew the strength from a man and made him a victim of his own dire illusions.

They had to get him married quickly, Brenda and her mother, because he would have been warned by her strange moods and rages had he known her longer. And his rage, he told Lilly, when he discovered they wanted his money, his ability to keep them in style, had been boundless. Then there were four years in a house filled with duplicity and frequent quarreling. He worked harder, avoiding his wife, but still kept the public pretense of having a marriage because he had delayed in divorcing her when he should have quickly gotten that done. By the time he was desperate to be free of her, she was alone and ill.

With the death of Mrs. Waite and Brenda's insanity, the anger was somehow lost. He wished he could seize it again. "Explain to me, Lilly, how it is that I feel almost responsible for her agony? I had nothing whatever to do with Brenda's past, but when I discovered my wife had been a battered and raped child, a victim of the brutality of her family and Union soldiers, I had nothing left but pity, and the urge to protect her."

Lilly had heard Andrew speak of guilt before. He felt guilty because his mother had died in loneliness and poverty, guilty because he had not divorced Brenda when he should have, and now he was guilty because she was ill. "This business of being Catholic," she said, "seems to have a lot to do with those feelings. Guilt must be a chiefly Catholic occupation."

"Do you ever feel guilty, Lilly?"

"Never," she said honestly.

"When Brenda doesn't have strange visions or the voice of her mother in her head, she has asked my forgiveness and received it.

She has begged me not to abandon her, and I've promised. When I asked her to free me from marriage, she simply told me I was not her husband."

"I think, Andrew, your commitment to Brenda will outlast us all."

"And what would you like me to do?" he asked her.

"Nothing for me," she said. "But, since you did not create this disaster, stop acting as though you did. Whatever else you do will be much easier if you are not guilt ridden."

"But you never ask me to hurry."

"I know if you could hurry, you would."

Lilly was learning that the grip Brenda had on Andrew's conscience was more powerful than the legal ties, the one-time love, the disappointment, or the shame. Sometimes she was more sorry for Andrew than for Brenda. She had never really believed free love was possible; she thought the cost would be higher for Andrew than for her. She felt trapped by her body and her desire, and this was something she almost welcomed; Andrew was trapped by a demon within himself.

When he made love to her, her body sang for hours afterward. He could arouse passion in her that took her out of the worldly state and into a trance that drove all earthly troubles from her mind. She had once feared not knowing this joy. Now she was beginning to fear knowing it only in this cottage, in their city flat, for a few hours here and there, in secret. Hopeless, but for Andrew, not for Lilly. Lilly knew what she wanted, what trades had to be made. Andrew wanted more, but could not seize it.

When he lost control again, he cursed. "Damn, there's a hex on this place! When I get inside you here, I can't protect you! You overwhelm me. Ah, Lilly, I love you so!"

She touched his cheek and gently told him it was all right; there was no need for concern.

Noel Padgett let the sheet drop over the still, cold features of Ned Armstrong. He turned to the doctor and handed him a slip of paper with Emily's name on it. "Send a telegram to this woman. This man's name is Ned Armstrong . . . and this is the address of his wife."

"You're sure?"

"Absolutely."

"How did you know him?"

"He was a friend of mine, on and off. I was at the table. He was a gambling man. He was a cheat. I've played cards with him sometimes. I come here from Wyoming where I ranch. I met him last year in the fall, he played for high stakes and was sometimes lucky. I swear I don't know the real name of the man who shot him—called himself Francis, and he made a big bunch of dust getting away. Has anyone else told you what happened?"

"It seems no one saw anything at all. Nobody but you. I'm afraid the constable doesn't want to let you go just yet."

"Makes no difference to me," Noel said. "I'm a patient man."

"Why did you want to see the body?"

He shrugged. "Wanted to make sure you knew he had kin."

"Well, I sure can't reason your interest. You might've got yourself more trouble than you need staying around. Now you're the only one to blame, and the law is going to close up that place."

"Don't matter. That's a godawful place."

A Chicago constable led Noel away. He hoped this affair would solve itself quickly.

Noel hadn't been back to Wyoming for two years. His ranching was falling apart back there and he couldn't quite get himself interested in saving it. He was getting ready to sell at a loss. Money was no real problem. He had a little less than before, but he had enough to live out his days simply and without scrimping by too much.

He'd been stalking Ned Armstrong. He had meant to kill him. It was the purest luck someone else had.

Noel spent months in Chicago looking for him for two winters. When he did find a man by that name, he wasn't sure it was really he until he overheard some fabrication of a rich wife in Philly who owned a big hotel named after him. Ned didn't run with a famous crowd; he was gambling and trying to sell false land certificates for property out West. Noel could see that in his younger, more agile years Ned could have successfully seduced young girls, but middle-aged women with lots of money must have proven a little harder to trick. Ned had to alter his philandering, and so he went after men with money to invest. Noel befriended him, led him along, offered to help him make a lot of money easy, and set him up.

It wasn't difficult to convince a fraud and gambler to get involved with a lot of frauds and gamblers. Noel found every back-street card game and bordello in Chicago and staked Ned. When Ned was finally in real deep, Noel was going to shoot him and leave his body somewhere with Emily's name and address in his pocket. But they got into a bad card game, Ned drank too much whiskey and cheated stupidly, and a drifter by the name of Francis pulled out his gun and shot him through his heart. Noel couldn't get scarce like everyone else at that card game and still be sure some authority would get the message to Emily that she was a widow; Noel stayed with Ned's body when everyone else ran and the proprietor of the place went for the law.

Chicago was growing into a pretty, new, rich city, but in the parts Noel and Ned had frequented, people still strapped on guns. It was obvious that Noel's gun was cold and the body still warm. The owner of the place was pretty reluctant to tell the law who had been gambling in his place; he didn't want some angry varmint coming around and shooting him. Now everyone was fooling around trying to decide if Noel had actually killed the man and tried to blame it on someone else.

After a week in jail, Noel paid a big fine and was released. The man had no family, he was told. There was no one to bury him. There were still a lot of killings in that part of town and too many possible criminals to put in jail. Noel realized he could have killed Ned, lied about it, bought his way out of jail, and done so much sooner than he had. He also believed that Emily would have sent money for a burial. "Did anyone get word to the widow?" he asked.

"Yessir."

"And she didn't offer to get him planted?"

"You know her?" he was asked.

"Nope, nor do I intend to introduce myself," Noel said.

"Well, there ain't no one to plant him. He's gone over to the Sanitary Commission."

"Uh-huh," Noel said, and left to gather his things and take the first train to Philadelphia. He went around by the tavern where Ned had died; they were doing a right fine business. The owner must have parted with a little money of his own to keep the place open. The illustrious Chicago officials had done all right for themselves on Ned's death, between Emily's money, Noel's fine, and a little bribery.

He hoped his name had not been connected to the death, but figured he'd know soon enough. If nothing about him had been telegrammed to Emily, he wouldn't be leaving Philadelphia again.

Lilly spent nineteen days with Andrew. When he left the cottage to go back to his work in New York City, she stayed a few days longer. The ocean was slowly warming up, and buds were starting to pop open. She was beginning to feel ready to leave and confront the hotel again; she felt as full as spring. Her cheeks were bright, her eyes deep, and a certain peace filled her. It was peace and certainty she had come here to find.

The apartments at the Arms were as full as ever, and she had been missed. The family that surrounded her made her feel safe; she was more sure of herself than ever before. She embraced each one: Sophia, Fletcher, Bertie, Amanda, Mama, Katherine, even Cleaves. Elizabeth was not yet home from her visiting but was due to return soon. The only one absent was Patricia, and after a big, noisy meal, Lilly went down the stairs to her sister's suite. For some reason she hadn't fully figured out, she felt the need to make peace with Patricia.

The maid was reluctant to let Lilly enter, and waves of worry began to intrude on Lilly's peace of mind. "Is she asleep? I'd like to talk to her tonight even though it's late and—"

Patricia stood in the doorway of her bedroom in her dressing gown. "It's all right," she told the maid. "Let her come in."

"I know it's late, Patricia, but—"

"Am I in trouble again?" she asked crisply.

"No, I only wanted to talk to you. You didn't join us for dinner, and I thought, since I've just came home, I would—"

"Talk to *me?* About what, for goodness' sake?"

"Oh, Patricia, never mind. If you're too busy or have something better to do—I only wanted to tell you I'm sorry everyone's been so hard on you. That book doesn't bother me."

"Really?" she asked with a sarcastic laugh. "How amazing! All this time you've completely ignored me, threatened me, hatefully criticized me, and now you're *sorry.*"

"We were friends once," Lilly said.

"Years and years ago! When Grandmother returned, this family cast me off. I haven't been part of the family since." She turned and walked into her bedroom, leaving the door ajar.

Lilly followed. "Patricia," she began. But when she got to the door and looked in, the sight of many opened trunks and bags scattered about froze Lilly's words. All of Patricia's dresses, shoes, hats, gloves, parasols were scattered about to be packed. "What is this?" she finally asked.

"I'm leaving. I thought you would be pleased."

"Where are you going? Why?"

"John is going to live in New York and write. He has the means to live anywhere in the world. I'm going with him."

"But what about Katherine? Mama?"

"Katherine isn't mine," Patricia said, not looking at Lilly. She continued to fold chemises.

The maid came to the doorway, but Lilly pushed her out. "Give us a minute," she said, closing the door. "Katherine is your *daughter*. Every time she sees you she holds out her arms to you and—"

"She belongs to Mama. And you. I can barely look at her. She only reminds me of how awful my life was. Awful and horrid. I don't want her. I never did."

"What the devil *do* you want? My God, Patricia, what is it you think you're going to have now? Are you going to live in sin with him, then? Are you going to try to divorce Dale? I can't believe you would—"

Patricia sighed almost wearily. "John is going to write, I am going to inspire him, and Dale can go to hell."

"Are you planning to say good-bye to anyone? Are you going to run off in the dark of night and—"

"Whom should I say good-bye to, Lilly? My family who can barely tolerate me? I really don't know what I've done to earn the absolute scorn of everyone around me. I made a dreadful mistake in marrying Dale, and when I discovered it, I went to Grandmother and begged her to let me come home! Once I had been tied to a bed and nearly killed, I was *allowed* home, but to what? To a prison! Your hotel, you said. I was not allowed to socialize with the guests, help the family entertain. I was never a good enough mother, daughter, sister. All any of you ever did was complain about me, *constantly*."

"Patricia, let's try," Lilly said. "Let's try to mend our fences. Don't run away."

"No, Lilly. I've finally found something I'm good at. John understands me, he thinks I'm wonderful, and he never criticizes me or makes me do things I don't want to do. He isn't a very public person, but he doesn't mind that I am. I talk about him when he doesn't wish to talk about himself. People, I've found, are very interested in me—they notice that I'm like the woman in his book and they like talking to me.

"I have nothing here. No one cares about me here. Everyone cares what people might *think*. Everyone calls me selfish! Why should I stay where I'm not wanted?"

Lilly suddenly recalled that carriage ride home from the Montaine household just after Katherine's birth. "If we could get Patricia a position on a throne where she is worshiped . . ."

"What could we have done, Patsy?" she asked. "What could any of us have done to make you happy?"

"You could have brought me into the family. All you did was give me a bed and tell me to behave myself! You could have treated me like one of you rather than the naughty girl who ran away from her marriage! You could have been *proud* of me when I inspired a whole novel, but you were ashamed of me! All of you! You invite that wretch into my home to visit his child. You won't let me go to the parties because someone might notice me and figure out that I'm not with Dale, and you wouldn't pay any attention to me *ever*."

"How will John make you happy, Patsy?"

Patricia's eyes were clear. She lifted her chin in that notorious defiance that she had been born with. "He will do as he's always done—tell me he understands how I feel and that I deserve to have what I desire because I am *good*. He's kind and gentle and strong in ways no one understands. He thinks I'm *smart*. You're the only one allowed to be smart here! And now he is also rich. He'll deny me *nothing*! He will never force *anything* on me that I don't want! To him I am something I have never been to any of you—I am *important!*"

Patricia's eyes were hard and fiercely blue. Her utter contempt for anyone who didn't think her *most* important glowed like a beacon through her eyes. It was Lilly whose eyes filled with tears, and they began to run slowly down her cheeks. She saw what was going to happen to her sister, and for the first time in all her life she understood completely. John would lay his body over a bed of nails for her to walk across, denying her nothing, claiming nothing for himself, and worshiping her beauty and charm even when she was at her most cruel. Patricia would go away with him to New York, or anywhere, and play the heroine in his books. The cities she visited would become her stage, and she would have fame and admiration where she had failed to find it before.

She couldn't puncture the thick walls of society with her marriage. She couldn't reign over the hotel while Amanda held court and Lilly was seen as the heiress. This she *could* do: she could be a famous writer's inspiration. As long as she was careful not to be too well known among her acquaintances, they might believe she was a good, generous, sweet woman. The only one really to suffer would be John; he apparently welcomed the pain of being used.

"Say good-bye to Mama, Patsy. Please."

"You may tell her I'm leaving if you like. I'm not going upstairs. I can't believe anyone will care that I'm leaving."

"We all care. We all wanted you to be happy, only none of us was willing to let you use us. You'll never understand that."

"I think I understand well enough what the lot of you have in store for me! None of you has ever loved me! Damn, if I had known you'd build a bloody famous hotel, do you think I'd have married that wretch? But you couldn't forgive me one mistake! You couldn't let me in your fancy world! Use you? I only wanted to be *one* of you!"

"We work very hard, Patsy. You didn't want to—"

"I can't *work!* I don't know how!"

Lilly sniffed back her tears and wiped her cheeks. "Mama will come down here to see you . . . I feel certain. If no one else tells you this, I'd like you to know—you may come home when you need us. But the terms will always be the same. This place is not here to serve you. We can give you lodging—but we can't give you all the adoration you seem to need."

Patricia folded a shawl. She didn't look up.

"I love you, Patsy," Lilly said.

"Don't *lie!*" Patricia snapped. "It's too late!"

"But I do love you. You just always mistook love for something else."

Lilly was the only one who attempted to stop Patricia. Both Amanda and Emily went to her suite to say good-bye, but neither argued with her. Emily asked her to write to them; she promised to take good care of Katherine and hoped Patricia would be happy.

Patricia had her baggage loaded onto a cart that followed an Armstrong Arms coach that took her to the train station. Emily watched the departure of the cart and coach from the roof. Her tears of loss were silent. Then a darkness settled over the household while each of the women tried to fathom what tactic she might have used to reach Patricia and save her from her own greed. Each one attempted to decide, personally, where she had failed.

The next day a telegram arrived. Emily Armstrong solemnly told Lilly that Ned was killed during a card game in Chicago. But she put the telegram away without letting anyone see it.

Andrew's face in the Reading station was familiar after over three years of monthly visits with his wife. He would routinely take the town coach to the picturesque little country house that he'd bought for Brenda and Mr. and Mrs. Sherman. The hills that surrounded the two-storey stone farmhouse were coming alive with greenery; a stream ran nearby and a barn stood apart from the house. A few animals grazed—sheep, goats, cows, and horses.

He always fought apprehension when the coach neared the house; he could never predict what he might find within. On his last visit Brenda had been a visitor in the sane world. The front door was open on top to let the spring breeze through and when Brenda came to the door, smiled and waved, he breathed an audible sigh of relief. She must be having a good spell.

She ran to him and put her arms around his neck. "Oh, Andrew, I knew you would come! I've been so lonely!"

"You look well," he said, smiling at her and walking with her into the house.

"I've been well for nearly two whole months. It's Father Demetrius, you know. He visits with me and prays with me. I've been feeling better right along."

"Hello, Mr. Devon," Mrs. Sherman greeted brightly. "I'm fixing tea. Give me a few more minutes."

"We'll go for a walk," Brenda said. "It's all right, Andrew, I've been walking a lot lately. Father says it's good for me. We'll go down to the stream and come back."

She took him by the hand in a girlish way, leading him out of the house. He could see Mr. Sherman with a pitchfork full of hay down the hill by the barn, feeding stock. There had been visits when Brenda looked good, just as there had been visits during which she had become so agitated she had to be given a heavy dose of laudanum. Her appearance today was almost too good to be true: her cheeks had filled in; her back was straighter.

"Tell me what you've been doing," he said, holding her hand and walking with her. It was his routine to be cautious in conversation until he knew how she would react.

"I've been sewing and baking with Mrs. Sherman. I've been to town twice—there isn't much to do there, but it's an outing. And I see Father Demetrius almost every afternoon. I'm resting better because of him. Andrew," she said, stopping and turning toward him. "Andrew, I'm going to be well."

"Good," he said, moving on.

"No, I mean it! You have to believe me this time! I haven't had any bad spells. I'm not so sick anymore! I know they told you it was hopeless—Mrs. Sherman said as much. But you must believe me— I'm getting well!"

"Who is this priest?" he asked. "Are you sure he's good for you?"

"He has the local parish—he's something of a celebrity around here. His prayers have helped more than one ailing person."

"And you like him?"

"I adore him, Andrew. He is the kindest, most wonderful— What more can I tell you? I haven't felt this well in years."

"Good, Brenda, good. I do believe you. Don't excite yourself. Let's not borrow trouble."

"Andrew, take me home, please . . . I want to go home. I'll be good, I promise. Please."

"I told you, Brenda, I sold the house. I have a small flat and this. There just isn't anything more. I have nowhere to take—"

"I'll go with you to your flat," she said.

"I think it's too soon, Brenda."

"You're afraid of me, aren't you?"

"No, I—"

"You are! I'll show you I'm getting well. I'll prove it to you. I don't hear people talking to me anymore, Andrew. I know that was all that was ever wrong. Mother! She just wouldn't leave me alone. She just wouldn't *die*. But Father has taken care of that."

368

"What? What has he done, Brenda?"

"Just prayer," she said, smiling confidently. Andrew looked at her closely. Her eyes were calm, not wild, and although she sounded a bit desperate, she appeared to be sane. "He simply helped me pray her into a quiet rest. He helped me give up my suffering to God. I'm going to be all right now."

He studied her eyes as she spoke. His hand moved to touch the dark hair at her temple, hair that was clean and shiny rather than wilted and mussed as on some other occasions.

"You've become gray, Andrew. That's my fault, I think. Somehow, I'll make it up to you. No one really tells me what I've done in sickness, but I have nightmares sometimes . . . I think I know how terrible I've been. It's all right if you can't ever forgive me. I—"

"Brenda, forgiveness or the lack of it is not an issue. I would like you to be well. It's all I've wanted for you."

She chattered on about the priest, about newfound sleep and health and forgiveness. She led him to the narrow stream on the property and sat down on the grass. It was remarkable how much like a farm girl she looked in a cotton print dress with her dark hair curled in a braid. Her skin was smooth and healthy, her voice clear and sane. He braced himself for a momentary lapse that did not come.

"Will you think about taking me home?" she asked him.

"Of course," he lied, his brow furrowing. "But I don't want you to rush back into the city, Brenda. I'd like us to be sure."

"If I stay well? If I don't have spells, will you?"

"Just give it time, Brenda."

"Do you still love me, Andrew?" she asked. When he hesitated, she ran on. "Oh, I promised Father I wasn't going to do that! Forgive me, Andrew! I can't expect so much of you. You were the only person in the world to stand by me, take care of me. Mr. Sherman told me all about the horrible asylums I could have been locked away in, places where people *can't* become well. You must believe me, Andrew, I know I owe my life to you! I know I don't deserve you. I can't force you to forget or forgive! I won't try."

"Brenda, tell me how this has happened to you. Was it only prayer? The priest?"

She shrugged and looked down. "Father Demetrius said that the demons I ran from were only memories that I tried too hard to fight. I locked the past inside and it festered there making terrible sores

369

in me. He said I didn't really have mania, but fear and confusion. We talked a lot about the kinds of things I was afraid of, and finally I began to realize I'm safe."

"I knew the priest had been visiting you, but—"

"It took a very long time for me to even be aware of his visits, his prayers. I'm not sure why he took this special interest in me. He's quite a nice gent; Mrs. Sherman invites him to dinner, and I know he wants to meet you. I know what worries you, Andrew. You're afraid it's a passing thing. I was afraid too. It isn't."

He smiled at her then, amazed and troubled by what seemed to be recovery. *Afraid* of what seemed to be recovery. He thought of Lilly.

"I want you to be well," he said again.

"Andrew, don't leave me. Stay here with me."

"I can't, Brenda. You know I can't."

"It's other women, isn't it? Mrs. Sherman told me it's been three years. I just didn't feel the time. She reminded me about an annulment. I can't stop you from that, Andrew. I remember, you know. I remember what Mother made me do to you. It was terrible of me, and I don't blame you if you can't love me again."

"Brenda, let's not resurrect all the suffering that—"

"But if I can be well—if I can be a good wife, will you think about giving me another chance? I promise not to blame you if you can't, but will you think about it?"

"Yes," he said, terrified of what saying no might do to her. "Of course."

Father Demetrius was an old priest rumored to have phenomenal spiritual strength. He'd been in Reading for twenty years and was credited with the cures of several ailments through prayer. Mrs. Sherman confirmed that Brenda did indeed seem to be improving, but warned Andrew that there were slippery days. They hadn't had a terrible time in months, but there had always been brief recoveries when Brenda had seemed normal. This was, however, the longest good spell. No one had wanted to give Andrew false hope. And fortunately, despite Brenda's impatience, no one, not even the priest, thought it a good idea to move her back to the city. If health was here, here was where Brenda belonged until it could be certain her health was safe.

He had a decent weekend there, having Sunday dinner with the priest and walks with Brenda. He took a saddle horse around the grounds and ate good country food prepared by Mrs. Sherman. Mr. Sherman took him to the train station on Monday morning.

"What do you really think, Martin?" Andrew asked as they rode.

The man sighed rather heavily. "I think her wellness or illness is the least of your troubles, son. Knowin' what the girl did to you on her mother's demand, I think I can guess the depth of your problems now."

"Don't worry about my problems. Do you think she's recovering?"

"I hope she's recovering, Andrew. The way of it is this, the priest visited her when she didn't know his name, when she sat like a stump and stared into the great beyond, answering questions none of us could hear. He talked to her anyway, said her name, prayed his prayers, blessed her. One day she recognized him and talked back. It's been steady since. Every day better than the one before. Me and the missus, we aren't of this faith, but the man's been given a lot of credit around here. Maybe it's true—maybe he's made her well."

Andrew nodded, knowing he should be more pleased.

"Give it a year, son," Martin Sherman said, "a year to be sure and a year to get her accustomed to what has to be."

"She's my wife," he said.

"You'll take care of her, one way or the other, that I know. You're a good enough man, given all that's happened. Me and the missus understand what it might be like—we had the boy, sometimes mighty hard to love, hard to be thankful for. We had each other, you know—someone to be a friend in a friendless time. More's the time we talked about what it might have been like, one of us so bad off and the other alone with the weight of it. We're fond of Brenda. She's a good girl—can't help what's been done to her. In some ways I suppose this is harder for you than the other. In some ways it must not be too easy to see the woman who hasn't been a wife to you in so many years want another chance. Don't get me wrong, son. I believe you want her well for her own sake. I'm only saying that I can believe in some ways this is harder to accept than the other."

Andrew was silent a long time. "In some ways," he finally said.

371

21

*L*illy was standing at the window of her office when Amanda came in. Amanda always gave two sharp taps and opened the door without being invited; Lilly often wondered what the knock was meant to do—give her time to hide what?

She had a good view of the grounds at the front of the hotel from her office window; she could see the Armstrong Arms coaches and horsecars arrive and depart, leaving and picking up guests at the broad portico below. She could see the rolling hills, manicured lawns, a large gazebo and bandstand, and the lower portion of what they had named the Queen Victoria Gardens, which was Lilly's favorite place to stroll in spring and summer. To the far right, if she strained, she could make out the edge of the large pond, almost a lake. Swans moved gracefully across the water. They had cleared and cleaned the area, constructed a dock and had a few small boats for the leisure of the guests.

"Lilly, have you made a contract with an orchestra for the Fourth of July afternoon?" Amanda asked. Lilly didn't have to turn around to know exactly how her grandmother looked: she would be wearing a high-necked afternoon suit and holding a sheaf of papers in her hand, and her reading spectacles balanced on her nose and attached to a ribbon that would be tacked to her jacket to keep from losing them.

"Not yet, Grandmother."

"Arranged the fireworks display?" she asked.

"I'll do that this week."

"All right, let's see . . ." Lilly heard the rustle of papers. "Ah, ordered beef for the barbecue?"

"Mama is taking care of that."

"Yes, that's right. The decoration of the ballroom?"

Lilly sighed. She turned around—there was the image she expected. She loved the sight of her grandmother working; without this work Amanda might become old. She still tinted her hair dark auburn, but had decided her sixties required she allow a little of the gray around her face to show; she called this her meager contribution to honesty. Lilly smiled appreciatively. "Will you come in and close the door, Grandmother? I'd like to tell you something."

Amanda finally looked up from her bundle of loose papers and notes. She closed the door and let her spectacles dangle over her bosom from the ribbon. There were two overstuffed chairs divided by a small table in Lilly's office, and she joined Lilly there.

"I haven't quite done my part around here, Gran," Lilly said. "I was away for a month . . . and since I've been back I've accomplished almost nothing."

"No one has complained about your work. With word of Ned's death, Patricia's antics, and all—all of us have moved slowly. It's been a dark time."

"My laziness has nothing to do with Patricia, nor with my departed father. I meant to speak to you immediately upon returning, but the household was so upset that I decided to wait a few days. It's personal—rather delicate I suppose."

"Well, now Lilly—"

"I'm pregnant."

Amanda's mouth dropped open and her eyes widened considerably. She gripped her papers suddenly, crumbling them. Lilly was relieved that her grandmother didn't clutch at her heart.

"Lilly, that's absurd!"

Lilly smiled in spite of herself. "No, it's quite real."

"You don't even have a man in your life!"

"Of course I do, Grandmother. I'm not going to give birth to the Christ child."

"But who? You haven't even . . . you've expressed no affection for any . . . God above! Who is it?"

"Now Gran, I'm afraid I don't want to tell you that. You see, he isn't going to marry me and so his name is rather irrelevant."

Amanda reached for Lilly's hand, but grasped her wrist. "But do you love him?"

"Oh yes, certainly."

"Then he *will* marry you, or I'll—"

"In this instance, your influence won't help. He already has a wife. I'm afraid we were careless."

"Careless? That's a hell of a way of putting it! Careless!"

"Hush now. It's a little soon to tell the entire staff, don't you think?"

Amanda lowered her voice to a coarse whisper. "That man? The one who so long ago kissed you and disappeared? He's the one?"

"Please, Gran, it just isn't important. Not really." She saw that Amanda's lips were pursed, her eyes were slits. "All right then—the same man. I came across him again. Not that it matters," Lilly shrugged.

"Oh, Lilly, what were you *thinking?*"

"I love him," she said lamely, "and just couldn't help myself."

Amanda gave a sharp, cruel laugh. "I assure you, that one's been done to death!"

"Well, I have no excuse. None. And I'm quiet pleased about the baby. I don't intend to get rid of it."

"Of course you're not—that's deadly." Amanda put a hand on her bad knee to get to her feet. She dropped her papers in the chair and began to pace about the small space. "I can't believe my ears. Not you, Lilly! You haven't found the man who can hold your interest through dinner!" She peered over her shoulder at her granddaughter. "I trust you stayed through the fruit and wine . . . at least once."

Lilly was concerned about the pregnancy, not quite sure how she could handle it, but was not yet unhappy or afraid. She hoped she wouldn't be. In fact, she had never felt more wonderful in her life. "Yes, Gran, the fruit and wine," she said wistfully. *The wine that filled my cup and was magically empty to be filled again and again! The fruit of life, growing within me.* She looked at her grandmother, and her look was serene, calm.

"That cottage of yours?" Amanda asked.

"No, I'm afraid not. I suspected, you see, and thought a little time away . . . solitude, might help me to understand what I want. By the time I left the cottage, I knew for certain."

"You've been to a doctor?"

"No, not yet. But I assure you, Gran, I am going to have a child, perhaps for Katherine's fourth birthday. And I suppose I should see a doctor to be certain—"

"How *could* you let this happen? How *could* you do this to us?"

Lilly stiffened in surprise. "Gran, don't. You know I wouldn't ever deliberately hurt you. It's too late for threats and recriminations. It can't be undone."

"But you were *careless,* you said! Careless! You should not have let him touch you in the first place! I'll find out who that son of a—"

"How long did you imagine I would be content to not have a whole life, Gran? Did you think I'd marry some dolt who'd lose all our money for us just to have—This may seem scandalous, but I assure you, it's far more decent than some contrived marriage! At least I love him!"

"And do you suppose, in your wildest dreams, that you'll have the luxury of carrying on with this—"

"Of course not! I know I can't!"

"The wretch took advantage of you when—"

"He's not a wretch! He's good and decent and—"

"And compromised you! Gave you his child! No marriage, but a child! Don't bother me with defending his *decency,* damn it all! No decent man would—"

"Stop pacing—your knee will be crippled tomorrow."

"The bloody tomcat! You'll have to go away, that's all. We can't have an illegitimate child born under our roof."

"I don't want to go away," she said flatly.

"Oh? And what do you propose? To grow round and fat and have the guests asking a lot of questions about where your *husband* happens to be? Fortunately I still have good friends in Europe who would be willing—"

"I don't want to go to Europe!"

"There are no alternatives, Lilly!"

"Of course there are! People get bored with scandal. Patricia and Dale didn't live under the same roof for years and there was hardly a snicker. Mama pretended to be a widow all her life and no one was the wiser. No one really *cares* for long."

"Good God! You mean it! Lilly, you're *different!* You've become one of the most admired young women in Philly! Don't you understand what role you've filled for people? Your mother left society, and they left her alone. Your sister was never one of them, so she was easy to ignore. But you—"

"They *created* me, Grandmother! They didn't know what I was, so they created me! I can't help that!"

"Lord, you mean to stay right here and get large and bulky and—I won't have it, that's all. We'll make some arrangements for you. You can return after a year."

"With my child?"

"Lilly, my *dear,* how can you hope to raise a child in circumstances like—"

"I won't do it! I won't go away or give up my child! What is it you expect of me?"

"I had expected intelligence and control, foolish old hen that I am!"

"Oh, don't speak to me of control! I haven't married three times, left my husband, or pretended to be a widow when I'm not!"

"Oh? Oh, miss brave and bright hotel owner, you think you can bear the way people will look at you, pregnant and unmarried, but you are *wrong.* You are so much in the eye—seen as my heir!"

"I'm not an *heir!* That's what people pretend I am because they don't know what to make of me! This hotel was my idea, my design, my—"

"Just how long has this little conspiracy been—"

"None of your business!"

"Lilly, you *will* tell me who—"

Lilly stood abruptly. "I won't! Be as angry and demanding as you like! There are certain things you *can't* control! You can't send me away if I don't want to go! I won't tell you any more, and I won't

377

be scolded! I am a woman, I am going to have a child, and it is done!"

Lilly's cheeks were colored from her anger, and she quickly went to the office door.

"Lilly!" Amanda whispered furiously.

But Lilly walked out. She went hurriedly down the hall toward the elevator and then down. A couple of people who worked for the hotel greeted her, but she walked past them. She wasn't any closer to having the problem resolved and had not expected Amanda to have that particular solution at the ready. Lilly didn't care what people said. She wasn't going to make a spectacle of her pregnancy, but she'd be damned if she'd be hustled out of her own home. And go away only to leave her child behind? Never!

What am I supposed to do? she thought furiously. I wanted love in my life, and there was only one man to love, only one man who was right. I wanted a child, and I'll have one. I can't help that it isn't tidy—I regret none of it!

This was the price of free love. What is a whole life worth? No matter how terrible it was, no matter the gossip, she would not go to Europe, would not give up her child.

She walked through the foyer of the hotel to the portico. Fletcher was just getting out of his coach and said hello to her, but with her mind elsewhere and her cheeks hot with anger, tears threatening in her eyes, she passed Fletcher without a word and walked briskly toward the gardens.

Lilly wondered if she should have expected her grandmother's rage and shame. How else could she have responded, as concerned with appearances as Amanda could be? Dealing with Patricia hadn't ruffled her too much because every family has *one* spot of trouble. But Amanda had decided on Lilly as an heir. There was the crux of the trouble! Amanda had created that image herself and delighted in it. Lilly wanted to be an independent woman, but the world wanted something else.

She wants the villain named, Lilly thought furiously. Villain? She'd seduced him with such purpose! Oh, what would she think if she knew this was *exactly* what I wanted? His love, his body, his child! Andrew can't be named and remain in the good graces of the family. I will not have him cast away from the household where his child grows. Now perhaps I will compromise. But now I know why!

She slowed once in the garden, relieved to be alone. Of course hotel guests could come down the path at any moment and she would have to be pleasant. She went to the gazebo, hoping she wouldn't have to spread that proprietress smile across her lips.

"Whatever it was, it certainly opened your sails!"

She turned to see Fletcher, his hand on the pillar and his foot on the gazebo step. "Fletcher, I'm sorry," she said, just realizing that she had ignored him. "This isn't a good time."

He stepped into the gazebo anyway, chuckling under his breath. "It doesn't look like a good time, Lilly. No, indeed. What on earth is it?"

She sighed heavily. "I had a disagreement with my grand-mother."

"Oh?" he laughed. "I always wanted to witness that. I'm amazed it's been this long—the two strongest female wills I have ever known were bound to come to blows sometime. I'm sure you can smooth it over."

"Not this time."

"Lilly, she's not getting any younger, nor any gentler. But she loves you."

Fletcher sat down on the gazebo bench, one leg outstretched and one arm over the back of the bench.

"She can be very stubborn. And when she comes up against that rare circumstance she can't control! Unbearable!"

"Yes," he laughed. "What uncontrollable challenge did you give her?"

"A small one," she said with a deep sigh. "You may as well know. You've been trusted with bigger secrets than this, and this one isn't going to be a secret for very long." She looked at him; she had always thought Fletcher so steady. She was almost eager to see if he would start shouting and accusing. "I'm afraid I'm pregnant."

His eyes widened briefly; he composed himself quickly. "I see," he said.

"I don't happen to have a husband."

"Yes, I was aware of that."

"I'm not going to be able to get one."

"The father isn't—?"

"Available," she finished for him.

He made a sound, not quite shock or laughter or disapproval. Perhaps it was his wry humor. "I'm glad you didn't say 'interested.' "

"He is indisposed."

379

"Married, you mean."

Her eyes shot to his face.

"Well, it's the single reason I can imagine the father of your child wouldn't marry you. A lot of men want to marry you before they even meet you."

"Yes, don't I know it."

"Even now—"

"Put that instantly from your mind!" she snapped. "If you think I'm taking this little bundle with me to dupe some poor, ignorant idiot who wants to get his hands on a hotel—"

"Well," he said, leaning back, unruffled, "What *is* your plan?"

"I don't have one yet. I'm still working on that."

"It must have taken you quite by surprise," he said.

"It shouldn't have. I'm not one for trifling affairs—it's not as though I engaged in a scandalous weekend."

"I shouldn't think so, as deliberate as you are."

"Well, damn it all, there you have it. I've gone and done it, and Grandmother is furious with me. I might as well have been wearing red on Canal Street!"

"Nonsense. She'll calm down. Though she'll be looking at you strangely—this is a part of you that Amanda, naively, didn't know existed. Did you tell her who—"

"No! And I think that alone makes her angrier than this result. You know how awful she is when she isn't in on a secret!"

"You'll be under sharp scrutiny, in that case. Your every conversation, your every glance, your—"

"It won't do any good," Lilly said.

"Ah," he acknowledged. "You intend to go it alone?"

"Can you think of any alternative?"

"Have you told him?"

"I meant to," she said, her voice softening. "But you see, there's nothing he can do. Nothing reasonable, that is. I've decided to tell him later, when I've thought this through."

"Well, Lilly, how are you otherwise?"

She looked at him and smiled. "That's what I'd hoped Grandmother would ask me. After all this family has been through, the number of times we've brushed up against scandal and escaped by the merest sliver . . . I feel wonderful, Fletcher! I feel better than I've felt in my life! What do you suppose would happen, really, if I simply refused to be ashamed? If I simply grew and grew till I popped and had a child, a loved and wanted child, and continued to work? Do you think all the world would refuse to cross my threshold? Do you think John would write another book?" She leaned toward him. "Do you think me shabby now? Have I lost all respectability?"

"Don't be ridiculous, Lilly! But remember, I'm very tolerant. If you truly love the man, I think what you've done makes more sense than what a lot of people do, but then I—"

"And I won't be able to continue to see him now," she said, her voice quiet. "Because of the baby, because of the way everyone will look at me, expecting to see some sort of acknowledgment in my eyes. It's a shame, a dreadful trade. That place where I was happiest is gone for now. I was so very happy with him."

He reached for her hand and squeezed it. "Love, Lilly, is very respectable. Unfortunately, it can also be very risky."

"I wish I could feel sorry. I don't, that's all. I have done exactly as I intended all along. Oh, I didn't mean to have a baby. I thought it best that I shouldn't. But, well, here it is." She shifted a bit on the bench. "Grandmother wants to send me away. She mentioned friends in Europe who would take me in. She even suggested that I couldn't keep my—" She stopped suddenly at that intolerable thought.

"Consider one thing, Lilly. As much as Amanda loves you, that would be a difficult suggestion for her—meant, I'm sure, only to protect you. It's her great-grandchild, too."

"It's her great-grandchild *second*."

"Don't expect this to be easy when you're going to be as stubborn as Amanda. Have you talked to your mother?"

"That is coming, I assure you. By the time I return to the apartments, she will have been told."

"Elizabeth?" he asked.

Lilly laughed suddenly. "Oh, she'll be the last. She has never quite overcome her terrible fretting!"

"Well, may I say one thing?"

"Anything you like, Fletcher."

"When you decide to love as you will, despite all the fancy little rules society has made up, you become a part of that person you love, more dramatically when you are going to have his child. You have to tell him before you decide, finally, what you're going to do."

"Why? He isn't having a baby!"

Fletcher laughed at her. "No, but you're having *his*. You don't have to do as he suggests, but you do owe him the decency of telling him and letting him speak his mind."

She thought about this for a moment. What good it was likely to do, she wasn't sure. "I thought, if I was patient—"

"That he would divorce his wife? Lilly, does that really seem likely?"

"No," she said quietly. "In fact, I always knew it possible he never would. But now—"

Fletcher stood and reached out a hand toward her. "Come on, Lilly. There's going to be a lot of blustering and swearing and interrogation. Let's get it behind us. I'll stand by you."

"Then you agree with me? I should be allowed to do as I please about this?"

"I think some solution will show itself when the wind calms and the sun comes out. Right now there's a lot of yelling to endure. Nothing will surface until Amanda has exhausted herself and Emily recovers. Let's just get the worst of it over."

"Oh, this is going to be horrible," she said, standing up and taking his arm to walk back.

"Soon, Lilly, you'll have to go see him. When you've heard all that has to be said, then it's time to decide. This week, Lilly, don't wait."

"Thank you, Fletcher, for not being ashamed of me."

"Lilly, I couldn't be that. I understand. I'm only sorry the circumstances aren't a bit happier for you. You'll make a wonderful mother."

"Wonderful or not, I already *am* a mother. Damn pity is, I'm not a wife!"

"Dear God!" was Emily's exclamation.

"Doesn't anyone in this family get married *first?*" Bertie chirped.

"Oh, don't judge," Amanda scolded. "We've only mixed that up a couple of times . . . It's not as though it hasn't ever happened before!"

"Lilly, who is the father?"

"Don't waste your breath, Emily. She isn't talking."

"It isn't *relevant*," Lilly said.

"If the father is not able to marry her," Fletcher said, "then his name will only confuse the issue."

"Hush up, Fletcher!"

"Fletcher is as much involved as anyone else in this family," Lilly argued. "At least he didn't scold me!"

"It's that miner from Minnesota," Bertie said, picking up a tray from the table and walking toward the kitchen to fix tea and whatever else would take the sting out of this meeting.

"That miner from Minnesota is a dolt!" Lilly said.

"Did the dolt compromise you? is the question," Emily said, her voice flat.

"I wasn't compromised," Lilly replied. "I was in love."

"She's going to have to take an extended holiday. There is simply no other way."

"Mother, surely there's some tale we can come up with to cover this?"

"Aren't we quite done with *tales?* Lord, I'm still trying to think of some story to explain Patricia!"

"What kind of tale could you use to cover this?" Lilly asked in astonishment.

"You could go away briefly," Emily said. "Katherine and I would go with you. We'll contrive some husband who will die before the wedding trip is over, and then we'll come home."

"Oh, Mother," Lilly sighed. "I am to go away a virgin and come home in three months, six months pregnant? Do you think *that* will cure gossip?"

"It could slow gossip."

"Do you see the world we live in?" Lilly said, flustered. "A world in which you're more respectable for attempting a terrible, stupid lie that no one believes for one second than if you simply bear your circumstances without playing everyone for fools!"

"Lilly, it is not as though *we* made these rules. We certainly won't get away with breaking them!"

"They've already been broken. Now all anyone can think of is how to confuse all the rules with lies and schemes!"

"The women in this family know nothing at all about men!" Bertie exclaimed, returning with tea and brandy.

"Well, some of us are learning a few things about men!" Amanda returned, glaring at Lilly.

383

Fletcher made a sound that could have been a laugh, and four women glared at him.

"Can't this be discussed without accusations concerning a person's character?" he asked somewhat lamely.

"If you're going to stay, be quiet! This is women's trouble," Amanda barked.

"I *want* Fletcher to stay," Lilly said, "And I don't intend to be scuttled off to Europe!"

On they went. Amanda was in search of an extended tour. Emily was seeking a story that would explain away the indiscretion of a sudden pregnancy. Bertie listed all the names of gentlemen she could remember. Fletcher watched and listened. There was a lot of pacing, a lot of swearing, and through it all Lilly was stoic, refusing to cry, refusing to name the man, refusing to let their upset cloud her decision. However it had to be managed, she intended to have her baby, hold it, love it, raise it.

It was the only thing, she supposed, that she and Andrew would ever have together. And he had thought the cottage would be their legacy!

Lilly began to believe they would be arguing over what must be done with her for so long that the baby would arrive and there would be nothing further to discuss. Later, when she was sitting on her bed brushing out her hair, Emily came into her bedroom and sat down beside her. She put a gentle hand on Lilly's shoulder, and Lilly put a hand over her mother's. "Mama, I'm sorry I disappointed you."

"I love you, Lilly. And I'll love your child. That's all there really is."

"Mama, I know it's wrong, but I'm actually happy. I've always wanted a child. This isn't quite the way I hoped it would be, but . . . I will try to be a good mother. As good as you."

"Lilly, what do you plan to do about him?"

"Oh, Mama, this really isn't his fault. He warned me—he tried to talk sense to me. I knew from the start he wasn't mine to keep. I thought there might be some solution to carry with the news."

"You are going to tell him?"

"Yes, certainly," she said.

"Are you going to put this man behind you, Lilly?"

"I suppose I must. I don't think I can accept this challenge regularly."

"I don't have the stamina. I don't know why you let it begin— you're smarter than most women."

"Mama, I've never learned to compromise, and I've never had the right sort of scruples. I couldn't be happier married to someone I don't love, and I couldn't be happier not having this baby growing in me. Oh, Mama," she said, a mist finally coming to her eyes, "I've never been the least attracted to conventional behavior! I'm perfectly hopeless!"

"You've carried such a big secret, Lilly, you must be filled with hope. My heart breaks for you."

"But I'll have a child," she said. "However big a mess this situation becomes, I will have and raise my child."

Lilly frequently carried a veiled hat in her large tote bag when she went to the flat Andrew had leased. Small, tidy, sparsely furnished, it was not very much. There was a bed, chest and bureau, armoire, table and chairs, a few dishes and pots, although they rarely shared a meal there. There was a wood stove, sink pump, and plenty of linens, and Andrew had hired someone to clean the place weekly. Lilly routinely had the coach leave her near the lending library, and from there she would walk to the little flat. Occasionally she passed residents who lived in the building and sometimes they would nod toward her. No one questioned Andrew about the place. Men, Lilly learned, could do as they pleased with their bodies; women were looked at with disapproval for the very same thing. Lilly's coat and shoes were of high quality, and she assumed those few people who saw her thought she was a prostitute or a married woman engaged in a secret affair. Her veil was for the sake of discretion. She really believed meeting Andrew here made as much sense in her life as any other thing she did.

Andrew had not yet arrived when she unlocked the door. She removed her hat and tossed it on the table. Then she sat on the settee and looked around the place. It seemed so reasonable, she thought, to choose carefully whom you loved and be true to that love.

When he arrived, letting himself in, he smiled, kissed her cheek, and went directly to the wood stove to light it. Making

tea for her was one of his rituals. He removed his jacket and unbuttoned his shirt at the collar before he drew her to her feet to
embrace her.

"Do you think we fool anyone?" she asked him. "The people I
pass look at me as though they can see through me."

"Do you care?" he said. "Lord, I missed you. Has it really only
been a week?"

She welcomed his kiss, that deep and wonderful kiss that had
become so familiar and comforting. All those predictable feelings
rose in her. How she loved him! But she finally wrenched herself free.
"Darling, stop. We have to talk. I have something important to tell
you."

"Can't you tell me while I—"

"I'm pregnant, Andrew," she blurted out.

He was momentarily startled and still. "You're sure?" he asked,
looking into her eyes.

"Yes, I'm sure. I haven't been to a doctor yet, but I'm sure.
Andrew, I—"

"Oh, Lilly!" he exclaimed, embracing her fiercely, covering her
cheeks with kisses, running his hands all over her. He finally held
her face in his hands and kissed her deeply. "Oh Lilly! Are you afraid?
Worried?"

"No," she said, laughing a little bit. "I know it isn't going to
be easy . . . and I've upset the family, as you can imagine . . . but I
feel wonderful and I'm happy. You?"

"My God! As terrible a thing as it could be . . . Lord, I've always
wanted a child, and I've never thought of anyone but you having my
child! I tried to prevent it, but I always knew if I failed I would be
overjoyed. The cottage!"

"No," she said, laughing again. "I meant to tell you at the
cottage. I'm afraid you were wasting your time with all your safe
measures. It must have happened right here where you were always
careful."

He picked her up, spinning her around in carefree abandon.
"Lilly, Lilly, how I love you. Don't worry. You mustn't worry. I'll
take care of you!"

"Andrew! Put me down!"

"Is Amanda loading her Flintwood?" he asked.

"I wouldn't tell them whose it is. Funny, with all the boring, stupid men I've been forced to dine with, your name didn't come up. Even when I said my lover was married!"

"Well, I'm sure they'll find out. Not that I care. I'm proud, Lilly. I'll do right by you. Both of you."

"Andrew, I knew you'd be happy! You mustn't tell them, they'd be so angry with you. They would never believe that it was I who—"

"I can transfer all my business to New York, Lilly. I'll build you a house in the country. I'll take care of you. The neighborhood won't even know we're not married."

Her eyes grew round. "Andrew, I don't want to go to New York. The hotel—"

"The hotel will be fine without you. You're having my child— you can't stay in the hotel now."

"Of course I can. It's my home, my work. I'll manage. I suppose people will gossip, but they will always gossip. Sooner or later it will become dull. It just won't matter that much for that long."

"Don't be absurd. They would ask you questions, stare at you—"

"Andrew, they stare at me now. When people don't know what to make of me, they make something up. I don't care. The hotel draws its own guests because it's good. I don't want to leave."

He put his arms around her waist. "Think about this, Lilly. You're going to have a child, my child," he said, his hand resting over her tummy. "Did you think you would just go on as always if this happened? You have to let me take care of you now."

"But I can take care of myself. I have plenty of money, and I have my work."

"Your family will be your work now. And I'll be with you."

She laughed hollowly. "I wouldn't survive without work," she said. "You know that."

"That was before, darling," he said, kissing her neck.

"A house in the country?" she asked, frowning. But he didn't see her frown.

"A beautiful house in the country," he murmured.

"Just how many women do you propose to stash away in the country in your lifetime, Andrew? I'll be the second . . . perhaps you have a number in mind."

He pulled away from her and looked at her face. "You know Brenda's circumstances are special. And that will be resolved, as soon as possible."

"Do you suggest I go to the country, temporarily, until you can have your annulment or divorce? Then back to the hotel?"

"Not actually," he said, frowning himself. "Perhaps someday. Until we can be a real, legal family, we'll do the best we can. We can't be apart. Don't you want a home to raise your children in?"

"Children? I think there's just this one!"

"I thought you would want to be with me—especially now."

"Of course I want to be with you," she said. "But I can't be. You're married, and I don't want to be stowed away in the country until you can be *un*married. It could take years!"

"I told you ours was another kind of life. You said it was what you wanted."

"I wanted to be your mistress, not your property. I don't like this idea any better than Grandmother's solution—she would have me go to Europe and give away my child. Mama thinks I should make up some lie and pretend to have a husband just long enough to get caught. You want to hide me in the country. Can't anyone just accept that it's happened, I'm having a child? Lord, is gossip *that* important?"

"You're not giving us a lot of choices. What do you propose? To stay in the hotel doing what you do and—"

"Well, Andrew, I don't intend to parade around the foyer or grounds in a delicate condition, and I don't plan to answer any questions. I suppose people will speculate, as they often do, but I'm only concerned about providing a good home for my—"

"And my child? How am I to take care of my child?"

"Until you can manage to marry me, I suppose you'll have to remain a friend of the family—"

"Friend of the family! Listen to what you're saying!"

"What do you want me to do? Oh never mind, you want me to grow fat in the country—at your haven, where you may visit as the man of the house and your child can call you Father, where the neighbors need not even know we're not married! Andrew, I can wait. I can wait for years if need be, but darling, I can't sit in the country and make believe you're my—"

"Wait? You mean to end it, now that you carry my child? Put

me back into that friendly and hospitable mime as a family friend until we can publicly court?"

"I can't be having a lot of children and no husband," she said, amazed by his anger.

"Lilly, stop it. You always knew this could happen!"

"I always knew I might become pregnant! I didn't know everyone would have a plan to hide me away, each one worse than the last! I want to stay in my own home, doing my work, and if the time comes when you're free to take your place in my life, you will be welcome!"

"You knew that might never happen! You knew we might have to make do!"

"We? How do *you* plan to make do? Your plan serves you very well. What do you have to sacrifice but a few dollars to have me sequestered away in secret, hidden from family and friends, breeding a lot of illegitimate children for you? You wouldn't—"

"If I were a woman who could come with child, I would! If I were a woman who chose an affair in lieu of a marriage, I would be willing to pay the price, meet the cost!"

"I am meeting the cost, damn you! I'm going to give birth, protect my reputation and child as well as possible without a lot of lies, and wait for you. Why—why do people prefer lies to the truth? Wouldn't it be better for us both if you are near and welcomed in the home where your child lives than to have an unhappy woman stuck away in the country?"

"How do you suppose you'll bear the shame of—"

"I *refuse* to be ashamed! Damn it, don't you see? There is no lie that will make life better than enduring whatever is said and loving my child! There is nothing that would be believed! I don't intend to spit in their eyes—I only mean to carry on!"

"And if word gets out that Lilly Armstrong is giving birth with no husband? How do you think that will sit with your precious hotel guests?"

"I don't care! If their prissy morals are outraged by my private behavior, let them find a better hotel! Let them *try!* Lord above, look how they snickered about Patricia! No one seems to mention the fact that Ned Armstrong was seen long after he was supposed to be dead, and Grandmother saved her status by marrying as quickly as possible. If society puts them all above me, to hell with them. If you think

you're going to tempt me into the country where I'll be quiet and mannerly and not draw attention to the fact that I'm having a—"
She stopped herself.

"Lilly, how do you expect me to behave? Do you see me as a pleasant dinner guest, watching you round out? Will he call me 'Uncle Andrew' and bounce on my knee?"

"The only reason I haven't told it's your baby is because I want you to be near. Andrew, I'm not ashamed that it's you; I'm proud that it's you I love. I hope that someday—"

"What if I tell them? What if I confront the whole bunch, Lady Nesbitt and all? Then what will you do?"

She lifted her chin. "My condition will be unchanged. You might be banned from the premises, the loss would be greater for you. That someday may be further than—"

"There may never be a someday! Brenda's sick, damn it! Don't you know what could happen to her if I push too hard? Is that what you want from me?"

"I never asked that of you. Never! You were the one who said that you were never married, that you were tricked and lied to and wanted to get free of it all. God, do you think I could love you as I do if you were the kind of man who couldn't take care of her and forgive her?"

"And if I had never uttered those words—that I wanted to be free? Then what would you be saying now?"

"The same things," she said, her voice trembling.

"That we would now become *friends*? You made a commitment to me, God damn it!"

"A commitment to love you! I wanted you! We never had any agreement about how I would handle a—"

"You can't walk away!"

"How can you speak to me like this? I don't understand you anymore. I'm not walking away from anything. I'm offering to deal with this alone and protect you as well! Protect you so that my outraged family won't expel you, so you can be near your child."

"Near? A distant part of his life, a friendly part of yours!"

"And it would be better to admit what I am to you, flee to some private, lonely country house, and go on and on forever? I can't believe you'd ask that of me!"

"Lilly, please," he said. "Please, let me take care of you. Please don't lock me away from my child this way."

"If you ask me to give up everything I've built, my family and my life, you can't really love me. I love you, and I will always love you. But you take too much for granted."

"I believed you," he said. "You seemed so sure of yourself, of what you wanted. Now—"

"I'm still sure," she said. She could feel her heart thumping with the pain of loss. She knew she couldn't carry on with this affair as she had, she would have a child to raise and couldn't keep adding siblings. But she had hope! Hope that in time he could be hers! She could be stronger than desire for the sake of Andrew's child! She knew that she could wait for him, for years, if need be. She had not imagined this sort of end until she heard him explain how he would handle her and their child. "I didn't want anything of you; I didn't ask anything. I'm sorry for Brenda; I'm sorry for us. If you can't stand beside me any other way than in a house in the country—I'm sorry, I wouldn't survive. If my grandmother can only accept me if I flee and give away my child, if Mama can only accept a lie, a tale . . . I will be more alone than I thought."

"If you saw her, you'd understand! She's mad, she's sorry, she begs for forgiveness and is barely clinging to some kind of hope that she'll get well!"

"Her hope is you. Funny, we had that in common."

"Come away with me, Lilly. Just give me time," he begged.

"If I let you scuttle me off to the country, our affair will go on, just like this, forever." She sighed, fighting tears. "I'm sorry, Andrew. I didn't know it would be like this."

He reached for her and covered her lips with his; his kiss was brutal and filled with pain. Tears came to Lilly's eyes. In spite of herself, she clung to him. "Can you live without this better than me, Lilly?" he asked her, his hand running up her rib cage and covering a breast. "All we've had, all we've been and shared together—can you so easily brush me aside and demand I act like a family friend while I watch my child grow up without me?"

She shook her head, and the tears came loose. "No," she said in a breath.

"I gave you everything I had. I never lied to you. You knew what I had to deal with!"

"I said I would wait. I didn't say where or how."

"You could wait with *me!*"

She shook her head. "No," she said. "I'll wait at home. As best I can."

"How can you betray me while you carry my child?" he asked pleadingly.

"Betray you? Oh, Andrew, is that what it is when a woman doesn't follow your orders?" She shook her head again and the tears dropped freely from her eyes. "I thought you were different! I thought you understood me."

"I thought I did, too!"

She pulled away from him and walked toward the table. She picked up her hat and looked at it, fingering the short veil that was meant to conceal her identity when she came to this little flat to have physical love. Free love. She tossed the hat back on the table. "I won't be needing this anymore," she said.

"Lilly, what do you mean to do?"

She looked at him for a long moment, wondering how she was going to live without him, how she would manage to give up the magic of an intimate life. "I'm going home, Andrew. Please, come and visit. Everyone loves seeing you."

"Lilly! Damn it!"

"Good-bye, darling."

When Fletcher found her, she was in her favorite place in the gazebo in the middle of the Queen Victoria Garden. Her tears had long since dried.

"Your mother suggested you might be here," he said. "Mind if I join you?"

"I'm not likely to be good company," she warned him.

"Your eyes are red. You've been crying," he said. "I suppose that means you've spoken to him."

"Oh yes," she said, adding a derisive grunt of disapproval.

"And . . . ?"

"He has a perfect solution—for himself. I should put myself in his tender and protective custody now, in a house in the country where he can come and go as he pleases and the neighbors need not even *know* we are not married."

"Oh?" Fletcher said, laughing in spite of himself.

"I'm glad *you're* amused!"

"I hoped I would guess wrong, but that seems to be a common solution to this type of problem. With effort he could find you a whole town of mistresses raising the offspring of married men!"

"Lord, what a thought!"

"In all fairness to the man, Lilly, even if he went straightaway to a solicitor and courts, getting a divorce is a damnable thing to get through. It takes a long time."

"Yes, I know that. But if he had me in his country house, having a lot of babies, do you suppose he would *ever* feel the need to get on with that? The amazing thing is that it was never my suggestion that he get free of his wife. She was there when this started. I knew she could be there still when it—" She had trouble with that word: *ended.*

"And you haven't come up with any good ideas, have you?"

"Just the same one. I'll try not to draw attention to myself. The accounting ledgers won't be offended by my expanding girth, I'm quite sure. I doubt there would be more or less talk if I were to marry a divorced man. People stay so busy with talk! When haven't they?"

"There seems to be one thing you haven't considered. I know you're strong enough to withstand the worst gossip. I know you don't care what people say. But what about the child, Lilly?"

"Would the child be better off given away? Or raised by an unhappy mother in the country?"

"No, certainly not. But here? With the gossip? Don't you think he would suffer? Would his playmates call him bastard?"

"I don't know that we've established he is going to be fatherless forever. Would everyone cling to gossip so heartily for five years? Ten? Why would they? Why wouldn't my child, loved and wanted, be happy with me? With us?"

"Sometimes you act as though this child will always be a baby. What if you never marry, Lilly? What if there is no steamier gossip than about your determination to have and raise an illegitimate child? Do you mean to keep him locked inside your apartments, apart from the world, apart from life? Will he ask you, someday, why he can't know his father's name? Will you give him a false name, a name that he can't uncover?"

"No! Of course not! When he's old enough—" She stopped suddenly. She hadn't thought about her child. Neither had anyone else until Fletcher did. Andrew thought of himself; he would keep his secret family in the country where he could have his fill of them and bide his time. Amanda would save her reputation by sending Lilly away. Emily would cover it up with some tale. And Lilly had devised a method of grasping her child in an I-don't-care-what-they-say world as if he would never grow up and ask questions!

"Will he be angry someday at all you contrived to have at his expense? We might all learn to live with this plan of yours, but will he?"

"Oh, Fletcher! What *am* I going to do?" she asked, suddenly feeling she must choose between Europe or a country estate as the mistress of a man who would only expect more of her sacrifices.

"I have a thought. Not a great one," he said. "I've given it some consideration. I suppose you could marry me."

"You?" she asked, shocked.

"They would snicker just the same. The age difference and all. I'm fifty."

"Oh, Fletcher, how could you make such a noble offer?"

He laughed and looked around. "The answer is not romantic, Lilly. I can make the offer because I'm not the least bit in love with you. Nor can I be. I'm very fond of you. I really don't think it would be good for the hotel or the women if you went away. And I don't know that your little plan bears the least resemblance to a solution. No one would accept you, you know, that way. You're too unconventional, Lilly. I think you're brilliant, and I think you're *right*. But that simply won't help you now."

"But, Fletcher! You have so many women!"

"Yes," he laughed. "I would have to be discreet, wouldn't I? Lilly, I won't lie to you, I don't want you for a wife—I think of you as a daughter at most. I'm not even sure I can bear to have a small child around much of the time—I'm impatient and set in my ways. I've always lived a solitary bachelor's life, and I'd like to continue that. When I was younger, I wished for a child—my own childhood was terrible and I thought I could do better. I'm afraid I've long since

394

stopped wishing for that. But . . . I could give you a name. A paternity. That's about all. It wouldn't be the kind of life you would expect as a wife."

"And my child? Would you want a child to whom you are only a legal paternity to call you Father?"

"That seems reasonable," he said, shrugging. "My greatest concern for him is that he wouldn't see much affection between us. Just ordinary, polite behavior, but that's better than having only one parent. We're good friends, Lilly, and that's all we'll ever be. Your child would probably be more drawn to the likes of . . . say . . . our friend Andrew Devon."

22

*E*mily Armstrong was in the foyer when the hotel coach brought Noel Padgett back to her. She went to the portico to greet him.

"Welcome home, Mr. Padgett," she said. "Fortunately your favorite suite is vacant."

"Thank you, Mrs. Armstrong," he said, smiling at her and tipping his hat. "It's good to be back."

"Frank," she said to the doorman, "please have Mr. Padgett's things taken to his suite. Mr. Padgett, I would love to show you Lilly's new gardens if you're interested. She's so proud of what's been done there."

"I'd be honored, ma'am," he said, offering his arm. "I'm a might dusty from the road."

"Now, Mr. Padgett, you could hardly help that," she said, walking away from the portico with him. "You'll welcome a warm tub and good meal tonight, I suppose."

"I'd welcome a damn sight more than that," he said, patting her hand and strolling with her toward the Queen Victoria Garden.

"Since you're always made welcome at Mother's table, I thought I should explain that the household is in an absolute dither. Ah, now where did it begin? With which one of my daughters? Yes, Patricia was the first."

"She seems to hold that distinction in every problem."

"Oh, but Lilly won't have her outdone. It was Patricia first—she decided to run off with John Giddings."

"Now you're spinning tales!"

"No indeed! It was quite a night—Patricia packing and Mother fuming and Lilly crying. She didn't take Katherine. I feel so terrible about that—not that I could live without Katherine. I suppose I'm devastated that she left her child, but I would have been more devastated had she taken her."

"I can't believe John spirited her away," he said.

"With him she can be her best self. He adores her, Lilly tells me. I can't fathom it. I don't know how he persuaded her. But Patricia has always wanted some kind of unbelievable life, and John's novel has invented her all over again. He gives her credit for it all, and I believe she must ride through Central Park imagining she is Chloe Tillets."

"Who?"

"Oh," Emily laughed, "the heroine, of course."

"You don't seem all that devastated," he pointed out as they neared the garden.

"Sometimes when there is so much—too much, actually—the only thing to do is let it all happen and carry on. Mother was always the one to try to change things, control them. Lilly will be like Mother in some ways. She is certainly her equal in stubbornness. But you see, this place and all its opulence and luxury were never what I needed to be happy. I have that old boardinghouse, and I wouldn't be miserable going back there. Sometimes I think I'll do just that! The simple life isn't a bad life. I was happy there."

"And Lilly?"

"Lilly is pregnant. We're keeping it in the family while we can, but you should know why Mother and Lilly spend a good share of time snipping at each other. You're like family. I thought you might welcome the warning. She's a large girl, so she will be able to conceal it for a while."

Noel whistled in astonishment. "Is she getting married?"

"Oh no, there will be no wedding. The man she claims is responsible, some man whose name we are not invited to know, is already married. Mother wants to send her away to Europe to have her child in secret, and Lilly won't go. Simple as that! She is very determined that her circumstances—choosing a man for love and refusing to be ashamed of it—are more respectable circumstances than some of ours—Mother's, mine, Patricia's."

"I see," he said, brooding on this for a while. "And when this child is born?"

"She says she will not lie, nor pretend it isn't her very own child, and if anyone has the audacity to ask her directly if she is indeed an unmarried mother, that person will deserve the answer it will bring."

"This could reflect on you, on Amanda."

"Well, there you are—I don't care. Mother is outraged, but she loves Lilly."

"What about the hotel? What if—"

"This place keeps Mother young, but if the whole monster emptied out, if no self-respecting family on holiday would even consider such a shameful abode, Mother could get a buyer in a second. Wilson Montaine makes an offer almost monthly, though he's old and slowing down and does less business every year. It's a legacy the two of them have. A kind of struggle for power. They have to try to beat each other somehow. At least it's become a more affectionate kind of competitiveness they play."

Noel gave a huff of laughter in sheer disbelief. "I can remember a time when I couldn't ask for a spittoon without being evicted!"

"Yes, well, that has certainly changed. Our family is tumbling about. I'm sure we'll provide some very entertaining gossip for anyone interested enough to have a look. I admire Lilly in a way—I certainly never had that kind of courage."

"Is her courage going to be good for her child?" he asked.

"That argument has been done, over and over. She asks simply would it be better for her child to grow up believing his father is dead? Better to be abandoned when she runs off with a man other than her husband to inspire fairy tales? Better to grow up knowing some man as his father and have that be a lie? Lilly intends to raise her child and tell that child, at the right age, the absolute truth. She says her child will find something to be angry about if he's an angry child—and at least he can be angry at being told the truth. I don't

399

know what to think, Noel. It isn't going to be an easy life for her, the one she's chosen."

"Or for you," he said sympathetically.

"As the years go by and all these people I love choose their various rebellious methods of confronting life, I have less and less of a grasp of what is right and what is wrong. Have I ever told you how furious I was that my own mother went off to marry? She was so determined to marry well, she had to do it twice more before she perfected it! I couldn't bear that my own mother would marry some rich man she was barely acquainted with—and I suddenly found myself begging Lilly to marry anyone at all just to save her reputation."

"Yours hasn't been a strictly conventional life, though your secret was better kept."

"I received the telegram, Noel."

"What telegram?" he asked.

"The one from Chicago. It said that you identified the body of Ned Armstrong."

"Oh," he said, "that telegram."

"Do you want to try to explain?"

"I don't dare. Nope, I don't think I want to."

"I won't marry you until I have the truth."

"No, Emily," he said, still walking, "you won't marry me when you get it."

"Then I guess I won't be marrying you at all."

He stopped walking and stood looking out over those lovely gardens, thinking. She waited patiently. He finally turned to her and looked in her eyes. "I went looking for him, Emily. I found him and helped him bury himself deeper in his messes, the same kind of lying, cheating messes he's been making all his life."

"I doubt he required much help," she said.

"Emily, I meant to shoot him in a card game. Cheaters still get shot out West and in some rough parts of most cities. It was only because someone else beat me to it that I didn't shoot him myself."

"Noel, you wouldn't have killed him."

"Yes, ma'am, I would have. I meant to. Now, that's the only truth there is. I want you. I wanted you to be able to marry me, and I aimed to help it along."

"Have you ever killed a man?" she asked him.

"Yep."

"When?"

"In the war. Once on a cattle drive when we were ambushed."

"No, no. Have you ever murdered a man?"

"Nope, but only because—"

"How long were you acquainted with Ned before he was killed?"

"I knew where he was for a long time—I was acquainted with him for several months. When I left you that first time, I didn't go to Wyoming. I went—"

"There, you see. You wouldn't have done that. You thought you would, you see. But if that had really been your intention, you wouldn't have waited so long—you would have killed him in the first card game. If someone else hadn't, you would have just come back."

"Emily, I—"

"Hush, Noel. You didn't. That's what matters. Remember who you're talking to—I pointed a gun at him myself! And if you hadn't been there, I never would have known he was dead. I know you believe yourself a powerful man, but Ned created plenty of his own trouble. It would have happened eventually. I'm surprised it didn't happen long ago."

"Will you marry me?" he asked her.

"Of course," she said. "Although my family seems to be getting out of the tradition."

"You really believe that? That I wouldn't have—"

"Do you really believe you would have?"

He turned to walk with her again. "I sure as hell did, until this very moment."

"Well, forget such nonsense. You're not that kind of man."

"Emily, I swear before God, until I met you I had a whole lot of ideas about what kind of man I was, and you plumb blew every one of them apart."

"Noel, you don't swear before God!"

"Yes, ma'am," he laughed. "I mean, no ma'am."

"You're not such a ruthless cowboy—at least not with me."

"With you, Emily, I am more than I thought I was."

It was July when Andrew went to Reading to see Father Demetrius. This time he wouldn't see Brenda; he was relieved that he wouldn't have to. In May she had had a brief relapse but the priest had tried to persuade her out of it. He had made excuses; it had not been a *real* relapse. She had only suffered for a few days and was convinced that if there were future incidents, they wouldn't last long. Andrew wasn't as convinced and he thought this miracle was more of a coincidence.

"It's an un-Christian thing you're asking me to do," the priest said.

"I've already been to confession, Father. It's been an un-Christian thing that's gone on for ten years in a hopeless, loveless marriage, and my penance has been dutifully paid. Over and over."

"If you haven't already considered what this could do to her, do so now. Her health is fragile and her mind is—"

"Listen to me," Andrew said impatiently, "she's been fragile since the day I met her. You've heard the whole thing from her own lips. It isn't her crime—it isn't mine. The church will approve an annulment for a marriage that was based in trickery and deceit."

"Part of her ability to be well lies in your forgiveness."

"My forgiveness or my continual sacrifice? When do I benefit from this holy forgiveness?"

"She's your legal wife, and the marriage was consummated—"

"She consummated things all over town in the early days! Oh hell, that's not the point! I didn't make her sick, and I can't make her well. I can only do what I've been doing—provide for her, encourage her. I have forgiven her. That doesn't mean I have to give up the rest of my life for—"

"It's a noble and honorable sacrifice. Marriage is a holy—"

"It's not just me. Other people have sacrificed too much, continue to sacrifice too much for this illusion a mad woman has of a marriage that has never existed. Father, she was not my wife for longer than four months! What do you think I've done the last ten years? I've started a life for myself. I've worked like a farm beast to earn what it takes to live three lives—the caretaker here, the businessman somewhere else, and—"

The priest looked over his spectacles, waiting.

"There's a woman, Father. She's going to have my child."

"I see," the priest said, looking at the papers on his desk.

"I'm thirty-six years old, Father. I *want* this child."

"The issue of adultery could complicate your petition for an annulment, Andrew. Not to mention what this development could do to Brenda. And of course I've already written many letters about her condition to the archdiocese in—"

"Letters about her? What kind of letters?"

"The church is very interested in the healing works of priests and in those who have experienced the miracles of prayer. It's a long tradition among us to share these benefits of faith."

Andrew listened to the priest without interruption and felt the hair on the back of his neck begin to prickle.

"We have been blessed in Reading. Cases of cholera have been healed, there was a woman who had never in her life spoken who was healed by prayer, and a deaf child can now hear. All healed by the love of Christ."

By you, Andrew thought. He was suddenly sure of something; he'd met very few honest people in his life. The honest ones were the most criticized. Wilson. Lilly.

"Brenda was a major achievement for you, Father," he said shrewdly.

"I was fortunate to be the vessel through which—"

"You might achieve immortality through your good works," Andrew said. "Her condition of madness must surely be the most rare, the most difficult."

"We have immortality through Christ," the priest said. "The work we're given is special, difficult, and if I could make you see one thing, Andrew, for the sake of your own soul, it is that sacrifice of one's worldly attachments can be the path through which we have life everlasting and joy while we're alive."

"Also fame," Andrew said. "Possibly sainthood."

"I think you've missed the point. What we have is a more meaningful life, a greater eternal pleasure."

But Andrew didn't think he had missed the point. The priest was going to add Brenda's recovery to a list of achievements he had written about to the church leaders. He had made himself a savior; many people in Reading were cognizant of his healing powers and he was visited often by the sick. If the word continued to spread, if the priest had many cures to his credit, he would be worshipped. He might get power in the church.

He had power over Brenda—that was the cure. Brenda had been overcome by her mother, then her dead mother, now the priest. Who knew how well she was? She could be controlled by Mrs. Waite. It was only the period after her mother's death and before Father Demetrius discovered her that she had been out of control, completely unmanageable.

"I think it would be a shame to mention adultery and somehow fail to get the annulment," Andrew said. "I suppose the best tactic would be to mention in your petition that the husband has suffered too long and must be given an opportunity to have a family to carry on the name. Brenda cannot be encouraged to have children."

"I don't know that we've established she can never have children. In fact—"

"She can't have them with me, Father. I can't be her husband anymore."

"I don't know that I can accommodate you, Andrew. The petition would absolutely require Brenda's endorsement, and . . ."

Andrew's concept of priests had been a very confused one all of his life. Taught to respect them, he couldn't dismiss his distrust. He often wondered if his father had been a good man who couldn't control his passion or an opportunist who used the power of his reverence to seduce a young girl. What excuses were used on his own mother? Had his father been decent, wouldn't he have left the church and married the mother of his child? What would God have expected of that priest? Of this one? "Convince her. I know you can. Tell her that it's the best possible way for her to become well. Tell her that she has to forgive me, you've convinced her to forgive the ones who really hurt her. I'll see that she's cared for. That's as much as I'm willing to do."

"I'm sorry, Andrew, I can't—"

"If you refuse, I'll take her away from here. I'll put her in an asylum. They'll keep her from hurting anyone."

The priest's eyes grew narrow and angry. "That would be a cruel and heartless thing to do!"

"This is cruel and heartless! I don't think God would love me any better if I let others live in pain and humiliation because you would like to have credit for healing Brenda! Perhaps if this were my fault, perhaps if my own hand or terrible words dealt her this madness, perhaps then you could convince me to carry on out of guilt, but that isn't the way of it. I know you can help me. You won't get much credit for it, but you can do it."

"And if I won't?"

"Then say good-bye to her on your next visit. I mean it, Father. I'll take her out of here. And I'll write my own letters, bring in priests to judge her condition, whatever I have to do."

"You will be dealing the death blow."

"Not if you do your part. Not if you continue to tell her what she wants and feels. The pity is that even you can't keep her going forever."

"I'll have to think," the priest said. "I'll have to pray."

"Good," Andrew said. "Think, pray, and visit my wife. I will see you in two weeks."

The gamble he had taken did not worry Andrew until he was away from Reading. It was then that sleeplessness and guilt had their day; he added prayers of his own. He prayed he had not misjudged what seemed obvious. The full two weeks passed slowly. He had not seen Lilly since May; he had not had the courage to look at her until he had resolved part of his burden.

Brenda seemed not to notice his exhaustion, his worry. She was plagued with her own. "I have to tell you something important," she said during their walk. "I'm afraid it's very bad news, Andrew. I hope you will forgive me."

"Whatever it is, I'm sure you've thought it through."

"It's been very difficult, but if I'm to have the kind of life that isn't marred by illness, I have to break free of the past. Oh, Andrew, I'm so sorry. I know you were hopeful that we could build some kind of life together—but it's important that I find a way to start over. Father Demetrius believes a good thing to do would be to ask for an annulment of our marriage. I don't know how I'll live, but I'll manage something with the help of——"

"You don't have to worry about how you'll live," he said. "I won't abandon you. I'll pay for your care until you don't need me anymore."

"Oh, Andrew," she said, tears coming to her eyes, "Father is so right about you! You're such a generous, wonderful man."

Generous, wonderful, and late, he thought. He saw the priest on his way out of town. "Thank you," he said.

"It won't be in time for your child," the priest glumly informed him. "I suspect a year, perhaps two."

"Don't drag it out, Father."

"I told you, it takes—"

"I'll be here in September to see how she is. She thinks my visits will be good for her, even under the circumstances."

"September, then," Father Demetrius said unhappily, more than aware that Andrew intended to monitor the sanity of his wife, prepared to write those letters, prepared to expose the priest as a fraud. Extortion had worked better for Andrew than all the forgiveness, responsibility, and honorable suffering had. It left him bitter and angry when he left Reading. It left him wondering if he could really live without guilt. Which guilt? Remaining the long suffering husband while Lilly and his child endured alone? Staying with Lilly while Brenda remained the pawn of a power-hungry priest?

Lilly had not really considered Fletcher's offer of marriage. She had said she couldn't be happier married to a man she didn't love. She had said there was no lie that could be better than bravely bearing the circumstances. But she had spoken all those words before she began to feel her child move within her, before she found the need for loose clothing, before she heard someone mutter *poule de luxe* as she passed. It was French for "prostitute deluxe."

The last time she ventured out publicly had been to attend a small party for her mother and Noel Padgett on the July day they married. It was the single happy day in her summer, seeing her mother achieve the joy of a marriage of love. There had been very few present at the simple ceremony, only the friends and staff members who held Emily dear. And of course, Sophia Washington, who grew ever more beautiful in Lilly's eyes as her face wrinkled and her eyes burned with that bright fire.

"Your Mama never been happier than this," she whispered to Lilly. "Miz Em waited her whole life for this man."

"I hope I don't have to wait my whole life," Lilly said quietly.

"That baby kickin' you yet, child?" Sophia asked.

"You know?" Lilly asked in surprise.

"Now, how you gwine to keep a secret 'round this house?" Sophia laughed, her grin wide and sparkling. "Jes' see you don't make it no worse on yourself."

"Your advice hasn't changed in twenty years," Lilly told her.

"World hasn't changed in longer than that," she said.

Noel Padgett entered the apartments as comfortably as a husband as he had as a tenant or guest. He didn't promise not to travel west again, but he sold his ranch and banked the money. He became a natural grandfather for Katherine.

Seeing Emily happy was not enough to ease Lilly's loneliness. However determined she was, she did not find herself able to ignore blithely the looks, the insensitive comments. She began to use the back stairs to go to the stables to fetch herself transportation from the hotel rather than going through the foyer to the portico where she would have to face guests. She greeted Jake, a hand she had hired herself, and found her greeting was answered with downcast eyes; as politely as possible, he did not look at her. She was informed that two maids had left her employ because they feared the hotel was soon to become a house of ill repute. Though it was only two, it felt like two hundred.

Lilly could enjoy the gardens only at dawn; at dusk hotel guests walked there. Her accounts were not insulted by her growing girth, but her secretary was and could barely look into Lilly's eyes when work was being assigned.

She kept whatever tears of self-pity she had to herself. Elizabeth bravely and sorrowfully resigned.

"Lilly, your grandmother has asked me who it was. Your resolve to have him has caused you too much pain for me to watch. They're all talking—in the offices, in the dining room, in the stables. I'm afraid—"

"That this will stain you," Lilly finished for her. Elizabeth promptly cried. "It's all right, Bethie, darling. I do understand. You've never been brave, but you've been a good, good friend. Did you tell?"

"No," she said, weeping.

"Well, thank you for that. I shouldn't have asked you not to in the first place."

"Lilly, it's not too late to go away somewhere and—"

"Yes, it is," she said flatly. "That won't fool anyone now."

"If he comes around, Lilly, I don't know if I can—"

"Of course you can't protect him—that's not your job. I'm not going to insist you stay. You're not a bondslave for goodness' sake. But Bethie, this will pass. Come to visit us when my motherhood is not all the rage," she said, pretending more courage than she felt. Losing Elizabeth was the second of many difficult revelations. Andrew's absence, which had not seemed to raise the curiosity of anyone else, had been the first.

September brought cooler weather and Lilly's increasing size. She found herself all but hiding. There were very few places she could go and not suffer averted eyes, muttered recriminations, or outright staring. There were a few surprises that she hadn't counted on—the sympathy of a laundress who met her eyes and asked her forthrightly if she was feeling well and offered a home remedy for dizziness that had been in her family for years. There was the gift of a hand-sewn quilt from the wife of a groundskeeper. This led Lilly to believe that people wanted to rise above prejudice and intolerance, but didn't quite know how. Those minor things helped her ease her distress in a difficult time.

The hotel maintained its reservations, but Lilly worried that if she were seen among them in her delicate condition, she would infect the business; even married women who were with child did not socialize publicly. The staff and her grandmother's friends were having a gossip feast, but to guests she was anonymous; if they became acquainted only with Amanda, the business might endure. She realized that if she was completely wrong, if the behavior all around her didn't adjust and improve, she would end up in the country or perhaps some other city, starting over. This suffering she could bear, but as her child became older, she would not be able to raise it among such reproof. She wouldn't have her son or daughter shunned, friendless, and scrutinized. She might be forced to adopt some convenient lie after all—but she would not do it for all the wrong reasons.

When the weather was cold enough late in September for large capes, Lilly could entertain herself by taking a coach to Rittenhouse Square or the theater where she wasn't known. She visited Fletcher's townhouse for luncheon or tea and began to think of him as her dearest friend outside the family. With him she could be completely herself; she found a new hospitality with him in her condition. She had been meeting with him for years about business; there was a different kind of friendship with him when she called on him socially. He always worried about her comfort and health, and he talked to her about books and plays, subjects they hadn't indulged before. Fletcher's solicitous valet, Michael, would make them tea, stoke the fire, and sometimes shyly offer to get a lap robe for Lilly. It was Fletcher's house where she felt the most nurtured.

"I should have married you," she told him one day. "I could be happy here. I could work as well."

"You'll work again, Lilly. And you're always welcome here."

Even the outings to the city were going to become rare as her pregnancy threatened to exceed the winter capes she hid under. She took an Armstrong Arms coach to Philly to walk about in the cold air, and though she hadn't asked Fletcher if she could visit, when the thought came, it was natural for her to walk to his house. She didn't realize she shouldn't presume on an open invitation.

No one answered her knock and she turned to walk away. Then, thinking perhaps Michael was out and Fletcher could be at work in his upstairs office, she tried the door and found it unlocked. She smiled to see the fire in the hearth on this cold fall day. Fletcher must be buried in paperwork. She began up the stairs when she heard Fletcher's voice.

"When you touch me like that, I can't concentrate on work."

Lilly felt embarrassment rush to her cheeks. She turned very quietly to sneak away; she had not considered the obvious—that Fletcher might have a woman with him.

"Forget about work for a while. Come downstairs and let me fix you a drink."

Lilly stopped suddenly. The voice was Michael's. She felt confusion; her eyes began to shift in bewilderment. She had misheard. No, she had heard. A riot of confounding, unbelievable possibilities rushed to her head all at once. All she was sure of was that she couldn't be found on the stair.

She fled from the house as quietly as she had come and walked briskly away, her cheeks on fire and her pulse racing. It was the need to sit down and think, slow her heartbeat and take stock that sent her back to the park where she could deal sensibly with her flood of emotions. Her first conclusion upset and disgusted her. Fletcher and Michael! She couldn't fathom it. She had heard of such things but had never considered them really possible. Lilly, who had asked such blatant questions in her life, had never found that one on her lips.

She sat and stared, her mind awash in confusion, while she began to believe what she had heard. All these many years! Fletcher left the British courts because he could not be seduced by a public life, because fame in the courts often preceded a political life and he had no interest in leaving himself so disposed to the whims of the public. He liked his work for Amanda in which he could be private, anonymous. His reputation as a ladies' man reminded her of the number of times he had been asked why he didn't marry. Being seen with women must have been a necessity to protect his private obsession.

A bachelor's life, he had told her. His was much more than that. She shivered to think she might have married him. But then she felt tears come to her eyes. Whether or not she understood what she had just discovered, they cared for each other very deeply. What an enormous risk he had exposed himself to, offering to bring Lilly and a child into his life with Michael! She would have discovered them eventually. He couldn't possibly have known what her reaction might be! She could expose him! Humiliate and destroy him! In outrage she could have easily cost him his secret. She could have cost him his happiness—Michael.

Yet, they had never been anything but kind to her. What had Fletcher told her? He was more tolerant than most. Love was decent and right, but risky. Of course he was tolerant—his secret was far more shocking than hers. How complex and confusing the world felt, suddenly. When she thought about the chances she took with her child, her love affair, her reputation, it all became far less overwhelming than what others faced in their intense, private lives.

She doubted this was a thing she would ever understand. She also knew that her ability to comprehend the true meaning of freedom hit a snag that she might not overcome. But there was one thing she was sure of: her own courage and the depth of her love. No one had ever risked as much for her as Fletcher had. How unselfish he had been. Though she did not go back to Fletcher's house, she did not tell anyone what she had heard. And she did not confront Fletcher. That she was forever changed by this reality was her secret.

When Fletcher came to the apartments as a dinner guest, she found him as companionable as ever before. When he asked why she had not called on him, she said, "My expanding world has made even the cloaks a poor attempt at discretion."

"Well, Lilly," he said very kindly, "I think you look even more beautiful. Michael asked about your health."

"Thank him," she said. "And do give him my regards."

Understanding, she decided, was not the same as accepting. There were more rules to be broken than Lilly had ever considered. Someday, she thought, perhaps the world will become more kind to people like us.

As the weather grew colder and Lilly grew larger, she finished reading *The Found Fortune*. She tried to imagine another twelve months and twelve segments of Chloe Tillets' unrequited passion for the man of her dreams. She dropped the last installment into what was left of her lap and thought about those letters she had read. She wondered if Patricia's peculiar aversion from physical love and her erotic letters continued to fuel their bizarre affair. She thought about Fletcher and Michael. The world had become almost too large.

"How are you finding that book, Lilly?" Emily asked. "Is it as shocking as it was? I hear it's been banned in certain cities."

"I find it rather amazing, Mama, given what I've learned in the past couple of years, that my condition is shocking enough to be censored. What I've done can't really be the worst thing."

Emily laughed. "Not the worst, darling. Just the most obvious right now."

She smoothed her hands over her round, hard middle. "Not for long," she muttered. "Soon it will be the loudest."

23

The cold rain in mid-November threatened to yield to snow, the first snowfall of the year. Emily was surprised and delighted to have Andrew Devon ushered into the cozy sitting room.

"Oh, Andrew, I've been wondering about you," she said, rising quickly. "We haven't seen you in such a long time. Let me get you something hot to—"

"No, Emily, please don't trouble yourself. I really can't stay long." He nodded toward Lady Nesbitt, put a hand toward Noel, and smiled at Katherine, who was busy with blocks in front of the fireplace. "She's growing more beautiful all the time."

"She does have the good looks of her parents," Emily said with pride. "You'll want to tell Dale, when you see him next, that Patricia is all right. We've had letters from her and—"

"Where's Lilly?" he asked, looking around. "Working?"

"No, she's out walking, if you can believe that! She never was one to do reasonable things!"

"No, I guess she never was," he said. He had not been in this household since the March before. By the way he was greeted he had to assume that the family still did not know that he had been a participant in Lilly's "unreasonable" behavior. Out walking in this cold drizzle? He frowned, then looked back to Emily.

"I apologize for missing your wedding. I—"

"Never mind that. Don't explain. No one has more going on than you. How is Wilson?"

"I'm sorry I haven't been keeping you better informed, there have been so many complications that I've been too busy to come for a visit. That's why I'm here. Wilson has gotten worse—he's very seriously ill. And I'm afraid things in the Montaine household are in an uproar. Dale is . . . well, Dale is unable to help very much. Wilson is failing, growing weaker, but he has an uncanny determination to have all his business settled once and for all. I'm sure it has to do with the fact that he doesn't think those of us he will leave behind are capable."

"Good Lord," Amanda said, "he's gotten that bad without us knowing? Why hasn't someone—"

"I'm sorry for not calling on you. My own business and the trouble with Brenda have had me literally running between Wilson's house, Reading, New York, and my own flat. I can barely keep up. That's the reason I'm here—I have to explain a great deal in a short time.

"Wilson is dying, it's no use pretending. Although I haven't done business on his behalf for a long time, I was needed. Dale has made a greater attempt to work for his father than ever before and may finally redeem himself as he loses Wilson, but I'm afraid he just isn't a businessman. That's all well and good, so long as he can overcome his other problems. Wilson has divided his property. He's commanding from the bed, and I'm seeing everything transferred for him. He knows the only way Dale will have a chance of being his own man is if what he's left behind is in a neat, worry-free bundle.

"Some of the estate is bequeathed to Katherine. Wilson isn't sure Katherine's father won't make serious mistakes in the management, despite Dale's newfound earnestness."

"Dale visits us when he can, although it has been well over a month. As I recall, he was very charming the last time, and he wasn't—" Emily didn't finish.

Andrew smiled, appreciating Emily's tact but finding it ludicrous at this late date. "He wasn't drunk? Well, there's still some of that going on, but his effort to stay sober and agreeable is greater than I dared hope. Emily, you will be named custodian for Katherine's inheritance."

"Me? But I—"

"You can find someone to help you, I'm sure. The thing you need to know is that Wilson is worried about what her parents might do with that money—it's a considerable amount. The conditions of his will are specific: you have to try to preserve it for her."

"Of course," she said, somewhat shaken by such an alien responsibility.

"And if you can spare the time and the weather improves, would you take Katherine to the house to see him? I don't think it would be a terrible ordeal for her. He's very weak but not frightening in appearance. Deanna—"

"Is she all right?"

He couldn't help but smile. "She is, Emily. She's doing very well. I think you're to be credited for the happiness Wilson and his wife shared the past few years. Your kindness and acceptance brought a wonderful change over Deanna, and Wilson for that matter. She'll be lonely without him, which is a wonder in itself. Not too long ago they couldn't sit at the dinner table together without harsh words. She could use some company, if you could see your way clear."

"I'll go the minute the rain stops and the roads are half decent. Oh, Andrew, I'm so sorry for all you have to go through."

"Wilson's done a lot for me. This is the least I can do. I meant to come sooner. I'm sorry for the rush. I don't want to be away too long. When all this is past, I promise to spend some time with you."

"And Brenda?" she asked when he would turn to go.

He turned back slowly. He sighed heavily. "She has brief periods of respite," he said, thinking over his words carefully. "But there's no point in hiding it—she's not well. She slips in and out. There's a priest there who can sometimes be a big help to her, but nothing can make that mania disappear forever. I don't know what's harder to see, her optimism when she thinks she will be well or her hysteria when she's in the grip of some other world where everyone is plotting against her and she's frightened all the time. I . . ." he looked down

415

and twisted his hat. "I don't know that you'll approve, but the marriage is going to be annulled. I'll continue to see that she's cared for, of course."

"Oh Andrew! That must have been such a hard decision for you."

"There's no point in doing anything else. I'm afraid it has never been a very fulfilling marriage for either of us. Brenda is in better hands in Reading than she's ever been elsewhere, especially with me. I think it's the right thing. There don't seem to be any good alternatives."

"An annulment must be a sticky wicket," Amanda said, "with her illness and all."

"Well, it is. It takes a long time. Another year I suppose. But the priest suggested it to Brenda, to help her break free of the past. I'm doing all I can for her."

"Of course you are," Emily said. "Are you going back to the Montaine home now?"

"Yes. I hate to be away very long. It's all there is right now. A man can't be left alone in his last days."

When he left them, Emily turned to Amanda. "That poor man has had the worst time of it. I don't think there's a more generous soul than Andrew. I hope he can be rewarded someday for all his unselfishness."

"Unselfishness?" Amanda questioned. "Without Wilson he would have nothing at all. I'm sure he's right—this is the least he should do."

"Oh, Mother, sometimes you are so harsh!"

"Yes, yes, I'm harsh. Somebody around here has to be made of nails."

Lilly walked in the drizzle because the hotel guests would not. She stayed indoors so much of the time that even an ugly day like this one lifted her spirits because she could indulge in a little air and exercise.

Her boots were sodden and her umbrella dripped. She was beginning to shiver from her walk through the brown, drooping gardens, down to the pond, and was on her way back to the rear of the hotel where she would climb the back stairs. She heard her name called.

She lifted her umbrella to see him standing there, not ten feet from her, water pouring off his hat. "Andrew?"

He walked slowly toward her. "I've missed you."

"You haven't let me know that," she said. Inside she longed to embrace him, kiss the moisture from his face. She held herself in check, afraid he didn't love her anymore.

"I wanted a chance to take care of a few things before seeing you. I needed to bolster myself; I wasn't sure I was up to the masquerade of being just a family friend."

She couldn't control a trembling smile, and she lifted her umbrella to let him share it. His arm went around her waist, their child held them apart. He brushed his cheek against hers. "My God. Oh, my God." He felt the sting of tears in his eyes, and she heard the shaking in his voice.

"It's a strong baby, Andrew. And Mama says it will be large."

"Are you all right?"

"I'm in perfect health."

"And otherwise?"

"Otherwise? Oh, it's difficult, but I knew it would be."

"Lilly, it's not too late. You can come away with me. I'll go right back upstairs with you, tell them the truth, and take you with me."

She fought the urge to cry, to throw her arms around him. At this moment good sense was harder to achieve than ever before in her life. She had never wanted anything so much as to do just what he suggested.

"I want to, Andrew. I want to go with you right now, but I can't. I can expect this child to make an appearance soon. Two weeks, perhaps three, perhaps less. I might not make it through the coach ride as far as your flat in the city."

His lips touched her cheek. "I'll take care of you. I would never let anything happen to you."

"I don't want to be away from my mother now, Andrew. Please understand. The family . . . they've been all I . . . without them I could not be as well as I am."

"Has it been terrible, Lilly? Worse than you thought?"

She couldn't hold back the tears through that question. She leaned against him. "It's been much harder than I thought. I must have been mad to insist on this damnable honesty. Most of the people I pass can't meet my eyes. The things they'll say just loud enough for me to hear would singe your ears. Elizabeth has left me."

"You don't have to suffer like this. Come away—"

"Perhaps I will, after the baby is born. Oh, Andrew, I made so many mistakes! I shouldn't have thought myself so strong! I'm not." She leaned against him and cried. He stroked her back. With the umbrella over them, they could appear to be a couple sharing an umbrella, chatting in the rain.

"Just to have you in my arms, just for a moment, even if it's while you cry! Lord, I've been half a man without you!"

"I thought you didn't love me anymore," she admitted.

"Oh, darling, of course I love you. I was trying to accomplish something toward our future together. The Reading priest who has been helping Brenda has petitioned for an annulment. I believe it's going to happen. Not in time, of course," he said, his large hand resting on her swollen middle. "But the moment it does—"

"Oh, Andrew, do you mean it?"

"Yes, I mean it."

"And Brenda?"

"She's not well, Lilly. There's nothing to do except what's already being done. Enduring it as her husband won't cure her."

"But will the annulment . . . will it—"

"Make her worse? I hope not, but it's too late now. It's moving along, and she has cooperated with the request. There's so much happening right now. Wilson is dying, and I'm the only one capable of untangling all his financial affairs. Fortunately I've been too busy to think of myself, but I have thought of you."

"Do you think you can come here now? Do you think you're up to it?"

"I'll try, Lilly." His arm tightened around her. "I'll try."

"We can't stand here in the rain all day," she sniffed.

He touched her lips with his. "Will you be all right?"

She nodded. "Better now than I've been in months."

"Go inside. You're freezing. I'll try to come back to you soon."

"I love you," she whispered.

"I love you. Be strong. We'll get it fixed. Somehow."

Andrew backed away from her. He took ten slow steps before he raised his hand in farewell. He turned and walked away from her, and she stood, her umbrella shielding her and watched until he was out of sight. Then she slowly turned and continued her trek toward the back of the hotel.

Amanda let the curtain in Lilly's fifth-floor office window drop. "Damn him!"

When the good smells of cooking permeated the apartments on the afternoon of Thanksgiving Day and all manner of friend and family had gathered for a feast, Lilly excused herself. She had not meant to disrupt the household on a day of fellowship and had therefore kept to herself the fierce tightening she felt. When she knew it would show on her face, she went to her room. It was then that she told her mother that the baby was going to make demands.

Lilly had waited too long. The day was cold and the doctor had to be fetched from his own dinner table. When he arrived two hours later, Emily had delivered Lilly of a large, bellowing son, and Lilly was already holding him.

Amanda waited until all the fuss was over before going in to Lilly's room to view the infant. She looked down at the baby through her spectacles. "Amazing," she said, smiling at her granddaughter. "You hardly delayed dinner."

An hour or so later, when the doctor had gone and Lilly rested comfortably, Amanda ordered a hotel coach and waited on the portico, her cloak pulled tightly around her. She instructed the driver to take her to the Montaine household.

She had no idea what to expect there, but Amanda had spent her life playing on hunches. She found the remnants of Wilson's family—Dale, Deanna, Andrew—all gathered, but not for the celebration of a feast day. She made much pretense of visiting, sitting quietly with Wilson, Deanna at her side. The poor old man was a withered version of his former self, and his room smelled of a death that would not be easy. His rasping breath made conversation impossible for him, and she made do with promising that Katherine would always be protected.

She then gave Deanna some of her time and encouraged her to come to the Armstrong Arms with as much sincerity as Emily would have used. She spoke at length to Dale, telling him that the mettle she always knew he possessed but had never quite received credit for would rise to this occasion. "Make your father proud of you, Dale. Make Katherine proud. This will require all your strength, but you can salvage a very satisfactory life for yourself."

It wasn't until she had duly paid her respects to the sick and grief-stricken that she approached Andrew. "I wonder if I could have a moment of your time. There's a business matter of some concern that you can help me with."

"Certainly," he said, offering Wilson's study.

When the doors were closed, she faced him. He gestured toward a chair for her, but she shook her head. "I'll be brief. You have a son. He's a big boy and healthy."

He was momentarily shocked, amazed. He had known the child would come soon. "Then Lilly—"

"She didn't tell me it's your son. She doesn't know that I know. I saw you that day, in the rain. That was *very* foolish."

"I'm sorry if you were embarrassed, but since you know now, I'll go to her and—"

"Wait a minute, young man. I want you to listen to me, and listen carefully. I know you're constructing some kind of trumped-up annulment. Is this thing really going to happen? Are you actually *leaving* your marriage?"

"Yes. I actually am. Not my responsibility for Brenda's care, but the marriage. The annulment is not trumped up, not in the least. I'm justified in this action. I plan to have a life with Lilly."

"Very well, I wouldn't want to hinder that. The girl is too damned stubborn to be trifled with—she will have whom she'll have and not settle, whether or not I approve."

"And do you?"

"Had I been consulted a year ago, I might have given you my answer with a pistol, but what's done is done. Now pay attention, young man. Stay away from her, do you hear me? I want to see your face only when your annulment is over with and you're an unmarried man. Then you may come around, politely, and begin your reacquaintance with my granddaughter. There's still a hope this ridiculous notion of hers can work—if you are discreet."

"What do you plan to tell Lilly?"

"Not a damned thing. She'll only defy me as she always has. As her mother did, as her sister did. The women in my family, Andrew, are all defiant. They all think they know better than the one who went before them. It's a curse.

"It's been worse for Lilly than she'll admit. She has suffered enormously, carrying this burden as she has. People who were her former friends won't speak to her. Staff who respected her call her names behind her back. The only reason we have hotel guests is that they don't know what she's done. It's still possible to salvage something, if you can restrain yourself."

"She won't understand my absence. She extracted a promise from me that I would visit. I told her I would try to come."

"There *is* a better way. Get your business done. Don't tempt the gossips by cooing over this baby, by not having the strength to keep your arms from embracing Lilly. Some damned cook or maid will see you, and that'll be it for you. Then the story that will follow you all will be worse, far worse. It will grow and grow, and your own past—your poor wife, your annulment, your affair while your wife suffered—all of it will follow the three of you. You'll make it worse by coming around now. Right now my great-grandson has some phantom father unknown to the world. The rumors of how he got his start, during your marriage, before your petition, could follow him all his life."

"Lilly is not one for lies, Lady Nesbitt. She likes the truth even when it's hard."

"She's beginning to discover the merits of a good lie, you can believe me. Think about it—if you know her at all, you know how headstrong she is. Sometimes foolish—at least where you're concerned. Here is a chance for you to help her. You will be a marriageable man, known to be a friend of the family. You're in good standing in the community, and your charitable act of rescuing this woman whose reputation is terribly, terribly scarred will help take the sting out of the rumors. They may always speculate as to who fathered that boy, but you can rise above it. If you start coming around now, however, perhaps a year before you're free to be a husband and father, you'll bungle it. Or she will.

"Andrew," Amanda continued, "you're clever enough to understand society. A woman of good standing can marry a bricklayer and lose her status forever. A man of good standing can marry the chamber maid and elevate hers. Exercise your acumen now, your understanding of how things work and how things don't—for *his* sake."

"I'm not the elite. What I do has no impact on——"

"Oh, drat that, it's all starting to blend, and will be blended by the time my great-grandson is a grandfather himself. I don't know that these morals will ever relax, but I promise you that a parvenu with manners will not be held out of society!"

"Do you think it good form for me to ignore and avoid my child? Now? When Lilly needs me?"

"I think it would be vulgar and cruel to test the patience of the gossips any further. Lilly would not be happy away from her home, she wouldn't like having no business. If the two of you push this thing any further, you'll have worse than you do."

"You should tell her, at least."

"If I attempt to explain, she may sneak away to see you. Then what? What if she's seen? Think of the child. She has the love and devotion of her family. She has the baby. Get your affairs in order. Then come around acting as if this conversation has never taken place."

There was a knock at the study door and it opened. A housemaid looked in. "Mr. Devon? Mr. Montaine has passed away."

"Dear God," Amanda said in a breath.

"I'll have to go to them," Andrew said.

"Yes, do. But first, tell me you'll cooperate."

"I'll think it over."

"I am seldom asked for my advice in time, Andrew. I tried to keep my daughter from running off with a fraud, and she nearly ruined her life. I tried to keep Patricia out of this family. I tried to convince Lilly to protect her reputation better. This once I do know what I'm saying is true: if you'll be patient and stay away until you're available to step into her life, she and your child can escape much pain. And I'm not advising. I am *demanding!*"

He stared at her for a long moment. He finally gave a brief, small nod. "I have to go," he said.

"It's fitting in a way. One leaves, one arrives. He's a beautiful boy, Andrew. You'll be proud of him one day."

"Thank you."

Amanda was unable to keep her secret. When Lilly couldn't hold back her tears on Christmas morning, Amanda explained things. Lilly was as angry as Amanda expected, but the mood passed for she was enchanted with her son and her vitality carried her through a brief dark spell.

The baby was called Richard for the grandfather Lilly never knew, and on most days the mere fact of his existence was enough to buoy her spirits. When the February chill descended and people were frozen into their houses, Lilly spoke of going away, perhaps starting a hotel like the Armstrong Arms in another city. But Amanda urged her to be patient; nothing could be done while the baby was so young. Again, Lilly's strength proved greater than her loneliness and the fear that she had been abandoned.

What keeps that young man? Amanda often wondered.

When the trees began to bud, Lilly grew impatient and discontent. Her account books received her as unconditionally as ever, but others did not. Not only had she been pregnant, she had actually delivered a fatherless child. It was not a state of grace for a woman.

Amanda, tired of the strain, urged Lilly again to give all of it time. She had warned her that this plan of hers would be at odds with society. They wouldn't forgive her easily. Again, Lilly bolstered herself. She was of such formidable strength that Amanda was filled with awe.

In Reading, Brenda fought her mother's voice. There were the voices of war; Mr. and Mrs. Sherman sometimes spoke with the voices of Union soldiers, and she felt the danger creep nearer and nearer. Father Demetrius had been called to Vienna to greet the sick and infirm, and sometimes she could hear him from that great distance. Without him her health was elusive and impossible to maintain.

They gave her poison in her food; they caused her to sleep for days on end—this she *knew*. Her mother called; her father raged; her stepfather threatened; the priest accused. She crept out of her bed in the dark of night to pray under the stars, to pray for peace in her mind. Why did God send these tormenters? Had she not been forgiving enough? Had she not endured enough?

She found a rope that was used to lead cattle and tied it around a beam in the barn. She could not endure the voices, the threats, the constant fear. She pulled a milking stool over to the bottom of the rope and stood on it. When the rope was tight and fashioned into an unforgiving knot, she kicked away the stool.

The voices were quiet for the first time in many, many years.

Andrew Devon received a letter from the archdiocese in Pittsburgh on the same day he received a letter from the Shermans. The first letter did not end his marriage but gave him legal recourse to use in a court of law to seek a divorce. The second letter made him a widower. Above all the Shermans wished him to know that this tragedy was not his doing—Brenda mourned the absence of the priest and had not been well since Father Demetrius left the country.

When word of Brenda Devon's suicide reached Lilly through Dale Montaine, she did not understand Andrew's failure to appear. She didn't know if he blamed her for having complicated his life, for having caused such pain.

The baby was almost six months old, and Lilly remembered a time when she could hear her own mind very clearly above the clamor of duty, responsibility, and worry. She had trouble convincing her mother and grandmother, but in an adamant argument she won the acquiescence if not the approval of her family. She went to the only place she was herself.

Richard was a contented baby, husky and full on mother's milk. He could sit up early and laughed at the waves that tickled his feet. This time Lilly was not able to make her own nonschedule; she let the baby decide. She could tell he would one day be a strong and unconventional man—he liked the night sky, he squealed at birds, he liked to put his fingers into her mouth while she nursed him. He was free, beautiful, and curious.

She chopped her own wood and cooked for herself for two weeks. She needed help to buy food for her cupboard and found a woman in the seaside village who was willing to shop, clean, and sometimes keep the baby. She apologized to God for all she had dared, professing a wider understanding now, and gave thanks every day for the same thing—her son. She found her mind was no more difficult to hear through a baby's laughter or complaints, and she came alive with the sea. By the time she believed herself restored, he came.

He walked onto the sandy beach, still wearing his coat and shoes. She heard the coach that brought him depart. She looked back at the cottage and saw his bags below the step at the door. She had been playing on the sand with Richard and stood to watch him approach. She didn't speak a word until he stood a foot from her. "I'm sorry for your loss," she said.

"I came as quickly as I could," he said.

"It's been such a long time since that day . . . since the rain, when you said—"

"I can explain. And for once, there's going to be plenty of time."

"Are you sure?" she asked him.

"Oh yes, Lilly. I'm sure."

"I was afraid you would blame me. All the pain . . . all the tears . . . all that I demanded."

He smiled, then laughed. "Blame you? Yes! I blame you, Lilly, for without your courage, none of us could have all this!"

She stooped to pick up his child. She hoisted the heavy, handsome baby on her hip. "Then I take the blame," she said.